PRAISE FOR

The Husband's Secret

"Emotionally astute, immensely smart, and as cinematically plotted as any Tom Perrotta novel destined for critical accolades and a big-screen adaptation."

—*Entertainment Weekly*

"Brilliant."

—Sophie Hannah, *New York Times* bestselling author

"Shocking, complex, and thought-provoking, this is a story reading groups will devour."

—Emily Giffin, *New York Times* bestselling author

"What a wonderful writer—smart, wise, funny."

—Anne Lamott, *New York Times* bestselling author

"Perfect for vacation reading: there's humor, suspense, a circle of appealing women." —*People*

"Secrets can be sinister; they can eat you alive. But they can also set you free. *The Husband's Secret* demonstrates this power with one of the most entertaining stories I have read in ages. Perfect for book clubs—lots to debate in these pages. I just loved it."

—Dorothea Benton Frank,
New York Times bestselling author

continued . . .

TITLES BY LIANE MORIARTY

Big Little Lies

The Husband's Secret

The Hypnotist's Love Story

What Alice Forgot

The Last Anniversary

Three Wishes

THE
HUSBAND'S SECRET

Liane Moriarty

BERKLEY

New York

BERKLEY
An imprint of Penguin Random House LLC
375 Hudson Street, New York, New York 10014

ISBN: 9780451490049

Pan MacMillan Australia edition / January 2013
G. P. Putnam's Sons hardcover edition / July 2013
Berkley trade paperback edition / March 2015
Berkley premium edition / July 2017

Printed in the United States of America
13   15   17   19   20   18   16   14

Cover art by: *Exploding Pink Rose* © Dan Farrall/Image Bank/Getty Images
Cover design by Lisa Amoroso

For Adam, George and Anna.

And for Amelia.

To err is human; to forgive, divine.

—ALEXANDER POPE

Poor, poor Pandora. Zeus sends her off to marry Epimetheus, a not especially bright man she's never even met, along with a mysterious covered jar. Nobody tells Pandora a word about the jar. Nobody tells her *not* to open the jar. Naturally, she opens the jar. What else has she got to do? How was she to know that all those dreadful ills would go whooshing out to plague mankind forevermore, and that the only thing left in the jar would be hope? Why wasn't there a warning label? And then everyone's like, Oh, Pandora. Where's your willpower? You were told not to open that box, you snoopy girl, you typical woman with your insatiable curiosity; now look what you've gone and done. When for one thing it was a *jar*, not a box, and for another—how many times does she have to say it?—nobody said a *word* about not opening it!

ONE

I t was all because of the Berlin Wall.

If it weren't for the Berlin Wall, Cecilia would never have found the letter, and then she wouldn't be sitting here, at the kitchen table, willing herself not to rip it open.

The envelope was gray with a fine layer of dust. The words on the front were written in a scratchy blue ballpoint pen, the handwriting as familiar as her own. She turned it over. It was sealed with a yellowing piece of sticky tape. When was it written? It felt old, like it was written years ago, but there was no way of knowing for sure.

She wasn't going to open it. It was absolutely clear that she should not open it. She was the most decisive person she knew, and she'd already decided not to open the letter, so there was nothing more to think about.

Although, honestly, if she did open it, what would be the big deal? Any woman would open it like a shot. She listed all her friends and what their responses would be if she were to ring them up right now and ask what they thought.

Miriam Oppenheimer: *Yup. Open it.*

Erica Edgecliff: *Are you kidding, open it right this second.*

Laura Marks: *Yes, you should open it and then you should read it out loud to me.*

Sarah Sacks: . . .

There would be no point asking Sarah because she was incapable of making a decision. If Cecilia asked her if she wanted tea or coffee, she would sit for a full minute, her forehead furrowed as she agonized over the pros and cons of each beverage, before finally saying, "Coffee! No, wait, tea!" A decision like this one would give her a seizure.

Mahalia Ramachandran: *Absolutely not. It would be completely disrespectful to your husband. You must not open it.*

Mahalia could be a little too sure of herself at times with those huge brown ethical eyes.

Cecilia left the letter sitting on the kitchen table and went to put the kettle on.

Damn that Berlin Wall, and that Cold War, and whoever it was who sat there back in nineteen forty-whenever-it-was, mulling over the problem of what to do with those ungrateful Germans; the guy who suddenly clicked his fingers and said, "Got it, by Jove! We'll build a great big bloody wall and keep the buggers in!"

Presumably he hadn't sounded like a British sergeant major.

Esther would know who first came up with the idea for

the Berlin Wall. Esther would probably be able to give her his date of birth. It would have been a man, of course. Only a man could come up with something so ruthless, so essentially stupid and yet brutally effective.

Was that sexist?

She filled the kettle, switched it on and cleaned the droplets of water in the sink with a paper towel so that it shone.

One of the mums from school, who had three sons almost exactly the same ages as Cecilia's three daughters, had said that some remark Cecilia had made was "a teeny-weeny bit sexist," just before they started the Fete Committee meeting last week. Cecilia couldn't remember what she'd said, but she'd only been joking. Anyway, weren't women allowed to be sexist for the next two thousand years or so, until they'd evened up the score?

Maybe she *was* sexist.

The kettle boiled. She swirled an Earl Grey tea bag and watched the curls of black spread through the water like ink. There were worse things to be than sexist. For example, you could be the sort of person who pinched your fingers together while using the word "teeny-weeny."

She looked at her tea and sighed. A glass of wine would be nice right now, but she'd given up alcohol for Lent. Only six days to go. She had a bottle of expensive Shiraz ready to open on Easter Sunday, when thirty-five adults and twenty-three children were coming to lunch, so she'd need it. Although she was an old hand at entertaining. She hosted Easter, Mother's Day, Father's Day and Christmas.

John-Paul had five younger brothers, all married with kids. So it was quite a crowd. Planning was the key. Meticulous planning.

She picked up her tea and took it over to the table. Why did she give up wine for Lent? Polly was more sensible. She had given up strawberry jam. Cecilia had never seen Polly show more than a passing interest in strawberry jam, although now, of course, she was always catching her standing at the open fridge, staring at it longingly. The power of denial.

"Esther!" she called out.

Esther was in the next room with her sisters watching *The Biggest Loser* while they shared a giant bag of salt-and-vinegar chips left over from the Australia Day barbecue months earlier. Cecilia did not know why her three slender daughters loved watching overweight people sweat and cry and starve. It didn't appear to be teaching them healthier eating habits. She should go in and confiscate the bag of chips, except they'd all eaten salmon and steamed broccoli for dinner without complaint, and she didn't have the strength for an argument.

She heard a voice from the television boom, "You get nothing for nothing!"

That wasn't such a bad sentiment for her daughters to hear. No one knew it better than Cecilia! But still, she didn't like the expressions of faint revulsion that flitted across their smooth young faces. She was always so vigilant about not making negative body-image comments in front of her daughters, although the same could not be said for her friends. Just the other day, Miriam Oppenheimer had said, loud enough for all their impressionable daughters to hear, "God, would you look at my stomach!" and squeezed her flesh between her fingertips as if it were something vile. Great, Miriam, as if our daughters don't already get a million messages every day telling them to hate their bodies.

Actually, Miriam's stomach *was* getting a little pudgy.

"Esther!" she called out again.

"What is it?" Esther called back, in a patient, put-upon voice that Cecilia suspected was an unconscious imitation of her own.

"Whose idea was it to build the Berlin Wall?"

"Well, they're pretty sure it was Nikita Khrushchev's!" Esther answered immediately, pronouncing the exotic-sounding name with great relish and her own peculiar interpretation of a Russian accent. "He was, like, the prime minister of Russia, except he was the premier. But it could have been—"

Her sisters responded instantly with their usual impeccable courtesy.

"Shut up, Esther!"

"Esther! I can't *hear* the *television*!"

"Thank you, darling!" Cecilia sipped her tea and imagined herself going back through time and putting that Khrushchev in his place.

No, Mr. Khrushchev, you may not have a wall. It will not prove that communism works. It will not work out well at all. Now, look, I agree capitalism isn't the be-all and end-all! Let me show you my last credit card bill. But you really need to put your thinking cap back on.

And then fifty-one years later, Cecilia wouldn't have

found this letter that was making her feel so . . . What was the word?

Unfocused. That was it.

She liked to feel focused. She was proud of her ability to focus. Her daily life was made up of a thousand tiny pieces—"Need coriander"; "Isabel's haircut"; "Who will watch Polly at ballet on Tuesday while I take Esther to speech therapy?"—like one of those terrible giant jigsaws that Isabel used to spend hours doing. And yet Cecilia, who had no patience for puzzles, knew exactly where each tiny piece of her life belonged and where it needed to be slotted in next.

And okay, maybe the life Cecilia was leading wasn't that unusual or impressive. She was a school mum and a part-time Tupperware consultant, not an actress or an actuary or a . . . poet living in Vermont. (Cecilia had recently discovered that Liz Brogan, a girl from high school, was now a prizewinning poet living in Vermont. Liz, who ate cheese-and-Vegemite sandwiches and was always losing her bus pass. It took all of Cecilia's considerable strength of character not to find that annoying. Not that she wanted to write poetry. But still. You would have thought that if anyone was going to lead an ordinary life, it would have been Liz Brogan.) Of course, Cecilia had never aspired to anything other than ordinariness. *Here I am, a typical suburban mum,* she sometimes caught herself thinking, as if someone had accused her of holding herself out to be something else, something superior.

Other mothers talked about feeling overwhelmed, about the difficulties of focusing on one thing, and they were always saying, "How do you do it all, Cecilia?" and she didn't know how to answer them. She didn't actually understand what they found so difficult.

But now, for some reason, something to do with this silly letter, everything felt somehow at risk. It wasn't logical.

Maybe it wasn't anything to do with the letter. Maybe it was hormonal. She was "possibly perimenopausal," according to Dr. McArthur. ("Oh, I am *not*!" Cecilia had said automatically, as if responding to a gentle, humorous insult.)

Perhaps this was a case of that vague anxiety she knew some women experienced. *Other* women. She'd always thought anxious people were cute. Dear little anxious people like Sarah Sacks. She wanted to pat their worry-filled heads.

Perhaps if she opened the letter and saw that it was nothing, she would get everything back in focus. She had things to do. Two baskets of laundry to fold. Three urgent phone calls to make. Gluten-free muffins to bake for the gluten-intolerant members of the School Website Project Group (i.e., Janine Davidson), which would be meeting tomorrow.

There were other things besides the letter that could be making her feel anxious.

The sex thing, for example. That was always at the back of her mind.

She frowned and ran her hands down the sides of her waist. Her oblique muscles, according to her Pilates teacher. Oh, look, the sex thing was *nothing*. It was not actually on her mind. She refused to let it be on her mind. It was of no consequence.

It was true, perhaps, that ever since that morning last year, she'd been aware of an underlying sense of fragility, a new understanding that a life of coriander and laundry could be stolen in an instant, that your ordinariness could vanish, and suddenly you're a woman on your knees, your face lifted to the sky, and some women are running to help, but others are already averting their heads, with the words not articulated, but felt: Don't let this touch me.

Cecilia saw it again for the thousandth time: little Spider-Man flying. She was one of the women who ran. Well, of course she was, throwing open her car door, even though she knew that nothing she did could make any difference. It wasn't her school, her neighborhood, her parish. None of her children had ever played with the little Spider-Man. She'd never had coffee with the woman on her knees. She just happened to be stopped at the lights on the other side of the intersection when it happened. A little boy, probably about five, dressed in a red and blue full-body Spider-Man suit was waiting at the side of the road, holding his mother's hand. It was Book Week. That's why the little boy was dressed up. Cecilia was watching him, thinking, *Mmmm, actually Spider-Man is not a character from a book*, when for no reason that she could see, the little boy dropped his mother's hand and stepped off the curb into the traffic. Cecilia screamed. She also, she remembered later, instinctively banged her fist on her horn.

If Cecilia had driven by just ten minutes later, or even five minutes later, she would have missed seeing it happen. The little boy's death would have meant nothing more to her than another traffic detour. Now it was a memory that would probably cause her grandchildren to one day say, "Don't hold my hand so *tight*, Grandma."

Obviously there was no connection between little Spider-Man and this letter. He just came into her mind at strange times.

Cecilia flicked the letter across the table with her fingertip and picked up Esther's library book: *The Rise and Fall of the Berlin Wall*.

So, the Berlin Wall. Wonderful.

The first she knew that the Berlin Wall was about to become a significant part of her life had been at breakfast this morning.

It had been just Cecilia and Esther sitting at the kitchen table. John-Paul was overseas, in Chicago until Friday, and Isabel and Polly were still in bed.

Cecilia didn't normally sit down in the mornings. She generally ate her breakfast standing at the breakfast counter while she made lunches, checked her Tupperware orders on her iPad, unpacked the dishwasher, texted clients about their parties, whatever, but it was a rare opportunity to have some time alone with her odd, darling middle daughter, so she sat down with her Bircher muesli, while Esther powered her way through a bowl of rice bubbles, and waited.

She'd learned that with her daughters. Don't say a word. Don't ask a question. Give them enough time and they'll finally tell you what's on their minds. It was like fishing. It took silence and patience. (Or so she'd heard. Cecilia would rather hammer nails into her forehead than go fishing.)

Silence didn't come naturally to her. Cecilia was a talker. "Seriously, do you ever shut the hell up?" an ex-boyfriend had said to her once. She talked a lot when she was nervous. That ex-boyfriend must have made her nervous. Although she also talked a lot when she was happy.

But she didn't say anything that morning. She just ate, and waited, and sure enough, Esther started talking.

"Mum," she said, in her husky, precise little voice with its faint lisp. "Did you know that some people escaped over the Berlin Wall in a hot-air balloon they made themselves?"

"I did not know that," said Cecilia, although she might have known it.

So long, Titanic; *hello, Berlin Wall,* she thought.

She would have preferred it if Esther had shared something with her about how she was feeling at the moment, any worries she had about school, her friends, questions about sex. But no, she wanted to talk about the Berlin Wall.

Ever since Esther was three years old, she'd been developing these interests or, more accurately, obsessions. First it was dinosaurs. Sure, lots of kids are interested in dinosaurs, but Esther's interest was, well, exhausting, to be frank, and a little peculiar. Nothing else interested the child. She drew dinosaurs, she played with dinosaurs, she dressed up as a dinosaur. "I'm not Esther," she'd say. "I'm T. rex." Every bedtime story had to be about dinosaurs. Every conversation had to be related somehow to dinosaurs. It was lucky that John-Paul was interested, because Cecilia was bored after about five minutes. (They were extinct! They had nothing to say!) John-Paul took Esther on special trips to the museum. He brought home books for her. He sat with her for hours while they talked about herbivores and carnivores.

Since then Ether's "interests" had ranged from roller coasters to cane toads. Most recently it had been the *Titanic*. Now that she was ten, she was old enough to do her own research at the library and online, and Cecilia was amazed at the information she gathered. What ten-year-old lay in bed reading historical books that were so big and chunky, she could barely hold them up?

"Encourage it!" her schoolteachers said, but sometimes Cecilia worried. It seemed to her that Esther was possibly a touch autistic, or at least sitting somewhere on the autism spectrum. Although Cecilia's mother had laughed when she mentioned her concern. "But Esther is exactly like you were!" she said. This was not true.

"I actually have a piece of the Berlin Wall," Cecilia had said that morning to Esther, suddenly remembering this fact, and it had been gratifying to see Esther's eyes light up with interest. "I was there in Germany, after the Wall came down."

"Can I see it?" asked Esther.

"You can have it, darling."

Jewelry and clothes for Isabel and Polly. A piece of the Berlin Wall for Esther.

Cecilia, twenty years old at the time, had been on a six-week holiday traveling through Europe with her friend Sarah Sacks in 1990, just a few months after the announcement that the Wall was coming down. (Sarah's famous indecisiveness paired with Cecilia's famous decisiveness made them the perfect traveling companions. No conflict whatsoever.)

When they got to Berlin, they found tourists lined along

the Wall, trying to chip off pieces as souvenirs using keys, rocks, anything they could find. The Wall was like a giant carcass of a dragon that had once terrorized the city, and the tourists were crows pecking away at its remains.

Without proper tools it was almost impossible to chip off a proper piece, so Cecilia and Sarah (well, Cecilia) decided to buy their pieces from the enterprising locals who had set out rugs and were selling a variety of offerings. Capitalism really had triumphed. You could buy anything from gray-colored chips the size of marbles to giant boulder-size chunks complete with spray-painted graffiti.

Cecilia couldn't remember how much she had paid for the tiny gray stone that looked like it could have come from anyone's front garden. "It probably did," said Sarah as they caught the train out of Berlin that night, and they'd laughed at their own gullibility, but at least they'd felt like they were a part of history. Cecilia had put her chip in a paper bag and written "MY PIECE OF THE BERLIN WALL" on the front, and when she came back to Australia she'd thrown it in a box with all the other souvenirs she'd collected: drink coasters, train tickets, menus, foreign coins, hotel keys.

Cecilia wished now she'd concentrated more on the Wall, taken more photos, collected more anecdotes she could have shared with Esther. Actually, what she remembered most about that trip to Berlin was kissing a handsome, brown-haired German boy in a nightclub. He kept taking ice cubes from his drink and running them across her collarbone, which at the time had seemed incredibly sexy, but now seemed unhygienic and sticky.

If only she'd been the sort of curious, politically aware girl who had struck up conversations with the locals about what it had been like living in the shadow of the Wall. Instead, all she had to share with her daughter were stories about kissing and ice cubes. Of course, Isabel and Polly would *love* to hear about the kissing and ice cubes. Or Polly would; maybe Isabel had reached the age where the thought of her mother kissing anybody would be appalling.

Cecilia had put "Find piece of Berlin Wall for E" on her list of things to do that day (there were twenty-five items—she used an iPhone app to list them), and at about two p.m., she had gone into the attic to find it.

"Attic" was probably too generous a word for the storage area in their roof space. You reached it by pulling down a ladder from a trapdoor in the ceiling.

Once she was up there, she had to keep her knees bent so as not to bang her head. John-Paul point-blank refused to go up there. He suffered from terrible claustrophobia and walked six flights of stairs every day to his office so he could avoid taking the elevator. The poor man had regular nightmares about being trapped in a room where the walls were contracting. "The walls!" he'd shout, just before he woke up, sweaty and wild-eyed. "Do you think you were locked in a cupboard as a child?" Cecilia had asked him once (she wouldn't have put it past his mother), but he said he was pretty sure he wasn't. "Actually, John-Paul never had nightmares when he was a little boy," his mother had told Cecilia when she asked. "He was a *beautiful* sleeper. Perhaps you give him too much rich food late at night?" Cecilia was used to the nightmares now.

The attic was small and crammed, but tidy and well organized, of course. Over recent years, "organized" seemed to have become her most defining characteristic. It was like she was a minor celebrity with this one claim to fame. It was funny how once it became a thing that her family and friends commented on and teased her about, it seemed to perpetuate itself, so that her life was now *extraordinarily* well organized, as if motherhood were a sport and she were a top athlete. It was like she was thinking, *How far can I go with this? How much more can I fit in my life without losing control?*

And that was why other people, like her sister, had rooms full of dusty junk, whereas Cecilia's attic was stacked with clearly labeled white plastic storage containers. The only part that didn't look quite Cecilia-ish was the tower of shoe boxes in the corner. They were John-Paul's. He liked to keep each financial year's receipts in a different shoe box. It was something he'd been doing for years, before he met Cecilia. He was proud of his shoe boxes, so she managed to restrain herself from telling him that a filing cabinet would be a far more effective use of space.

Thanks to her labeled storage containers, she found her piece of the Berlin Wall almost straightaway. She peeled off the lid of the container marked "Cecilia: Travel/Souvenirs. 1985–1990," and there it was in its faded brown paper bag. Her little piece of history. She took out the piece of rock (cement?) and held it in her palm. It was even smaller than she remembered. It didn't look especially impressive, but hopefully it would be enough for the reward of one of Esther's rare, lopsided little smiles. You had to work hard for a smile from Esther.

Then Cecilia let herself get distracted (yes, she achieved a lot every day, but she wasn't a *machine*, she did sometimes fritter away a little time) looking through the box and laughing at the photo of herself with the German boy who did the ice cube thing. He, like her piece of the Berlin Wall, wasn't quite as impressive as she remembered. Then the house phone rang, startling her out of the past, and she stood up too fast and banged the side of her head painfully against the ceiling. The walls, the walls! She swore, reeled back, and her elbow knocked against John-Paul's tower of shoe boxes.

At least three lost their lids and their contents, causing a mini landslide of paperwork. This was precisely why the shoe boxes were not such a good idea.

Cecilia swore again and rubbed her head, which really did hurt. She looked at the shoe boxes and saw that they were all for financial years dating back to the eighties. She began stuffing the pile of receipts into one of the boxes when her eye was caught by her own name on a white business envelope.

She picked it up and saw that it was John-Paul's handwriting.

It said:

For my wife, Cecilia Fitzpatrick
To be opened only in the event of my death

She laughed out loud, and then abruptly stopped, as if she were at a party and she'd laughed at something somebody said and then realized that it wasn't a joke, it was actually quite serious.

She read it again—"For my wife, Cecilia Fitzpatrick"—and oddly, for just a moment, she'd felt her cheeks go warm, like she was embarrassed. For him or for her? She wasn't sure. It felt like she'd stumbled upon something shameful, as if she'd caught him masturbating in the shower. (Miriam Oppenheimer had once caught Doug masturbating in the shower. It was just so *dreadful* that they all knew that, but once Miriam was on to her second glass of champagne, the secrets just bubbled out of her, and once they knew it was impossible to un-know it.)

What did it *say*? She considered tearing it open right that second, before she had time to think about it, like the way she sometimes (not very often) shoved the last piece of chocolate in her mouth, before her conscience had time to catch up with her greed.

The phone rang again. She wasn't wearing her watch, and suddenly she felt like she'd lost all sense of time.

She threw the rest of the paperwork back into one of the shoe boxes and took the piece of the Berlin Wall and the letter back downstairs.

As soon as she left the attic, she was picked up and swept along by the fast-running current of her life. There was a big Tupperware order to deliver, the girls to be picked up from school, the fish to be bought for tonight's dinner (they ate a lot of fish when John-Paul was away for work because he hated it), phone calls to return. The parish priest, Father

Joe, had been calling to remind her that it was Sister Ursula's funeral tomorrow. There seemed to be some concern about numbers. She would go, of course. She left John-Paul's mysterious letter on top of the fridge, and gave Esther the piece of the Berlin Wall just before they sat down for dinner.

"Thank you." Esther handled the little piece of rock with touching reverence. "Exactly which part of the Wall did it come from?"

"Well, I think it was quite near Checkpoint Charlie," said Cecilia with jolly confidence. She had no idea.

But I can tell you that boy with the ice cube wore a red T-shirt and white jeans and he picked up my ponytail and held it between his fingertips and said, "Very pretty."

"Is it worth any money?" asked Polly.

"I doubt it. How could you prove it really was from the Wall?" asked Isabel. "It just looks like a piece of rock."

"DMA testing," said Polly. The child watched far too much television.

"It's DNA, not DMA, and that comes from people," said Esther.

"I *know* that!" Polly had arrived in the world outraged to discover that her sisters had gotten there before her. "Well, then why—"

"So who do you reckon is going to get voted off *The Biggest Loser* tonight?" asked Cecilia, while simultaneously thinking, *Why, yes, whoever that is observing my life, I am changing the subject from a fascinating period of modern history that might actually teach my children something to a trashy television show that will teach them nothing, but will keep the peace and not make my head hurt.* If John-Paul had been at home, she probably wouldn't have changed the subject. She was a far better mother when she had an audience.

The girls talked about *The Biggest Loser* for the rest of dinner, while Cecilia pretended to be interested and thought about the letter sitting on top of the fridge. Once the table was cleared and the girls were all watching TV, she took it down to stare at it.

Now she put down her cup of tea and held the envelope up to the light, half laughing at herself. It looked like a handwritten letter on lined notebook paper. She couldn't decipher a word.

Had John-Paul perhaps seen something on television about how the soldiers in Afghanistan wrote letters to their families to be sent in the event of their deaths, like messages from the grave, and had he thought that it might be nice to do something similar?

She just couldn't imagine him sitting down to do such a thing. It was so sentimental.

Lovely though. If he died, he wanted them to know how much he loved them.

". . . in the event of my death." Why was he thinking about death? Was he sick? But this letter appeared to have been written a long time ago, and he was still alive. Besides, he'd had a checkup a few weeks back, and Dr. Kluger had said he was as "fit as a stallion." He'd spent the next few days tossing his head back and whinnying and neighing around the house, while Polly rode on his back swinging a tea towel around her head like a whip.

Cecilia smiled at the memory, and her anxiety dissipated.

So a few years ago, John-Paul had done something unchar-
acteristically sentimental and written this letter. It was
nothing to get all worked up about, and of course she
shouldn't open it just for the sake of curiosity.

She looked at the clock. Nearly eight p.m. He'd be calling soon. He generally called around this time each night
when he was away.

She wasn't even going to mention the letter to him. It
would embarrass him, and it wasn't really an appropriate
topic of conversation for the phone.

One thing: How exactly was she meant to have found
this letter if he *had* died? She might never have found it!
Why hadn't he given it to their solicitor, Miriam's husband,
Doug Oppenheimer? So difficult not to think of him in
the shower every time he came to mind. Of course it had
no bearing on his abilities as a lawyer; perhaps it said more
about Miriam's abilities in the bedroom. (Cecilia had a
mildly competitive relationship with Miriam.)

Of course, given the current circumstances, now was
not the time to be feeling smug about sex. *Stop it. Do not
think about the sex thing.*

Anyway, it was dumb of John-Paul not to have given the
letter to Doug. If he'd died she probably would have thrown
out all his shoe boxes in one of her decluttering frenzies
without even bothering to go through them. If he'd wanted
her to find the letter, it was crazy to just shove it in a random shoe box. Why not put it in the file with the copies of
their wills, life insurance and so on? John-Paul was one of
the smartest people she knew, except when it came to the
logistics of life.

"I seriously don't understand how men came to rule the world," she'd said to her sister, Bridget, this morning, after she'd told her about how John-Paul had lost his rental car keys in Chicago. It had driven Cecilia bananas seeing that text message from him. There was nothing she could do!

This type of thing was always happening to John-Paul. Last time he went overseas he'd left his laptop in a cab. The man lost things constantly. Wallets, phones, keys, his wedding ring. His possessions just slid right off him.

"They're pretty good at building stuff," her sister said. "Like bridges and roads. I mean, could you even build a hut? Your basic mud hut?"

"I could build a hut," said Cecilia.

"You probably could," groaned Bridget, as if this were a failing. "Anyway, men don't rule the world. We have a female prime minister. And you rule your world. You rule the Fitzpatrick household. You rule St. Angela's. You rule the world of Tupperware."

Cecilia was president of St. Angela's Primary Parents and Friends Association. She was also the eleventh top-selling Tupperware consultant in Australia. Her sister found both of these roles hugely comical.

"I don't rule the Fitzpatrick household," said Cecilia.

"Sure you don't," guffawed Bridget.

It was true that if Cecilia died, the Fitzpatrick household would just . . . Well, it was unbearable to think about what would happen. John-Paul would need more than a letter from her. He'd need a whole manual, including a floor plan of the house pointing out the locations of the laundry and the linen cupboard.

The phone rang, and she snatched it up.

"Let me guess. Our daughters are watching the chubby people, right?" said John-Paul. She'd always loved his voice on the phone: deep, warm and comforting. Oh, yes, her husband was hopeless, and lost things and ran late, but he took care of his wife and daughters, in that old-fashioned, responsible, I-am-the-man-and-this-is-my-job way. Bridget was right: Cecilia ruled her world, but she'd always known that if there was a crisis—a crazed gunman, a flood, a fire—John-Paul would be the one to save their lives. He'd throw himself in front of the bullet, build the raft, drive them safely through the raging inferno, and once that was done, he'd hand back control to Cecilia, pat his pockets and say, "Has anyone seen my wallet?"

After she saw the little Spider-Man die, the first thing she did was call John-Paul, her fingers shaking as she pressed the buttons.

"I found this letter," said Cecilia. She ran her fingertips over his handwriting on the front of the envelope. As soon as she heard his voice, she knew she was going to ask him about it that very second. They'd been married for fifteen years. There had never been secrets.

"What letter?"

"A letter from you," said Cecilia. She was trying to sound light, jokey, so that this whole situation would stay in the right perspective, so that whatever was in the letter would mean nothing, would change nothing. "To me, to be opened in the event of your death." It was impossible to use the words "event of your death" to your husband without your voice coming out odd.

There was silence. For a moment she thought they'd been cut off, except that she could hear a gentle hum of chatter and clatter in the background. It sounded like he was calling from a restaurant.

Her stomach contracted.

"John-Paul?"

TWO

I f this is a joke," said Tess, "it's not funny."

Will put his hand on her arm. Felicity put her hand on her other arm. They were like matching bookends holding her up.

"We're so very, very sorry," said Felicity.

"So sorry," echoed Will, as if they were singing a duet together.

They were sitting at the big round wooden table they used for client meetings, but mostly for eating pizza. Will's face was dead white. Tess could see each tiny black hair of his stubble in sharp definition, standing upright, like some sort of miniature crop growing across his shockingly white skin. Felicity had three distinct red blotches on her neck.

For a moment Tess was transfixed by those three blotches, as if they held the answer. They looked like fingerprints on Felicity's brand-new slender neck. Finally, Tess raised her eyes and saw that Felicity's eyes—her famously beautiful almond-shaped green eyes; *The fat girl has such beautiful eyes!*—were red and watery.

"So this realization," said Tess. "This realization that you two . . ." She stopped. Swallowed.

"We want you to know that nothing has actually happened," interrupted Felicity.

"We haven't—you know," said Will.

"You haven't slept together." Tess saw that they were both proud of this, that they almost expected her to admire them for their restraint.

"Absolutely not," said Will.

"But you want to," said Tess. She was almost laughing at the absurdity of it. "That's what you're telling me, right? You want to sleep together."

They must have kissed. That was worse than if they'd slept together. Everyone knew that a stolen kiss was the most erotic thing in the world.

The blotches on Felicity's neck began to slink up her jawline. She looked like she was coming down with a rare infectious disease.

"We're so sorry," said Will again. "We tried so hard to—to make it not happen."

"We really did," said Felicity. "For months, you know, we just—"

"Months? This has been going on for months!"

"Nothing has actually gone on," intoned Will, as solemnly as if he were in church.

"Well, something has gone on," said Tess. "Something rather significant has gone on." Who knew she was capable of speaking with such hardness? Each word sounded like a block of concrete.

"Sorry," said Will. "Of course—I just meant—you know."

Felicity pressed her fingertips to her forehead and began to weep. "Oh, Tess."

Tess's hand went out of its own accord to comfort her. They were closer than sisters. She always told people that. Their mothers were twins, and Felicity and Tess were only children, born within six months of each other. They'd done everything together.

Tess had once punched a boy—a proper closed-fist right hook across the jaw—because he called Felicity a baby elephant, which was exactly what Felicity had looked like all through her school days. Felicity had grown into a fat adult, "a big girl with a pretty face." She drank Coke like it was water and never dieted or exercised or seemed particularly bothered by her weight. And then, about six months ago, Felicity had joined Weight Watchers, given up Coke, joined a gym, lost forty kilos and turned beautiful. Extremely beautiful. She was exactly the type of person they wanted for that *Biggest Loser* show: a stunning woman trapped in a fat person's body.

Tess had been thrilled for her. "Maybe she'll meet someone really nice now," she'd said to Will. "Now that she's got more confidence."

It seemed that Felicity *had* met someone really nice. Will. The nicest man Tess knew. That took a lot of confidence, to steal your cousin's husband.

"I'm so sorry, I just want to die," wept Felicity.

Tess pulled back her hand. Felicity—snarky, sarcastic, funny, clever, fat Felicity—sounded like an American cheerleader.

Will tipped his head back and stared at the ceiling with a clenched jaw. He was trying not to cry too. The last time Tess had seen him cry was when Liam was born.

Tess's eyes were dry. Her heart hammered as if she were terrified, as if her life were in danger. The phone rang.

"Leave it," said Will. "It's after hours."

Tess stood, went over to her desk and picked up the phone.

"TWF Advertising," she said.

"Tess, my love, I know it's late, but we've got us a little problem."

It was Dirk Freeman, marketing director of Petra Pharmaceuticals, their most important and best-paying client. It was Tess's job to make Dirk feel important, to reassure him that although he was fifty-six and was never going to climb any higher in the ranks of senior management, he was the big kahuna and Tess was his servant, his maid, his lowly chambermaid, in fact, and he could tell her what to do and be flirty, or grumpy, or stern, and she'd pretend to give him a bit of lip, but when it came down to it, *she had to do what he said*. It had occurred to her recently that the service she was providing Dirk Freeman bordered on sexual.

"The color of the dragon on the Cough Stop packaging is all wrong," said Dirk. "It's too purple. Much too purple. Have we gone to print?"

Yes, they'd gone to print. Fifty thousand little cardboard

boxes had rolled off the presses that day. Fifty thousand perfectly purple, toothily grinning dragons.

The work that had gone into those dragons. The e-mails, the discussions. And while Tess was talking about dragons, Will and Felicity were falling in love.

"No," said Tess, her eyes on her husband and cousin, who were both still sitting at the meeting table in the center of the room, their heads bowed, examining their fingertips, like teenagers in detention. "It's your lucky day, Dirk."

"Oh, I thought it would have—well, good." He could barely hide his disappointment. He'd wanted Tess all breathless and worried. He'd wanted to hear the tremor of panic in her voice.

His voice deepened, became as abrupt and authoritative as if he were about to lead his troops onto the battlefield. "I need you to hold everything on Cough Stop, right? The lot. Got it?"

"Got it. Hold everything on Cough Stop."

"I'll get back to you."

He hung up. There was nothing wrong with the color. He'd call back the next day and say it was fine. He'd just needed to feel powerful for a few minutes. One of the younger hotshots had just made him feel inferior in a meeting.

"The Cough Stop boxes went to print today." Felicity turned in her seat and looked worriedly at Tess.

"It's fine," said Tess.

"But if he's going to change—" said Will.

"I *said* it's fine."

She didn't feel angry yet. Not really. But she could feel the possibility of a fury worse than anything she'd ever experienced, a simmering vat of anger that could explode like a fireball, destroying everything in its sight.

She didn't sit down again. Instead she turned and examined the whiteboard where they recorded all their work in progress.

Cough Stop packaging!!!

Bedstuff website ☺

It was humiliating to see her own scrawly, carefree, confident handwriting with its flippant exclamation marks. The smiley face next to the Bedstuff website, because they'd worked so hard to get that job, pitching against bigger companies, and then, yes! They'd won it. She'd drawn that smiley face yesterday, when she was ignorant of the secret that Will and Felicity were sharing. Had they exchanged rueful looks behind her back when she'd drawn the smiley face? *She won't be so smiley-faced once we confess our little secret, will she?*

The phone rang again.

This time Tess let it go to the answering service.

TWF Advertising. Their names entwined together to form their little dream business. The idle "what if" conversation they'd actually made happen.

The Christmas before last they'd been in Sydney for the holiday. As was traditional, they spent Christmas Eve at Felicity's parents' house. Tess's Aunt Mary and Uncle Phil. Felicity was still fat. Pretty and pink and perspiring in a size eighteen dress. They had the traditional sausages on the barbecue, the traditional creamy pasta salad, the traditional pavlova. She and Felicity and Will had all been whining about their jobs. Incompetent management. Stupid colleagues. Drafty offices. And so on and so forth. "Geez, you're a miserable bunch, aren't you?" said Uncle Phil, who didn't have anything to whine about now that he was retired.

"Why don't you go into business together?" said Tess's mother.

It was true that they were all in similar fields. Tess was the marketing communications manager for a but-this-is-the-way-we've-always-done-it legal publishing company. Will was the creative director of a large, prestigious, extremely pleased with themselves advertising agency. (That's how they'd met. Tess had been Will's client.) Felicity was a graphic designer working for a nasty tyrant.

Once they'd started talking about it, the ideas had fallen into place so fast. *Click, click, click!* By the time they were eating the last mouthfuls of pavlova, it was all set. Will would be the creative director! Obviously! Felicity would be the art director! Of course! Tess would be the account executive! That one wasn't quite so obvious. She'd never held a role like that. She'd always been on the client side, and she considered herself something of a social introvert.

In fact, a few weeks ago she'd done a *Reader's Digest* quiz in a doctor's waiting room called "Do You Suffer from Social Anxiety?" and her answers (all *C*s) confirmed that she did, in fact, suffer from social anxiety and should seek professional help or "join a support group." Everybody who did that quiz probably got the same result. If you didn't suspect you had social anxiety, you wouldn't bother doing the quiz; you'd be too busy chatting with the receptionist.

She certainly did not seek professional help, nor tell a single soul. Not Will. Not even Felicity. If she talked about it, then it would make it real. The two of them would watch her in social situations and be kindly empathetic when they saw the humiliating evidence of her shyness. The important thing was to *cover it up*. When she was a child her mother had once told her shyness was almost a form of selfishness. "You see, when you hang your head like that, darling, people think you don't like them!" Tess had taken that to heart. She grew up and learned how to make small talk with a thumping heart. She forced herself to make eye contact, even when her nerves were screaming at her to *look away, look away!* "Bit of a cold," she'd say to explain away the dryness of her throat. She learned to live with it, the way other people learned to live with lactose intolerance or sensitive skin.

Anyway, Tess wasn't overly concerned that Christmas Eve two years ago. It was all just talk, and they'd been drinking a lot of Aunt Mary's punch. They weren't *really* going to start a business together. She wouldn't really have to be the account executive.

But then, in the new year, when they got back to Melbourne, Will and Felicity had kept going on about it. Will and Tess's house had a huge downstairs area that the previous owners had used as a teenagers' retreat. It had its own separate entrance. What did they have to lose? The start-up costs would be negligible. Will and Tess had been putting extra money on their mortgage. Felicity was sharing an apartment. If they failed, they could all go back out and get jobs.

Tess had been swept along on the wave of their enthusiasm. She'd been happy enough to resign from her job, but the first time she sat outside a potential client's office, she had to cram her hands between her knees to stop them from trembling. Often she could actually feel her *head* wobbling. Even now, after eighteen months, she still suffered debilitating nerves each time she met a new client. Yet she was oddly successful in her role. "You're different from other agency people," one client told her at the end of their first meeting, as he shook her hand to seal the deal. "You actually listen more than you talk."

The horrible nerves were balanced by the glorious euphoria she felt each time she walked out of a meeting. It was like walking on air. She'd done it again. She'd battled the monster and won. And best of all, nobody suspected her secret. She brought in the clients. The business flourished. A product launch they did for a cosmetics company had even been nominated for a marketing award.

Tess's role meant that she was often out of the office, leaving Will and Felicity alone for hours at a time. If someone had asked her if that worried her, she would have laughed. "Felicity is like a sister to Will," she would have said.

She turned from the whiteboard. Her legs felt weak. She went and sat back down, choosing a chair at the other end of the table from them. She tried to get her bearings.

It was six o'clock on a Monday night. She was right in the middle of her life.

There had been so many other things distracting her when Will came upstairs and said he and Felicity needed to talk to her about something. Tess had just put down the phone from speaking with her mother, who had rung to say she'd broken her ankle playing tennis. She was going to be on crutches for the next eight weeks, and she was very sorry, but could Easter be in Sydney instead of Melbourne this year?

It was the first time in the fifteen years since Tess and Felicity had moved interstate that Tess had felt bad about not living closer to her mother.

"We'll get a flight straight after school on Thursday," Tess had said. "Can you cope until then?"

"Oh, I'll be fine. Mary will help. And the neighbors."

But Aunt Mary didn't drive, and Uncle Phil couldn't be expected to drive her over every day. Besides, Mary and Phil were both starting to look frail themselves. And Tess's mother's neighbors were ancient old ladies or busy young families who barely had time to wave hello as they backed their big cars out of their driveways. It didn't seem likely that they'd be bringing over casseroles.

Tess had been fretting over whether she should book a flight to Sydney for the very next day, and then perhaps organize a home helper for her mother. Lucy would hate to have a stranger in the house, but how would she shower? How would she cook?

It was tricky. They had so much work on, and she didn't like to leave Liam. He wasn't quite himself. There was a boy in his class, Marcus, who was giving him grief. He wasn't exactly bullying him; that would have been nice and clear-cut and they could have followed the school's sternly bullet-pointed "We Take a Zero-Tolerance Approach to Bullying" code of practice. Marcus was more complicated than that. He was a charming little psychopath.

Something new and awful had gone on with Marcus that day at school, Tess was sure of it. She'd been giving Liam his dinner while Will and Felicity were downstairs working. Most nights she and Will and Liam, and often Felicity too, managed to eat as a family, but the Bedstuff website was meant to go live that Friday, so they were all working long hours.

Liam had been quieter than usual while he was eating his dinner. He was a dreamy, reflective little boy; he'd never been a chatterbox, but there had been something so grown-up and sad about the way he mechanically speared each piece of sausage with his fork and dunked it in the tomato sauce.

"Did you play with Marcus today?" Tess had asked.

"Nah," said Liam. "Today's Monday."

"So what?"

But he'd closed down and refused to say another word about it, and Tess had felt rage fill her heart. She needed to talk to his teacher again. She had the strongest feeling that her child was in an abusive relationship and nobody could see it. The school playground was like a battlefield.

That's what had been on Tess's mind when Will had asked her if she'd come downstairs: her mother's ankle and Marcus.

Will and Felicity were sitting at the meeting table waiting for her. Before Tess joined them, she collected all the coffee mugs that were sitting around the office. Felicity had a habit of making herself fresh cups of coffee that she never finished. Tess put the mugs in a row on the meeting table and said, as she sat down, "New record, Felicity. *Five* half-drunk cups."

Felicity hadn't said anything. She looked oddly at Tess, as if she felt *really* bad about the coffee cups, and then Will made his extraordinary announcement.

"Tess, I don't know how to say this," he said. "But Felicity and I have fallen in love."

"Very funny." Tess had grouped the coffee cups together and smiled. "Hilarious."

But it seemed it wasn't a joke.

Now she studied her hands on the honey-gold pine of the desk. Her pale, blue-veined, knuckly hands. An ex-boyfriend had once told her that he was in love with her hands. Will had a lot of trouble getting the wedding ring over her knuckle at their wedding. Their guests had laughed softly. Will had pretended to exhale with relief once he got it on, while he secretly caressed her hand.

Tess looked up and saw Will and Felicity exchange covert worried glances.

"So it's true love, is it?" said Tess. "You're *soul mates*, are you?"

A nerve throbbed in Will's cheek. Felicity tugged at her hair.

Yes. That's what they were both thinking. *Yes, it is true love. Yes, we are soul mates.*

"When exactly did this start?" she asked. "When did these feelings between you develop?"

"That doesn't matter," said Will hurriedly.

"It matters to *me*!" Tess's voice rose.

"I guess, I'm not sure, maybe, about six months ago?" mumbled Felicity, looking at the desk.

"So when you started to lose weight," said Tess.

Felicity shrugged.

Tess said to Will, "Funny that you never looked twice at her when she was fat."

The bitter taste of nastiness flooded her mouth. How long since she'd let herself say something that was purely nasty? Not since she was a teenager.

She had never called Felicity fat. Never said a critical word about her weight.

"Tess, please . . ." said Will, without any censure in his voice, just a soft, desperate pleading.

"It's fine," said Felicity. "I deserve it. We deserve it."

She lifted her chin and looked at Tess with naked, brave humility.

So Tess was going to be allowed to kick and scratch as much as she wanted. They were just going to sit there and take it for as long as it took. They weren't going to fight back. Will and Felicity were fundamentally good. She knew this. They were good people, and that's why they were going to be so *nice* about this, so understanding and accepting of Tess's rage, so that in the end *Tess* would be the bad person, not them. They hadn't actually slept together; they hadn't betrayed her. They'd fallen in love! It wasn't an ordinary grubby little affair. It was fate. Predestined. Nobody could think that badly of them.

It was genius.

"Why didn't you tell me on your own?" Tess tried to lock eyes with Will, as if the strength of her gaze could bring him back from wherever he'd gone. His eyes, his strange hazel eyes, the color of beaten copper, with thick black eyelashes, eyes that were so different from Tess's own run-of-the-mill pale blue ones; the eyes that her son had inherited and that Tess thought of now as somehow *belonging* to her, a beloved possession for which she gracefully accepted compliments: "Your son has lovely eyes." "He gets them from my husband. Nothing to do with me." But everything to do with her. Hers. They were *hers*. Will's gold eyes were normally amused; he was always ready to laugh at the world, he found day-to-day life generally pretty funny. It was one of the things she loved about him most. But right now they were looking at her imploringly, the way Liam looked at her when he wanted something at the supermarket.

Please, Mum, I want that sugary treat with all the preservatives and the cleverly branded packaging and I know I promised I wouldn't ask for anything but I want it.

Please, Tess, I want your delicious-looking cousin and I know I promised to be true to you in good times and bad, in sickness and health, but pleeeease.

No. You may not have her. I said no.

"We couldn't work out the right time or the right place," said Will. "And we both wanted to tell you. We couldn't—and then we just thought, we couldn't go any longer without you knowing—so we just . . ." His jaw shifted, turkeylike, in and out, back and forth. "We thought there would never be a good time for a conversation like this."

We. They were a "we." They'd talked about this. Without her. Well, of course they'd talked without her. They'd fallen in love without her.

"I thought I should be here too," said Felicity.

"Did you, now?" said Tess. She couldn't bear to look at Felicity. "So what happens next?"

Asking the question filled her with a fresh nauseated wave of disbelief. Surely nothing was going to happen. Surely Felicity would rush off to one of her new gym classes and Will would come upstairs and talk to Liam while he had his bath, maybe get to the bottom of the Marcus problem, while Tess cooked a stir-fry for dinner; she had the ingredients ready. It was too bizarre, thinking of the little plastic-wrapped tray of chicken strips sitting staidly in the refrigerator. Surely she and Will were still going to have a glass of that half-empty bottle of wine and talk about potential men for the brand-new, slender Felicity. They'd already canvassed so many possibilities. Their Italian bank manager. The big quiet guy who supplied all their gourmet jams. Never once had Will slapped his hand to his forehead and said, "Of course! How could I have missed it? *Me!* I'd be perfect for her!"

It was a joke. She couldn't stop thinking that the whole thing was a terrible joke.

"We know nothing can make this easy, or right, or better," said Will. "But we'll do *whatever* you want, whatever you think is right for you and for Liam."

"For Liam," repeated Tess, dumbstruck.

For some reason it hadn't occurred to her that Liam would have to be told about this, that Liam would have anything to do with it, or be in any way affected. Liam, who was upstairs right now, lying on his stomach, watching television, his six-year-old little mind filled with giant-size worries of Marcus.

No, she thought. *No, no, no. Absolutely not.*

She saw her mother appearing at her bedroom door. "Daddy and I want to talk to you about something."

It would not happen to Liam the way it had happened to her. Over her dead body. It was the one thing she'd always known she could and would spare him from. Her beautiful, grave-faced little boy would not feel the loss and confusion she'd felt that awful summer all those years ago. He would *not* pack a little overnight bag every second Friday. He would *not* have to check a calendar on the refrigerator to see where he was sleeping each weekend. He would *not* learn to think before he spoke whenever one parent asked a seemingly innocuous question about the other.

Her mind raced.

All that mattered now was Liam. Her own feelings were irrelevant. How could she save this? How could she stop it?

"We never, ever meant for this to happen." Will's eyes were big and guileless. "And we want to do this the right way. The best way for all of us. We even wondered—"

Tess saw Felicity shake her head slightly at Will.

"You even wondered what?" said Tess. Here was more evidence of their talking. She could imagine the enjoyable intensity of these conversations. Teary eyes demonstrating what good people they were, how they were suffering at the thought of hurting Tess, but what choice did they have in the face of their passion, their love?

"It's too soon to talk about what we're going to do." Felicity's voice was firmer suddenly. Tess's fingernails dug into her palms. How dare she? How dare she talk in her normal voice, as if this were a normal situation, a normal problem?

"You even wondered *what*?" Tess kept her eyes on Will.

Forget about Felicity, she told herself. *You don't have time to feel angry. Think, Tess, think.*

Will's face went from white to red. "We wondered if it would be possible for all of us to live together. Here. For Liam's sake. It's not like this is a normal breakup. We're all . . . family. So that's why we thought, I mean, maybe it's crazy, but we just thought it might be possible. Eventually."

Tess guffawed. A hard, almost guttural sound. Were they out of their minds? "You mean, I just move out of my bedroom and Felicity moves in? So we just say to Liam, 'Don't worry, honey, Daddy sleeps with Felicity now and Mummy is in the spare room'?"

Felicity looked mortified. "Of course not."

"When you put it like that—" began Will.

"But what other way is there to put it?"

Will exhaled. He leaned forward. "Look," he said. "We don't need to work anything out right this second." Sometimes Will used a particularly masculine, reasonable but authoritative tone in the office when he wanted things done a certain way. Tess and Felicity gave him absolute hell about it. He was using that tone now, as if it was time to get things under control.

How *dare* he?

Tess lifted her closed fists and slammed them down so hard on the table that it rattled. She'd never done such a thing before. It felt farcical and absurd and somewhat thrilling. She was pleased to see both Will and Felicity flinch.

"I'll tell you what's going to happen," she said, because all at once it was perfectly clear.

It was simple.

Will and Felicity needed to have a proper affair. The sooner, the better. This smoldering thing they had going had to run its course. At the moment it was sweet and sexy. They were star-crossed lovers, Romeo and Juliet gazing soulfully at each other over the purple Cough Stop dragon. It needed to get sweaty and sticky and sleazy and eventually—hopefully, God willing—banal and dull. Will loved his son, and once the fog of lust cleared, he'd see that he'd made a ghastly but not irretrievable, mistake.

This could all be fixed.

The only way forward was for Tess to leave. Right now.

"Liam and I will go and stay in Sydney," she said. "With Mum. She called just a minute ago to say she's broken her ankle. She needs someone there to help her."

"Oh, no! How? Is she okay?" said Felicity.

Tess ignored her. Felicity didn't get to be the caring niece anymore. She was the other woman. Tess was the wife. And she was going to fight this. For Liam's sake. She would fight it and she would win.

"We'll stay with her until her ankle is better."

"But, Tess, you can't take Liam to live in *Sydney*." Will's bossy tone vanished. He was a Melbourne boy. There had never been any question that they would live anywhere else. He looked at Tess with a wounded expression, as if he were Liam being unjustly told off for something. Then his brow cleared. "What about school?" he said. "He can't miss school."

"He can go to St. Angela's for a term. He needs to get away from Marcus. This will be good for him. A complete change of scenery. He can walk to school, like I did."

"You wouldn't be able to get him in," said Will frantically. "He's not Catholic!"

"Who says he's not Catholic?" said Tess. "He's baptized in the Catholic Church."

Felicity opened her mouth and shut it again.

"I'll get him in," said Tess. She had no idea how hard it would be to get him in. "Mum knows people at the church."

As Tess spoke, images of St. Angela's, the tiny local Catholic school she and Felicity had both attended, filled her head. Playing hopscotch in the shadows of the church spires. The sound of church bells. The sweet rotting smell of forgotten bananas in the bottom of school bags. It was a five-minute walk from Tess's mother's home. The school was at the end of a tree-lined cul-de-sac, and in the summer, the trees formed a canopy overhead like a cathedral. It was autumn now, still warm enough to swim in Sydney. The leaves of the liquidambars would be green and gold. Liam would walk through puddles of pale pink rose petals on uneven footpaths.

Some of Tess's old teachers were still teaching at St. Angela's. Kids whom Tess and Felicity had been at school with had grown up and turned into mums and dads who sent their own children there. Tess's mother mentioned their names sometimes, and Tess could never quite believe they still existed. Like the gorgeous Fitzpatrick boys. Six blond, square-jawed boys who were so similar, they looked like they'd been purchased in bulk. They were so good-looking, Tess used to blush whenever one of them walked by. One of the altar boys was always a Fitzpatrick boy. Each of them left St. Angela's in Year 4 and went off to that exclusive Catholic boys' school on the harbor. They were wealthy as well as gorgeous. Apparently the eldest Fitzpatrick boy had three daughters, who were all at St. Angela's. She hadn't seen a Fitzpatrick boy in years.

Could she really do it? Take Liam to Sydney and send him to her old primary school? It felt impossible, like she was trying to send him back through time to her childhood. For a moment she felt dizzy again. This wasn't happening. Of course she couldn't take Liam out of school. His sea creature project was due on Friday. He had Little Athletics on Saturday. She had a load of washing ready to go on the line and a potential new client to see first thing tomorrow morning.

But she saw that Will and Felicity were exchanging glances again, and her heart twisted. She looked at her watch. It was six thirty p.m. From upstairs she could hear the theme music for that unbearable show *The Biggest Loser*. Liam must have switched off his DVD and changed it over to normal TV. In a minute he'd flick the channel looking for something with guns.

"You get nothing for nothing!" shouted someone from the television set.

Tess hated the empty motivational phrases they used on that show.

"I'll get us on a flight tonight," she said.

"Tonight?" said Will. "You can't take Liam on a flight tonight."

"Yes I can. There'll be a nine p.m. flight. We'll make it easily."

"Tess," Felicity said. "This is over the top. You really don't need to—"

"We'll get out of your way," said Tess. "So you and Will can sleep together. Finally. Take my bed! I changed the sheets this morning."

Other things came into her head. Far worse things she could say.

To Felicity: "He likes you on top, so lucky you lost all that weight!"

To Will: "Don't look too closely at all the stretch marks."

But no, they were the ones who should be feeling as sordid as a roadside motel. She stood up and smoothed down the front of her skirt.

"So that's that. You'll just have to deal with the agency without me. Tell the clients there's been a family emergency."

There certainly had been a family emergency.

She went to pick up the row of Felicity's half-full coffee

cups, linking her fingers through as many handles as she could carry. Then she changed her mind, put the cups back down, and while Will and Felicity watched, she carefully selected the two fullest cups, lifted them up in the palms of her hands and, with a netballer's careful aim, threw cold coffee straight at their stupid, earnest, sorry faces.

THREE

Rachel thought they were going to tell her that they were having another baby. That's what made it so much worse. As soon as they walked into the house, she knew there was big news. They had the self-conscious, smug expressions of people who know they are about to make you sit up and listen.

Rob was talking more than usual. Lauren was talking less than usual. Only Jacob was his normal self, tearing through the house this way and that, flinging open the cupboards and drawers where he knew Rachel kept little treasure troves of toys and things that she thought might interest him.

Of course, Rachel didn't ask Lauren or Rob if they had something they wanted to tell her. She wasn't that sort of grandma, not her. She took meticulous care when Lauren visited to be the perfect mother-in-law: caring but not cloying, interested but not nosy. She never criticized or even made so much as a suggestion about Jacob, not even to Rob when he was on his own, because she knew how much worse that would be for Lauren to hear: "Mum says . . ." This wasn't easy. A steady stream of suggestions ran silently through her head like those snippets of news that ran along the bottom of the TV on CNN.

For one thing, the child needed a haircut! The two of them must be blind not to notice the way Jacob kept blowing his hair out of his eyes. Also, the fabric of that dreadful Thomas the Tank Engine shirt was much too scratchy on his skin. If he was wearing it on the day she had him, she always took it straight off and dressed him in a nice old soft T-shirt, and then madly re-dressed him when they were coming up the driveway.

But what good had it done her? All her careful mother-in-lawing? She may as well have been the mother-in-law from hell. Because they were leaving, and taking Jacob with them, as if they had every right—which they did, she guessed, technically.

There was no new baby. Lauren had been offered a job. A wonderful job in New York. It was a two-year contract. They told her at the dinner table when they were having dessert (Sara Lee apple custard turnover and ice cream). From their breathless elation, you'd think she'd been offered a job in bloody paradise.

Jacob was sitting on Rachel's lap when they told her, his solid, square little body melting against hers with the divine limpness of a tired toddler. Rachel was breathing in the scent of his hair, her lips against the little dip in the center of his neck.

When she had first held Jacob in her arms and pressed

her lips to his tender, fragile scalp, it had felt as though she were being brought back to life, like a wilting plant being watered. His new-baby scent had filled her lungs with oxygen. She'd actually felt her spine straighten, as if someone had finally released her from a heavy weight she'd been forced to carry for years. When she'd walked out into the hospital parking lot, she could see color seeping back into the world.

"We're hoping you'll come and visit us," said Lauren.

Lauren was a "career woman." She worked for the Commonwealth Bank doing something very high up and stressful and important. She earned more than Rob. This wasn't a secret. In fact, Rob seemed proud of it, mentioning it more than seemed necessary. If Ed had ever heard his son showing off about his wife's salary, he would have curled up and died, so it was lucky that he had . . . well, curled up and died.

Rachel had also worked for the Commonwealth Bank before she got married, although this coincidence had never come up in their conversations about Lauren's work. Rachel didn't know if her son had forgotten this fact about his mother's life, or never knew it, or just didn't find it that interesting. Of course, Rachel understood very well that her little bank job, the one she gave up as soon as she got married, had no similarity to Lauren's "career." Rachel couldn't conceive what Lauren actually did each day. The most she knew was that it was something to do with "project management."

You would think someone so good at project management could manage the project of packing a bag for Jacob when he came to stay the night, but apparently not. Lauren always seemed to forget something essential.

No more nights with Jacob. No more bath time. No more stories. No more dancing to the Wiggles in the living room. It felt like he was dying. She had to remind herself that he was still alive, sitting right here on her lap.

"Yeah, you've got to come and see us in New York City, Mum!" said Rob. He sounded like he already had an American accent. His teeth caught the light as he smiled at his mother. Those teeth had cost Ed and Rachel a small fortune. Rob's strong, straight, piano-key teeth would be right at home in America.

"Get yourself your first-ever passport, Mum! You could even see a bit of America if you wanted. Go on one of those bus tours. Or, I know, do one of those Alaskan cruises!"

She wondered sometimes if their lives hadn't been divided so cleanly as if by a giant wall—before April 6, 1984, after April 6, 1984—if Rob would have grown up differently. Not quite so relentlessly upbeat, not quite so much like a real estate agent. Mind you, he *was* a real estate agent, so it shouldn't have come as a surprise when he behaved like one.

"I want to do one of those Alaskan cruises," said Lauren. She put her hand over Rob's. "I always imagined us doing one when we're old and gray."

Then she coughed, probably because she remembered that Rachel was old and gray.

"It certainly would be interesting." Rachel took a sip of her tea. "Maybe a little chilly."

Were they mad? Rachel did not want to do an Alaskan

cruise. She wanted to sit on the back step in the sunshine and blow bubbles for Jacob in the backyard and watch him laugh. She wanted to see him grow week by week.

And she wanted them to have another baby. Soon. Lauren was thirty-nine! Just last week Rachel had told Marla that there was plenty of time for Lauren to have another baby. They had them so late these days, she'd said. But that was when she'd secretly thought there was going to be an announcement any minute. In fact, she'd been *planning* for that second baby (just like an ordinary, interfering mother-in-law). She had decided that when the baby came, she'd retire. She loved her job at St. Angela's, but in two years she'd be seventy (seventy!) and she was getting tired. Looking after two children two days a week would be enough for her. She'd assumed this was her future. She could almost feel the weight of the new baby in her arms.

Why didn't the damned girl want another baby? Didn't they want to give Jacob a little brother or sister? What was so special about New York, with all those beeping horns and steam billowing oddly from holes in the street? For Pete's sake, the girl went back to work *three months* after Jacob was born. It wasn't like having a baby would be that big an inconvenience for her.

If someone had asked Rachel that morning about her life, she would have said that it was full and satisfying. She looked after Jacob on Mondays and Fridays, and the rest of the time he was in day care while Lauren sat at her desk in the city, managing her projects. When Jacob was at day care, Rachel worked at St. Angela's as the school secretary. She had her work, her gardening, her friend Marla, her

stack of library books and two whole precious days a week
with her grandson. Jacob often stayed overnight with her
on the weekend too, so that Rob and Lauren could go out.
They liked going out, those two, to their fancy restaurants,
the theater and the *opera*, do you mind. Ed would have
guffawed over that. *Is my son a nancy boy or what?*

If someone had asked, "Are you happy?" she would have
said, "I'm as happy as I can be."

She had no idea that her life was so flimsily constructed,
like a house of cards, and that Rob and Lauren could march
in here on a Monday night and cheerfully help themselves
to the one card that mattered. Remove the Jacob card and
her life collapsed, floated softly to the ground.

Rachel pressed her lips to Jacob's head and tears filled
her eyes.

Not fair. Not fair. Not fair.

"Two years will go so quickly," said Lauren, her eyes on
Rachel.

"Like this!" Rob clicked his fingers.

For you, thought Rachel.

"Or we might not even stay the full two years," said
Lauren.

"Then again, you might end up staying for good!" said
Rachel, with a big bright smile to show that she was a
woman of the world and she knew how these things
worked.

She thought of the Russell twins, Lucy and Mary, and
how both their daughters had gone to live in Melbourne.
"They'll end up staying there," Lucy had said sadly to Ra-

chel one Sunday after church. It was years and years ago, but it had stuck in Rachel's head, because she was right. The last Rachel heard, the cousins—Lucy's shy little girl and Mary's plump daughter with the beautiful eyes—were still in Melbourne and were there for good.

But Melbourne was a hop, skip and a jump away. You could fly to Melbourne for the day if you wanted. Lucy and Mary did it all the time. You couldn't fly to New York for the day.

And then there were people like Virginia Fitzpatrick, who job-shared (in a manner of speaking) the school secretary's position with Rachel. Virginia had six sons and fourteen grandchildren, and most of them lived within a twenty-minute radius on Sydney's North Shore. If one of Virginia's children decided to go to New York, she probably wouldn't even notice; she had so many grandchildren to spare.

Rachel should have had more children. She should have been a good Catholic wife and mother and had at least six, but no, she didn't, because of her vanity, because she secretly thought she was special; different from all those other women. God knows exactly *how* she thought she was special. It wasn't like she had any specific aspirations of career, or travel, or whatever, not like girls did these days.

"When do you leave?" Rachel said to Lauren and Rob, as Jacob slid from her lap unexpectedly and bolted into the living room on one of his urgent missions. A moment later she heard the sound of the television start up. The clever little thing had worked out how to use the remote control.

"Not till the new year," said Lauren. "We've got lots to sort out. Visas and so on. We'll have to find an apartment, a nanny for Jacob."

A nanny for Jacob.

"Job for me." Rob sounded a little nervous.

"Oh, yes, darling," said Rachel. She did try to take her son seriously. She really did. "A job for you. In real estate, do you think?"

"Not sure yet," said Rob. "We'll have to see. I might end up being a househusband."

"So sorry I never taught him how to cook," said Rachel to Lauren, not especially sorry. Rachel had never been much interested in cooking or that good at it; it was just another job that had to be done, like doing the laundry. The way people went *on* these days about cooking.

"That's okay." Lauren beamed. "We'll probably eat out a lot in New York. The city that never sleeps, you know!"

"Although, of course, Jacob will need to sleep," said Rachel. "Or will the nanny feed him while you're out for dinner?"

Lauren's smile wavered and she glanced at Rob, who was oblivious, of course.

The volume of the television suddenly increased, so the house boomed with cinematic sound. A male voice shouted, "You get nothing for nothing!"

Rachel recognized the voice. It was one of the trainers on *The Biggest Loser*. She liked that show. She found it soothing to get caught up in a brightly colored, plastic world where all that mattered was how much you ate and exercised, where pain and anguish were suffered over no greater tragedy than push-ups, where people spoke intensely about calories and sobbed joyfully over lost kilos. And then they all lived happily, skinnily ever after.

"You playing with the remote again, Jake?" called out Rob over the noise of the TV. He left the table and went into the living room.

He was always the first to get up and go to Jacob. Never Lauren. Right from the beginning he'd changed nappies. Ed never changed a nappy in his life. Of course, all the daddies changed nappies these days. It probably didn't hurt them. It just made Rachel feel awkward, almost embarrassed, as if they were doing something inappropriate, too feminine. How the girls of today would shriek if she were to ever admit to that!

"Rachel," said Lauren.

Rachel saw that Lauren was looking at her nervously, as if she had a large favor to ask. *Yes, Lauren, I'll take care of Jacob while you and Rob live in New York! For two years? No problem. Off you go. Have a lovely time.*

"This Friday," said Lauren. "Good Friday. I know that it's, ah, the anniversary . . ."

Rachel froze. "Yes," she said in her chilliest voice. "Yes it is." She had no desire to discuss this Friday with Lauren, of all people. Her body had known weeks ago that Friday was coming up. It happened every year in the last days of summer, when she felt that very first hint of crispness in the air. She'd feel a tension in her muscles, a prickling sense of horror, and then she'd remember: *Of course. Here comes another autumn.* A pity. She used to love autumn.

"I understand that you go to the park," said Lauren, as

if they were discussing the venue for an upcoming cocktail party. "It's just that I wondered—"

Rachel couldn't bear it.

"Would you mind if we didn't talk about it? Just not right now? Another time?"

"Of course!" Lauren flushed, and Rachel felt a pang of guilt. She rarely played that card. It was so easy to make people feel terrible.

"I'll make us a cup of tea," she said, and began to stack the plates.

"Let me help." Lauren half stood.

"Leave that," ordered Rachel.

"If you're sure." Lauren pushed a lock of strawberry-blond hair behind her ear. She was a pretty girl. The first time Rob brought her home to meet Rachel, he could barely contain his pride. It reminded her of his rosy, plump face when he'd brought home a new painting from pre-school.

What happened to their family in 1984 should have made Rachel love her son even more, but it didn't. It was like she'd lost her ability to love—until Jacob was born. By then, she and Rob had developed a relationship that was perfectly nice, but it was like that dreadful carob chocolate. As soon as you tasted it, you knew that it was just a wrong, sad imitation. So Rob had every right to take Jacob away from her. She deserved it for not loving him enough. This was her penance. Two hundred Hail Marys and your grandson goes to New York. There was always a price, and Rachel always had to pay it in full. No discounts. Just like she'd paid for her mistake in 1984.

Rob was making Jacob giggle now. Wrestling with him, probably, hanging him upside down by his ankles, the same way Ed used to wrestle with him.

"Here comes the . . . TICKLE MONSTER!" cried Rob.

Peal after peal of Jacob's laughter floated into the room like streams of bubbles, and Rachel and Lauren both laughed together. It was irresistible, like they were being tickled themselves. Their eyes met across the table, and at that instant, Rachel's laughter turned into a sob.

"Oh, *Rachel*." Lauren half rose from her seat and reached out a perfectly manicured hand. (She had a manicure, a pedicure and a massage every third Saturday. She called it "Lauren time." Rob brought Jacob over to Rachel's place whenever it was "Lauren time," and they walked to the park on the corner and ate egg sandwiches.) "I'm so sorry. I know how much you'll miss Jacob, but—"

Rachel took a deep, shaky breath and pulled herself together with all the strength that she had, as if she were heaving herself back up from a cliff edge.

"Don't be silly," she said so sharply that Lauren flinched and dropped back into her seat. "I'll be fine. This is a wonderful opportunity for you all."

She began stacking their dessert plates, roughly scraping leftover Sara Lee into a messy, unappealing pile of food.

"By the way," she said, just before she left the room. "That child needs a haircut."

FOUR

John-Paul? Are you there?"

Cecilia pressed the phone so hard to her ear that it hurt.

Finally he spoke. "Have you opened it?" His voice was thin and reedy, like a querulous old man in a nursing home.

"No," said Cecilia. "You're not dead, so I thought I'd better not." She'd been trying for a flippant tone, but she sounded shrill, as if she were nagging him.

There was silence again. She heard someone with an American accent call out, "Sir! This way, sir!"

"Hello?" said Cecilia.

"Could you please not open it? Would you mind? I wrote it a long time ago, when Isabel was a baby, I think. It's sort of embarrassing. I thought I'd lost it, actually. Where did you find it?"

He sounded self-conscious, as if he were talking to her in front of people he didn't know that well.

"Are you with someone?" asked Cecilia.

"No. I'm just having breakfast here in the hotel restaurant."

"I found it when I was in the attic, looking for my piece of the Berlin . . . Anyway, I knocked over one of your shoe boxes, and there it was."

"I must have been doing my taxes around the same time I wrote it," said John-Paul. "What an idiot. I remember I looked and looked for it. I thought I was losing my mind. I couldn't *believe* I would lose . . ." His voice faded. "Well."

He sounded so contrite, so full of what seemed like over-the-top remorse.

"Well, that doesn't matter." Now she sounded motherly, like she was talking to one of the girls. "But what made you write it in the first place?"

"Just an impulse. I guess I was all emotional. Our first baby. It got me thinking about my dad and the things he didn't get to say after he died. Things left unsaid. All the clichés. It just says sappy stuff, about how much I love you. Nothing earth-shattering. I can't really remember, to be honest."

"So why can't I open it, then?" She put on a wheedling voice that slightly sickened her. "What's the big deal?"

Silence again.

"It's not a big deal, but, Cecilia, please, I'm asking you not to open it." He sounded quite desperate. For heaven's sake! What a fuss. Men were so ridiculous about emotional stuff.

"Fine. I won't open it. Let's hope I don't get to read it for another fifty years."

"Unless I outlast you."

"No chance. You eat too much red meat. I bet you're eating bacon right now."

"And I bet you fed those poor girls fish tonight, didn't you?" He was making a joke, but he still sounded tense.

"Is that Daddy?" Polly skidded into the room. "I need to talk to him urgently!"

"Here's Polly," said Cecilia as Polly attempted to pull the cordless phone from her grasp. "*Polly*, stop it. Just a *moment*. Talk to you tomorrow. Love you."

"Love you too," she heard him say as Polly grabbed the phone. She ran from the room with it pressed to her ear. "Daddy, listen, I need to tell you something, and it's quite a big *secret*."

Polly loved secrets. She hadn't stopped talking about them, or sharing them, ever since she'd learned of their existence at the age of two.

"Let your sisters talk to him too!" called out Cecilia.

She picked up her cup of tea and placed the letter next to her, squaring it up with the edge of the table. So that was that. Nothing to worry about. She would file it away and forget about it.

He'd been embarrassed. That was all. It was sweet.

Of course, now that she'd promised not to open it, she couldn't. It would have been better not to have mentioned it. She'd finish her tea and make a start on those muffins.

She pulled Esther's book about the Berlin Wall over, flipped the pages and stopped at a photo of a young boy with an angelic, serious face that reminded her a little of John-Paul, the way he'd looked as a young man, when she first fell in love with him. John-Paul always took great care with his hair, using a lot of gel to sculpt it into place, and he was quite adorably serious, even when he was drunk (they were often drunk in those early days). His gravity used to make Cecilia feel girly and giggly. They'd been together for ages before he revealed a lighter side.

The boy, she read, was Peter Fechter, an eighteen-year-old bricklayer who was one of the first people to die trying to escape over the Berlin Wall. He was shot in the pelvis and fell back into the "death strip" on the Eastern side, where he took an hour to bleed to death. Hundreds of witnesses on both sides watched, but nobody offered him medical assistance, although some people threw him bandages.

"For heaven's sake," said Cecilia crossly, and pushed the book away. What a thing for Esther to read, to know, that such things were possible.

Cecilia would have helped that boy. She would have marched straight out there. She would have called for an ambulance. She would have shouted, "What's wrong with you people?"

Who knew what she would have done really; probably nothing, if it meant the risk of being shot herself. She was a mother. She needed to be alive. Death strips were not part of her life. Nature strips. Shopping strips. She'd never been tested. She probably never would be tested.

"Polly! You've been talking to him for hours! Dad is probably bored!" yelled Isabel.

Why must they always be yelling? The girls missed their father desperately when he was away. He was more patient with them than Cecilia was, and right from when they were little he'd always been prepared to be involved in their lives in ways in which Cecilia quite honestly couldn't be bothered. He played endless tea parties with Polly, holding tiny teacups with his little finger held out. He listened thoughtfully to Isabel talk on and on about the latest drama with her friends. It was always a relief for all of them when John-Paul came home. "Take the little darlings!" Cecilia would cry, and he would, driving them off on some adventure, bringing them back hours later, sandy and sticky.

"Daddy does not think I'm boring!" screamed Polly.

"Give the phone to your sister right *now*!" yelled Cecilia.

There was a scuffle in the hallway, and Polly reappeared in the kitchen. She came and sat down at the table with Cecilia and put her head in her hands.

Cecilia slid John-Paul's letter in between the pages of Esther's book and looked at her six-year-old daughter's beautiful little heart-shaped face. Polly was a genetic anomaly. John-Paul was good-looking (a spunk, they used to call him) and Cecilia was attractive enough in low lighting, but somehow they'd managed to produce one daughter who was in a different league altogether. Polly looked just like Snow White: black hair, brilliant blue eyes and ruby lips. *Genuinely* ruby lips; people thought she was wearing lipstick. Her two elder sisters with their ash-blond hair and freckled noses were beautiful to her parents, but it was only Polly who consistently turned heads in shopping centers. "Far too pretty for her own good," Cecilia's mother-in-law had observed the other day, and Cecilia was irritated, but at the same time she understood. What did it do to your personality to have the one thing that every woman craved?

Cecilia had noticed that beautiful women held themselves differently; they swayed like palm trees in the breeze of all that attention. Cecilia wanted her daughters to run and stride and stomp. She didn't want Polly to bloody sway.

"Do you want to know the secret I told Daddy?" Polly looked up at her through her eyelashes.

Polly would sway, all right. Cecilia could see it already.

"That's okay," said Cecilia. "You don't need to tell me."

"The secret is that I've decided to invite Mr. Whitby to my pirate party," said Polly.

Polly's seventh birthday was the week after Easter. Her pirate party had been a popular topic of conversation for the last month.

"Polly," said Cecilia. "We've talked about this."

Mr. Whitby was the PE teacher at St. Angela's, and Polly was in love with him. Cecilia didn't know what it said about Polly's future relationships that her first crush was a man who appeared to be about the same age as her father. She was meant to be in love with teenage pop stars, not a middle-aged man with a shaved head. It was true that Mr. Whitby had *something*. He was very broad-chested and athletic-looking and he rode a motorbike and listened with his eyes, but it was the school mums who were meant to feel his sex appeal (which they certainly did; Cecilia herself was not immune), not his six-year-old students.

"We're not asking Mr. Whitby to your party," said Cecilia. "It wouldn't be fair. Otherwise he'd feel like he had to come to everyone's parties."

"He'd want to come to mine."

"No."

"We'll talk about it another time," said Polly airily, pushing her chair back from the table.

"We won't!" Cecilia called after her, but Polly had sauntered off.

Cecilia sighed. Well. Lots to do. She stood and pulled John-Paul's letter from Esther's book. First, she would file this damned thing.

He said he'd written it just after Isabel was born, and that he didn't remember exactly what it said. That was understandable. Isabel was twelve, and John-Paul was often so vague. He was always relying on Cecilia to be his memory.

It was just that she was pretty sure he'd been lying.

FIVE

aybe we should break in." Liam's voice pierced the silent night air like the shriek of a whistle. "We could smash a window with a rock. Like, for example, that rock right there! See, Mum, look, see, see, can you see—"

"Shhh," said Tess. "Keep your voice down!" She banged the door knocker against the wood of the door over and over.

Nothing.

It was eleven o'clock at night, and she and Liam were standing at her mother's front door. The house was completely dark, the blinds drawn. It looked deserted. In fact, the whole street seemed eerily silent. Was no one up watching the late news? The only light came from a streetlight on the corner. The sky was starless, moonless. The only sound was a single plaintive cicada, the last survivor of summer, and the soft sigh of far-off traffic. She could smell the soft perfume of her mother's gardenias. Tess's mobile phone had run out of battery. She couldn't call anyone, not even a taxi to take them to a hotel. Maybe they *would* have to break in, but Tess's mother had become so security-conscious over the last few years. Didn't Mum have an alarm now? Tess imagined the sudden *woop, woop* of an alarm shattering the neighborhood.

I can't believe this is happening to me.

She hadn't thought it through. She should have called earlier in the night to let her mother know that they were coming, but she'd been in such a state, booking the flight, packing, getting to the airport, finding the right gate, Liam trotting alongside her, talking the whole time. He was so excited, he wouldn't shut up the whole flight, and now he was so exhausted he was virtually delirious.

He thought they were on a rescue mission to help Grandma.

"Grandma has broken her ankle," Tess had told him. "So we're going to stay and help her for a little while."

"What about school?" he'd asked.

"You can miss a few days of school," she'd told him, and his face lit up like a Christmas tree. She hadn't mentioned anything about attending a new school. Obviously.

Felicity had left, and while Tess and Liam packed, Will had slunk about the house, pale and sniffing. When they were alone and she was throwing clothes into a bag, he'd tried to talk to her, and she'd turned on him like a cobra rising to strike, hissing through clenched, crazy teeth, "Leave me alone."

"I'm sorry," he said, taking a step backward. "I'm so sorry."

He and Felicity must have used the word "sorry" about five hundred times by now.

"I promise you," said Will, lowering his voice, presumably so Liam wouldn't overhear, "if there's any doubt in your mind, I want you to know that we never slept together."

"You keep saying that, Will," she said. "I don't know why you think that makes it better. It makes it worse. It never occurred to me that you *would* sleep together! Like, thank you so much for your restraint. I mean, for God's sake . . ." Her voice trembled.

"I'm sorry," he said again, and wiped the back of his hand across his nose, sniffing loudly.

Will had behaved perfectly normally in front of Liam. He'd helped him find his favorite baseball cap under his bed, and when the cab had arrived, he'd squatted down on his knees and half cuddled, half wrestled him in that rough, loving way of fathers with their sons. Tess had seen exactly how Will had managed to keep this thing with Felicity a secret for so long. Family life, even with just one little boy, had its own familiar rhythms, and it was perfectly possible to keep right on dancing like you always have, even when your mind is somewhere else.

And now here she was, stranded in this sleepy, silent little North Shore suburb of Sydney with a delirious six-year-old.

"Well," she said carefully to Liam. "I guess we should . . ."

What? Wake up a neighbor? Risk the alarm?

"Wait!" said Liam. He put a finger to his lips; his big

eyes were pools of shining blackness in the dark. "I think I hear something from inside."

He pressed his ear to the front door. Tess did the same. "Hear it?"

She did hear something. A strange, rhythmic thumping sound from overhead.

"It must be Grandma's crutches," said Tess.

Her poor mother. She'd probably been in bed. Her bedroom was right at the other end of the house. Bloody Will. Bloody Felicity. Dragging her poor crippled mum out of bed.

When exactly did this thing between Will and Felicity start? Was there an actual moment where something changed? How could she have missed it? She saw them together every single day of her life and she'd never noticed a thing. Felicity had stayed for dinner last Friday night. Maybe Will had been a little quieter than usual. Tess had thought it was because his back was playing up. He was tired. They'd all been working so hard. But Felicity had been in fine form. Luminous, even. Tess had caught herself staring a few times. Felicity's beauty was still so new, and it made everything about her beautiful. Her laugh. Her voice.

Yet Tess hadn't been wary. She'd been stupidly secure of Will's love. Secure enough to wear her old jeans with that black T-shirt that Will said made her look like a biker chick. Secure enough to tease him for his mild grumpiness. He'd whacked her bottom with the edge of the tea towel when they were cleaning up the kitchen afterward.

They hadn't seen Felicity over the weekend, which was unusual. She'd been busy, she said. It was rainy and cold. Tess and Will and Liam had watched TV, played snap, made pancakes together. It had been a good weekend. Hadn't it?

It occurred to her that Felicity was luminous on Friday night because she was in love.

The door swung open and light flooded the hallway. "What in the world?" said Tess's mother. She was wearing a blue quilted dressing gown and leaning heavily on a pair of crutches, her eyes blinking myopically, her face dragged down with pain and effort.

Tess looked at her mother's white-bandaged ankle and imagined her waking up, hauling herself out of bed, hobbling around trying to find her dressing gown and then the crutches.

"Oh, Mum," she said. "I'm so sorry."

"Why are you sorry? What are you doing here?"

"We've come . . ." she began, but her throat closed up.

"To help you, Grandma!" cried Liam. "Because of your ankle! We flew here in the dark!"

"Well, that's very lovely of you, my darling boy." Tess's mother moved on her crutches to the side to let them in. "Come in, come in. Sorry I took so long coming to the door. I had no idea crutches were so damned tricky. I imagined myself swinging jauntily along, but they dig into your armpits like I don't know what. Liam, go turn on the light in the kitchen and we'll have some hot milk and cinnamon toast."

"Cool!" Liam headed toward the kitchen, and for some

inexplicable six-year-old-boy reason, began moving his arms and legs jerkily like a robot. "I compute! I compute! Affirmative—to—cinnamon toast!"

Tess carried their bags inside.

"Sorry," she said again as she put them down in the hallway and looked up at her mother. "I should have called. Is your ankle very painful?"

"What happened?" said her mother.

"Nothing."

"Rubbish."

"Will . . ." she began, and stopped.

"My darling girl." Her mother lurched about alarmingly as she tried to reach for her without losing hold of the crutches.

"Don't break another bone." Tess steadied her. She could smell her mother's toothpaste, her face cream and soap, and beneath it all that familiar musky, musty Mum smell. On the hallway wall behind her mother's head was a framed photo of herself and Felicity at seven years old, in their white lacy Communion dresses and veils, their palms piously pressed together at the center of their chests in the traditional first Communion pose. Aunt Mary had an identical photo in the same spot in her hallway. Now Felicity was an atheist, and Tess described herself as "lapsed."

"Hurry up and tell me," said Lucy.

"Will . . ." Tess tried again. "And, and . . ." She couldn't finish.

"Felicity," supplied her mother. "Am I right? Yes." She lifted one elbow and thumped a crutch hard against the floor so that the first Communion photo rattled. "The little bitch."

———

1961. The Cold War was at its iciest. Thousands of East Germans were fleeing for the West. "No one has any intention of building a wall," announced East Germany's chancellor, Walter Ulbricht, described by some as Stalin's robot. People looked at one another with raised eyebrows. What the . . . ? Who said anything about a wall? *Thousands more packed their bags.*

In Sydney, Australia, a young girl called Rachel Fisher sat on the high wall overlooking Manly Beach, swinging her long, tanned legs, while her boyfriend, Ed Crowley, flipped through the Sydney Morning Herald, *annoyingly engrossed. There was an article in the paper about the developments in Europe, but neither Ed nor Rachel had much interest in Europe.*

Finally Ed spoke. "Hey, Rach, why don't we get you one of those?" he said, and pointed at the page in front of him.

Rachel peered over his shoulder without much interest. The paper was open to a full-page advertisement for Angus & Coote. Ed's finger was on an engagement ring. He grabbed her elbow just before she toppled off the wall onto the beach.

———

They were gone. Rachel was in bed with the television on, the *Women's Weekly* in her lap, a cup of Earl Grey tea on the bedside table, along with the flat cardboard box of macarons that Lauren had brought along tonight. Rachel should have offered them around at the end of the night, but she'd forgotten. It may have been deliberate; she could never be sure just how much she disliked her daughter-in-law. It was possible she hated her.

Why not go on your own to New York, my dear girl? Get two years' worth of Lauren time!

Rachel slid the cardboard tray onto the bed in front of her and examined the six garishly colored biscuits. They didn't look that special to her. Supposedly they were the latest thing among people who cared about the latest things. These ones were from a shop in the city where people lined up for hours to buy them. Fools. Did they have nothing better to do? Although it seemed unlikely that Lauren had lined up for hours. After all, Lauren had better things to do than everyone! Rachel had a feeling there might have been a story about the procurement of the macarons, but she didn't really listen when Lauren was speaking about anything that didn't involve Jacob.

She selected a red one and took a tentative bite.

"Oh, God," she moaned a moment later, and thought, for the first time in she didn't know how long, of sex. She took a bigger bite. "Mother *Mary*." She laughed out loud. No wonder people lined up for them. It was exquisite; the raspberry flavor of the creamy center was like the barest touch of fingertips on her skin, the meringue light and tender, like eating a cloud.

Wait. Who said that?

"It's like eating a cloud, Mummy!" An entranced little face.

Janie. About four years old. Her first taste of pink, sticky, sugary fairy floss at—Luna Park? A church fete? Rachel couldn't zoom back her memory. It was focused only on Janie's shining face and her words: "It's like eating a cloud, Mummy!"

Janie would have loved these macarons.

Without warning, the biscuit slipped from Rachel's fingers and she hunched over, as if she could duck the first punch, but it was too late, it had her. It had been a long time since it was as bad as this. A wave of pain, as fresh and shocking as that first year when she woke up each morning and for one instant forgot before she was punched in the face with the realization that Janie wasn't in the room down the hallway, spraying herself with too much sickly Impulse deodorant, pasting orange makeup over her perfect seventeen-year-old skin, dancing to Madonna.

The almighty, towering injustice of it tore and twisted her heart like contractions. *My daughter would have loved these silly biscuits. My daughter would have had a career. My daughter could have gone to New York.*

A steel vise wrapped around her chest and squeezed so she felt like she was suffocating and she gasped for air, but beneath her panic she could hear the weary, calm voice of experience: *You've been here before. It won't kill you. It feels like you can't breathe, but you actually are breathing. It feels like you'll never stop crying, but you actually will.*

Finally, little by little, the vise around her chest loosened its grip enough for her to breathe again. It never went away completely. She'd accepted that a long time ago. She'd die with the clamp of grief still wrapped around her chest. She didn't want it to go away. That would be like Janie had never existed.

She was reminded of those Christmas cards from the first year.

Dear Rachel, Ed and Rob, We wish you a merry Christmas and a happy new year.

It was as if they'd just closed up the space where Janie had been. And "*merry*"! Were they out of their silly little minds? She swore each time she'd opened another card, ripping it into tiny pieces.

"Mum, give them a break, they just don't know what else to say," Rob had said to her tiredly. He was just fifteen, and his face seemed to belong to a sad, pale fifty-year-old with acne.

Rachel swept the macaron crumbs off the sheets with the back of her hand. "Crumbs! Christ Almighty, look at these crumbs!" Ed would have said. He thought eating in bed was immoral. Also, if he could see the television sitting there on the chest of drawers, he'd have a fit. Ed believed that people who had televisions in their bedrooms were akin to cocaine addicts; weak, debauched types. The bedroom, according to Ed, was for a prayer on your knees next to the bed, your head resting on your fingertips, lips moving rapidly (very rapidly; he didn't believe in wasting too much of the Big Guy's time), followed by sex (preferably every night), followed by sleep.

She picked up the remote and pointed it at the television, flicking through the channels.

A documentary about the Berlin Wall.

No. Too sad.

One of those crime investigation shows.

Never.

A family sitcom.

She left it there for a moment, but it was a husband and a wife shouting at each other, and their voices were horrible and high-pitched. Instead, she switched it over to a cooking show and turned the sound down. Ever since she'd been living alone, she'd gone to bed with the television on, the comforting banality of the murmuring voices and flickering images warding off the feeling of terror that could sometimes overwhelm her.

She lay on her side and closed her eyes. She slept with the lights on. After Janie died she and Ed couldn't stand the dark. They couldn't go to sleep like normal people. They had to trick themselves and pretend that they weren't going to sleep.

Behind her closed eyelids, she saw Jacob toddling along a New York street, wearing his little denim overalls, crouching down with his fat little hands on his knees to examine the steam billowing out of the vents in the road. Was that steam *hot*?

Had she been crying for Janie before, or had she really been crying for Jacob? All she knew was that once they took him from her, life would go back to being unendurable, except—and this was the worst part—she *would* in fact endure it, it wouldn't kill her, she'd keep on living day after day after day, an endless loop of glorious sunrises and sunsets that Janie never got to see.

Did you call for me, Janie?

That thought was like the tip of a knife twisting and turning at her very core. It was excruciating every time, but she never stopped asking the question, because one, she deserved it, and two, it was the only way she could answer her if she had called. *I'm here. I'm still here.*

She'd read somewhere that wounded soldiers called for morphine and their mothers as they died on the battlefield. The Italian soldiers especially. "Mamma mia!" they called.

In a sudden movement that wrenched her back, Rachel sat up and hopped out of bed in Ed's pajamas (she'd started wearing them straight after he died and never stopped; they didn't really smell of him anymore, but she could almost imagine that they did). She got down on her knees next to her chest of drawers and pulled out an old photo album with a soft, faded green vinyl cover.

She sat back up on the bed and slowly flipped the pages. Janie laughing. Janie dancing. Janie eating. Janie sulking. Janie with her friends.

Including him. That boy. His head turned away from the camera, looking at Janie, as if she'd just said something smart and funny. What did she say? Every time, she always wondered that. *What did you just say, Janie?*

Rachel pressed her fingertip to his grinning, freckled face, and watched her mildly arthritic, age-spotted hand curl into a fist.

SIX

The first thing Janie Crowley did when she got out of bed that chilly April morning was jam the back of a chair beneath her door handle so neither of her parents could walk in on her. Then she got down on her knees next to her bed and heaved up the corner of her mattress to retrieve a pale blue box. She sat on the edge of her bed and removed a tiny yellow pill from the packet, holding it up on her fingertip to the light, considering it and all that it symbolized before placing it on the center of her tongue as reverently as a Communion wafer. Then she rehid the packet under her mattress and jumped back into her warm bed, pulled the covers up and turned on her clock radio to the tinny sound of Madonna singing "Like a Virgin."

The tiny pill tasted chemical, sweet and deliciously sinful.

"Think of your virginity as a gift. Don't just hand it over to any old fellow," her mother had said to her in one of those conversations where she was trying to pretend to be cool, as if any form of premarital sex would be okay, as if her father wouldn't fall to his knees and pray a thousand novenas at the thought of someone touching his pristine little girl.

Janie had no intention of handing it over to just anyone. There had been an application process, and today she would be informing the successful candidate.

The news came on, and most of it was boring, sliding right off her consciousness, nothing to do with her. The only part that was interesting was that Canada's first test-tube baby had been born. Australia already had a test-tube baby! *So we win, Canada! Ha, ha.* (She had older Canadian cousins who made her feel inferior with their sophisticated niceness and their not-quite-American accents.) She sat up in bed, grabbed her school diary and drew a long, thin baby squashed into a test tube, its little hands pressed up against the glass, its mouth gaping. *Let me out, let me out!* It would make the girls at school laugh. She snapped the diary shut. The idea of a test-tube baby was somehow repellent. It reminded her of that day when her science teacher started talking about a woman's eggs. Dis-gus-ting! And the worst part? Their science teacher was a man. A man talking about a woman's eggs. That was just so inappropriate. Janie and her friends were furious. Also, he probably wanted to look down all their shirts. They'd never actually caught him in the act, but they sensed his repulsive desire.

It was a shame that Janie's life was going to end in just

over eight hours, because she wasn't her nicest self. She had been an adorable baby, a winsome little girl, a shy, sweet young teen, but around the time of her seventeenth birthday last May, she'd changed. She was dimly aware of her mild awfulness. It wasn't her fault. She was terrified of everything (university, driving a car, ringing up to make a hairdresser's appointment), and her hormones were making her crazy, and so many boys were starting to act kind of angrily interested in her, as if maybe she was pretty, which was nice but confusing, because when she looked in the mirror all she could see was her ordinary, loathsome face and her weird, long, skinny body. She looked like a praying mantis. One of the girls at school had told her that, and it was true. Her limbs were too long. Her arms, especially. She was all out of proportion.

Also, her mother had something odd going on at the moment, which meant she wasn't concentrating on Janie, and up until recently she'd always concentrated on her with such irritating fierceness. (Her mother was *forty years old*! What could possibly be going on in her life that was so interesting?) It was unsettling to have that bright spotlight of attention vanish without warning. Hurtful, really, although she wouldn't have admitted that, or even been aware that she was hurt.

If Janie had lived, her mother would have returned to her normal, fiercely concentrating self, and Janie would have become lovely again around the time of her nineteenth birthday, and they would have been as close as a mother and daughter can be, and Janie would have buried her mother instead of the other way around.

If Janie had lived, she would have dabbled in soft drugs and rough boys, water aerobics and gardening, Botox and tantric sex. During the course of her lifetime, she would have had three minor car crashes, thirty-four bad colds and two major surgeries. She would have been a moderately successful graphic designer, a nervy scuba diver, a whiny camper, an enthusiastic bushwalker and an earlier adopter of the iPod, the iPhone and the iPad. She would have divorced her first husband and had IVF twins with her second, and the words "test-tube babies" would have flitted like an old joke across her mind while she posted their photos on Facebook for her Canadian cousins to Like. She would have changed her name to Jane when she was twenty and back to Janie when she was thirty.

If Janie Crowley had lived, she would have traveled and dieted, danced and cooked, laughed and cried, watched a lot of television and tried her very best.

But none of that was going to happen, because it was the morning of the last day of her life, and although she would have enjoyed watching the mascara-streaked faces of her friends as they made a spectacle of themselves, clutching one another and sobbing at her gravesite in an orgy of grief, she really would have preferred to have found out all the things that were waiting to happen to her.

SEVEN

Cecilia spent most of Sister Ursula's funeral thinking about sex. Not kinky sex. Nice, married, approved-by-the-Pope sex. But still. Sister Ursula probably wouldn't have appreciated it.

"Sister Ursula was devoted to the children of St. Angela's." Father Joe gripped both sides of the lectern, gazing earnestly at the tiny group of mourners (although, truthfully now, was anyone in this entire church really *mourning* Sister Ursula?), and for a moment his eyes seemed to meet Cecilia's as if for approval. Cecilia bobbed her head and smiled slightly to show him that he was doing a good job.

Father Joe was only thirty and not an unattractive man. What made a man in this day and age choose the priesthood? *Choose* celibacy?

So back to sex. Sorry, Sister Ursula.

She first remembered noticing that there was a problem

with their sex life last Christmas. She and John-Paul didn't seem to be going to bed at the same time. Either he'd be up late, working or surfing the net, and she'd be asleep before he came to bed, or else he'd suddenly announce he was exhausted and go to bed at nine o'clock. The weeks slipped on by, and every now and then she'd think, *Gosh, it's been a while*, and then forget about it.

Then there was that night back in February when she went out to dinner with some of the Year 4 mums and she'd drunk more than usual because Penny Maroni was driving. Cecilia had felt amorous when she got into bed, but John-Paul had brushed her hand away and mumbled, "Too tired. Leave me alone, you drunken woman." She'd laughed and fallen asleep, not at all offended. The next time he initiated sex she was going to make a jokey remark, like, "Oh, so now you want it." But she never got the opportunity. That's when she started to register the days ticking on by. What was going on?

She thought it had probably been about six months now, and the more time that passed, the more confused she got. Yet whenever the words started to form in her mouth—*Hey, what's going on, honey?*—something stopped her. Sex had never been an issue of contention between them, the way she knew it was between many couples. She didn't use it as a weapon or a bargaining tool. It was something unspoken and natural and beautiful. She didn't want to ruin that.

Maybe she just didn't want to hear his answer.

Or, worse, his *lack* of an answer. Last year John-Paul had taken up rowing. He loved it and came home each Sunday raving about how much he enjoyed it. But then he'd unexpectedly, inexplicably quit the team. "I don't want to talk about it," he'd said when she kept asking, desperate for a reason. "Give it a rest."

John-Paul could be so odd at times.

She hurried over the thought. Besides, she was pretty sure all men were odd at times.

Also, six months wasn't actually that long, was it? Not for a married middle-aged couple. Penny Maroni said they did it once a year if they were lucky.

Recently, though, Cecilia had felt like a teenage boy, thinking constantly about sex, mildly pornographic images flitting across her mind as she stood at the checkout, standing with the other parents watching the kids play sports and thinking of a hotel in Canberra where John-Paul had tied her wrists together with the blue plastic band the physical therapist had given her for her ankle exercises.

They left the blue band in the hotel room.

Cecilia's ankle still clicked when she turned it a certain way.

How did Father Joe cope? She was a forty-two-year-old woman, an exhausted mother of three daughters, with menopause right there on the horizon, and *she* was desperate for sex, so surely Father Joe Mackenzie, a fit young man who got plenty of sleep, found it difficult.

Did he masturbate? Were Catholic priests allowed, or was that considered not within the spirit of the whole celibacy thing?

Wait, wasn't masturbation a sin for everyone? This was something her non-Catholic friends would expect her to know. They seemed to think she was a walking Bible.

When truth be told, if she ever had time to think about it, she wasn't sure if she was even that enthusiastic a fan of God anymore. He seemed to have dropped the ball a long time ago. Appalling things happened to children, across the world, every single day. It was inexcusable.

Little Spider-Man.

She closed her eyes, blinked the image away.

Cecilia didn't care what the fine print said about free will and God's mysterious ways and blahdy-blah. If God had a supervisor, she would have sent off one of her famous letters of complaint a long time ago. "You have lost me as a customer."

She looked at Father Joe's earnest, smooth-skinned face. Once he'd told her that he found it "really interesting when people questioned their faith." But she didn't find her doubts all that relevant. She believed in St. Angela's with all her heart: the school, the parish, the community it represented. She believed that "love one another" was a lovely moral code by which to live her life. The sacraments were beautiful, timeless ceremonies. The Catholic Church was the team for which she'd always barracked. As for God, and whether he (or she—seemed more likely!) actually existed or not, well, maybe when the kids were all in high school she might have more time to think about it.

And yet, everyone thought she was the ultimate Catholic.

She thought of Bridget, saying at dinner the other night, "How did you get to be so *Catholic*?" when Cecilia mentioned something perfectly ordinary about Polly's first confession next year (or reconciliation, as they called it these days), as if her sister hadn't been quite the little liturgical dance queen when they were at school.

Cecilia would have given her little sister a kidney without hesitation, but sometimes she really wanted to straddle her and hold a pillow over her face. It had been an effective way of keeping her in line when they were kids. It was unfortunate the way adults had to repress their true feelings.

Of course, Bridget would give Cecilia a kidney too. She'd just groan a lot more during the recovery process, and mention it at every opportunity, and make sure Cecilia covered all her expenses.

Father Joe had wrapped things up. The scattered group of people in the church got to their feet for the final hymn with a gentle murmur of suppressed sighs, subdued coughs and the cracking of middle-aged knees. Cecilia caught Melissa McNulty's eye across the aisle; Melissa raised her eyebrows to indicate, *Aren't we good people for coming to Sister Ursula's funeral when she was so awful and we're so busy?*

Cecilia gave her a rueful half shrug that said, *But isn't that always the way?*

She had a Tupperware order in the car to give to Melissa after the funeral, and she must remember to confirm with her that she would be taking care of Polly at ballet this afternoon, because she had Esther's speech therapy and Isabel's haircut. Speaking of which, Melissa really needed to get her color redone. Her black roots looked dreadful. It was uncharitable of Cecilia to notice, but she couldn't help but remember being on canteen with Melissa last month and hearing her complain about how her husband wanted sex every second day, like clockwork.

As Cecilia sang along to "How Great Thou Art," she thought about Bridget's teasing remark at dinner and knew why it had bothered her.

It was because of the sex. Because if she wasn't having sex, she wasn't anything else except an uncool, middle-aged, frumpy mum. And, by the way, she was not frumpy. Just yesterday, a truck driver had given her a long, slow wolf whistle when she was running against the lights in her netball uniform to buy coriander.

The whistle was definitely for her. She was alone and she'd checked to make sure there hadn't been any other younger, more attractive women in sight. The previous week she'd had the disconcerting experience of hearing someone whistle when she was walking with the girls through the shopping center, and she'd turned to see Isabel looking resolutely ahead, her cheeks flushed pink. Isabel had suddenly shot up: She was already as tall as Cecilia, and she was starting to curve in at the waist, out at the hips and bust. Lately she'd been wearing her hair up in a high po-nytail with a heavy straight fringe hanging too low over her eyes. She was growing up, and it wasn't only her mother who was noticing.

It's starting, Cecilia had thought sadly. She wished she could give Isabel a shield, like the ones riot police held, to protect her from male attention, that feeling of being scored each time you walked down a street, the demeaning com-ments yelled out of cars, that casual sweep of the eyes. She'd wanted to sit down and talk to Isabel about it, but then she hadn't known what to say. She'd never quite gotten her head around it herself. It's no big deal. It is a big deal. They have no right to make you feel that way. Or, just ignore it, one day you'll turn forty and you'll slowly realize you don't feel the eyes anymore, and the freedom is a relief, but you'll also sort of miss it, and when a truck driver whistles at you while you're crossing the road, you'll think, *Really? For me?*

It had seemed like a really genuine, friendly whistle too.

It was a little humiliating just how much time she'd devoted to analyzing that whistle.

Well, anyway, she certainly was not worried that John-Paul was having an affair. Definitely not. It wasn't a possibility. Not even a remote possibility. He wouldn't have time for an affair! When would he fit it in?

He did travel a bit. He could fit in an affair then.

Sister Ursula's coffin was being carried from the church by four broad-shouldered, tousle-haired young men in suits and ties, with careful blank faces, who were supposedly her nephews. Fancy Sister Ursula sharing the same DNA as such attractive young boys. They'd probably spent the whole funeral thinking about sex too. Young boys like that with their roaring young libidos. The tallest one really was particularly good-looking with those dark, flashing eyes . . .

Dear God. Now she was imagining having sex with one of Sister Ursula's pallbearers. A *child*, by the look of him. He was probably still in high school. Her thoughts were not only immoral and inappropriate, but illegal. (Was it illegal to think? To covet your third-grade teacher's pallbearer?)

When John-Paul got home from Chicago on Good Friday, they would have sex every single night. They would rediscover their sex lives. It would be great. They'd always been so good together. She'd always assumed that they were having better-quality sex than everyone else. It had been such a cheering thought at school functions.

John-Paul couldn't *get* better sex anywhere else. (Cecilia had read a lot of books. She kept her skills up-to-date, as if it were a professional obligation.) He had no need for an affair. Not to mention that he was one of the most ethical, moral, rule-following people she knew. He wouldn't cross a double yellow line for a million dollars. Infidelity was not an option for him. He just would not do it.

That letter had nothing to do with an affair. She wasn't even thinking about the letter! That's how unconcerned she was about it. That fleeting moment last night when she thought he'd been lying on the phone was completely silly. The awkwardness over the letter was just because of the innate awkwardness of all long-distance phone calls. They were unnatural. You were on opposite sides of the world, at opposite ends of the day, so you couldn't quite synchronize your voices: one person too upbeat, the other too mellow.

Opening the letter would not result in some shocking revelation. It was not, for example, about another, secret family he was supporting. John-Paul did not have the requisite organizational abilities to handle bigamy. He would have slipped up long ago. Turned up at the wrong house. Called one of his wives by the wrong name. He'd be constantly leaving his possessions at the other place.

Unless, of course, his hopelessness was all part of his duplicitous cover.

Perhaps he was gay. That's why he'd gone off sex. He'd

been faking his heterosexuality all these years. Well, he'd certainly done a good job of it. She thought back to the early years, when they used to have sex three or four times in one day. That would really have been above and beyond the call of duty if he was only faking his interest.

He quite enjoyed musicals. He loved *Cats*! And he was better at doing the girls' hair than she was. Whenever Polly had a ballet concert, she insisted that John-Paul be the one to put her hair in a bun. He could talk arabesques and pirouettes with Polly as well as he could talk soccer with Isabel and the *Titanic* with Esther. Also, he adored his mother. Weren't gay men particularly close to their mothers? Or was that a myth?

He owned an apricot polo shirt, and ironed it himself.

Yes, he was probably gay.

The hymn finished. Sister Ursula's coffin left the church, and there was a sense of a job well done as people picked up their bags and jackets and got ready to get on with their days.

Cecilia put down her hymn book. For heaven's sake. Her husband was not gay. An image came to her of John-Paul, marching up and down the sidelines at Isabel's soccer match last weekend, calling out encouragement. Along with a day's worth of silver stubble, he had two purple ballerina stickers stuck on each cheek. Polly had put them there to amuse herself. Cecilia felt a surge of love as she remembered. There was nothing effeminate about John-Paul. He was just comfortable in his own skin. He didn't need to prove himself.

The letter had nothing to do with the sex lull. It had

nothing to do with anything. It was safely locked away in the filing cabinet in the red manila folder with the copies of their wills.

She'd promised not to open it. So she couldn't, and she wouldn't.

EIGHT

D o you know who died?" asked Tess.

"What's that?" Her mother had her eyes closed,
her face lifted to the sun.

They were in the St. Angela's primary school playground. Tess's mother was in a wheelchair they'd hired
from the local pharmacy, with her ankle propped up on the
footrest. Tess had thought that her mother would hate
being in a wheelchair, but she seemed to quite enjoy it,
sitting with perfect, straight-backed posture, as if she were
at a dinner party.

They'd stopped for a moment in the morning sunshine
while Liam explored the school yard. There were a few
minutes to spare before they saw the school secretary to
arrange Liam's enrollment.

Tess's mother had arranged everything this morning.
There would be no problem enrolling Liam in St. Angela's,
Lucy told Tess proudly. In fact, they could do it that very
day if they liked! "There's no rush," said Tess. "We don't

need to do anything until after Easter." She hadn't asked her mother to ring the school. Wasn't she entitled to do nothing but feel flabbergasted for at least twenty-four hours? Her mother was making everything seem far too real and irrevocable, as if this nightmarish practical joke were actually happening.

"I can cancel the appointment if you like," Lucy had said with a martyred air.

"You made an appointment?" asked Tess. "Without asking me?"

"Well, I just thought we might as well bite the bullet."

"Fine," said Tess with a sigh. "Let's just do it."

Naturally, Lucy had insisted on coming along today. She would probably answer questions on Tess's behalf, like she used to do when Tess was little and overcome with shyness when a stranger approached. Her mother had never really lost the habit of speaking on her behalf. It was a little embarrassing, but also quite nice and relaxing, like five-star service at a hotel. Why not sit back and let someone else do all the hard work for you?

"Do you know who died?" said Tess again.

"Died?"

"The *funeral*," said Tess.

The school playground adjoined the grounds of St. Angela's Church, and Tess could see a coffin being carried out to a hearse by four young pallbearers.

Someone's life was over. Someone would never feel the sunshine on their face again. Tess tried to let that thought put her own pain into its proper perspective, but it didn't help. She wondered if Will and Felicity were having sex right at this minute, in her bed. It was midmorning. They didn't have anywhere else to go. The thought of it felt like incest to her. Dirty and wrong. She shuddered. There was a bitter taste at the back of her throat, as if she'd had a night out drinking bad cheap wine. Her eyes felt gritty.

The weather wasn't helping. It was far too lovely, mocking her pain. Sydney was bathed in a haze of gold. The Japanese maples at the front of the school were aflame with color, and the camellia blossoms were a rich, lush crimson. There were pots of bright red, yellow, apricot and cream begonias outside the classrooms. The long sandstone lines of St. Angela's Church were sharply defined against the cobalt blue of the sky. *The world is so beautiful,* said Sydney to Tess. *What's your problem?*

She tried to smooth away the jagged edge of her voice. "You don't know whose funeral it is?"

She didn't really care whose funeral it was. She just wanted to hear words, words about anything, to make those images of Will's hands on Felicity's newly slender white body go away. Porcelain skin. Tess's skin was darker, a legacy from her father's side of the family. There was a Lebanese great-grandmother who had died before Tess was born.

Will had called her mobile that morning. She should have ignored it, but when she saw his name she felt an involuntary spark of hope and snatched up the phone. He was calling to tell her that this was all a mistake. Of course he was.

But as soon as he spoke in that horrible new, heavy, solemn voice, without a hint of laughter, the hope vanished.

"Are you okay?" he'd asked. "Is Liam all right?" He was speaking as if there had been a recent tragedy in their lives that had nothing to do with him.

She was desperate to tell the real Will what this new Will, this humorless intruder, had done; how he'd crushed her heart. The real Will would want to fix things for her. The real Will would be straight on the phone, making a complaint about the way his wife had been treated, demanding recompense. The real Will would make her a cup of tea, run her a bath and finally, make her see the funny side of what had just happened to her.

Except, this time, there was no funny side.

Her mother opened her eyes and turned her head to squint up at Tess. "I think it must be for that dreadful little nun."

Tess raised her eyebrows to indicate mild shock, and her mother grinned, pleased with herself. She was so determined to make Tess happy, she was like a club entertainer, frantically trying out edgy new material to keep the crowd in their seats. This morning, when she was struggling with the lid on the Vegemite jar, she'd actually used the word "motherfucker," carefully sounding out the syllables so that the word didn't sound any more profane than "leprechaun."

Her mother had pulled out the most shocking swearword in her vocabulary because she was ablaze with anger on her behalf. Lucy saying "motherfucker" was like a meek and mild, law-abiding citizen suddenly transformed into a gun-wielding vigilante. That's why she'd phoned the school so fast. Tess understood. She wanted to take action, to do something, anything, on Tess's behalf.

"Which particular dreadful little nun?"

"Where's Liam?" Her mother twisted around awkwardly in her wheelchair.

"Right there," said Tess. Liam was wandering about, checking out the playground equipment with the jaded eye of a six-year-old expert. He hunkered down on his knees at the bottom of a big yellow funnel-shaped slide and poked his head up inside as if he were doing a safety audit.

"I lost sight of him for a moment."

"You don't have to keep him in sight all the time," said Tess mildly. "That's sort of my job."

"Of course it is."

At breakfast this morning, they'd both wanted to take care of each other. Tess had the advantage because she had two working ankles and could therefore already have the kettle boiled and the tea made in the time it took for her mother to reach for her crutches.

Tess watched Liam wander over to the corner of the playground under the fig tree where she and Felicity used to sit and eat their lunches with Eloise Bungonia. Eloise had introduced them to cannelloni. (A mistake for someone with Felicity's metabolism.) Mrs. Bungonia used to send enough for the three of them. It was before childhood obesity was an issue. Tess could still taste it. Divine.

She watched Liam become still, staring off into space as if he could see his mother eating cannelloni for the first time.

It was disconcerting, being here at her old school, as if time were a blanket that had been folded up so that different times were overlapping, pressed against each other. She would have to remind Felicity about Mrs. Bungonia's cannelloni.

No. No, she wouldn't.

Liam suddenly pivoted and karate-kicked the rubbish bin so that it clanged.

"Liam," remonstrated Tess, but not really loud enough for him to hear.

"Liam! Shhh!" called her mother, louder, putting a finger to her lips and pointing toward the church. A small group of mourners had come out and were standing about talking to one another in that restrained, relieved way of funeral attendees.

Liam didn't kick the rubbish bin again. He was an obedient child. Instead he picked up a stick and held it in two hands like a ninja sword, swirling it above his head, while the sound of sweet little voices singing "Eensy Weensy Spider" floated out of one of the kindergarten classrooms. *Oh, God,* thought Tess; where had he learned to do that? She had to be more vigilant about those computer games, although she couldn't help admiring the authentic way he handled the sword. She would tell Will about it later. He'd laugh.

No, she wouldn't tell Will about it later.

Her brain couldn't seem to catch up with the news. It was like the way she'd kept rolling toward Will last night in her sleep, only to find empty space where he should have been, and then waking up with a jolt. She and Will slept well together. No twitching or snoring or battling for blankets. "I can't sleep properly without you now," Will complained after they'd only been dating a few months. "You're like a favorite pillow. I have to pack you wherever I go."

"Which particular dreadful nun died?" Tess asked her mother again, her eyes on the mourners. Now was not the time to be pulling out old memories like that.

"They weren't all dreadful," reflected her mother. "Most of them were lovely. What about that Sister Margaret Ann, who came to your tenth birthday party? She was beautiful. I think your father quite fancied her."

"Seriously?"

"Well, probably not." Her mother shrugged as if not being attracted to beautiful nuns was yet another example of her ex-husband's failings. "Anyway, this must be the funeral for Sister Ursula. I read in the parish newsletter last week that she died. I don't think she ever taught you, did she? Apparently she was a great one for smacking with the handle of the feather duster. Nobody uses feather dusters much these days, do they? Is the world a dustier place for it, I wonder?"

"I think I remember Sister Ursula," said Tess. "Red face and caterpillar eyebrows. We used to hide from her when she was on playground duty."

"I'm not sure if there are *any* nuns teaching at the school anymore," said her mother. "They're a dying breed."

"Literally," said Tess.

Her mother chortled. "Oh, dear, I didn't mean . . ." She

stopped, distracted by something at the church entrance. "Okay, darling, steel yourself. We've just been spotted by one of the parish ladies."

"What?" Tess was immediately filled with a sense of dread, as if her mother had said they'd just been spotted by a wild animal.

A petite blond woman had detached herself from the mourners and was briskly walking toward the school yard.

"Cecilia Fitzpatrick," said her mother. "The eldest Bell girl. Married John-Paul, the eldest Fitzpatrick boy. The best-looking one, if you want my opinion, although they're all much of muchness. Cecilia had a younger sister, I think, who might have been in your year. Let's see now. Bridget Bell?"

Tess was about to say she'd never heard of them, but a memory of the Bell girls was gradually emerging in her mind like a reflection on water. She couldn't visualize their faces, just their long, blond, stringy plaits flying behind them as they ran through the school, doing whatever those kids who were at the center of things did.

"Cecilia sells Tupperware," said Tess's mother. "Makes an absolute *fortune* from it."

"But she doesn't know us, does she?" Tess looked hopefully over her shoulder to see if there might be someone else waving back at Cecilia. There was no one. Was she on her way over to spruik Tupperware?

"Cecilia knows everyone," said her mother.

"Can't we make a run for it?"

"Too late now." Her mother spoke through the side of her mouth as she smiled her toothy social smile.

"Lucy!" said Cecilia as she arrived in front of them, faster than Tess had thought possible. It was like she'd just teleported herself there. She bent to kiss Tess's mother. "What have you done to yourself?"

Don't you call my mother Lucy, thought Tess, taking an instant, childish dislike. *Mrs. O'Leary, thank you!* Now that she was right in front of them, Tess remembered Cecilia's face perfectly well. She had a small, neat head—the plaits had been replaced with one of those crisp, artful bobs—an eager, open face, a noticeable overbite, and two ridiculously huge dimples. She was like a pretty little ferret.

And yet she'd landed a Fitzpatrick boy.

"I saw you when I came out of the church. Sister Ursula's funeral; did you hear she'd passed? Anyway, I caught sight of you, and I thought, *That's Lucy O'Leary in a wheelchair! What's going on?* So being the nosy parker that I am, I came over to say hello! Looks like a good-quality wheelchair; did you hire it from the pharmacist? But what happened, Lucy? Your ankle, is it?"

Oh, Lord. Tess could feel her entire personality being drained from her body. Those talkative, energetic people always left her feeling that way.

"It's nothing too serious, thanks, Cecilia," said Tess's mother. "Just a broken ankle."

"Oh, no, but that *is* serious, you poor thing! How are you coping? How are you getting about? I'll bring over a lasagna for you. No, I will. I insist. You're not vegetarian, are you? But that's why you're here, I guess, is it?" Without warning, Cecilia suddenly turned to look at Tess, who took an involuntary step backward. What did she mean? Something to do with vegetarianism? "To look after your mum? I'm Cecilia, by the way, if you don't remember me!"

"Cecilia, this is my daughter—" began Tess's mother, only to be cut off by Cecilia.

"Of course. Tess, isn't it?" Cecilia turned and to Tess's surprise held out her hand to shake in a businesslike way. Tess had been thinking of Cecilia as someone from her mother's era, an old-fashioned Catholic lady who used Catholic words like "passed" and would therefore stand back smiling sweetly while the men did the manly business of shaking hands. Her hand was small and dry, her grip strong.

"And this must be your son?" Cecilia smiled brightly in Liam's direction. "Liam?"

Jesus. She even knew Liam's name. How was that possible? Tess didn't even know if Cecilia had children. She'd forgotten her very existence until thirty seconds ago.

Liam looked over, aimed his stick straight at Cecilia and pulled the imaginary trigger.

"Liam!" said Tess, at the same time as Cecilia groaned, clutched her chest and buckled at the knees. She did it so well, for an awful moment Tess worried that she really was collapsing.

Liam held the stick up to his mouth, blew on it and grinned, delighted.

"How long do you think you'll be in Sydney for?" Cecilia locked eyes with Tess. She was one of those people who held eye contact for too long. The polar opposite of Tess. "Just until you've got Lucy back on her feet? You run a business in Melbourne, don't you? I guess you can't be away for too long! And Liam must be in school?"

Tess found herself unable to speak.

"Tess is actually enrolling Liam in St. Angela's for a . . . short time," spoke up Lucy.

"Oh, that's wonderful!" said Cecilia. Her eyes were still fixed on Tess. Good Lord, did the woman ever blink? "So let's see now, how old is Liam?"

"Six," said Tess. She dropped her eyes, unable to bear it any longer.

"Well, then he'll be in Polly's class. We had a little girl leave earlier in the year, so you'll be in with us. One-J. Mrs. Jeffers. Mary Jeffers. She's *wonderful*, by the way. Very sociable too, which is nice!"

"Great," said Tess weakly. Fabulous.

"Liam! Now you've shot me, come and say hello! I hear you're coming to St. Angela's!" Cecilia beckoned to Liam, and he wandered over, dragging his stick behind him.

Cecilia bent at the knees so she was at Liam's eye level. "I have a little girl who will be in your class. Her name is Polly. She's having her seventh birthday party the week after Easter. Would you like to come?" Liam's face instantly got that blank look that always made Tess worry that people might think he had some kind of disability.

"It's going to be a pirate party." Cecilia straightened and turned to Tess. "I hope you can come. It will be a good way for you to meet all the mums. We'll have a private little oasis for the grown-ups. Guzzle champagne while the little pirates rampage about."

Tess felt her own face fold up. Liam had probably inherited his catatonic look from her. She could not meet another brand-new group of mothers. She'd found socializing with the school mums difficult enough when her life was in perfect order. The chat, chat, chat, the swirls of laughter, the warmth, the friendliness (most mums were so very nice) and the gentle hint of bitchiness that ran beneath it all. She'd done it in Melbourne. She'd made a few friends on the outskirts of the inner social circle, but she couldn't do it again. Not now. She didn't have the strength. It was like someone had cheerfully suggested she run a marathon when she'd just dragged herself out of bed after suffering from the flu.

"Great," she said. She would make up an excuse later.

"I'll make Liam a pirate costume," said Tess's mother. "An eye patch, a red-and-white-striped top, ooh, and a sword! You'd love a sword, wouldn't you, Liam?"

She looked around for Liam, but he'd run off and was using his stick like a drill against the back fence.

"Of course, we'd love to have you at the party too, Lucy," said Cecilia. She was highly irritating, but her social skills were impeccable. For Tess, it was like watching someone play the violin beautifully. You couldn't conceive how they did it.

"Oh, well, thank you, Cecilia!" Tess's mother was delighted. She loved parties. Especially the food. "Let's see now, a red-and-white-striped top for a pirate costume. Has he already got one, Tess?"

If Cecilia was a violinist, Tess's mother was a folksy,

well-meaning guitarist trying her best to play the same tune.

"I mustn't keep you. I guess you're off to see Rachel now in the office?" asked Cecilia.

"We've got an appointment with the school secretary," said Tess. She had no idea of the woman's name.

"Yes, Rachel Crowley," said Cecilia. "So efficient. Runs the place like a Swiss watch. She actually shares the job with my mother-in-law, although between you and me and the gatepost, I think Rachel does all the work. Virginia just chats on her days. Not that I can talk. Well, actually, that's my point—I can talk." She laughed merrily at herself.

"How *is* Rachel these days?" asked Tess's mother significantly.

Cecilia's ferrety face got all somber. "I don't know her that well, but I do know she has a beautiful little grandson. Jacob. He just turned two."

"Ah," breathed Lucy, as if that solved everything. "That's good to hear. Jacob."

"Well, it was so nice to meet you, Tess," said Cecilia, fixing her again with her unblinking stare. "I must skedaddle. I've got to get to my Zumba class—I go to the gym down the road; it's great, you should try it sometime, just hilarious—and then I'm going straight to this party supply place in Strathfield; it's a bit of a drive, but it's worth it because the prices are amazing, seriously, you can get a helium balloon kit for under fifty dollars, and that gives you over a hundred balloons, and I'm doing so many parties over the next few months—Polly's pirate party, and the

Year One parents' party, which of course you'll be invited to as well!—and then I'm dropping off a few Tupperware orders; I do Tupperware, by the way, Tess, if you need anything, especially if you're looking for some early Christmas present ideas. Anyway, all that before school pickup! You know how it is."

Tess blinked. It was like being buried in an avalanche of detail. The myriad of tiny logistical maneuvers that made up someone else's life. It wasn't that it was dull. Although it was a little dull. It was mainly the sheer *quantity* of words that flowed so effortlessly from Cecilia's mouth.

Oh God, she's stopped talking. Tess registered with a start that it was her turn to speak.

"Busy," she said finally. "You sure are busy." She forced her lips into something she hoped resembled a smile.

"See you at the pirate party!" called out Cecilia to Liam, who turned from drilling his tree to look at her with that funny, inscrutable, masculine expression he sometimes got, an expression that painfully reminded Tess of Will.

Cecilia lifted her hand like a claw. "Aha, me hearties!"

Liam grinned, as if he couldn't help himself, and Tess knew she'd be taking him to the pirate party, whatever it cost her.

"Oh my," said Tess's mother when Cecilia was out of earshot. "Her mother was exactly the same. Very nice, but exhausting. I always felt like I needed a cup of tea and a lie-down after talking with her."

"What's the story with this Rachel Crowley?" asked Tess as they headed toward the school office, she and Liam pushing one handle each of the wheelchair.

Her mother grimaced. "Do you remember the name Janie Crowley?"

"Not the girl they found with the rosary beads—"

"That's the one. She was Rachel's daughter."

———

Rachel could tell that Lucy O'Leary and her daughter were both thinking about Janie while they enrolled Tess's little boy in St. Angela's. They were both being just a little chattier than was obviously natural for them. Tess couldn't quite meet Rachel's eyes, while Lucy was doing that tender-eyed, tilted-head thing that so many women of a certain age did when they talked to Rachel, as if they were visiting her in a nursing home.

When Lucy asked if the photo on Rachel's desk was her grandson, both she and Tess went quite over the top with compliments—not that it wasn't a beautiful photo of Jacob, of course, but you didn't need to be a rocket scientist to see that what they really meant was *We know your daughter was murdered all those years ago, but does this little boy make up for it? Please let him make up for it so we can stop feeling so strange and uncomfortable!*

"I look after him two days a week," Rachel told them, her eyes on the computer screen while she printed off some paperwork for Tess. "But not for much longer. His parents are taking him off to New York for two years." Her voice cracked without her permission, and she cleared her throat irritably.

She waited for the reaction she'd been getting from everyone all day: *How exciting for them! What an opportunity! Will you go for a visit?*

"Well that just takes the cake!" exploded Lucy, and she banged her elbows on the arms of her wheelchair like a cranky toddler. Her daughter, who had been busy filling in a form, looked up, startled. Tess was one of those plain-looking women with a short, boyish haircut and strong, austere features, who sometimes stun you with a flash of raw beauty. Her little boy, who looked a lot like Tess, except for his strange, gold-colored eyes, also turned to stare at his grandmother.

Lucy rubbed her elbows. "Of course I'm sure it's exciting for your son and daughter-in-law. It's just that after all you've been through, losing Janie like—the way you did, and then your husband . . . I'm so sorry, I can't actually remember his name, but I know you lost him too—well, this just doesn't seem fair."

By the time she finished talking, her cheeks were crimson. Rachel could tell she was horrified at herself. People were always worrying that they'd inadvertently reminded her of her daughter's death, as if it were something that slipped her mind.

"I'm so sorry, Rachel, I shouldn't have . . ." Poor Lucy looked distraught.

Rachel waved a hand to swat away her apologies. "Don't be sorry. Thank you. It does take the cake, actually. I'll miss him terribly."

"Well, now, who have we here?"

Rachel's boss, Trudy McDuff, the school principal, floated into the room, one of her trademark crocheted shawls slipping off her bony shoulders, strands of gray frizzy hair floating around her face, a smudge of red paint on her left cheekbone. She'd probably been on the floor painting with the kindergarten children. True to form, Trudy looked straight past Lucy and Tess to the little boy, Liam. She had no interest in grown-ups, and this would one day be her downfall. Rachel had seen three school principals come and go since she'd been secretary, and in her experience it wasn't possible to run a school while ignoring the grown-ups. It was a political job.

Also, Trudy didn't seem to be quite Catholic enough for the job. Not that she went around breaking the commandments, but she had an impious, sparkly-eyed expression on her face during Mass. Before she died, Sister Ursula (whose funeral Rachel had just boycotted, because she'd never forgiven her for hitting Janie with a feather duster) had probably written to the Vatican to complain about her.

"This is the boy I mentioned earlier," said Rachel. "Liam Curtis. He's enrolling in Year One."

"Of course, of course, welcome to St. Angela's, Liam! I was just thinking as I walked up the stairs that today I was meeting someone whose name begins with the letter *L*, which happens to be one of my favorite letters. Tell me, Liam, out of these three things, which do you like best?" She folded back her fingers with each item. "Dinosaurs? Aliens? Superheroes?"

Liam considered the question gravely.

"He quite likes dino—" began Lucy O'Leary. Tess put her hand on her mother's arm.

"Aliens," said Liam finally.

"Aliens!" Trudy nodded. "Well, I will be keeping that in mind, Liam Curtis. And this is your mum and your grandmother, I'm guessing?"

"Yes, indeed, I'm—" began Lucy O'Leary.

"Lovely to meet you both." Trudy smiled vaguely in their general direction. She turned back to Liam. "When are you starting with us, Liam? Tomorrow?"

"No!" Tess looked alarmed. "Not until after Easter."

"Oh, live a little, I say! Jump right in while the iron is hot!" said Trudy. "Do you like Easter eggs, Liam?"

"Yes," said Liam adamantly.

"Because we're planning a gigantic Easter egg hunt tomorrow."

"I'm super good at Easter egg hunts," said Liam.

"Are you? Excellent! Well, then I'd better make it a super challenging hunt." Trudy glanced at Rachel. "Everything under control here, Rachel, with all the . . . ?" She gestured sorrowfully at the paperwork, of which she knew nothing.

"All under control," said Rachel. Just like Cecilia, she was helping keep Trudy in a job too, because she didn't see why the children of St. Angela's shouldn't have a school principal from fairyland.

"Lovely, lovely! I'll leave you to it!" said Trudy, and she wandered off into her office, pulling the door shut behind her, presumably so she could scatter fairy dust over her keyboard, as she certainly didn't do too much else on her computer.

"My goodness, she's a different kettle of fish from Sister Veronica-Mary!" said Lucy quietly.

Rachel snorted in appreciation. She remembered Sister Veronica-Mary, who had been principal from 1965 through to 1980, very well.

There was a knock, and Rachel looked up to see the tall, imposing shadow of a man through the frosted glass panel of her office, before his head appeared inquiringly around the door.

Him. She flinched and took a deep breath in through her nostrils, as if at the sight of a furry black spider, not a perfectly plain-looking man. (Actually, Rachel had heard other women call him gorgeous, which she found preposterous.)

"Excuse me, ah, Mrs. Crowley."

He could never get far enough away from his schoolboy self to call her Rachel like the rest of the staff. Their eyes met, and as usual, his slid away first to rest somewhere above her head.

Lies in his eyes, thought Rachel, as she did virtually every time she saw him, as if it was an incantation or prayer. *Lies in his eyes.*

"Sorry to interrupt," said Connor Whitby. "I just wondered if I could pick up those tennis camp forms."

"There's something that Whitby boy isn't telling us," Sergeant Rodney Bellach had said all those years ago, when he had a head full of startlingly curly black hair. "That kid has got lies in his eyes."

Rodney Bellach was retired now. As bald as a bandicoot. He called every year on Janie's birthday, when he liked to tell Rachel about his latest ailments. Someone else who got old while Janie stayed seventeen.

Rachel handed over the tennis camp forms, and Connor's eyes fell on Tess.

"Tess O'Leary!" His face was transformed so that he looked for a moment like the boy in Janie's photo album.

Tess looked up, her face wary. She didn't seem to recognize Connor at all.

"Connor!" He tapped his broad chest. "Connor Whitby!"

"Oh, Connor, of course. It's so nice to . . ." Tess half rose, and then found herself trapped by her mother's wheelchair.

"Don't get up, don't get up," said Connor. He went to kiss Tess on the cheek just as she was starting to sit down again, so that his lips met her earlobe.

"What are you doing here?" asked Tess. She didn't seem especially pleased to see Connor.

"I work here," he said.

"As an accountant?"

"No, no, I had a career change a few years back. I'm the PE teacher."

"You are?" she said. "Well, that's . . ." Her voice drifted, and she finally said, ". . . nice."

Connor cleared his throat. "Well, anyway, it's very good to see you." He glanced at Liam, went to speak and then changed his mind and held up the sheaf of tennis forms. "Thanks for this, Rachel."

"My pleasure, Connor," said Rachel coldly.

Lucy turned to her daughter as soon as Connor left. "Who was that?"

"Just someone I used to know. Years ago."

"I don't think I remember him. Was he a boyfriend?"

"Mum." Tess gestured at Rachel and the paperwork in front of her.

"Sorry!" Lucy smiled guiltily, while Liam looked up at the ceiling, stretched out his legs and yawned.

Rachel saw that the grandmother, mother and grandson all had identical full upper lips. It was like a trick. Those bee-stung lips made them more beautiful than they actually were.

She was suddenly inexplicably furious with all three of them.

"Well, if you could just sign the allergies and medications sections *here*," she said to Tess, jabbing at the form with her fingertip. "No, not there. Here. Then we'll be done and dusted."

———

Tess had her keys in the ignition to drive them home from the school when her mobile rang. She lifted it from the console to check who was calling.

When she saw the name on the screen, she held up the phone for her mother to see.

Her mother squinted at the phone and sat back with a shrug. "Well, I had to tell him. I promised him I'd always keep him up-to-date with what was going on in your life."

"You promised him that when I was ten!" said Tess. She held the phone up, trying to decide whether or not to answer it or let it go to voice mail.

"Is it Dad?" said Liam from the backseat.

"It's *my* dad," said Tess. She'd have to talk to him some-time. It might as well be now. She took a breath and pressed the Answer button. "Hi, Dad."

There was a pause. There was always a pause.

"Hello, love," said her father.

"How are you?" asked Tess in the hearty tone of voice she reserved for her father. When had they last spoken? It must have been Christmas Day.

"I'm great," said her father dolefully.

Another pause.

"I'm actually in the car with—" began Tess at the same time as her father said, "Your mother told me—"

They both stopped. It was always excruciating. No mat-ter how hard she tried, she could never seem to synchronize her conversations with her father. Even when they were face-to-face they never achieved a natural rhythm. Would their relationship have been less awkward if he and her mother had stayed together? She'd always wondered.

Her father cleared his throat. "Your mother mentioned you were having a spot of . . . trouble."

Pause.

"Thanks, Dad," said Tess at the same time as her father said, "I'm sorry to hear that."

Tess could see her mother rolling her eyes, and she turned away slightly toward the car window, as if to protect her poor, hopeless father from her mother's scorn.

"If there's anything I can do," said her father, "just . . . you know, call."

"Absolutely," said Tess.

Pause.

"Well, I should go," said Tess at the same time as her father said, "I liked the fellow."

"Tell him I e-mailed him a link for that wine appreciation course I was telling him about," said her mother.

"Shhh." Tess waved her hand irritably at Lucy. "What's that, Dad?"

"Will," said her father. "I thought he was a good bloke. That's no bloody help to you, though, is it, love?"

"He'll never do it, of course," murmured her mother to herself, examining her cuticles. "Don't know why I bother. The man doesn't *want* to be happy."

"Thanks for calling, Dad," said Tess, at the same time as her father said, "How's the little man doing?"

"Liam is great," said Tess. "He's right here. Do you want—"

"I'll let you go, love. You take care, now."

He was gone. He always finished the call in a sudden, frantic rush, as if the phone were bugged by the police and he had to get off before they tracked down his location. His location was a small, flat, treeless town on the opposite side of the country, in Western Australia, where he had mysteriously chosen to live twenty-five years ago.

"Had a whole heap of helpful advice then, did he?" said Lucy wryly.

"He did his best, Mum," said Tess.

"Oh, I'm sure he did," said her mother with satisfaction.

NINE

"So it was a Sunday when they put the Wall up. They called it Barbed Wire Sunday. You want to know why?" said Esther from the backseat of the car. It was a rhetorical question. Of course they did. "Because everyone woke up in the morning and there was, like, this long barbed wire fence right through the city."

"So what?" said Polly. "I've seen a barbed wire fence before."

"But you weren't allowed to cross it!" said Esther. "You were stuck! You know how we live on *this* side of the Pacific Highway and Grandma lives on the other side?"

"Yeah," said Polly uncertainly. She wasn't too clear on where anyone lived.

"It would be like there was a barbed wire fence all along the Pacific Highway, and we couldn't visit Grandma anymore."

"That would be such a pity," murmured Cecilia as she looked over her shoulder to change lanes. She'd been to visit her mother this morning after her Zumba class and had spent twenty full minutes she couldn't spare looking through a "portfolio" of her nephew's preschool work. Bridget was sending Sam to an exclusive, obscenely priced preschool, and Cecilia's mother couldn't decide whether to be delighted or disgusted about it. She had settled for hysterical.

"I bet you didn't get a portfolio like this at that ordinary little preschool your girls went to," her mother had said, while Cecilia tried to flip the pages faster. She was going shopping for all the nonperishables in preparation for Sunday before she picked up the girls.

"Actually, I think most of the preschools do things like this these days," Cecilia had said, but her mother had been too busy exclaiming over Sam's finger-painted self-portrait.

"Imagine, Mum," said Esther, "if we kids were visiting Grandma in West Berlin for the weekend when the wall went up, and you and Dad were stuck in East Berlin. You'd have to say to us, 'Stay at Grandma's place, kids! Don't come back! For your *freedom*!'"

"That's awful," said Cecilia.

"I'd still go back to Mummy," said Polly. "Grandma makes you eat peas."

"It's history, Mum," said Esther. "It's what actually happened. Everyone got separated. They didn't care. Look! These people are holding up their babies to show their relatives on the other side."

"I really can't take my eyes off the road," said Cecilia with a sigh.

Thanks to Esther, Cecilia had spent the last six months

imagining herself scooping up drowning children from the icy waters of the Atlantic while the *Titanic* sank. Now she was going to be in Berlin, separated from her children by the Wall.

"When does Daddy get back from Chicago?" asked Polly.

"Friday morning!" Cecilia smiled at Polly in the rear-view mirror, grateful for the change of subject. "He's coming back on Good Friday. It will be a very good Friday because Daddy will be back!"

There was a disapproving silence in the backseat. Her daughters tried not to encourage deeply uncool talk.

They were right in the middle of their near-normal after-school frenzy of activity. Cecilia had just dropped Isabel at the hairdresser, and now they were on their way to Polly's ballet and Esther's speech therapy. (Esther's barely percep-tible lisp, which Cecilia found adorable, was apparently unacceptable in today's world.) After that, it would be rush, rush, rush to get dinner prepared and homework and read-ing done before her mother came over to watch the children while Cecilia went off to do a Tupperware party.

"I have another secret to tell Daddy," said Polly. "When he comes home."

"One man tried to abseil out of his apartment window, and the firemen in West Berlin tried to catch him with a safety net, but he missed, and he died."

"My secret is that I don't want a pirate party anymore," said Polly.

"He was thirty," said Esther. "So I guess he'd lived a pretty good life already."

"What?" said Cecilia.

"I said he was thirty," said Esther. "The man who died."

"Not you; Polly!"

A red traffic light loomed, and Cecilia slammed her foot on the brake. The fact that Polly no longer wanted a pirate party was breathtakingly insignificant in comparison to that poor man (*thirty!*) crashing to the ground for the freedom that Cecilia took for granted, but right now, she couldn't pause to honor his memory, because a last-minute change of party theme was unacceptable. That's what happened when you had freedom. You lost your mind over a pirate party.

"Polly." Cecilia tried to sound reasonable, not psychotic. "We've sent out the invitations. You're having a pirate party. You asked for a pirate party. You're getting a pirate party."

A nonrefundable deposit had been paid to Penelope the Singing and Dancing Pirate, who certainly charged like a pirate.

"It's a secret just for Daddy," said Polly. "Not for you."

"Fine, but I'm not changing the party."

She wanted the pirate party to be perfect. For some reason she particularly wanted to impress that Tess O'Leary. Cecilia had an illogical attraction to enigmatic, elegant people like Tess. Most of Cecilia's friends were talkers. Their voices overlapped in their desperation to tell their stories. *I've always hated vegetables . . . The only vegetable my child will eat is broccoli . . . My kid loves raw carrots . . . I love raw carrots!* You had to jump right in without waiting for a pause in the conversation, because otherwise you'd never get your turn. But women like Tess didn't seem to have that need to share the ordinary facts of their lives, and that made Cecilia desperate to know them. *Does* her *kid like broccoli?* she'd ponder. She'd talked too much when she met Tess and her mother after Sister Ursula's funeral this morning. Babbled. Sometimes she could hear herself doing it. Oh, well.

Cecilia listened to the tinny sound of voices shouting something passionate and German from the YouTube video Esther was watching on the iPad.

It was extraordinary how tumultuous historical moments could be replayed right here in this ordinary little moment as she drove down the Pacific Highway toward Hornsby, and yet, at the same time, it gave Cecilia a hazy sense of dissatisfaction. She longed to feel something momentous. Sometimes her life seemed so *little*.

Did she *want* something huge and terrible to happen, like a wall being built across her city, so she could appreciate her ordinary life? Did she want to be a tragic figure like Rachel Crowley? Rachel seemed almost disfigured by the terrible thing that had happened to her daughter, so that Cecilia sometimes had to force herself not to look away, as if she were a burn victim, not a perfectly pleasant-looking, well-groomed woman with good cheekbones.

Is that what you want, Cecilia? Some nice big exciting tragedy?

Of course she didn't.

The German voices from Esther's computer tickled irritatingly at her ear.

"Can you please turn that off?" Cecilia said to Esther. "It's distracting."

"Just let me—"

"Turn it off! Couldn't one of you children do what I ask just once, the first time? Without negotiating? Just once?"

The sound went off.

In the rearview mirror she saw Polly raise her eyebrows and Esther shrug and lift her palms. *What's with her? No idea.* Cecilia could remember similar silent conversations with Bridget in the back of her mother's car.

"Sorry," said Cecilia humbly after a few seconds. "I'm sorry, girls. I'm just . . ."

Worried that your father is lying to me about something? In need of sex? Wishing I hadn't babbled on the way I did to Tess O'Leary in the school yard this morning? Perimenopausal?

". . . missing Daddy," she finished. "It will be nice when he's home from America, won't it? He'll be so happy to see you girls!"

"Yeah, he will," said Polly, sighing. She paused. "And Isabel."

"Of course," said Cecilia. "Isabel too, of course."

"Daddy looks at Isabel a funny way," said Polly conversationally.

That was way out of left field.

"What do you mean?" asked Cecilia. Sometimes Polly came up with the strangest things.

"All the time," said Polly. "He looks at her weirdly."

"No he doesn't," said Esther.

"Yeah, he looks at her like it's hurting his eyes. Like he's angry and sad at the same time. Especially when she wears that new skirt."

"Well, that's a silly sort of thing to say," said Cecilia. What in the world did the child mean? If she didn't know any better, she would think that Polly was describing John-Paul looking at Isabel in a *sexual* way.

"Maybe Daddy is mad with Isabel about something," said Polly. "Or he just feels sad that she's his daughter. Mum, do you know why Daddy is mad at Isabel? Did she do something bad?"

A panicky feeling rose in Cecilia's throat.

"He probably wanted to watch the cricket on TV," mused Polly. "And Isabel wanted to watch something else. Or, I don't know."

Isabel had been so grumpy lately, refusing to answer questions and slamming the door, but wasn't that what all twelve-year-old girls did?

Cecilia thought of those stories she'd read about sexual abuse. Stories in the *Daily Telegraph* where the mother said, "I had no idea," and Cecilia thought, *How could you not know?* She always finished those stories with a comfortable sense of superiority. *This could not happen to my daughters.*

John-Paul could be strangely moody at times. His face turned to granite. You couldn't reason with him. But didn't all men do that at times? Cecilia remembered how she and her mother and sister tiptoed around her father's moods.

But John-Paul would *never* harm his daughters. This was ridiculous. This was Jerry Springer stuff. It was a betrayal of John-Paul to allow the faintest shadow of a doubt to cross her mind. Cecilia would stake her life on the fact that John-Paul wouldn't abuse one of his daughters.

But would she stake one of her daughters' lives?

No. If there was the smallest risk . . .

Dear God, what was she meant to do? Ask Isabel, "Has Daddy ever touched you?" Victims lied. Their abusers told them to lie. She knew how it worked. She read all those trashy stories. She *liked* having a quick cathartic little weep before folding up the newspaper, putting it in the recycling bin and forgetting all about it. Those stories gave her a sick sort of pleasure, whereas John-Paul always refused to read them. Was that a clue to his guilt? Aha! If you don't like reading about sick people, you're sick yourself!

"Mum!" said Polly.

How could she possibly confront John-Paul? "Have you ever done anything inappropriate to one of our daughters?" If he asked a question like that of her, she would never forgive him. How could a marriage continue when a question like that was asked? "No, I haven't ever molested our daughters. Pass the peanut butter, please."

"Mum!" said Polly again.

"What?"

You shouldn't have to ask, he'd say. *If you don't know the answer, you don't know me.*

She did know the answer. She did!

But then all those other stupid mothers thought they knew the answer too.

And John-Paul had been so strange on the phone when she asked him about that letter. He had been lying about something. She was sure of it.

And there was the sex thing. Perhaps he'd lost interest in Cecilia because he was lusting after Isabel's changing young body? It was laughable. It was revolting. She felt sick.

"MUM!"

"Mmm?"

"Look! You drove right past the street! We're going to be late!"

"Sorry. Damn it. Sorry."

She slammed on her brakes to do a U-turn. There was a furious shriek of a horn from behind them, and Cecilia's heart leapt into her chest as she looked in her rearview mirror and saw a huge truck.

"Shit." She raised a hand in apology. "Sorry. Yes, yes, I know!"

The truck driver wouldn't forgive her and kept his hand pressed on the horn.

"Sorry, sorry!" As she completed her U-turn she looked up to wave her apology again (she had the Tupperware name emblazoned down one side of her car—she didn't want to damage the company's reputation). The driver had wound down his window and was leaning almost halfway out, his face ugly with rage as he slammed his fist over and over into the palm of his hand.

"Oh, for heaven's sake," she muttered.

"I think that man wants to kill you," said Polly.

"That man is very *naughty*," said Cecilia severely. Her heart sped as she sedately drove back to the dance studio, double-checking all her mirrors and indicating her intentions well in advance to other drivers.

She wound down her window and watched as Polly ran into the studio, her pink tulle tutu bobbing, her delicate shoulder blades jutting out like wings beneath the straps of her leotard.

Melissa McNulty appeared at the door and waved to indicate that as per their arrangement she was taking care of Polly. Cecilia waved back and reversed.

"If this was Berlin and Caroline's office was on the other side of the Wall, I wouldn't be able to go to speech therapy," said Esther.

"Good point," said Cecilia.

"We could help her *escape*! We could put her in the boot of the car. She's pretty little. I think she'd fit. Unless she gets that claustrophobia like Daddy."

"I feel like Caroline is the sort of person who would probably organize her own escape," said Cecilia. *We've already spent enough on her! We're not going to help her escape from East Berlin!* Esther's speech therapist was intimidating, with her perfect vowels. Whenever Cecilia spoke to her, she caught herself articulating all syllables ve-ry care-ful-ly, as if she were doing an elocution test.

"I don't think Daddy looks at Isabel funny," said Esther.

"Don't you?" said Cecilia happily. Good Lord. How melodramatic she'd been. Polly made one of her peculiar little observations and Cecilia's mind jumped straight to sexual abuse. She must be watching too much trashy television.

"But he was crying the other day before he went to Chicago," said Esther.

"What?"

"In the shower," said Esther. "I went into your bathroom to get the nail scissors and Daddy was crying."

"Well, darling, did you ask him *why* he was crying?" said Cecilia, trying not to show just how much she cared about the answer.

"Nope," said Esther breezily. "When I'm crying I don't like to be interrupted."

Damn it. If it had been Polly, she would have pulled back the shower curtain and demanded an immediate answer from her father.

"I was going to ask you why Daddy was crying," said Esther. "But then I forgot. I had a lot on my mind."

"I really don't think he was crying. He was probably just . . . sneezing or something," said Cecilia. The idea of John-Paul crying in the shower was so foreign, so weird. Why would he be crying, except over something truly terrible? He was not a crier. When the girls were born his eyes got a shiny quality to them, and when his father died unexpectedly he put down the phone and made a strange, fragile noise, as if he were choking on something small and fluffy. But apart from that she'd never seen him cry.

"He wasn't *sneezing*," said Esther.

"Maybe he had one of his migraines," said Cecilia, although she knew that whenever John-Paul was afflicted by one of his debilitating migraines, the last thing he would do was take a shower. He needed to be alone, in bed, in a dark, quiet room.

"Uh, Mum, Daddy never takes a *shower* when he has a migraine," said Esther, who knew her father just as well as Cecilia knew her husband.

Depression? It seemed to be going around at the moment. At a recent dinner party half the guests revealed they were on Prozac. After all, John-Paul had always gone through . . . patches. They often followed the migraines. There would be a week or so where it was like he was just going through the motions. He'd been saying and doing all the right things, but there'd be something vacant in his eyes, as if the real John-Paul had checked out for a while and sent this very authentic-looking replica to take his place. "You okay?" Cecilia would ask, and he'd always take a few moments to focus on her before saying, "Sure. I'm fine."

But it was always temporary. Suddenly he'd be back, fully present, listening to her and the girls with all his attention, and Cecilia would convince herself that she imagined the whole thing. The patches were probably just a lingering effect of the migraines.

But crying in the shower. What did he have to *cry* about? Things were good at the moment.

John-Paul once tried to commit suicide.

The fact floated slowly, repellently, to the surface of her mind. It was something she tried not to think about too often.

It had happened when he was in his first year of university, before Cecilia had begun dating him. Apparently he'd gone off the rails for a while, and then one night he swallowed a bottle of sleeping pills. His flatmate, who was meant to be visiting his parents for the weekend, came home unexpectedly and found him. "What was going through your mind?" Cecilia asked him when she heard the story for the first time. "Everything just seemed too hard," said John-Paul. "Going to sleep forever just seemed like an easier option."

Over the years, Cecilia had often prodded him for more information about this time in his life. "But *why* did it seem so hard? What exactly was so hard?" But John-Paul didn't seem capable of clarifying further. "I guess I was just your typical anguished teenager," he said. Cecilia didn't get it. She was never anguished as a teenager. Eventually, she had to give up and accept John-Paul's suicide attempt as an out-of-character incident in his past. "I just needed a good woman," John-Paul told her. It was true there had never been a serious girlfriend until Cecilia came along. "I was honestly starting to think he might be gay," one of his brothers had confided in her once.

There was the gay thing again.

But his brother had been joking.

An unexplained suicide attempt in his teenage years, and now, all these years later, he was crying in the shower.

"Sometimes grown-ups have big things on their minds," said Cecilia carefully to Esther. Obviously her first responsibility was to make sure that Esther wasn't concerned. "So I'm sure Daddy was just—"

"Hey, Mum, can I please get this book on Amazon about the Berlin Wall for Christmas?" asked Esther. "Do you want me to order it now? All the reviews are five stars!"

"No," said Cecilia. "You can borrow it from the library." *God willing, we'll have escaped from Berlin by Christmas.*

She turned into the parking lot underneath the speech therapist's office, wound down the window and pressed the button on the intercom.

"Can I help you?"

"We're here to see Caroline Otto," she said. Even when she talked to the receptionist she rounded her vowels.

As she parked the car, she considered each new fact.

John-Paul giving Isabel strange, sad, angry looks.

John-Paul crying in the shower.

John-Paul losing interest in sex.

John-Paul lying about something.

It was all so strange and worrying, but there was something beneath it all that was not actually unpleasant, that was in fact giving her a mild sense of anticipation.

She turned off the ignition, pulled on the handbrake, undid her seat belt.

"Let's go," she said to Esther, and opened the car door. She knew what was giving her that little blip of pleasure. It was because she'd made a decision. Something was clearly not right. She had a moral obligation to do something immoral. It was the lesser of two evils. She was justified.

As soon as the girls were in bed tonight, she would do what she'd wanted to do from the very beginning. She was going to open that goddamned letter.

TEN

There was a knock at the door.

"Ignore it." Tess's mother didn't look up from her book.

Liam, Tess and her mother were sitting in separate armchairs in her mother's front room, reading their books with small bowls full of chocolate raisins resting on their laps. It had been one of Tess's daily routines as a child: eating chocolate raisins and reading with her mother. They always did star jumps afterward to counteract the chocolate.

"It might be Dad." Liam put his book down. Tess was surprised at how readily he'd agreed to sit and read. It must have been the chocolate raisins. She could never get him to do his reading for school.

And now, bizarrely, he was starting at a new school. Just like that. *Tomorrow.* It was disconcerting the way that peculiar woman had convinced him to start the very next day, with the promise of an Easter egg hunt.

"You spoke to your dad in Melbourne just a few hours

ago," she reminded Liam, keeping her voice neutral. He and Will had talked for twenty minutes. "I'll talk to Daddy later," Tess had said when Liam went to hand her the phone. She'd already spoken to Will once that morning. Nothing had changed. She didn't want to hear his horrible serious new voice again. And what could she say? Mention that she'd run into an ex-boyfriend at St. Angela's? Ask if he was jealous?

Connor Whitby. It must have been over fifteen years since she'd seen him. They'd gone out for less than a year. She hadn't even recognized him when he walked into the office. He'd lost all his hair and seemed a much bigger, broader version of the man she remembered. The whole thing had been so awkward. Bad enough that she was sitting across the desk from a woman whose daughter had been murdered.

"Maybe Daddy got on a plane to surprise us," said Liam.

There was a rap on the window right near Tess's head. "I know you're all in there!" said a voice.

"For God's sake." Tess's mother closed her book with a snap.

Tess turned and saw her aunt's face pressed flat against the living room window, her hands cupped around her eyes so she could peer inside.

"Mary, I *told* you not to come over!" Lucy's voice rocketed up several octaves. She always sounded forty years younger when she spoke to her twin sister.

"Open the door!" Aunt Mary rapped again on the glass. "I need to talk to Tess!"

"Tess doesn't want to talk to you!" Lucy lifted her crutch and jabbed it in the air in Mary's direction.

"Mum," said Tess.

"She's my niece! I have rights!" Aunt Mary tried to wrench the wooden window frame up.

"She has *rights*," snorted Tess's mother. "What a load of—"

"But why can't she come in?" Liam's brow knitted.

Tess and her mother looked at each other. They'd been so careful about what they said in front of Liam.

"Of course she can come in." Tess put her book to one side.

"Darling," said Mary when Tess opened the door. "And Liam! You've grown again! How does that keep happening?"

"Hi, Uncle Phil." Tess went to brush cheeks with her uncle, but to her surprise he suddenly pulled her to him in an awkward hug. He smelled of Old Spice and cigarettes. He said quietly into her ear, "I am deeply ashamed of my daughter."

Then he straightened and said, "I'll keep Liam company while you girls talk."

With Liam and Uncle Phil safely stashed in front of the television, Mary, Lucy and Tess sat at the kitchen table drinking tea.

"I made it very clear that you weren't to show up here," said Tess's mother, who wasn't so cranky with her sister that she would forgo her extremely good chocolate brownies.

Mary rolled her eyes, settled her elbows on the table and pressed Tess's hand between her warm, plump little palms. "Sweetheart, I'm just so sorry this has happened to you."

"This isn't something that just *happened* to her," exploded Lucy.

"The point is that I don't think Felicity really did have a choice," said Mary.

"Oh! I didn't realize! Poor Felicity! Someone put a gun to her head, did they?" Lucy put a pretend gun to her own head. Tess wondered when her mother had last had her blood pressure checked.

Mary resolutely ignored her sister and directed her conversation at Tess. "Sweetheart, you *know* Felicity would never have chosen for this to happen. This is torture for her. *Torture.*"

"Is this a joke?" Lucy took a savage bite of brownie. "Do you seriously expect Tess to feel sorry for Felicity?"

"I just hope you can find it in your heart to forgive her." Mary was doing a wonderful job of pretending that Lucy wasn't there.

"Okay, that's enough," said Lucy. "I don't want to hear another word come out of your mouth."

"Lucy, sometimes love just strikes!" Mary finally acknowledged her sister. "It just happens! Out of the blue!"

Tess stared into her teacup and swirled it around. Was this actually out of the blue? Or had it always been there, right in front of her eyes? Felicity and Will had gotten on famously from the moment they met. "Your cousin is a riot," Will had said to Tess after the three of them went out to dinner for the first time. Tess took it as a compliment, because Felicity was part of her. Her sparkling company was something Tess had to offer. And the fact that Will properly appreciated Felicity (not all her previous boyfriends had; some had actively disliked her) was a huge mark in his favor.

Felicity had taken an instant liking to Will too. "You can marry this one," she'd said to Tess the next day. "He's the one. I have spoken."

Did Felicity already have a crush on Will back then? Was this inevitable? Foreseeable?

Tess remembered the euphoria she'd felt that day after she'd introduced Will and Felicity. It felt like she'd reached a glorious destination, a mountaintop. "He's perfect, isn't he?" she'd said to Felicity. "He gets us. He's the first one who really gets us."

Gets *us*. Not gets *me*.

Her mother and aunt were still talking, oblivious of the fact that Tess wasn't contributing a word.

Lucy had slapped her hand over her eyes. "This isn't some wonderful love story, Mary!" She removed her hand and shook her head in disgust at her sister as if she were the worst kind of criminal. "What's wrong with you? Truly, what's wrong with you? Tess and Will are married. And have you forgotten there is an actual, real child involved? My grandson?"

"But you see, they're just so desperate to somehow make it right," said Mary to Tess. "They both love you so much."

"That's nice," said Tess.

Over the last ten years Will had never once complained about the fact that Felicity spent so much time with them. Perhaps that had been a sign. A sign that Tess wasn't enough for him. What ordinary husband would be prepared to have his wife's fat cousin come along on their annual summer holiday? Unless he was in love with her. Tess was a fool not to have seen it. She'd enjoyed watching Will and Felicity banter and argue and tease each other. She'd never felt excluded. Everything was better, sharper, funnier, edgier, when Felicity was around. Tess felt like she was more herself when Felicity was around, because Felicity knew her better than anyone. Felicity let Tess shine. Felicity laughed the loudest at Tess's jokes. She helped define and shape Tess's personality, so that Will could see Tess as she truly was.

And Tess felt prettier when Felicity was around.

She pressed cold fingertips to her burning cheeks. It was shameful but true. She had never felt repelled by Felicity's obesity, but she had felt particularly slim and lithe when she stood next to her.

And yet, nothing changed in Tess's mind when Felicity lost weight. It had not occurred to her that Will would ever look at Felicity in a sexual way. She was so sure of her position in their strange little threesome. Tess was at the apex of the triangle. Will loved her best. Felicity loved her best. How very self-centered of her.

"Tess?" said Mary.

"Let's talk about something else." Tess put her hand on her aunt's arm.

Two fat tears slid snail paths down Mary's pink, powdery cheeks. Tess had the oddest feeling that she was looking at her properly for the first time, as if she'd never even bothered to meet Mary's eyes before. Was it possible that Tess had never really thought of her mother and aunt as people, except in relation to her? Whenever she and Felicity were with their mothers, they let their thirty-five-year-old bodies slouch, they became offhand and chatty, full of the confidence that comes from being adored. Their mothers fussed and clucked while Tess and Felicity generously told them what life was like out in the real world. But now Tess and Lucy and Mary were just three women sitting around a table, grappling with this absurd, sad situation.

Mary dabbed at her face with a crumpled tissue. "Phil didn't want me to come. He said I'd do more harm than good, but I just thought I could find a way to make it all right. I spent all morning looking at photos of you and Felicity when you were growing up. The fun you two had together! That's the worst of this. I can't bear it if you become estranged from each other."

Tess patted her aunt's arm. Her own eyes felt dry and clear. Her heart was clenched like a fist.

"I think you might have to bear it," she said.

ELEVEN

You're not seriously expecting me to go to a Tupperware party," Rachel had said to Marla when she asked her a few weeks back while they were having coffee.

"You're my best friend." Marla stirred sugar into her soy decaf cappuccino.

"My daughter was murdered," said Rachel. "That gives me a permanent 'get out of party' card for the rest of my life."

Marla raised her eyebrows. She'd always had particularly eloquent eyebrows.

Marla had the right to raise her eyebrows. Ed had been in Adelaide for work (Ed was always away for work) when the two policemen turned up at Rachel's door. Marla went with Rachel to the morgue and was standing right next to her when they lifted that ordinary white bedsheet to reveal Janie's face. Marla was ready the moment Rachel's legs gave way and caught her instantly, expertly, one hand cupping her elbow, the other grabbing her upper arm. She was a midwife. She had a lot of practice catching burly husbands just before they hit the floor.

"Sorry," said Rachel.

"Janie would have come to my party," said Marla. Her eyes filled. "Janie loved me."

It was true. Janie had adored Marla. She was always telling Rachel to dress more like Marla. And then, of course, on the one occasion Rachel wore a dress that Marla had helped her buy, look what happened.

"I wonder if Janie would have liked Tupperware parties," said Rachel as she watched a middle-aged woman arguing with her primary-schooler at the table next to them. She tried, and failed, as she always did, to imagine Janie as a forty-five-year-old woman. She sometimes ran into Janie's old friends in the shops, and it was always such a shock to see their seventeen-year-old selves emerge from those puffy, generic middle-aged faces. Rachel had to stop herself from exclaiming, "Good Lord, darling, look how *old* you've become!" in the same way that you said, "Look how tall you've grown!" to children.

"I remember Janie was very tidy," said Marla. "She liked to be organized. I bet she would have been right into Tupperware."

The wonderful thing about Marla was that she understood Rachel's desire to talk endlessly about the sort of adult that Janie might have become, to wonder how many children she would have had and the sort of man she would have married. It kept her alive, for just those few moments. Ed had hated those hypothetical conversations so much, he'd leave the room. He couldn't understand Rachel's need to wonder what could have been, rather than just accepting that it never would be. "Excuse me, I was *talking*!" Rachel would yell after him.

"Please come to my Tupperware party," said Marla.

"All right," said Rachel. "But just so you know, I'm not buying anything."

And so here she was sitting in Marla's living room, crowded and noisy with women drinking cocktails. Rachel was sandwiched on a couch in between Marla's two daughters-in-law, Eve and Arianna, who had no plans to move to New York and were *both* pregnant with Marla's first grandchildren.

"I'm just not into pain," Eve was telling Arianna. "I told my obstetrician, I said, 'Look, I have zero tolerance for pain. Zero. Don't even talk to me about it.'"

"Well, I guess nobody really likes pain?" said Arianna, who seemed to doubt every word that came out of her mouth. "Except masochists?"

"It's unacceptable," said Eve. "In this day and age. I refuse it. I say no thank you to pain."

Ah, so that was my mistake, thought Rachel. *I should have said no thank you to pain.*

"Look who's here, ladies!" Marla appeared with a tray of sausage rolls in hand and Cecilia Fitzpatrick by her side. Cecilia looked polished and shiny and was wheeling a neat black suitcase behind her.

Apparently it was something of a coup to get Cecilia to do a party for you, because she was so booked up. She had six Tupperware consultants working beneath her, according to her mother-in-law, and was sent on all sorts of overseas jaunts and the like. "I'll tell you this in confidence, of course," Cecilia's mother-in-law, Virginia Fitzpatrick, had said to Rachel once, "but I think Cecilia actually makes more money than John-Paul, and he's an *engineer.*"

"So, now, Cecilia." Marla was flustered with responsibility, and the sausage rolls slid about on the tray in her hand. "Would you like a drink?"

Cecilia wheeled her bag to a neat stop and rescued the sausage rolls just in the nick of time.

"Just a glass of water would be lovely, Marla," she said. "Why don't I hand these out for you while I introduce myself, although I think I know a lot of faces, of course. Hello, I'm Cecilia, it's Arianna, isn't it? Sausage roll?" Arianna looked blankly at Cecilia as she took a sausage roll. "Your younger sister teaches my daughter Polly ballet. I'm going to show you the perfect little containers for freezing purees for your baby! And Rachel, it's so nice to see you. How's little Jacob?"

"Moving to New York for two years." Rachel took a sausage roll and gave Cecilia a wry smile. Cecilia wasn't everyone's cup of tea, but Rachel didn't mind her, because she returned phone calls, and every time she said she'd do something, she actually did it. The last Parents & Friends president, Gary Morgan, had been deeply in love with himself, and the only thing you could rely on was that the smell of his aftershave would linger for a good three hours after he'd visited the school office.

Cecilia stopped. "Oh, Rachel, what a bugger," she said sympathetically, but then, in typical Cecilia style, she instantly shifted into solution mode. "But listen, you'll visit, right? Someone was telling me recently about this website with amazing deals on New York apartments. I'll e-mail you the link, promise." She moved on. "Hi there, I'm Cecilia. Sausage roll?"

And on she went about the room, serving food and compliments, fixing every guest with that strange piercing gaze of hers, so that by the time she finished and was ready to do her demonstration, everyone obediently swung their knees in her direction, their faces attentive, ready to be sold Tupperware, as if a firm but fair teacher had taken control of a rowdy classroom.

Rachel was surprised by how much she ended up enjoying the night. It was partly the very good cocktails that Marla was serving, but it was also thanks to Cecilia, who interspersed her lively and somewhat evangelical product demonstration ("I'm a Tupperware freak," she told them. "I just *love* this stuff." Rachel found her genuine passion touching. And compelling! It would be *great* if her carrots stayed crunchier for longer!) with a trivia competition. Each guest who got a trivia question right was awarded a gold-foil-wrapped chocolate coin. At the end of the night the person with the most gold coins would win a prize.

Some of the questions were about Tupperware. Rachel did not know, or particularly feel the need to know, that a Tupperware party began somewhere in the world every 2.7 seconds ("One second, two seconds—that's another Tupperware party starting!" chirped Cecilia), or that a man named Earl Tupper created the famous "burping seal." But she did have quite good general knowledge and she began to feel quite competitive about the growing pile of gold coins in front of her.

In the end it was a fierce battle between Rachel and Marla's friend from her midwifery days, Jenny Cruise, and Rachel actually punched her fist in the air when she won by a single gold coin on the question, "Who played Pat the Rat on the soapie *Sons and Daughters*?"

Rachel knew the answer (Rowena Wallace) because Janie had been obsessed with that silly show when she was a teenager. She sent up a word of thanks to Janie.

She'd forgotten how much she enjoyed winning.

In fact, she was on such a high that she ended up ordering over three hundred dollars' worth of Tupperware that Cecilia assured her would transform her pantry and her life. By the end of the night she was a little drunk.

Actually, everyone was a little drunk, except for Marla's pregnant daughters-in-law, who left early, and Cecilia, who was presumably drunk on the joy of Tupperware.

There was much shrieking. Husbands were telephoned. Lifts home were negotiated. Rachel sat on the couch happily eating her way through her pile of chocolate coins.

"What about you, Rachel? Have you arranged a lift home?" said Cecilia, when Marla was at the front door shouting good-byes to her tennis friends. Cecilia had all her Tupperware packed away into her black bag and was still as immaculate as at the start of the night, except for two spots of color high on her cheeks.

"Me?" Rachel looked around and realized she was the last guest. "I'm fine. I'll drive home."

For some reason it hadn't really occurred to her that she

needed to find a way to get home too. It was something to do with her sense of always feeling separate from everybody else, as if things that worried them couldn't possibly worry her, as if she were immune from the ordinariness of life.

"Don't be ridiculous!" Marla swooped back into the room. The night had been a triumph. "You can't drive, you crazy girl! You'd be way over the limit. Mac can drive you home. He hasn't got anything better to do."

"That's okay. I'll catch a cab." Rachel roused herself. Her head did feel fuzzy. She didn't want Mac to drive her home. Mac, who had stayed in his study throughout the Tupperware party, was a man's man and had got on great with Ed, but he was always so painfully shy in one-on-one conversations with women. It would be excruciating being alone in the car with him.

"You live down near the Wycombe Road tennis courts, don't you, Rachel?" said Cecilia. "I'll drive you home. You're right on my way."

Moments later, they'd waved Marla off and Rachel was in the passenger seat of Cecilia's white Ford Territory with the giant Tupperware logo along the side. The car was very comfortable, quiet and clean and nice-smelling. Cecilia drove just as she did everything, capably and briskly, and Rachel put her head back against the headrest and waited for Cecilia's reliable, soothing stream of conversation about raffles, carnivals, newsletters and everything else pertaining to St. Angela's.

Instead, there was silence. Rachel glanced over at Cecilia's profile. She was chewing on her bottom lip and squinting, as if at some thought that was giving her pain.

Marriage problems? Something to do with the kids? Rachel remembered all the time she used to devote to giant-seeming problems about sex, misbehaving children and misunderstood comments, broken appliances and money.

It wasn't that she now knew those problems didn't matter. Not at all. She longed for them to matter. She longed for the tricky tussle of life as a mother and a wife. How wonderful to be Cecilia Fitzpatrick driving home to her daughters after hosting a successful Tupperware party, worrying over whatever was quite rightfully worrying her.

In the end it was Rachel who broke the silence. "I had fun tonight," she said. "You did a great job. No wonder you're so successful at it."

Cecilia gave a small shrug. "Thank you. I love it." She gave Rachel a wry smile. "My sister makes fun of me over it."

"Jealous," said Rachel.

Cecilia shrugged and yawned. She seemed like a different person from the performer at Marla's house and the woman who zoomed around St. Angela's.

"I'd love to see your pantry," mused Rachel. "I bet everything is all labeled and in the perfect container. Mine looks like a disaster zone."

"I am proud of my pantry." Cecilia smiled. "John-Paul says it's like a filing cabinet of food. The girls get in terrible trouble if they put something back in the wrong spot."

"How are your girls?" asked Rachel.

"Wonderful," said Cecilia, although Rachel saw a shadow of a frown. "Growing up fast. Giving me cheek."

"Your eldest daughter," said Rachel. "Isabel. I saw her

the other day in assembly. She reminds me a little of my daughter. Of Janie."

Cecilia didn't respond.

Why did I tell her that? thought Rachel. *I must be drunker than I realize. No woman wants to hear that her daughter looks like a girl who was strangled.*

But then Cecilia said, with her eyes on the road ahead, "I have just one memory of your daughter."

TWELVE

have just one memory of your daughter."

Was it the right thing to do? What if she made Rachel cry? She'd just won the Heat 'N Eat Everyday Set and she seemed so happy about it.

Cecilia never felt comfortable around Rachel. She felt trivial, because surely the whole world was trivial to a woman who had lost a child in such circumstances. She always wanted to somehow convey to Rachel that she *knew* she was trivial. Any time Cecilia imagined losing one of her daughters, a silent, primal scream would get trapped in her throat. If she couldn't stand imagining it, how could Rachel actually live it? "Time heals," Cecilia's mother-in-law intoned whenever the subject of Rachel's grief had come up, as if sharing a job with Rachel qualified her as an expert, and Cecilia had thought, *I bet it doesn't.*

Years ago, she'd seen something in a magazine article about how grieving parents appreciated hearing people tell them memories of their children. There would be no more new memories, so it was a gift to share one with them. Ever since then, whenever Cecilia saw Rachel, she thought of her memory of Janie, paltry though it was, and wondered how she could share it with her. But there was never an opportunity. You couldn't bring it up in the school office in between conversations about the uniform shop and the netball timetable.

Now was the perfect time. The only time. And Rachel was the one who had brought up Janie.

"Of course, I didn't actually know her at all," said Cecilia. "She was four years ahead of me. But I do have this memory." She faltered.

"Go on." Rachel straightened in her seat. "I love to hear memories of Janie. Actually, I love to hear her name. It makes other people uncomfortable talking about her. Not me."

"Well, it's just something really tiny," said Cecilia. Now she was terrified she wouldn't deliver enough. She wondered if she should embellish. "I was in Year Two. Janie was in Year Six. I knew her name because she was house captain of Red."

"Ah, yes." Rachel smiled. "We dyed everything red. One of Ed's work shirts accidentally got dyed red. Funny how you forget all that stuff."

"So it was the school carnival, and do you remember how we used to do marching? Each house had to march around the oval. I'm always telling Connor Whitby that we should bring back the marching. He just laughs at me."

Cecilia glanced over and saw that Rachel's smile had withered a little. She plowed on. Was it too upsetting? Not that interesting?

"I was the sort of child who took the marching *very* seriously. And I desperately wanted Red to win, but I tripped over, and because I fell, all these other children crashed into the back of me, Sister Ursula was screaming like a banshee, and that was the end of it for Red. I was sobbing my heart out; I thought it was the absolute end of the world, and Janie Crowley, your Janie, came over and helped me up, and brushed off the back of my uniform, and she said very quietly in my ear, 'It doesn't matter. It's only stupid marching.'"

Rachel didn't say anything.

"That's it," said Cecilia humbly. "It wasn't much, but I just always—"

"Thank you, darling," said Rachel, and Cecilia was reminded of an adult thanking a child for a homemade bookmark made out of cardboard and glitter. Rachel lifted a hand, as if she were about to wave at someone, and then she let it brush gently against Cecilia's shoulder before dropping it in her lap. "That's just so Janie. 'Only stupid marching.' You know what? I think I remember it. All the children tumbling to the ground. Marla and I giggling our heads off." She paused. Cecilia's stomach tensed. Was she about to burst into tears?

"Gosh, you know, I am a tiny bit drunk," said Rachel. "I actually thought about driving myself home. Imagine if I'd killed someone."

"I'm sure you wouldn't have," said Cecilia.

"I really did have fun tonight," said Rachel. Her head was turned so that she was addressing the car window. She gently knocked her forehead against the window. It seemed like something a much younger woman would do after she'd had too much to drink. "I should make the effort to go out more often."

"Oh, well!" said Cecilia. This was her thing. She could fix that! "You must come to Polly's birthday party the weekend after Easter! Saturday afternoon at two. It's a pirate party."

"That's very nice of you, but I'm sure Polly doesn't need me crashing her party," said Rachel.

"You must come! You'll know lots of people. John-Paul's mother. My mum. Lucy O'Leary is coming with Tess and her little boy, Liam." Cecilia was suddenly desperate for Rachel to come. "You could bring your grandson! Bring Jacob! The girls would *love* to have a toddler there."

Rachel's face lit up. "I did say I'd look after Jacob while Rob and Lauren are seeing real estate agents about renting out their house while they're in New York. Oh, this is me, just ahead."

Cecilia stopped the car in front of a redbrick bungalow. It seemed like every light in the house had been left on.

"Thanks so much for the lift." Rachel climbed out of the car with the same careful sideways slide of the hips as Cecilia's mother. There was a certain age, Cecilia had noticed, before people stooped or trembled, but where they didn't seem to trust their bodies in quite the same way as they once had.

"I'll send an invitation to you at the school!" Cecilia leaned across the seat to call out the window, wondering if she should be offering to walk Rachel to the door. Her own mother would be insulted if she did. John-Paul's mother would be insulted if she didn't.

"Lovely," said Rachel, and she walked off briskly, as if she'd read Cecilia's thoughts and wanted to prove she wasn't elderly just yet, thanks very much.

Cecilia turned the car around in the cul-de-sac, and by the time she came back, Rachel was already inside, the front door pulled firmly shut.

Cecilia looked for her silhouette through the windows but didn't see anything. She tried to imagine what Rachel was doing now and what she was feeling, alone in a house with the ghosts of her daughter and her husband.

Well. She had a slightly breathless feeling, as if she'd just driven home a minor celebrity. And she'd talked to her about Janie! It had gone pretty well, she thought. She'd given Rachel a memory, just like the magazine article said she should. She felt a mild sense of social achievement, and of satisfaction in finally ticking off a long-procrastinated task, and then she felt ashamed for feeling pride, or any sort of pleasure, in connection to Rachel's tragedy.

She stopped at a traffic light and remembered the angry truck driver from that afternoon, and with that thought, her own life came flooding back into her mind. While she'd been driving Rachel home, she'd temporarily forgotten everything: the strange things Polly and Esther had said about John-Paul today in the car, her decision to open his letter tonight.

Did she still feel justified?

Everything had seemed so ordinary after speech therapy.

There had been no more peculiar revelations from her daughters, and Isabel had seemed especially cheerful after her haircut. It was a short pixie cut, and from the way Isabel was holding herself, it was clear that she thought it made her look very sophisticated, when it actually made her look younger and sweeter.

There had been a postcard for the girls from John-Paul in the letterbox. He had a running joke with his daughters, where he sent them the silliest postcards he could find. Today's postcard featured one of those dogs with folds of wrinkly skin, wearing a tiara and beads, and Cecilia thought it was stupid, but true to form, the girls all fell about laughing and put it on the fridge.

"Oh, come on now," she said mildly, as a car suddenly pulled into the lane in front of her. She lifted her hand to toot the horn and then didn't bother.

Note how I didn't scream and yell like a mad person, she thought for the benefit of that afternoon's psychotic truck driver, just in case he happened to have stopped by to read her mind. It was a cab in front of her. He was doing that weird cabbie thing of testing the brakes every few seconds.

Great. He was heading the same direction as she was. The cab jerked its way down her street, and without warning suddenly stopped at the curb outside Cecilia's house.

The lights in the cab went on. The passenger was sitting in the front seat. One of the Kingston boys, thought Cecilia. The Kingstons lived across the road and had three sons in their twenties, still living at home, using their expensive private educations to do never-ending degrees and get drunk in city bars. "If a Kingston boy ever goes near one of our girls," John-Paul always said, "I'll be ready with the shotgun."

She pulled into her driveway, pressed the button on the remote for the garage and looked in her rearview mirror. The cabbie had popped the boot. A broad-shouldered man in a suit was pulling out his luggage.

It wasn't a Kingston boy.

It was John-Paul. He always looked so unfamiliar when she saw him unexpectedly like that in his work clothes, as if she were still twenty-three and he'd become all grown-up and gray-haired without her.

John-Paul was home three days early.

She was filled with equal parts pleasure and exasperation.

She'd lost her chance. She couldn't open the letter now. She turned off the ignition, pulled on the handbrake, undid her seat belt, opened the car door and ran down the driveway to meet him.

THIRTEEN

Hello?" said Tess warily, looking at her watch as she picked up her mother's home phone.

It was nine o'clock at night. Surely it couldn't be another telemarketer.

"It's me."

It was Felicity. Tess's stomach flipped. Felicity had been calling all day on her mobile and leaving voice-mail messages and texts that Tess left unheard and unread. It felt strange, ignoring Felicity, as if she were forcing herself to do something unnatural.

"I don't want to talk to you."

"Nothing has happened," said Felicity. "We still haven't slept together."

"For God's sake," said Tess, and then to her surprise, she laughed. It wasn't even a bitter laugh. It was a genuine laugh. This was ridiculous. "What's the holdup?"

But then she caught sight of herself in the mirror above

her mother's dining room table and saw her smile fade, like someone catching on to a cruel trick.

"All we can think about is you," said Felicity. "And Liam. The Bedstuff website crashed—anyway, I won't talk to you about work. I'm at my apartment. Will is at home. He looks like a wreck."

"You're pathetic." Tess turned away from her reflection in the mirror. "You're both so pathetic."

"I know," said Felicity. Her voice was so low, Tess had to press the phone hard against her ear to hear her. "I'm a bitch. I'm that woman we hate."

"Speak up!" said Tess irritably.

"I said, I'm a bitch!" repeated Felicity.

"Don't expect any arguments from me."

"I don't," said Felicity. "Of course I don't."

"You want me to be all right with it," marveled Tess. She knew them so well. "You want me to make everything all right."

That was her job. That was her role in their three-way relationship. Will and Felicity were the ones who ranted and raved, who let the clients upset them, who got their feelings hurt by strangers, who thumped the steering wheel and shouted, "Are you kidding me?" It was Tess's job to soothe them, to jolly them along, to do the whole glass-is-half-full, it-will-all-work-out, you'll-feel-better-in-the-morning thing. How could they possibly have an affair without her there to help? They needed *Tess* there to say, "It's not your fault!"

"I don't expect that," said Felicity. "I don't expect any-thing from you. Are you all right? Is Liam all right?"

"We're fine," said Tess coldly. "Liam is starting at St. Angela's tomorrow."

"*Tomorrow?* What's the rush?"

"There's an Easter egg hunt."

"Ah," said Felicity. "Chocolate. Liam's Kryptonite. He's not being taught by any of the psychotic nuns who taught us, is he?"

Tess thought, *Don't you* chat *with me, as if everything were normal!* But for some reason she went on talking anyway. It was too ingrained in her psyche. She'd chatted to Felicity every day of her life. She was her best friend. She was her only friend.

"The nuns are all dead," she said. "But the PE teacher is Connor Whitby. Remember him?"

"Connor Whitby," repeated Felicity. "He was that sad, sinister guy you were going out with before we came to Melbourne. But I thought he was an accountant."

"He retrained. He wasn't sinister, was he?" said Tess. Hadn't he been perfectly nice? He was the boyfriend who had loved her hands. She remembered that suddenly. How strange. She'd been thinking about him last night, and now he'd reappeared in her life.

"He was sinister," said Felicity definitely. "He was really old too."

"He was ten years older than me."

"Anyway, I remember there was something creepy about him. I bet he's even creepier now. There's something un-savory about PE teachers, with their tracksuits and whistles and clipboards."

Tess's hand tightened around the phone. Felicity's *smug-*

ness. She always thought she knew everything, that she was the superior judge of character, that she was more sophisticated and edgy than Tess.

"So I guess you weren't in love with Connor Whitby, then?" she said, brittle and bitchy. "Will is the first one to take your fancy?"

"Tess—"

"Don't bother," she cut her off. "Is there anything else?"

"I don't suppose I could say good night to Liam, could I?" said Felicity in a small, meek voice that didn't suit her.

"No," said Tess. "Anyway, he's asleep." He wasn't asleep. She'd walked by his bedroom (her father's old study) just a moment ago and seen him lying in bed, playing on his Nintendo DS.

"Tell him I said hello."

Liam had a certain chuckle he reserved especially for Felicity.

Tess sighed. "He's in bed. I'll just check—if he's awake, I'll put him on."

"Thank you," said Felicity humbly.

Tess pressed the phone against her chest and went to walk down the hall to Liam's bedroom. Then she stopped, pivoted and went to the other end of the house. She put the phone back to her ear.

"I don't care if you sleep with Will or not," she said. "Actually, I think you should sleep with him. Get it out of your system. But I will not have Liam growing up with divorced parents. You were there when Mum and Dad split up. You *know* what it was like for me. That's why I can't believe . . ."

There was a searing pain at the center of her chest. She pressed her palm to it. Felicity was silent.

"You're not going to live happily ever after with him," said Tess. "You know that, don't you? Because I'm prepared to wait this out. I will wait for you to finish with him." She took a deep, shaky breath. "Have your revolting little affair and then give my husband back."

———

October 7, 1977: Three teenagers were killed when East German police clashed with protestors demanding "Down with the wall!" Lucy O'Leary, pregnant with her first child, saw the story on the news and cried and cried. Her twin sister, Mary, who was also pregnant with her first child, rang her the next day and asked if the news was making her cry too. They talked for a while about tragedies happening around the world and then moved on to the far more interesting topic of their babies.

"I think we're having boys," said Mary. "And they'll be best friends."

"More likely they'll want to kill each other," said Lucy.

FOURTEEN

Rachel sat in a steaming hot bath, clinging to the sides while her head spun. It was a stupid idea to have a bath when she was tipsy from the Tupperware party. She'd probably slip when she got out and break her hip.

Perhaps that was a good strategy. Rob and Lauren would cancel New York and stay in Sydney to take care of her. Look at Lucy O'Leary. Her daughter came from Melbourne to look after her the moment she heard about her breaking her ankle. She even pulled her son out of his school in Melbourne, which seemed a bit over the top, now that Rachel thought about it.

Recalling the O'Learys made Rachel think of Connor Whitby and the expression on his face when he saw Tess. Rachel wondered if she should warn Lucy. *Just a heads-up. Connor Whitby might be a murderer.*

Or he might not be. He might also be a perfectly nice PE teacher.

Some days, when Rachel saw him with the children on the oval, in the sunshine, his whistle around his neck, eating a red apple, she would think, *There is no way on heaven and earth that nice man could have hurt Janie!* And then other bitter gray days, when she caught sight of him walking alone, his face impassive, his shoulders broad enough to kill, she thought, *You know what happened to my daughter.*

She rested her head against the back of the bath, closed her eyes and remembered the first time she'd heard of his existence. Sergeant Bellach told her that the last person to see Janie alive was a boy from the local public school called Connor Whitby, and Rachel had thought, *But that can't be, I've never heard of him.* She knew all of Janie's friends and their mothers.

Ed had told Janie she wasn't allowed a serious boyfriend until after she'd finished her very last HSC exam. He'd made such a big deal of it. But Janie hadn't argued, and Rachel had blithely assumed she wasn't even that interested in boys yet.

She and Ed met Connor for the first time at Janie's funeral. He shook Ed's hand and pressed his cold cheek against Rachel's. Connor was part of the nightmare, as unreal and wrong as the coffin. Months afterward Rachel found that one photo of them together at someone's party. He was laughing at something Janie had said.

And then all those years later, he got the job at St. Angela's. She hadn't even recognized him until she saw his name on the employment application.

"I don't know if you remember me, Mrs. Crowley," he

said to her a short time after he started, when they were alone together in the office.

"I remember you," she said icily.

"I still think about Janie," he said. "All the time."

She hadn't known what to say. *Why do you think of her? Because you killed her?*

There was definitely something like guilt in his eyes. She was not imagining it. She'd been working as a school secretary for fifteen years. Connor had the look of a kid sent to the principal's office. But was it guilt over murder? Or something else?

"I hope it's not uncomfortable for you, my working here," he'd said.

"It's perfectly fine," she'd said curtly, and that was the last time they ever spoke of it.

She had considered resigning. Working at Janie's old primary school had always been bittersweet. Little girls with skinny Bambi legs would streak past her in the playground and she'd catch a glimpse of Janie; on hot summer afternoons she'd watch the mothers picking up their children and remember long-ago summers, picking up Janie and Rob and taking them for ice cream; their flushed little faces. Janie had been at high school when she died, so Rachel's memories of St. Angela's weren't tarnished by her murder. That is, until Connor Whitby turned up, roaring his horrible motorbike through Rachel's soft, sepia-colored memories.

In the end, she'd stayed out of stubbornness. She enjoyed the work. Why should she be the one to leave? And, more important, she felt in a strange way that she owed it to Janie to not run away, to face up to this man, every day, and whatever it was he'd done.

If he had killed Janie, would he have taken a job at the same place as her mother? Would he have said, "I still think about her"?

Rachel opened her eyes and felt that hard ball of fury lodged permanently at the back of her throat, as if she'd not quite choked on something. It was the not knowing. The not fucking knowing.

She added more cold water to the bath.

"It's the not knowing," a tiny, refined-looking woman had said at that homicide victims support group she and Ed had gone to a few times, sitting on folding chairs in that cold community hall somewhere in Chatswood, holding their foam cups of instant coffee in shaky hands. The woman's son had been murdered on his way home from cricket practice. Nobody heard anything. Nobody saw anything. "The not fucking knowing."

There was a ripple of soft blinks around the circle. The woman had a sweet, cut-glass voice; it was like hearing the Queen swear.

"Hate to tell you this, love, but knowing doesn't help all that much," interrupted a stocky red-faced man, whose daughter's murderer had been sentenced to life in prison.

Rachel and Ed both took a mutual, violent dislike to the red-faced man, and they stopped going to the support group because of him.

People thought that tragedy made you wise, that it automatically elevated you to a higher, more spiritual level, but it seemed to Rachel that just the opposite was true.

Tragedy made you petty and spiteful. It didn't give you any great knowledge or insight. She didn't understand a damned thing about life except that it was arbitrary and cruel, and some people got away with murder while others made one tiny, careless mistake and paid a terrible price.

She held a washcloth under the cold tap, folded it and placed it across her forehead, as if she were a patient with a fever.

Seven minutes. Her mistake could be measured in minutes.

Marla was the only person who knew. Ed never knew.

Janie had been complaining that she was tired all the time. "Do more exercise," Rachel kept telling her. "Don't go to bed so late. Eat more!" She was so skinny and tall. And then she'd started complaining about some vague pain in her lower back. "Mum, I seriously think I've got glandular fever." Rachel had made the appointment with Dr. Buckley just so she could tell Janie there was nothing wrong with her, and that she needed to do all the things that her mother told her.

Janie normally caught the bus and walked home from the Wycombe Road bus stop. The plan was that Rachel would pick her up at the corner down from the high school and take her straight to Dr. Buckley's office in Gordon. She'd reminded Janie of the plan that morning.

Except Rachel was seven minutes late, and when she got to the corner, Janie wasn't waiting. *She's forgotten,* Rachel had thought, drumming her fingers on the steering wheel. *Or she got sick of waiting.* The child was so impatient, act-ing as if Rachel were a convenient form of public transportation with an obligation to run on a schedule. There were no mobile phones in those days. There wasn't anything Rachel could do except wait in the car for another ten minutes (she didn't actually like waiting much herself) before finally going home and ringing Dr. Buckley's receptionist to cancel the appointment.

She hadn't been worried. She was aggravated. Rachel knew there was nothing particularly wrong with Janie. It was typical that Rachel would go to the trouble of making the doctor's appointment and then Janie wouldn't bother. It wasn't until much later, when Rob said, his mouth full of sandwich, "Where's Janie?" that Rachel looked up at the kitchen clock and felt that first icy thread of fear.

Nobody had seen Janie waiting on the corner, or if they did they never came forward. Rachel never knew what difference those seven minutes had made.

What she did eventually learn from the police investigation was that Janie turned up at Connor Whitby's house at something like three thirty, and they watched a video together (*Nine to Five* with Dolly Parton), before Janie said she "had something to do in Chatswood," and Connor walked her to the railway station. Nobody else ever saw her alive. Nobody remembered seeing her on the train or anywhere in Chatswood.

Her body was found the next morning by two nine-year-old boys who were riding their BMX bikes through Wattle Valley Park. They stopped at the playground and found her lying at the bottom of the slide. She had her school blazer placed over her like a blanket, as if to keep her warm from the cold, and a pair of rosary beads in her hands. She'd been strangled by someone with their bare hands. Traumatic asphyxiation was the cause of death. No signs of a struggle. Nothing to scrape from her fingernails. No usable fingerprints. No hairs. No DNA. Rachel asked the question when she read about cases being solved through DNA testing in the late nineties. No suspects.

"But where was she going?" Ed kept asking, as if she'd finally remember the answer if he asked the question often enough. "Why was she walking through that park?"

Sometimes, after he'd asked her over and over, he'd end up sobbing with rage and frustration. Rachel couldn't bear it. She wanted nothing to do with his grief. She didn't want to know about it, or feel it, or share it. Hers was bad enough. How could she cope with carrying his as well?

She wondered now why they couldn't turn to each other to share their grief. She knew they loved each other, but when Janie died, neither of them could bear the sight of the other's tears. They'd held on to each other the way strangers do in a natural disaster, their bodies stiff, awkwardly patting shoulders. And there was poor little Rob caught in the middle, a teenage boy clumsily trying to make everything right, all false smiles and cheery lies. No wonder he'd become a real estate agent.

The water was too cold now.

Rachel began to shiver uncontrollably, as if she had hypothermia. She put her hands on the sides of the bath and went to stand up.

She couldn't do it. She was stuck in here for the night. Her arms, her dead-white, sticklike arms, had no strength in them. How was it possible that this useless, frail, blue-veined body was the same one that had once been so brown, firm and strong?

"That's a good tan for April," Toby Murphy had said to her that day. "Sunbathe do you, Rachel?"

That's why she had been seven minutes late. She was flirting with Toby Murphy. Toby was married to her friend Jackie. He was a plumber and needed an office assistant. Rachel had gone for an interview, and she stayed in Toby's office for over an hour, flirting. Toby was an incorrigible flirt, and she was wearing the new dress that Marla had convinced her to buy, and Toby kept looking at her bare legs. Rachel would never have been unfaithful to Ed, and Toby adored his wife, so everyone's marriage vows were safe, but still, he was looking at her legs, and she liked it.

Ed wouldn't have been happy if she'd worked for Toby. He didn't know about the interview. Rachel sensed he felt competitive toward Toby, something to do with Toby being a "tradie" and Ed being a less masculine pharmaceutical salesman. Ed and Toby played tennis together, and Ed generally lost. He pretended it didn't matter, but Rachel could tell that it always rankled.

So it was particularly mean of her to enjoy Toby looking at her legs.

Her sins that day had been so trite. Vanity. Self-indulgence. A tiny betrayal of Ed. A tiny betrayal of Jackie Murphy. But maybe those trite little sins were the worst. The person who killed Janie had probably been sick, crazy in the head, whereas Rachel was sane and self-aware, and she knew exactly what she was doing when she let her dress ride a bit farther up her knees.

The bubble bath she'd poured into the bathwater floated on the surface like drops of oil, slimy and greasy. Rachel tried again to heave herself out of the bath and failed.

Maybe it would be easier if she let the water out first.

She let the plug out with her toe, and the roar of the water going down the drain sounded as it always did, like the roar of a dragon. Rob had been terrified of that drain. "Raaah!" Janie used to yell, making her hands into claws. When the water was gone, Rachel turned herself over onto her front. She got onto her hands and knees. Her kneecaps felt like they were being crushed.

She pulled herself to a half-standing position, held on to the side and tentatively put one leg out, then the other. She was out. Her heart settled. Thank God. No broken bones.

Perhaps that was her last-ever bath.

She toweled herself dry and pulled her dressing gown from the hook behind the door. The dressing gown was made out of beautiful, soft fabric. Another thoughtful gift chosen by Lauren. Rachel's home was filled with thoughtful gifts chosen by Lauren. For example, that chunky, vanilla-scented candle in the glass jar, sitting on her bathroom cabinet.

"Big smelly candle," Ed would have called it.

She missed Ed at funny times. Missed arguing with him. Missed sex. They kept having sex after Janie died. They were both surprised by this, and sickened that their bodies still responded the same way as before, but they kept doing it.

She missed them all: her mother, her father, her husband, her daughter. Each absence felt like its own separate vicious little wound. None of their deaths were fair. Janie's murderer was responsible for all of them. Natural causes be damned.

Don't you dare was the strange thought that came into Rachel's head when she saw Ed crash to his knees in the hallway one hot February morning. She meant, *Don't you dare leave me here to deal with this pain on my own.* She knew right away that he was dead. They said it was a massive stroke, but Ed and her parents had died of broken hearts. Only Rachel's heart had stubbornly refused to do the right thing and kept on beating. It made her feel ashamed, like the way her desire for sex had shamed her. She kept breathing, eating, fucking, living, while Janie rotted in the ground.

She ran the palm of her hand across the steamed-up mirror and considered her blurry reflection behind the drops of water. She thought of the way Jacob kissed her with both his little fat hands pressed to her cheeks, his big clear blue eyes staring straight into hers, and each time she'd feel amazed gratitude that her wrinkly face could inspire such adoration.

For something to do, she gently nudged at the chunky candle until it reached the edge of the cabinet, toppled and crashed to the floor in a shatter of vanilla-smelling glass.

FIFTEEN

Cecilia was having sex with her husband. Good sex. Very good sex. Extremely good sex! They were having sex again. Hooray!

"Oh God," said John-Paul from above her. His eyes closed.

"Oh God," said Cecilia agreeably.

It was like there hadn't been a problem at all. They'd gone to bed tonight and turned to each other as naturally as when they were first together as young lovers, back when it was inconceivable that they would ever sleep next to each other without first having sex.

"Jesus. Christ." John-Paul tipped his head back in ecstasy.

Cecilia moaned to let him know she was pretty happy too.

Very. Good. Sex. Very. Good. Sex. She repeated the words in rhythm with the movement of their bodies.

What was that? She strained her ears. Was it one of the

girls calling out for her? No. Nothing. Damn it to hell. She'd lost her concentration now. Lose focus for just a moment and that was the end of it. She was back at square one. Tantric sex was the solution, according to Miriam. Now she was thinking about Miriam. So that was the end of that.

"Oh God, oh *God*." John-Paul appeared to be having no problem maintaining focus.

Gay! Gay, my foot.

The girls, who should have been sound asleep but were only just going to bed (Cecilia's mother was disobedient when it came to schedules) had been ecstatic to see their father home earlier than anticipated.

They'd climbed all over him, talking over the top of one another, telling him about *The Biggest Loser*, the Berlin Wall, the really stupid thing that Harriet had said at ballet the other day, how much fish Mum had made them eat and so on.

Cecilia had watched John-Paul telling Isabel to turn around so he could admire her new haircut and had noted nothing strange about the way he looked at her. He was exhausted, with shadows under his eyes after the long flight (he'd been stuck in Auckland for most of the day after managing to get an earlier flight home that went via New Zealand), but he seemed happy, pleased with himself for surprising them. He did not seem like a man who cried secret tears in the shower. And now they were having sex! Great sex! Everything was fine. There was nothing to worry about. He hadn't even mentioned the letter. It couldn't be that significant if he wasn't even talking about it.

"Far . . . *out*."

John-Paul shuddered and fell against her.

"Did you just say 'far out'?" said Cecilia. "You seventies throwback."

"Yes, I did," said John-Paul. "It indicated satisfaction. Speaking of which, I sense that . . . ?"

"I'm fine," said Cecilia. "It was far out, man." It certainly would be next time.

John-Paul laughed, rolled off her and pulled her to him, wrapping his arms around her and kissing her neck.

"Been a while," observed Cecilia neutrally.

"I know," said John-Paul. "Why is that? That's why I came home early. I suddenly got horny as hell."

"I spent all of Sister Ursula's funeral thinking about sex," said Cecilia.

"That's the way," said John-Paul sleepily.

"A truck driver whistled at me the other day. I've still got it, just so you know."

"I don't need a bloody truck driver to tell me my wife's still got it. You were wearing your netball skirt, I bet."

"I was." She paused. "Someone whistled at Isabel the other day in the shops."

"Little fucker," said John-Paul, but without much heat. "She looks much younger with that haircut."

"I know. Don't tell her."

"Not stupid." He sounded like he was nearly asleep.

Everything was fine. Cecilia felt her breathing start to slow. She closed her eyes.

"Berlin Wall, eh?" said John-Paul.

"Yup."

"I was sick to death of the *Titanic*."

"Me too."

Cecilia let herself start to slide into sleep. *Everything back on track. Everything as it should be. So much to do tomorrow.*

"What did you do with that letter?"

Her eyes opened. She looked straight ahead in the darkness.

"I put it back up in the attic. In one of the shoe boxes."

It was a lie. A proper black lie sliding as easily from her lips as a white lie about satisfaction with a gift or sex. The letter was in the filing cabinet in the office just down the hallway.

"Did you open it?"

There was something about the quality of his voice. He was wide awake, but he was making his voice sound sleepy and disinterested. She could feel tension emanating from the length of his body like an electrical current.

"No," she said. She made her voice sound sleepy too. "You asked me not to . . . so I didn't."

His arms around her seemed to soften.

"Thank you. Feel embarrassed."

"Don't be stupid."

His breathing slowed. She let hers slow to match his.

She'd lied because she didn't want to lose the opportunity to read the letter, if and when she chose to read it. It was a real lie that lay between them now. Damn it. She just wanted to forget about the bloody letter.

She was so tired. She would think about it tomorrow.

It was impossible to know how long she'd been asleep

when she woke up again, in an empty bed. Cecilia squinted at the digital clock on the nightstand. She couldn't see it without her glasses.

"John-Paul?" she said, sitting up on her elbows. There was no sound from the en suite bathroom. Normally he slept like the dead after a long-haul flight.

There was a sound above her head.

She sat up, completely alert, her heart hammering with instant understanding. He was in the attic. *He never went in the attic.* She'd seen the tiny beads of sweat gathering above his lip when he suffered an attack of claustrophobia. He must want that letter very badly if he was prepared to go up there.

Hadn't he once said, "It would have to be a matter of life or death to get me up there"?

Was the letter a matter of life or death?

Cecilia didn't hesitate. She got out of bed, walked down the hallway in the dark and into the office. She switched on the desk lamp, slid open the top drawer of the filing cabinet and pulled out the red manila folder marked "Wills."

She sat down in the leather chair, swiveled it to face the desk and opened the file in the little pool of yellow light created by the desk light.

For my wife, Cecilia Fitzpatrick. To be opened only in the event of my death.

She opened the top drawer, took out the letter opener.

There were frantic footsteps above her head, a thud as something fell over. He sounded like a crazy man. It occurred to her that for him to be back in Australia now, he must have gone straight to the airport after she called last night.

For Christ's sake, John-Paul, what in the world is going on?

With one swift, vicious movement, she sliced the envelope open. She pulled out a handwritten letter. For a moment her eyes couldn't focus. The words danced about in front of her.

our baby girl, Isabel

so sorry to leave you with this

given me more happiness than I ever deserved

She forced herself to read it properly. Left to right. Sentence by sentence.

SIXTEEN

Tess woke up suddenly, irretrievably alert. She looked at the digital clock next to her bed and groaned. It was only eleven thirty p.m. She snapped on the bedside light and lay back on her pillow, staring up at the ceiling.

This was her old bedroom, but there wasn't anything much left in it to remind her of her childhood. Tess had barely been out the door before her mother had transformed it into an elegant guest bedroom with a good queen-size bed, matching bedside tables and lamps. This was in complete contrast to Aunt Mary, who had reverently left Felicity's bedroom exactly as she'd left it. Felicity's room was like a perfectly preserved archaeological site, with the *TV Week* posters still on the wall.

The only part of Tess's bedroom that had been left untouched was the ceiling. She let her eyes follow the rippled edge of the white cornices. She used to lie in bed staring at the ceiling on Sunday mornings, worrying about what she'd said at last night's party, or what she hadn't said, or what she should have said. Parties had terrified her. Parties still terrified her. It was the lack of structure, the casualness, the not knowing where to sit. If it weren't for Felicity she would never have gone, but Felicity was always keen to go. She'd stand with Tess in a corner, quietly delivering cutting critiques on all the guests and making Tess laugh.

Felicity had been her savior.

Wasn't that true?

Tonight, when she and her mother had sat down for a glass of brandy and too much chocolate—"This is how I coped when your father left," Lucy had explained. "It's medicinal"—they'd been talking about Felicity's phone call, and Tess said, "The other night, you guessed that it was Will and Felicity. How did you know?"

"Felicity never let you have anything just for yourself," said her mother.

"What?" Tess had been bemused, disbelieving. "That's not true."

"You wanted to learn the piano. Felicity learned the piano. You played netball. Felicity played netball. You got too good at netball, so Felicity was left behind; next thing—you've suddenly lost interest in netball. You get a career in advertising. What a surprise! Felicity gets a career in advertising."

"Oh, Mum," said Tess. "I don't know. You make it sound so calculated. We just liked doing the same things. Anyway, Felicity is a graphic designer! I was an advertising manager. They're quite different."

But not to her mother, who had pursed her lips as if she

knew better before draining the rest of her brandy. "Look, I'm not saying she's *evil* as such. But she suffocated you! When you were born, I remember thanking God that you weren't a twin, that you'd be able to live your life on your own terms, without all that comparing and competing. And then, somehow, you and Felicity end up just like Mary and me, like twins! *Worse* than twins! I wondered what sort of person you might have become if you didn't have her breathing down your neck all the time, what friends you might have made—"

"*Friends?* I wouldn't have made any other friends! I was too shy! I was so shy, I was practically disabled. I'm still sort of socially weird." She stopped short of telling her mother about her self-diagnosis.

"Felicity kept you shy," her mother had said. "It suited her. You weren't really that shy."

Now Tess wriggled her neck against her pillow. It was too hard; she missed her own pillow at home in Melbourne. Was what her mother said true? Had she spent most of her life in a dysfunctional relationship with her cousin?

She thought of that awful, strange, hot summer when her parents' marriage had ended, and her father packed his clothes into the suitcase they took on holidays and went to stay in a musty-smelling furnished apartment full of spindly old-lady furniture, and her mother wore the same old shapeless dress for eight days in a row and walked about the house laughing, crying and muttering, "Good riddance, mate." Tess was ten. It was Felicity who got Tess through that summer, who took her to the local pool and lay side by side with her on the concrete in the burning sun (and Felicity, with her beautiful white skin, hated sunbaking) for as long as Tess wanted, who spent *her own money* on a greatest-hits record just to make Tess feel better, who brought her bowls of ice cream with chocolate topping each time she sat on the couch and cried.

It was Felicity whom Tess called when she lost her virginity, when she lost her first job, when she was dumped for the first time, when Will said, "I love you," when he proposed, when her water broke, when Liam took his first steps, when she and Will had their first proper fight.

They'd shared everything throughout their lives. Toys. Bikes. Their first dollhouse. (It stayed at their grandmother's house.) Their first car. Their first apartments. Their first overseas holiday. Tess's husband.

She'd let Felicity share Will. Of course she had. She'd let Felicity be like a mother to Liam, and she'd let Felicity be like a wife to Will. She'd shared her whole life with her. Because Felicity was obviously too fat to find her own husband and her own life. Was that what Tess had been subconsciously thinking? Or because she thought Felicity was too fat to even *need* her own life?

And then Felicity got greedy. She wanted all of Will.

If it had been any other woman but Felicity, Tess would never had said, "Have your affair and then give my husband back." It wouldn't have been conceivable.

But because it was Felicity it was . . . okay? Forgivable? Is that what she meant? She'd share a toothbrush with Felicity, so she'd also let her use her husband? But at the same time, it also made the betrayal worse. A million times worse.

She rolled onto her stomach and pressed her face into the pillow. Her feelings about Felicity were irrelevant. She needed to think about Liam. ("What about *me*?" her ten-year-old self had kept thinking when her parents split up. "Don't I get a say in this?" She thought she was the center of their world, and then she'd discovered she had no vote. No control.)

There was no such thing as a good divorce for children. She'd read that somewhere, just a few weeks ago, before all this. Even when the split was perfectly amicable, even when both parents made a huge effort, the children suffered.

Tess threw back the covers and got out of bed. She needed to go somewhere, to get out of this house and away from her thoughts. *Will. Felicity. Liam. Will. Felicity. Liam.*

She would get in her mother's car and drive. She looked down at her striped pajama pants and T-shirt. Should she get dressed? She had nothing to wear anyway. She hadn't brought enough clothes with her. It didn't matter. She wouldn't get out of the car. She put on a pair of flat shoes and crept out of the room down the hallway, her eyes adjusting to the dark. The house was silent. She switched on a lamp in the dining room and left a note for her mother just in case she woke.

Back soon, gone for a drive around the block, Tess xx.

She grabbed her wallet, took her mother's car keys from the hook beside the door and crept out into the soft, sweet night air, breathing in deeply.

She drove her mother's Honda down the Pacific Highway with the windows down and the radio turned off. Sydney's North Shore was quiet, deserted. A man carrying a briefcase, who must have caught the train home after working late, hurried along the footpath.

A woman probably wouldn't walk home alone from the station at this time of night. Tess thought about how Will had once told her that he hated walking behind a woman late at night, in case she heard his footsteps and thought he was an ax murderer. "I always want to call out, 'It's all right! I'm not an ax murderer!'" he said. "I'd run for my life if someone called that out to me," Tess had told him. "See, we can't win," said Will.

Whenever something bad happened on the North Shore, the newspapers described it as "Sydney's *leafy* North Shore" so it would sound extra heinous.

Tess stopped at a traffic light, glanced down and saw the red warning light on the petrol gauge.

"Damn it," she said.

There was a brightly lit all-night service station on the next corner. She'd stop there. She pulled into the service station and got out. It was deserted, except for a man on a motorbike on the other side of the service station forecourt, readjusting his helmet after filling up.

She opened her mother's petrol tank and lifted the nozzle from its slot.

"Hello," said a man's voice.

She jumped and spun around. The man had wheeled his motorbike over, so he was on the other side of her car. He lifted his helmet. The petrol station's bright lights were shining in her eyes, blurring her vision. She couldn't distinguish his features, just a creepy white blob of a face.

Her eyes went to the empty counter inside the service

station. Where was the damned attendant? Tess put her arm protectively across her braless chest. She thought of an episode of *Oprah* she'd seen with Felicity where a policeman advised women what to do if they were ever accosted. You had to be extremely aggressive and shout something like, "No! Go away! I don't want trouble! Go! Go!" For a while she and Felicity had taken great pleasure in yelling it at Will whenever he walked into a room.

Tess cleared her throat and clenched her fists as if she were doing one of her body combat classes. It would be so much easier to be aggressive if she were wearing her bra.

"Tess," said the man. "It's just me. Connor. Connor Whitby."

SEVENTEEN

Rachel woke from a dream that dissolved and faded before she could catch it. All she could remember was panic. Something to do with water. Janie when she was a little girl. Or was it Jacob?

She sat up in bed and looked at the clock. It was eleven thirty p.m. The house smelled of sickly vanilla because of the candle that she'd smashed after she got stuck in the bath.

Her mouth felt dry from the alcohol she'd drunk at the Tupperware party. It seemed like years had passed since then, not hours. She got out of bed. No point trying to get back to sleep now. She would be up until the gray light of dawn crept through the house.

Moments later she had the ironing board set up and was using her remote to switch channels on the TV. There was nothing worth watching.

She went instead to the cupboard under the TV where she kept all her videocassettes. She kept her old VCR still set up so she could watch her old collection of movies. "Mum, all these movies of yours are on DVD now," Rob kept telling her worriedly, as if it were somehow illegal to still use a VCR. She ran her finger along the spines of the videocassettes, but she wasn't in the mood for Grace Kelly or Audrey Hepburn or even Cary Grant.

She pulled cassettes out willy-nilly and came upon one with a blank spine covered in handwriting: hers, Ed's, Janie's and Rob's. They'd crossed out shows as they'd recorded over each one. The children of today would probably consider this tape an ancient relic. Didn't they just download shows now? She went to toss the tape aside and got distracted looking at the names of the shows they used to watch in the eighties: *The Sullivans*, *A Country Practice*, *Sons and Daughters*. It looked like Janie had been the last one to use it. "Sons and Daughters" she'd written, in her scratchy, scrawly handwriting.

Funny. It was thanks to *Sons and Daughters* that she'd won the quiz tonight. She remembered Janie lying on the living room floor, transfixed by the silly show, singing along to the maudlin theme song. How did it go? Rachel could almost hear the tune in her head.

On impulse, she stuck the tape into the VCR and pressed Play.

She sat back on her haunches and watched the end of a margarine ad, with that comical, dated look and sound of old TV commercials. Then *Sons and Daughters* began. Rachel sang along in her head, amazed to find that all the words could be retrieved from her subconscious. There was Pat the Rat, younger and more attractive than Rachel had remembered. The tortured face of the male lead appeared on the screen, frowning deeply. He was still on TV, starring in some police rescue show. Everyone's lives had gone on. Even the lives of the stars of *Sons and Daughters*. Poor Janie was the only one stuck forever in 1984.

She went to press Eject when she heard Janie's voice say, "Is it on?"

Rachel's heart stopped. Her hand froze midair.

Janie's face filled the screen, peering straight at the camera with a gleeful, cheeky expression. She was wearing green eyeliner and too much mascara. There was a small pimple on the side of her nose. Rachel thought she knew her daughter's face by heart, but she'd forgotten things she hadn't known she'd forgotten—like the exact reality of Janie's teeth and Janie's nose. There was nothing particularly amazing about Janie's teeth and Janie's nose, except that they were *Janie's*, and there they were again. Her left eyetooth turned in just slightly. Her nose a fraction too long. In spite of that, or maybe because of it, she was beautiful, even more beautiful than Rachel remembered.

They never had a home video recorder. Ed didn't think they were worth the money. The only footage they had of Janie alive was from a friend's wedding, where Janie had been the flower girl. "Janie." Rachel put her hand to the television screen.

"You're standing too close to the camera," said a boy's voice.

Rachel dropped her hand.

Janie moved back. She was wearing high-waisted blue jeans, with a metallic silver belt and a long-sleeved purple top. Rachel remembered ironing that purple top. The sleeves were tricky, with a complicated arrangement of pleats.

Janie was truly beautiful, like a delicate bird, a heron perhaps, but good Lord, had the child really been *that* thin? Her arms and legs were so spindly. Had there been something wrong with her? Did she have anorexia? How had Rachel not noticed?

Janie sat down on the edge of a single bed. She was in a room Rachel had never seen before. The bed had a striped red-and-blue bedspread. The walls behind were dark brown wood paneling. Janie lowered her chin and looked up at the camera with a mock serious face while she lifted a pencil to her mouth as if it were a microphone.

Rachel laughed out loud and clasped her hands together as if in prayer. She'd forgotten that too. How could she have forgotten it? Janie used to pretend to be a reporter at the oddest times. She'd come into the kitchen, pick up a carrot and say, "Tell me, Mrs. Rachel Crowley, how was your day today? Ordinary? Extraordinary?" And then she'd hold the carrot in front of Rachel, and Rachel would lean in close to the carrot and say, "Ordinary."

Of course she said "ordinary." Her days were always so very ordinary.

"Good evening, I'm Janie Crowley reporting live from Turramurra, where I'm interviewing a reclusive young man by the name of Connor Whitby."

Rachel caught her breath. She turned her head and the word "Ed" caught in the back of her throat. *Ed. Come. You must see this.* It had been years since she'd done that.

Janie spoke into the pencil again. "If you could just scoot a little closer, Mr. Whitby, so my viewers can see you."

"Janie."

"Connor." Janie imitated his tone.

A broad-chested, dark-haired boy wearing a yellow-and-blue-striped rugby shirt and shorts slid over on the bed until he was sitting next to Janie. He glanced at the camera and looked away again, uncomfortably, as if he could see Janie's mother twenty-eight years in the future, watching them.

Connor had the body of a man and the face of a boy. Rachel could see a smattering of pimples across his forehead. He had that starved, frightened, sullen look you saw on so many teenage boys. It was as if they needed to both punch a wall and be cuddled. The Connor of thirty years ago didn't inhabit his body in the comfortable way he did now. He didn't know what to do with his limbs. He flung his legs out in front of him and tapped one open palm softly against his closed fist.

Rachel could hear herself breathing raggedy gasps. She wanted to lunge into the television and drag Janie away. What was she doing there? She must be in Connor's bedroom. She was not allowed to be on her own in a boy's bedroom. Ed would have a fit.

Janie Crowley, young lady, you come back home this minute.

"Why do you need me actually in it?" asked Connor, his eyes returning to the camera. "Can't I just sit off camera?"

"You can't have your interview subject off camera," said

Janie. "I might need this tape for when I apply for a job as a reporter on *60 Minutes*." She smiled at Connor, and he smiled back: an involuntary, smitten smile.

"Smitten" was the right word. The boy was smitten with her daughter. "We were just good friends," he'd told the police. "She wasn't my girlfriend." "But I know all her friends," Rachel told the police. "I know all their mothers." She could see the polite restraint on their faces.

"So, Connor, tell me about yourself." Janie held out the pencil.

"What do you want to know?"

"Well, for example, do you have a girlfriend?"

"I don't know," said Connor. He looked keenly at Janie and suddenly seemed more grown-up. He leaned forward and spoke into the pencil. "*Do* I have a girlfriend?"

"That would depend." Janie twisted her ponytail around her finger. "What do you have to offer? What are your strengths? What are your weaknesses? I mean, you need to sell yourself a bit, don't you know?"

She sounded silly now, strident and whiny, even. Rachel winced. *Oh, Janie, darling, stop it! Speak nicely. You can't talk to him like that.* It was only in the movies that teenagers flirted with beautiful sensuality. In real life it was excruciating to watch them flailing about.

"Geez, Janie, if you *still* can't give me a straight answer, I mean . . . fuck!"

Connor stood up from the bed and Janie gave a disdainful little laugh, while at the same time her face crumpled like a child's, but Connor only heard the laugh. He walked straight toward the camera. His hand reached out so that it filled the screen.

Rachel held out her hand to stop him. *No, don't turn it off. Don't take her away from me.*

The screen instantly filled with static, and Rachel's head jerked back as if she'd been slapped.

Bastard. Murderer.

She was filled with adrenaline, exhilarated with hatred. Why, this was *evidence*! New evidence after all these years!

"Call me anytime, Mrs. Crowley, if you think of anything. I don't care if it's the middle of the night." Sergeant Bellach had said that so many times, it had become boring.

She never had before. Now at least she had something for him. They would get him. She could sit in a courtroom and watch a judge pronounce Connor Whitby guilty.

As her fingers jabbed at Sergeant Bellach's number, she bounced up and down impatiently on the balls of her feet, while the image of Janie's crumpled face filled her head.

EIGHTEEN

Connor," said Tess. "I'm just getting some petrol."

"You're kidding," said Connor.

Tess took a moment to get it. "You gave me a fright," she said, with a touch of petulance because she was embarrassed. "I thought you were an ax murderer."

She placed the nozzle in the petrol spout. Connor kept standing there, without moving, his helmet tucked under one arm, looking at her as if he expected something. *Okay, well, that was enough chitchat, wasn't it? On your bike. Off you go.* Tess preferred people from her past to stay in the past. Ex-boyfriends, old school friends, past colleagues—really, what was the point of them? Lives moved on. Tess quite enjoyed reminiscing *about* people she once knew, not *with* them. She pulled on the petrol lever, smiling warily, politely at him, trying to remember exactly how their relationship had ended. Was it when she and Felicity moved to Melbourne? He was a boyfriend in between lots of other boyfriends. She usually broke up with them before they broke up with her. Normally after Felicity had made fun of them. There was always a new boy to take their place. She thought it was because she was the right level of attractiveness: not too intimidating. She always said yes to whoever asked her out. It wouldn't have occurred to her to say no.

She remembered that Connor had always been keener than she was—he was too old and serious, she'd thought. It was her first year at uni; she was only nineteen, and she'd been somewhat bemused by the intense interest this older, quiet boy was showing her.

She may well have treated him quite badly. She'd been lacking in so much confidence when she was a teenager, worrying all the time about what people thought of her and how they might hurt her, without even considering the impact she might have on their feelings.

"I've been thinking about you, actually," said Connor. "After I saw you at the school this morning, I was even wondering if you'd like to, ah, catch up? For a coffee, maybe?"

"Oh!" said Tess. A coffee with Connor Whitby. It just seemed so preposterously irrelevant, like those times that Liam suggested they do a jigsaw puzzle just when Tess was smack-bang in the middle of some computer or plumbing crisis. Her whole life had just imploded! She wasn't going to go for a coffee with this sweet, but essentially dull, ex-boyfriend from her teens.

Didn't he know she was married? She twisted her hands on the petrol pump so that her wedding ring was in full view. She still felt extremely married.

Apparently, moving back home was just like joining Facebook, when middle-aged ex-boyfriends came crawling out of the woodwork like cockroaches, suggesting drinks, putting out their nasty little feelers for potential affairs. Was Connor married? She glanced over at his hands, trying to see a ring.

"I didn't mean a *date*, if that's what you're thinking," said Connor.

"I wasn't thinking that."

"I know you're married, don't worry. I don't know if you remember my sister's son, Benjamin? Anyway, he's just finished uni and he wants to go into advertising or marketing. That's your field, isn't it? I was actually thinking of exploiting you for your professional expertise." He chewed on the side of his cheek. "Maybe 'exploiting' is the wrong choice of word."

"Benjamin has just finished uni?" Tess was startled. "But he couldn't have—he was only in preschool!"

Memories flooded back. A minute ago she wouldn't have been able to name Connor's nephew, or even remember that he had one. Now she could suddenly see the exact pale green color of the walls of Benjamin's bedroom.

"He was a preschooler sixteen years ago," said Connor. "Now he's six foot three, and very hairy, with a tattoo of a bar code on his neck. I'm not kidding. A bar code."

"We took him to the zoo," marveled Tess.

"We may well have."

"Your sister was sound asleep." Tess remembered a dark-haired woman curled up on a sofa. "She was sick." Hadn't she been a single mother? Not that Tess had appreciated that at the time. She should have offered to go out and buy groceries. "How is your sister?"

"Oh, well, we actually lost her a few years ago." He sounded apologetic. "A heart attack. She was only fifty. Very fit and healthy, so it was . . . a terrible shock. I'm Benjamin's guardian."

"God, I'm so sorry, Connor." Tess's voice fractured with the unexpectedness of it. The world was a desperately sad place. Hadn't he been especially close to his sister? What was her name? Lisa. It was Lisa.

"A coffee would be great," she said suddenly, impulsively. "You can pick my brain. For what it's worth." She wasn't the only one suffering. People lost their loved ones. Husbands fell in love with other people. Besides, a coffee with someone entirely unrelated to her current life would be the perfect distraction. Connor Whitby was not creepy.

"That'd be great." Connor smiled. She didn't remember him having such an attractive smile. He lifted his helmet. "I'll call, or e-mail."

"Okay, do you need my—" The petrol pump clicked to indicate her tank was full, and Tess lifted it out and placed it back on the bowser.

"You're a St. Angela's mum now," said Connor. "I can track you down."

"Oh. Good." A St. Angela's mum. She felt strangely exposed. She turned to face him with her car keys and wallet in her hand.

"Like your PJs, by the way." Connor looked her up and down and grinned.

"Thanks," said Tess. "I like your bike. I don't remember

you riding one." Didn't he drive a boring little sedan of some sort?

"It's my midlife crisis."

"I think my husband is having one of those," said Tess.

"Hope it's not costing you too much," said Connor.

Tess shrugged. Ha ha. She looked at the bike again and said, "When I was seventeen, my mother said she would pay me five hundred dollars if I signed a contract promising to never go on the back of a boy's motorbike."

"Did you sign it?"

"I did."

"Never breached the contract?"

"Nope."

"I'm forty-five," said Connor. "Not exactly a boy."

Their eyes met. Was this conversation becoming . . . flirtatious? She remembered waking up next to him, in a plain white room with a window that looked out on a busy highway. Didn't he have a *water bed*? Hadn't she and Felicity laughed themselves silly over that? He wore a St. Christopher medallion that dangled over her face when they made love. All at once she felt nauseated. Miserable. This was a mistake.

Connor seemed to recognize the change in her mood.

"Anyway, Tess, I'll give you a call sometime about that coffee." He put his helmet back on, revved his bike, lifted a black-gloved hand and roared off.

Tess watched him go, and it occurred to her with a jolt that she'd had her first-ever orgasm on that ridiculous water bed. Actually, now that she thought about it, there had been a few other firsts in that bed too. *Slosh, slosh* went the bed. Sex, especially for a good Catholic girl like Tess, had been so raw and dirty and new back then.

As she walked into the brightly lit service station to pay for the petrol, she glanced up and caught sight of herself in a security mirror. Her face, she noticed, was very pink.

NINETEEN

Y ou've read it, then," said John-Paul.

Cecilia looked at him as if she'd never seen him before. A middle-aged man who had once been very handsome and still was, to her at least. John-Paul had had one of those honest, trustworthy faces. You'd buy a used car from John-Paul. That famous Fitzpatrick jaw. All the Fitzpatrick boys had good strong jaws. He had a good head of hair, gray and thick. He was still vain about his hair. He liked to blow it dry. His brothers gave him hell about that. He stood at the door of the study, wearing his blue-and-white-striped boxer shorts and a red T-shirt. His face was pale and sweaty, as if he had food poisoning.

She hadn't heard him come down from the attic, or walk down the hallway. She didn't know how long he'd been standing there, while she sat, staring unseeingly at her hands, which she saw now were clasped angelically in her lap, like a little girl in church.

"I've read it," she said.

She pulled the sheet of paper over to her and read it again, slowly, as if this time, now that John-Paul was standing right in front of her, it would surely say something different.

It was written in blue ballpoint pen on a lined piece of paper. It felt ridged, like braille. He must have pressed hard with his pen, as if he had been trying to engrave each word into the paper. There were no paragraphs or spaces. The words were crammed together without a break.

My darling Cecilia,

If you're reading this, then I've died, which sounds so melodramatic to write down, but I guess everyone dies. You're in the hospital right now, with our baby girl, Isabel. She was born early this morning. She's so beautiful and tiny and helpless. I've never felt anything like what I felt when I held her for the first time. I'm already terrified that something will ever happen to her. And that's why I have to write this down. Just in case something does happen to me, at least I have done this. At least I have tried to make it right. I've had a few beers. I might not be making sense. I probably will tear this letter up. Cecilia, I have to tell you that when I was seventeen, I killed Janie Crowley. If her parents are still alive, will you please tell them that I'm sorry and that it was an accident. It wasn't planned. I lost my temper. I was seventeen and so fucking stupid. I can't believe it was me. It feels like a nightmare. It feels like I must

*have been on drugs, or drunk, but I wasn't. I was
perfectly sober. I just snapped. I had a brain snap, like
those idiot rugby players say. It sounds like I'm trying to
justify it, but I'm not trying to make excuses. I did this
terrible, unimaginable thing and I can't explain it. I
know what you're thinking, Cecilia, because everything
is black-and-white for you. You're thinking, why didn't
he confess? But you know why I couldn't go to jail,
Cecilia. You know I couldn't be locked up. I know I'm a
coward. That's why I tried to kill myself when I was
eighteen, but I didn't have the balls to go through with
it. Please tell Ed and Rachel Crowley that I never went
a day without thinking of their daughter. Tell them it
happened so fast. Janie was laughing just seconds before.
She was happy right up until the end. Maybe that just
sounds awful. It does sound awful. Don't tell them that.
It was an accident, Cecilia. Janie told me she was in
love with some other kid and then she laughed at me.
That's all she did. I lost my mind. Please tell the
Crowleys that I'm so sorry, I couldn't be sorrier. Please
tell Ed Crowley that now that I'm a dad I understand
exactly what I've done. The guilt has been like a tumor
eating away at me, and now it's worse than ever. I'm so
sorry to leave you with this, Cecilia, but I know you're
strong enough to handle it. I love you and our baby so
much, and you've given me more happiness than I ever
deserved. I deserved nothing and I got everything. I'm
so sorry.*

  With all my love,
  John-Paul

Cecilia thought she'd experienced anger before, plenty of times, but now she knew that she'd had no idea how real anger felt. The white-hot burning purity of it. It was a frantic, crazy, wonderful feeling. She felt like she could fly. She could fly across the room, like a demon, and claw bloody scratch marks down John-Paul's face.

"Is it true?" she said. She was disappointed by the sound of her voice. It was weak. It didn't sound like it came from someone who was wild with anger. "Is it true?" she said again, stronger.

She knew it was true, but her desire for it not to be true was so overpowering, she had to ask. She wanted to beg for it to be made untrue.

"I'm sorry," he said. His eyes were bloodshot and rolling about like a terrified horse.

"But you'd never," said Cecilia. "You wouldn't. You couldn't."

"I can't explain it."

"You didn't even know Janie Crowley." She corrected herself. "I didn't even know you knew her. You never even mentioned her."

At the mention of Janie's name, John-Paul began to visibly shake. He clung to the sides of the doorframe. Seeing him shake like that was even more shocking than the actual words he'd written.

"If you'd died," she said. "If you'd died and I'd found this letter . . ."

She stopped. She couldn't breathe for the fury.

"How could you just leave that for me? Leave me to do that for you? Expect me to turn up on Rachel Crowley's doorstep and tell her . . . this . . . thing?" She stood up, covered her face with her hands and turned around in circles. She was naked, she noted without particular interest. Her T-shirt had ended up at the bottom of the bed after they had sex and she hadn't bothered to find it. "I drove Rachel home tonight! I drove her home! I talked to her about Janie! I thought I was so great for telling her this memory I had of Janie, and all the time this letter was sitting here." She removed her hands and looked at him. "What if one of the girls had found it, John-Paul?" That had only just occurred to her. It was so momentous, so dreadful, she had to say it again. *"What if one of the girls had found it?"*

"I know," he whispered. He came into the room and stood with his back up against the wall and looked at her as if he were facing a firing squad. "I'm sorry."

She watched as his legs gave way and he slid to the carpet to a sitting position.

"Why would you write it?" She picked up the corner of the letter and dropped it again. "How could you put something like that in writing?"

"I'd had too much to drink, and then the next day, I tried to find it so I could tear it up." He looked up at her tearfully. "And I'd lost it. I nearly lost my mind looking for it. I must have been working on my tax return and then it got caught up in some of the papers. I thought I'd looked—"

"Stop it!" she shouted. She couldn't bear to hear him talking with his usual hopeless wonder about the way things got lost and then turned up again, as if this letter were something perfectly ordinary, like an unpaid car insurance bill.

John-Paul put a finger to his lips. "You'll wake the girls," he said tremulously.

His nervousness made her feel sick. *Be a man!* she wanted to scream. *Make this go away. Take this thing off me!* It was a disgusting, ugly, horrible creature *he* needed to destroy. It was an impossibly heavy box he needed to lift from her arms. And he wasn't doing anything.

A tiny voice floated down the hallway. "Daddy!"

It was Polly, their lightest sleeper. She always called for her father. Cecilia would not do. Only her father could make the monsters go away and slay the dragon. Only her father. Her father, who had killed a seventeen-year-old girl. Her father, who was a murderer. Her father, who had kept this terrible secret for all these years. It was like she hadn't properly understood any of it.

The shock winded her. She collapsed into the black leather chair.

"Daddy!"

"Coming, Polly!" John-Paul got slowly to his feet using the wall to support himself. He gave Cecilia a desperate look and headed down the hallway toward Polly's room.

Cecilia focused on her breathing. In through the nostrils. She saw Janie Crowley's eleven-year-old face. "It's only stupid marching." Out through the mouth. She saw the grainy black-and-white picture of Janie that had appeared on the front cover of the newspapers, a long blond ponytail falling down one shoulder. All murder victims looked exactly like murder victims: beautiful, innocent and doomed, as if it were preordained. In through the nostrils. She saw Rachel Crowley gently banging her forehead against the car window. Out through the mouth. What to do, Cecilia? What to do? How could she fix it? How could she make it right? She fixed things. She made things right. She put things in order. All you had to do was pick up the phone, get on the Internet, fill in the right forms, talk to the right people, arrange the refund, the replacement, the better model.

Except that nothing would ever bring Janie back. Her mind kept returning to that one cold, immovable, awful fact, like an enormous wall that couldn't be crossed.

She began ripping the letter into tiny pieces.

Confess. John-Paul would have to confess. That was obvious. He would have to come clean. Make it all clean and shiny. Scrub it away. Follow the rules. The law. He'd have to go to prison. He'd have to be sentenced. A sentence. Put behind bars. But he couldn't be locked up. He'd lose his mind. So, then, medication, therapy. She'd talk to people. Do the research. He wouldn't be the first prisoner with claustrophobia. Weren't those cells actually quite spacious? They had exercise yards, didn't they?

Claustrophobia didn't actually kill you. It just made you *feel* like you couldn't breathe.

Whereas two hands placed around the neck could kill you.

He'd strangled Janie Crowley. He'd actually put his hands around her thin girlish neck and squeezed. Didn't that make him evil? Yes. The answer had to be yes. John-Paul was evil.

She kept tearing at the letter, shredding the pieces into tinier and tinier fragments until she could roll them between her fingertips.

Her husband was evil. Therefore he must go to jail. Cecilia would be the wife of a prisoner. She wondered if there was a social club for the wives. She'd set one up if there wasn't. She giggled hysterically, like a crazy woman. Of course she would! She was Cecilia. She'd be president of the Prisoners' Wives Association and organize fundraising for air-conditioning units to be put in their poor husbands' cells. Did prisons have air-conditioning? Was it just primary schools that missed out? She imagined chatting with the other wives while they waited to go through the metal detectors. "What's your husband in for? Oh, bank robbery? Really? Mine's in for murder. Yep, strangled a girl. Off to the gym after this, are you?"

Would there be that subtle one-upmanship like there was between mothers? "It's so stressful having a gifted child." What would be the equivalent for a prison wife? "It's such a strain when your husband is a model prisoner! The others are constantly beating him up!"

She giggled some more. Dear Jesus. Dear God. Dear Saint Somebody-or-other. Who was the patron saint for wives of murderers?

"She's gone back off," said John-Paul. He was back in the study, standing in front of her, massaging little circles under his cheekbones, the way he did when he was exhausted.

He didn't look evil. He just looked like her husband. Unshaven. Messy hair. Shadows under his eyes. Her husband. The father of her children.

If he'd killed someone once, what was to stop him from doing it again? She'd just let him go into Polly's room. She'd just let a murderer go into her daughter's room.

But it was *John-Paul*! Their father. He was Daddy.

How could they tell the girls what John-Paul had done? *Daddy is going to jail.*

For a moment her mind stopped completely.

They could never tell the girls.

"I'm so sorry," said John-Paul. He held out his arms uselessly, as if he wanted to hold her but they were separated by something too vast to be crossed. "Darling, I'm just so sorry."

Cecilia wrapped her arms around her naked body. She trembled violently. Her teeth chattered. *I'm having a nervous breakdown,* she thought with relief. *I'm about to lose my mind, and that's just as well, because this cannot possibly be fixed. It is simply not fixable.*

TWENTY

There! See?"

Rachel hit the Pause button so that Connor Whitby's angry face was frozen on the screen. It was the face of a monster. His eyes were black evil holes. His lips were pulled back in a rabid sneer. Rachel had watched the footage four times now, and each time she became more convinced. It was, she thought, quite stunningly conclusive. Show this to any jury and they'd convict.

She turned to look at former Sergeant Rodney Bellach, sitting on her couch, leaning forward with his elbows on his knees, and caught him flattening his hand across his mouth to stifle a yawn.

Well, it *was* the middle of the night. Sergeant Bellach— "You can just call me plain old Rodney now," he kept telling her—had obviously been deeply asleep when she'd called. His wife had answered the phone, and Rachel had overheard her trying to wake him up. "Rodney. *Rodney*. It's for you!" When he'd finally taken the phone, his voice was thick and slurred with sleep. "I'll be right there, Mrs. Crowley," he'd finally said when she made him understand, and as he put down the phone Rachel heard his wife say, "Where, Rodney? You'll be right *where*? Why can't it wait until the morning?"

His wife sounded like a right old nag.

It probably could have waited until the morning, reflected Rachel now, as she saw Rodney valiantly struggling to repress another massive yawn and rubbing his knuckles into his bleary eyes. At least he would have been more alert then. He really didn't look well at all. Apparently he'd recently been diagnosed with type 2 diabetes. He'd made some dramatic changes to his diet. He'd mentioned all this as they were sitting down to watch the video. "Completely cut out all sugar," he'd said dolefully. "No more ice cream for dessert."

"Mrs. Crowley," he said finally. "I can certainly see why you would think that this proves that Connor had a motive of some sort, but I have to be honest with you, I just don't think it's enough to convince the boys to take a second look."

"He was in love with her!" said Rachel. "He was in love with her and she was rejecting him."

"Your daughter was a very pretty girl," said Sergeant Bellach. "Probably a lot of boys were in love with her."

Rachel was gobsmacked. How had she never noticed that Rodney was so stupid? So obtuse? Had the diabetes affected his IQ? Had the lack of ice cream shrunk his brain?

"But Connor wasn't just any boy. He was the last one

to see her before she died," she said slowly and carefully to make sure he understood.

"He had an alibi."

"His mother was his alibi!" said Rachel. "She lied, obviously!"

"And his mother's boyfriend backed it up too," said Rodney. "But more importantly, there was a neighbor who saw Connor put out the garbage at five p.m. The neighbor was a very reliable witness. A solicitor and a father of three. I remember every detail of Janie's case, Mrs. Crowley. I can assure you, if I thought we had *anything*—"

"Lies in his eyes!" interrupted Rachel. "You said Connor Whitby had lies in his eyes. Well, you were right! You were exactly right!"

Rodney said, "But, see, all this proves is that they had a little tiff."

"A little tiff!" cried Rachel. "Look at that boy's face! He killed her! I *know* he killed her. I know it in my heart, in my . . ." She was going to say "body," but she didn't want to sound like a loony. It was true, though. Her body was telling her what Connor had done. It was burning all over, as if she had a fever. Even her fingertips felt hot.

"Well, you know what, I'll see what I can do, Mrs. Crowley," said Rodney. "I'm not making any promises about whether it will go anywhere, but I *can* promise you this video will get into the right hands."

"Thank you. That's all I can ask." It was a lie. She could ask for a lot more. She wanted a police car with a shrieking, whirling siren to race to Connor Whitby's house right that second. She wanted Connor handcuffed, while a grim-faced burly police officer read him his rights. Oh, and she did *not* want that police officer to tenderly protect Connor's head when they put him in the back of the police car. She wanted Connor's head smashed over and over, until it was nothing but a bloody pulp.

"How's that little grandson of yours? Growing up?" Rodney picked up a framed photo of Jacob from the mantelpiece while Rachel ejected the videocassette.

"He's going to New York." Rachel handed him the cassette.

"No kidding?" Rodney took the cassette and carefully replaced Jacob's photo. "My oldest granddaughter is off to New York too. She's eighteen now. Little Emily. Got herself a scholarship to some top university. The Big Apple, they call it, don't they? Wonder why they call it that?"

Rachel gave him a sickly smile and led him to the front door. "I have absolutely no idea, Rodney. No idea at all."

TWENTY-ONE

On the morning of the last day of her life, Janie Crowley sat next to Connor Whitby on the bus.

She felt strangely breathless, and she tried to calm herself with slow deep breaths from her diaphragm, like her drama teacher had taught the class for dealing with stage fright. It didn't seem to help.

Calm down, she told herself.

"I've got something to say," she said.

He didn't say anything. He never did say much, thought Janie. She watched him studying his hands resting on his knees, and she studied them herself. He had very big hands, she saw with a shiver, of fear or anticipation, or both. Her own hands were icy cold. They were always cold. She slid them under her cardigan to warm them.

She said, "I've made a decision."

He turned his head suddenly to look at her. The bus

lurched as it went around a corner, and their bodies slid closer, so that their eyes were only inches apart.

She was breathing so fast, she wondered if there was something wrong with her.

"Tell me," he said.

TWENTY-TWO

WEDNESDAY

The alarm clock wrenched Cecilia cruelly, instantly awake at six thirty a.m. She was lying on her side, facing John-Paul, and their eyes opened simultaneously. They were so close, their noses were almost touching.

She looked at the delicate scribbles of red veins in the whites of John-Paul's blue eyes, the pores on his nose, the gray stubble on his strong, firm, honest chin.

Who was this man?

Last night they had gone back to bed and lain together in the darkness, staring blindly at the ceiling, while John-Paul had talked. How he'd talked. There had been no need to probe for information. She didn't ask a single question. He wanted to talk, to tell her everything. His voice had been low and fervent, without modulation, almost monotonous, except there was nothing monotonous about what he was telling her. The more he talked, the hoarser his voice got. It was like a nightmare, lying in the dark, listening to that raspy whisper of his going on and on and on. She'd had to bite her lip to stop herself from screaming, *Shut up, shut up, shut up!*

He'd been in love with Janie Crowley. Crazy in love. Obsessed, even. The way you think you're in love when you're a teenager. He met her one day at the Hornsby McDonald's when they were both filling in applications for part-time work. Janie recognized him from when they'd been at primary school together, before he'd gone off to his exclusive boys' school. They'd been in the same year at St. Angela's, but in different classes. He didn't actually remember Janie at all, although he sort of knew the Crowley name. Neither of them ended up working at McDonald's. Janie got a job at the dry cleaner, and John-Paul got a job at the deli, but they had this amazing intense conversation about God knows what, and she gave him her phone number, and he rang her the next day.

He thought she was his girlfriend. He thought he was going to lose his virginity to her. It all had to be really secretive, because Janie's dad was one of those crazy Catholic dads and he said she couldn't even have a boyfriend until she was eighteen. Their relationship, such as it was, had to be completely secret. That only made it more exciting. It was like they were secret agents. If he rang her house and anyone but Janie answered, the rule was that he had to hang up. They never held hands in public. None of their friends knew. Janie insisted on this. They went to the movies once and held hands in the dark. They kissed on a train in an empty carriage. They sat in the rotunda at Wattle

Valley Park and smoked cigarettes and talked about how they wanted to go to Europe before uni. And that was it, really. Except that he thought about her day and night. He wrote her poetry he was too embarrassed to give her.

He never wrote me *poetry,* thought Cecilia irrelevantly.

That night Janie asked him to meet her in Wattle Valley Park, where they'd met often before. It was always deserted, and there was the rotunda where they could sit and kiss. She said she had something to tell him. He thought she was going to tell him that she'd gone to the family planning center to get a prescription for the pill, they'd talked about that, but instead she said that she was sorry, but she was in love with another boy. John-Paul had been stunned. Bewildered. He didn't know there was another boy in the running! He said, "But I thought you were my girlfriend!" And she'd laughed. She'd seemed so happy, John-Paul said, so happy that she wasn't his girlfriend, and he was just crushed, and humiliated, and filled with this incredible rage. It was his pride more than anything. He felt like a fool, and for that, he *wanted to kill her.*

John-Paul seemed horribly desperate for Cecilia to know this. He said he didn't want to justify it, or mitigate it, or pretend it was an accident—because for a few seconds, he absolutely felt the desire to kill.

He didn't remember making the decision to put his hands around her neck. But he remembered the moment when he was suddenly aware of the slender, girlish neck between his hands and realized it wasn't one of his brothers he had in a choke hold. He was *hurting* a *girl.* He remembered thinking, *What the fuck am I doing?* and dropping his hands so fast, he actually felt relieved because he was so sure he'd caught himself in time, that he hadn't killed her. Except that she was limp in his arms, her eyes staring over his shoulder, and he thought, *No, this can't be possible*. He thought it had only been a second, maybe two seconds, of crazy rage; definitely not long enough to kill her.

He couldn't believe it. Even now. After all these years. He was still shocked and horrified by what he'd done.

She was still warm, but he knew, without a shadow of a doubt, that she was dead.

So he laid her carefully at the bottom of the slide, and he remembered thinking that the night was getting colder, so he put her school blazer over the top of her, and he had his mum's rosary beads in his pocket because he'd done an exam that day and he always took them for luck. So he carefully placed them in Janie's hands. It was his way of saying sorry, to Janie and to God. And then he ran. He ran and ran until he couldn't breathe.

He thought for sure he would be caught. He kept waiting for the heavy weight of a policeman's hand to drop on his shoulder.

But he was never even questioned. He and Janie weren't at the same school, or in the same youth group. Neither of their parents or friends had known about it. It seemed that nobody had ever seen them together. It was like it had never happened.

He said that if the police had ever questioned him, he would have confessed immediately. He said that if someone else had been accused of the murder, he would have given himself up. He wouldn't have let anyone else take the fall for it. He wasn't *that* evil.

It was just that nobody asked the question, so he never gave the answer.

During the nineties he started hearing news reports about crimes being solved through DNA evidence, and he wondered if he'd left a minuscule vestige of himself behind: a single hair, for example. But even if he had, they'd been together for such a short time and they'd played their undercover game so effectively. Nobody knew he knew Janie. He could almost convince himself that he *hadn't* known her, that it had never happened.

And then the years had just gone by, layers and layers of years piled on top of the memory of what he'd done. Sometimes, he whispered, he could go for months feeling relatively normal, and then other times he could think of nothing else except what he'd done and he thought he'd go crazy.

"It's like a monster trapped in my mind," he rasped into Cecilia's ear. "And sometimes it gets free and it goes rampaging about, and then I get it under control again. I chain it up. You know what I mean?"

No, thought Cecilia. *No, actually, I don't.*

"And then I met you," said John-Paul. "And I sensed something about you. A deep-down goodness. I fell in love with your goodness. It was like looking at a beautiful lake. It was like you were somehow purifying me."

Cecilia was appalled. *I'm not good*, she thought. *I smoked*

marijuana once! We used to get drunk together! I thought
you fell in love with my figure, my sparkling company, my
sense of humor, not my goodness, for God's sake!

He kept talking, seemingly desperate for her to know
every tiny detail.

When Isabel was born and he became a parent, he suddenly had a new and terrible understanding of exactly what
he'd done to Rachel and Ed Crowley.

"When we were living on Bell Avenue, I used to drive
by Janie's father walking his dog on my way to work," he
said. "And his *face*—it looked . . . I don't know how to
describe it. Like he was in such physical pain that he should
have been rolling about on the floor, except he wasn't, he
was walking the dog. And I'd think, *I did that to him. I'm*
responsible for that pain. I kept trying to leave the house at
different times, or drive different ways, but I kept seeing
him."

They'd lived in the house on Bell Avenue when Isabel
was a baby. Cecilia's memories of Bell Avenue smelled of
baby shampoo and nappy cream and mashed pear and ba-
nana. She and John-Paul had been besotted by their new
baby. Sometimes he'd go in late to work so he could spend
longer lying on the bed with Isabel in her little white all-
in-one suit, nuzzling her plump, firm tummy. Except that
wasn't the case. He was trying to avoid seeing the father
of the girl he'd murdered.

"I'd see Ed Crowley and I'd think, *That's it, I've got to*
confess," he said. "But then I'd think about you and the
baby. How could I do that to you? How could I tell you?
How could I leave you to bring up a baby on your own? I

thought about our leaving Sydney. But I knew you wouldn't want to leave your parents, and anyway it felt wrong. It felt like running away. I had to stay here, where at any moment I could run into Janie's parents and know what I'd done. I had to suffer. So that's when I had an idea. I had to find new ways to punish myself, to suffer—without making anyone else suffer. I had to do penance."

If anything gave him too much pleasure—pleasure that was solely for him—then he gave it up. That's why he gave up rowing. He loved it, so he had to stop because Janie never got to row. He sold his beloved Alfa Romeo because Janie never got to drive a car.

He devoted himself to the community, as if a judge had ordered him to do so many hours of community service.

Cecilia had thought becoming a father had been what made him so community-minded. She thought that was something they had in common, when in fact, the John-Paul she thought she knew didn't even exist. He was a fabrication. His whole life was an act: an act for God's benefit, to let him off the hook.

He said the community service thing was tricky, because what about when he enjoyed it? For example, he loved being a volunteer bushfire fighter—the camaraderie, the jokes and the adrenaline—so did his enjoyment outweigh his contribution to the community? He was always calculating, wondering what else God would expect of him, how much more he would have to pay. Of course, he knew that none of it was enough, and that he would probably go to hell when he died.

He's serious, thought Cecilia. *He really believes he's going to hell, as if hell is an actual physical place, not an abstract idea.* She went to say *Thank goodness for eternal damnation!* but she didn't. He was referring to God in a chillingly familiar way. They weren't that type of Catholics. They were Catholics, sure; they went to church, but for God's sake, they weren't *religious.* God didn't come into their day-to-day conversation.

Except, of course, this wasn't a day-to-day conversation.

He kept talking. It was endless. Cecilia thought of that urban myth about an exotic worm that lived in your body, and the only cure was to starve yourself and then place a hot dinner in front of your mouth, and wait for the worm to smell the food and slowly uncoil itself, sliding its way up your throat. John-Paul's voice was like that worm: an endless length of horror slipping from his mouth.

He told her that as the girls grew older, his guilt and regret had become almost unendurable. The nightmares, the migraines, the bouts of depression that he tried so hard to hide from her were all because of what he'd done.

"Earlier this year, Isabel started to remind me of Janie," said John-Paul. "Something about the way she was wearing her hair. I kept staring at her. It was terrible. I kept imagining someone hurting Isabel, the way I . . . the way I hurt Janie. An innocent little girl. I felt like I had to put myself through the grief that I put her parents through. I had to imagine her dead. I've been crying. In the shower. In the car. Sobbing."

"Esther heard you crying before you went to Chicago," said Cecilia. "In the shower."

"Did she?" John-Paul blinked. "I didn't realize."

For a moment there was beautiful silence as he digested this.

Okay, thought Cecilia, *we're done. He's stopped talking. Thank God.* She felt a physical and mental exhaustion she hadn't experienced since she went through labor.

"I gave up sex," said John-Paul.

For God's sake.

He wanted her to know that last November, he was trying to think of new ways to punish himself and he decided to give up sex for six months. He was ashamed that he'd never thought of it before. It was obviously one of the great pleasures of his life. It had nearly killed him. He'd been worried she might think he was having an affair, because obviously he couldn't tell her the real reason.

"Oh, John-*Paul.*" Cecilia sighed into the darkness.

This perpetual quest for redemption he'd been undertaking for all these years seemed so silly, so childish, so utterly pointless and so typically *unsystematic.*

"I invited Rachel Crowley to Polly's pirate party," said Cecilia, remembering, marveling at the idiotically innocent person she'd been just a few hours earlier as she stared into the inky darkness. "I drove her home tonight. I talked to her about Janie. I thought I was so great . . ."

Her voice broke.

She heard John-Paul take a deep breath in through his nostrils.

"I'm so sorry," he said. "I know I keep saying it. I know it's useless."

"It's all right," she said, and nearly laughed, because it was such a lie.

That was the last thing she remembered before the two of them must have suddenly fallen into a deep, drugged-like sleep.

"Are you okay?" said John-Paul now. "Do you feel all right?"

She smelled his stale morning breath. Her own mouth felt dry. Her head ached. She felt hungover, seedy and ashamed, as if the two of them had engaged in some disgusting debauchery the previous night.

She pressed two fingertips to her forehead and closed her eyes, unable to look at him any longer. Her neck ached. She must have slept at a funny angle.

"Do you think you still . . ." He stopped himself and cleared his throat convulsively. He finally spoke in a whisper. "Can you still be with me?"

She looked into his eyes and saw pure, primal terror.

Did one act define who you were forever? Did one evil act as a teenager counteract twenty years of marriage, of *good* marriage, twenty years of being a good husband and a good father? Murder and you are a murderer. That was how it worked for other people. For strangers. For people you read about in the newspaper. Cecilia was sure about that, but did different rules apply to John-Paul? And if so, why?

There was a rapid pitter-patter of footsteps down the hallway, and suddenly a small, warm body catapulted itself onto their bed.

"G'morning, Mum," said Polly as she breezily wriggled herself between them. She shoved her head onto Cecilia's pillow. Strands of her blue-black hair tickled Cecilia's nose. "Hello, Daddy."

Cecilia looked at her youngest daughter as if she'd never seen her before: her flawless skin, the long sweep of her eyelashes and the brilliant blue of her eyes. Everything about her was exquisite and pure.

Cecilia's eyes met John-Paul's with perfect, bloodshot understanding. This was why.

"Hello, Polly," they said together.

TWENTY-THREE

Liam said something Tess couldn't hear, dropped her hand and stopped suddenly right at the entrance to St. Angela's. The flood of parents and children changed course to cope with the sudden obstacle in their path, streaming around them. Tess bent down next to him, and someone's elbow banged against the back of her head.

"What is it?" she said, rubbing her head. She felt twitchy, nervy and overstimulated. School drop-off was just as bad here as in Melbourne: a very particular version of hell for someone like her. People, people everywhere.

"I want to go back home." Liam spoke to the ground. "I want Daddy."

"What's that?" said Tess, although she'd heard. She tried to take him by the hand. "Let's get out of everybody's way first."

She knew this was coming. It had all been suspiciously, oddly easy. Liam had seemed strangely sanguine about this abrupt, unplanned change of schools. "He's so adaptable,"

Tess's mother had marveled, but Tess had thought it had more to do with the problems he'd been experiencing at his old school than actual enthusiasm about starting a new one.

Liam dragged on her arm, so she had to bend back down again.

"You and Daddy and Felicity should stop fighting," he said, cupping his hand around Tess's ear. His breath was warm and toothpaste-scented. "Just say sorry to each other. Say you didn't mean it. So we can go back home."

Tess's heart stopped.

Stupid. Stupid, stupid, stupid. Did she really think she could put this over on Liam? He'd always surprised them with how well he observed what was going on around them.

"Grandma can come and stay with us in Melbourne," said Liam. "We can look after her there until her ankle gets better."

Funny. That had never actually occurred to Tess. It was as if she thought her life in Melbourne and her mother's life in Sydney took place on different planets.

"They have wheelchairs at the airport," said Liam solemnly, just as the edge of a little girl's backpack swung against his face and caught the corner of his eye. His face crumpled, and tears spilled from his beautiful golden eyes.

"Honey," she said helplessly, on the edge of tears herself. "Look. You don't have to go to school at all. This was a crazy idea—"

"Well, good morning, Liam. I was wondering if you were here yet!" It was that dotty school principal. She crouched down on her haunches next to Liam as easily as a child. *She must do yoga*, thought Tess.

A boy about the same age as Liam walking by gave her a loving pat on her gray, frizzy-haired head, as if she were the school dog, not the school principal. "Hello, Mrs. McDuff!"

"Good morning, Harrison!" Trudy lifted a hand, and her shawl slid off her shoulders.

"I'm sorry. We're creating a traffic jam here," began Tess, but Trudy just smiled slightly in her direction, readjusted her shawl with one hand and returned her attention to Liam.

"Do you know what your teacher, Mrs. Jeffers, and I did yesterday afternoon?"

Liam shrugged and roughly brushed his tears.

"We turned your classroom into another planet." Her eyes sparkled. "Our Easter egg hunt is in outer space."

Liam sniffed and looked extremely cynical. "How?" he said. "How'd you do that?"

"Come and see." Trudy stood up and took Liam's hand. "Say 'bye to your mum. You can tell her how many eggs you found in space this afternoon."

Tess kissed the top of his head. "Okay, well. Have a wonderful day, and don't forget I'll—"

"There's a spaceship, of course. Guess who gets to fly it?" said Trudy, leading him away, and Tess saw Liam glance up at her, his face suddenly bright with cautious hope, before he was swallowed up in a crowd of blue-and-white-checked uniforms.

Tess turned and headed back out onto the street. She felt that strangely untethered feeling she always felt when she left Liam in someone else's care, as if gravity had disappeared. What would she do with herself now? And what was she going to say to him after school today? She couldn't lie and tell him that there was nothing going on, but she couldn't tell him the truth, could she? *Daddy and Felicity are in love. Daddy is meant to love me best. So I'm feeling angry with them. I'm feeling very hurt.*

Supposedly the truth was always the best option.

She'd rushed into this. She'd pretended to herself that she was doing everything for Liam. She'd yanked her child from his home and his school and his life because in actual fact that was what *she* wanted to do; she wanted to be as far away from Will and Felicity as possible, and now Liam's happiness was dependent on a peculiar frizzy-haired woman called Trudy McDuff.

Maybe she should homeschool him until all this was sorted out. She could handle most of it. English, geography. It could be fun! But math. That was her downfall. Tess's math was terrible. Felicity had helped Tess pass math when they were at school, and now Tess was in charge of helping Liam with his math. Felicity had said just the other day that she was quite looking forward to rediscovering the quadratic equation when Liam was in high school, and Tess and Will had looked at each other, shuddered and laughed. Felicity and Will had behaved so *normally*! All that time. Hugging their nasty little secret to themselves.

She was walking along the street outside the school back toward her mother's house when she heard a voice behind her.

"Good morning, Tess."

It was Cecilia Fitzpatrick suddenly walking alongside

her in the same direction, chunky car keys jangling from one hand. There was something odd about the way she was walking, as if she had a limp.

Tess took a deep, bracing breath. "Morning!" she said.

"Just dropped Liam off for his first day, did you?" said Cecilia. She was wearing sunglasses, so Tess was spared the scary eye contact. She sounded as if she was coming down with a cold. "Was he okay? Always a bit tricky."

"Oh, well, not really, but Trudy . . ." Tess stopped, distracted, because she'd just noticed Cecilia's shoes. It seemed like they weren't matching. One was a black ballet shoe. The other was a gold sandal with a heel. No wonder she was walking funny. Tess looked away and remembered to keep talking. "But that school principal, Trudy. She was wonderful with him."

"Oh, yes, Trudy is one in a million, that's for sure," said Cecilia. "Anyway, this is my car here." She indicated a very shiny white four-wheel drive with the Tupperware logo along the side. "We forgot Polly had gym today. I never . . . Anyway, we forgot, so I've got to drive home and get her shoes. Polly is in love with the PE teacher, so I'll be in terrible trouble if I'm late."

"Connor," said Tess. "Connor Whitby. He's her PE teacher." She thought of him last night at the service station, his helmet under one arm.

"Yes, that's right. All the little girls are in love with him. Actually, half the mothers are too."

"Really." *Slosh, slosh* went that water bed.

"Good morning, Tess. Hi there, Cecilia." It was Rachel

Crowley, the school secretary, walking from the other direction, wearing a pair of white running shoes with her businesslike skirt and silk shirt. Tess wondered if anyone ever looked at Rachel without thinking about Janie Crowley and what happened to her in that park. It was impossible to think that Rachel had once been an ordinary woman, that no one could have sensed the tragedy that was waiting for her.

Rachel stopped in front of them. More conversation. It was endless. She looked tired and pale, her white hair not quite as beautifully blow-dried as it had been when Tess met her the day before. "Thanks again for the lift home last night," she said to Cecilia. She smiled at Tess. "I was at one of Cecilia's Tupperware parties last night and had too much to drink. That's why I'm on foot today." She gestured at her shoes. "Shameful, isn't it?"

There was an awkward silence. Tess had confidently expected Cecilia to speak next, but she seemed distracted by something off in the distance and was strangely, almost bizarrely silent.

"Sounds like you had a fun night," said Tess finally. Her voice sounded too loud and hearty. Why couldn't she just speak like a normal person?

"It was, actually." Rachel frowned slightly at Cecilia, who still hadn't said a word. She turned her attention back to Tess. "Did Liam go off to his classroom okay?"

"Mrs. McDuff took him under her wing," said Tess.

"That's good," said Rachel. "He'll be fine. Trudy takes special care of the new children. I'd better go start my day.

Get out of these ridiculous-looking clodhoppers. 'Bye, girls."

"Have a great . . ." Cecilia's voice came out husky, and she cleared her throat. "Have a great day, Rachel."

"You too."

Rachel headed off toward the school.

"Well," said Tess.

"Oh dear," said Cecilia. She pressed her fingertips to her mouth. "I think I'm going . . ." She looked around her agitatedly, as if she was searching for something. "Shit."

And suddenly she was crouched in the gutter being violently sick.

Oh God, thought Tess, as the terrible retching sounds went on and on. She did not want to see Cecilia Fitzpatrick being sick in a gutter. Was it a hangover from the previous night? Food poisoning? Should she crouch down beside her and hold back her hair like girlfriends did for each other in nightclub bathrooms after too many tequilas? Like she and Felicity had once done for each other? Or should she gently rub Cecilia's back in a circular motion like she did for Liam when he was sick? Should she at least make some soothing, sympathetic sounds as she stood here watching, to show she cared? Rather than just standing here, wincing and looking the other way? But she barely knew the woman.

When she was pregnant with Liam, Tess had suffered from chronic all-day-long morning sickness. She'd thrown up in numerous public places, and her only wish had been to be left alone. Perhaps she should just slip quietly away? But she couldn't just abandon the poor woman. She looked around her desperately for another school mum, one of those capable sorts who would know what to do. Cecilia would have dozens of friends at the school, but the street was suddenly deserted and quiet.

Then she was struck by wonderful inspiration: *tissues.* The thought of being able to offer Cecilia something both useful and appropriate filled her with something ridiculously akin to joy. She rustled through her handbag and found a small, unopened packet of tissues and a bottle of water.

"You're like a Boy Scout," Will had said to her early on in their relationship, when she'd pulled a small flashlight from her bag after he dropped his car keys on a dark street on their way home from a movie. "If we got stuck on a desert island, we could be self-sufficient thanks to Tess's handbag," Felicity had said, because, of course, Felicity had been there too, that night, she remembered now. When was Felicity ever not there?

"My goodness me," said Cecilia. She straightened up, plonked herself on the curb and wiped the back of her hand across her mouth. "How embarrassing."

"Here." Tess handed over the tissues. "Are you all right? Was it something you maybe ate?" Cecilia's hands, Tess noticed, were trembling badly, and her face was pasty white.

"I don't know." Cecilia blew her nose and looked up at Tess. There were purplish crescents under her streaming eyes and tiny flecks of mascara on her eyelids. She looked dreadful. "I'm so sorry about this. You must go. You've probably got a million things to do."

"I don't actually have a thing to do," said Tess. "Not a thing in the world." She undid the bottle cap. "Sip of water?"

"Thank you." Cecilia took the water bottle and drank. She went to stand up and staggered. Tess grabbed her arm just before she fell.

"Sorry, so sorry." Cecilia was almost sobbing.

"It's fine." Tess held her up. "It's perfectly fine. I think I should drive you home."

"Oh, no, no, that's so sweet of you, but I'm really fine."

"No you're not," said Tess. "I'll drive you home. You can hop into bed, and I'll drop your daughter's shoes back off at the school."

"I can't believe I nearly forgot Polly's damned shoes again," said Cecilia. She looked utterly appalled at herself, as if she'd put Polly's life at risk.

"Come on," said Tess. She took Cecilia's keys from her unresisting hand, pointed the key at the Tupperware car and pressed the Unlock button. She was filled with an unusual sense of capability and purpose.

"Thank you for this." Cecilia leaned heavily on Tess's arm as she helped her into the passenger side of her car.

"It's no problem at all," said Tess in a brisk, no-nonsense voice entirely unlike her own, closing the door and heading around to the driver's side.

How kind and civic of you! Felicity spoke up in her head. *Next thing you'll be joining the P&F!*

Fuck off, Felicity, thought Tess, and she turned Cecilia's key in the ignition with a deft flick of the wrist.

TWENTY-FOUR

What was wrong with Cecilia this morning? She was certainly not herself, mused Rachel as she walked into St. Angela's, feeling peculiar and self-conscious about her bouncy, flat-footed walk in her sneakers instead of her normal heels. She could feel moisture in her armpits and along her hairline, but actually, walking instead of driving to work had left her feeling quite invigorated. Before she'd left the house this morning, she'd momentarily considered calling a taxi because she felt so exhausted after the previous night. She'd been up for hours after Rodney Bellach had left, mentally replaying that video of Janie and Connor in her head over and over. Each time she remembered Connor's face it became more malevolent in her memory. Rodney was just being cautious, not wanting her to get her hopes up. He was old now, and a bit soft around the edges. Once a snappy, smart young police officer saw the video, he (or she!) would instantly see the implications and take decisive action.

What would she do if she ran into Connor Whitby at
the school today? Confront him? Ask the question? Make
the accusation? The thought made her feel dizzy. Her emotions would soar like mountains: grief, fury, hatred.

She took a deep breath. No, no, she would not confront
him. She wanted this done properly, and she didn't want
to forewarn him about the new evidence or say something
that might cost her a guilty verdict. Imagine if he got off
on a legal technicality because she couldn't keep her mouth
shut. She felt an unexpected sense of not quite happiness,
but something. Hope? Satisfaction? Yes, it was satisfaction,
because she was doing something for Janie. That was it. It
had been so long since she'd been able to do something,
anything, for her daughter: to go into her bedroom on a
cold night and place an extra blanket over those bony shoulders (she was always cold), to make her one of her favorite
cheese and pickle sandwiches (with heaps of butter—Rachel
was always secretly trying to fatten her up), to carefully
hand-wash her good clothes, to give her a ten-dollar bill
for no reason at all. For years she'd felt this desire to do
something again for Janie, to still be her mother, to look
after her again in some small way, and now at last she could.
I'm getting him, darling. Not much longer now.

Her mobile phone rang in her handbag and she fumbled
for it, anxious to catch the caller before the silly thing
stopped ringing and went to voice mail. It must be Rodney!
Who else would call at this time of the morning? With news
already? But surely it was too soon; it couldn't possibly be
him.

"Hello?"

She'd seen the name, just before she answered. Rob, not Rodney. The "Ro" had given her a moment of hope.

"Mum? Everything all right?"

She tried not to feel aggrieved with Rob for not being Rodney.

"Everything is fine, love. Just on my way in to work. What's up?"

Rob launched into a long story as Rachel kept walking toward the school office. She went by one of the Year 1 classrooms and heard bubbles of children's laughter floating out the door. As she glanced in, she saw her boss, Trudy McDuff, streak across the classroom with one arm lifted in the air like a superhero, while the Year 1 teacher put her hand over her eyes and giggled helplessly. Was that a disco strobe light flashing white lights around the room? Tess O'Leary's little boy certainly wouldn't be bored on his first day of school, that was for sure. As for that report Trudy was meant to be working on for the Department of Education . . . Rachel sighed. She'd give her until ten a.m. and then she'd drag her back to her desk.

"So is that okay, then?" said Rob. "You'll come to Lauren's parents' on Sunday?"

"What's that?" said Rachel. She walked into her office and put her handbag on her desk.

"I thought maybe you could bring a pavlova. If you like."

"Bring a pavlova where? When?" She couldn't process what Rob was going on about.

She heard Rob take a deep breath.

"On Easter Sunday. For lunch. With Lauren's family. I

know we said we'd go to you for lunch, but it's just impossible to fit everything in. We've been so busy with all the arrangements for New York. So then we thought if you came over to their place, we could see both families at once."

Lauren's family. Lauren's mother had always just been to the ballet or the opera or the theater the night before, and whatever it was would have been simply *extraordinary* or *exquisite*. Lauren's father was a retired barrister who would exchange a few courteous pleasantries with Rachel before abruptly turning away with a politely baffled expression on his face, as if he couldn't quite place who she was. There was always a stranger at the table, someone beautiful and exotic-looking who would dominate the conversation with endless talk of their recent fascinating trip to India or Iran, and everybody except for Rachel (and Jacob) would find them enthralling. There appeared to be an endless supply of these colorful guests, because Rachel had never met the same one twice. It was like they were hired as guest speakers for the occasion.

"Fine," said Rachel resignedly. She would take Jacob off and play with him in the garden. Anything was bearable if she had Jacob. "That's fine. I'll bring the pavlova."

Rob loved her pavlovas. Bless him. He never seemed to notice that Rachel's wonky-looking pavlovas were a somewhat lowbrow addition to the table.

"By the way, Lauren wanted to know if you want her to pick up any more of those macarons that we brought over the other night."

"That's nice of her, but actually they were a little sweet

for me," said Rachel. (In fact, Rachel was now obsessed with macarons, and Marla had asked her youngest son, who worked in the city as a something-or-other, to send "one of his underlings" out to buy another box. Poor underling. But better an underling should suffer than for Rachel to admit her daughter-in-law had done something right.)

"She also said to ask if you had fun at the Tupperware party last night."

Lauren must have noticed Marla's invitation on the fridge when she picked up Jacob on Monday. Show-off. *Look how interested I am in my mother-in-law's elderly little life!*

"It was perfectly fine," said Rachel. Would she tell him about the video? Would it upset him? Please him? He had a right to know. She sometimes felt uneasily aware of how little notice she'd taken of Rob's grief, how she'd just wanted him to stay out of her way, to go to bed, to watch TV, to let her cry in private.

"Bit boring, eh, Mum?"

"It was fine. Actually, when I got home—"

"Hey! I got Jacob's passport photo done before work yesterday. Wait till you see the photo. So cute."

Janie had never had a passport. Yet *Jacob*, at just two years old, had a passport that allowed him to leave the country at barely a moment's notice.

"I can't *wait* to see it," said Rachel. She would not tell Rob about the video. He was far too busy with his own important, jet-setting life to worry about an investigation into his sister's murder.

There was a pause. Rob wasn't stupid.

"We haven't forgotten about Friday," he said. "I know this time of year is always hard for you. Actually, speaking of Friday . . ."

He seemed to be waiting for her to say something. Was this in fact the whole point of the phone call?

"Yes," she said impatiently. "What about Friday?"

"Lauren tried to talk to you about it the other night. It's her idea. Well, it's not. It's not at all. It's my idea. It's just something she said that made me think it might . . . So, anyway, I know you always go to the park. To that park. I know you normally go on your own. But I wondered if maybe I could go too. With Lauren and Jacob, if that's all right."

"I don't need—"

"I know you don't *need* us there," interrupted Rob. He sounded unusually terse. "But *I'd* like to be there this time. For Janie. To show her that . . ."

Rachel heard his voice crack.

He cleared his throat and spoke again, in a deeper voice.

"And then afterward, there's that nice café near the station. Lauren said it's open on Good Friday. We could have breakfast afterward." He coughed and said hastily, "Or just coffee at least."

Rachel imagined Lauren standing in the park, looking solemn and stylish. She'd wear a cream trench coat, pulled in tight at the waist, and her hair would be in a shiny, low ponytail that didn't swing too jauntily, and her lipstick would be a neutral color, not too bright, and she'd say and do all the right things at all the right times, and somehow turn "marking the anniversary of my husband's sister's murder" into another perfectly managed event on her social calendar.

"I think I'd really prefer . . ." she began, but then she thought of the way Rob's voice had cracked. It was all orchestrated by Lauren, of course, but maybe it was something that Rob needed. Maybe he needed it more than Rachel needed to be alone.

"All right," she said. "That's fine with me. I normally get there very early, around six a.m., but Jacob is up at the crack of dawn these days, isn't he?"

"Yes! He is! So. We'll be there. Thank you. It means—"

"I've actually got a really full plate today, so if you don't mind . . ." They'd taken up the phone for long enough. Rodney might be about to call any minute. She didn't want him to leave a voice-mail message. She wanted to hear it firsthand.

"'Bye, Mum," said Rob sadly.

TWENTY-FIVE

Cecilia's home was beautiful, welcoming and light-filled, with big glass windows that looked out on a perfectly tended backyard and swimming pool. The walls were hung with sweet, funny family photos and framed children's drawings. Everything was shining and tidy, but not in an overly formal, forbidding way. The sofas looked comfy and squishy; there were bookshelves crammed with books and interesting-looking knickknacks. There was evidence of Cecilia's daughters everywhere: sports equipment, a cello, a pair of ballet slippers, but everything was in its absolutely correct place. It was like the house was up for sale and it was being marketed by the real estate agent as the "ideal family home."

"I love your house," said Tess as Cecilia led her through to the kitchen.

"Thank you, it's—oh!" Cecilia stopped abruptly at the kitchen door. "I do apologize for this mess!"

Walking in behind her, Tess said, "You're kidding,

right?" There were a handful of breakfast bowls on an island bench, a half-drunk glass of apple juice sitting on top
of the microwave, a solitary carton of Sultana Bran and a
small pile of books on the kitchen table. Everything else
was in perfect, shining order.

Tess watched in bemusement as Cecilia whirled around
the kitchen. Within seconds she'd stowed the dishes in the
dishwasher, put the cereal away in a giant pantry and was
polishing the kitchen sink with a paper towel.

"We ran unusually late this morning," explained Cecilia
as she scrubbed at the sink as if her life depended on it.
"Normally I can't leave the house unless everything is perfect. I know I'm ridiculous. My sister says I have that disorder. What is it? Obsessive-compulsive. That's it. OCD."

Tess thought Cecilia's sister might have a point.

"You should rest," she said.

"Have a seat. Would you like a cup of tea? Coffee?" said
Cecilia frantically. "I have muffins, biscuits . . ." She
stopped, pressed her hand to her forehead and briefly closed
her eyes. "Goodness. That is, ah, what was I saying?"

"I think I should make *you* a cup of tea."

"I might actually need to . . ." Cecilia pulled out a chair
and then stopped, transfixed by the sight of her shoes.

"My shoes don't match," she said, awestruck.

"No one would have noticed," said Tess.

Cecilia sat down and rested her elbows on the table. She
gave Tess a rueful, almost shy smile. "I have a reputation
at St. Angela's for being the opposite of this."

"Oh, well," said Tess. She filled a very shiny-looking
kettle with water and noticed that she'd left a few droplets

on Cecilia's perfect sink. "Your secret is safe with me." Worried that she'd implied that Cecilia's behavior was somehow shameful, she quickly changed the subject. "Is one of your daughters doing an assignment on the Berlin Wall?"

"My daughter Esther is learning about it for her own interest," said Cecilia. She pulled the pile of books toward her and opened one of them. "She gets crazily interested in these different topics. We all end up becoming experts. It can be a bit draining. Anyway." She took a deep breath and suddenly turned in her chair to face Tess as if they were at a dinner party and Cecilia had decided it was time to focus on her instead of the guest on her other side. "Have you been to Berlin, Tess?"

The pitch of her voice was not quite right. Was she about to be sick again? Could Cecilia be on drugs? Mentally ill?

"No, actually." Tess opened Cecilia's pantry door to find tea bags and her eyes widened at the array of labeled Tupperware containers of all shapes and sizes. It was like a magazine ad. "I've been to Europe a few times, but my cousin, Felicity . . ." She stopped. She'd been about to say that her cousin, Felicity, wasn't interested in Germany and so therefore she'd never been, and she was struck for the first time by what an odd thing that was to say. As if her own feelings about seeing Germany were of no consequence. (What *were* her own feelings about Germany?) She saw a tray set out with rows of tea bags. "Gosh. You've got everything. Which tea would you like?"

"Oh, Earl Grey, just black, no sugar. Really, please let me!" Cecilia went to stand up.

"Sit, sit," said Tess, almost bossily, as if she'd known Cecilia forever. If Cecilia was behaving unlike herself, so was Tess. Cecilia sat back down.

A thought occurred to Tess. "Will Polly need her sports shoes straightaway? Should I rush back to the school with them?"

Cecilia startled. "I forgot about Polly's shoes *again*! I completely forgot."

Tess smiled at how appalled Cecilia looked. It was like she was forgetting things for the first time in her whole life.

Cecilia said slowly, "They don't go up to the oval until ten."

"In that case I'll have a cup of tea with you," said Tess. She helped herself to an unopened packet of expensive-looking chocolate biscuits from Cecilia's extraordinary pantry, somewhat thrilled by her temerity. Oh, this was living life on the edge, all right. "And a biscuit?"

TWENTY-SIX

Cecilia watched Tess lift her cup of tea to her mouth (she'd used the wrong mugs—Cecilia never used those mugs for guests) and smile at her over the rim, unaware of the monologue running silently through Cecilia's head.

Want to know what I found out last night, Tess? My husband murdered Janie Crowley. I know! Wow, hey. Yep, Rachel Crowley's daughter, that's right, the nice white-haired lady with the sad eyes, the one who walked past us this morning and looked me right in the eyes and smiled. So! I'm in a bit of a pickle to be honest, Tess, as my mother would say. A real pickle.

What would Tess say if Cecilia actually spoke any of those words out loud? Cecilia had thought Tess was one of those mysterious, self-assured types who didn't need to fill silent gaps with conversation, but it occurred to her now that perhaps she was shy. There was something brave about the way she met Cecilia's eyes and sat with careful, straight-backed posture, as if she were a child behaving well at someone else's house.

She was really being very nice to Cecilia, driving her home after that terrible incident in the gutter. Was Cecilia going to throw up every time she saw Rachel Crowley from now on? Because that could be complicated.

Tess tilted her head at the Berlin Wall books. "I always like reading about the escape attempts."

"Me too," said Cecilia. "The successful ones, that is." She opened one of the books to the section of photos in the middle. "See this family?" She pointed at a black-and-white photo of a young man and woman and their four small, scruffy children. "This man hijacked a train. Cannonball Harry, they called him. He drove the train at full speed through these barriers. The conductor was saying, 'Are you crazy, comrade?' They all had to get down under the seats so they wouldn't get shot. Can you imagine? Not being him, being her. The mother. I keep thinking about it. Four children lying on the floor of a train. Bullets flying over their heads. She made up a fairy tale to keep them distracted. She said she'd never made up a story for them before. Actually, I never made up stories for my children either. I'm not creative. I bet you make up stories for your children, don't you?"

Tess seemed startled. "Sometimes, I guess."

I'm talking too much, thought Cecilia, and then she realized she'd said "your children" when Tess had only the one child, and she wondered if she should correct herself, but what if Tess desperately wanted more children but couldn't have them for some reason?

Tess turned the book around to face her and looked at the photo. "I guess it shows what you'll do for freedom. We just take it for granted."

"But I think if I'd been his wife, I would have said no," said Cecilia. She sounded too agitated, as if she really were faced with this choice. She made a conscious effort to calm her voice down. "I don't think I would have been brave enough. I would have said, *It's not worth it. Who cares if we're stuck behind this wall? At least we're alive. At least our children are alive.* Death is too high a price for freedom."

What was the price for John-Paul's freedom? Rachel Crowley? Was she the price? Her peace of mind? The peace of mind she would have in at last knowing what had happened to her daughter, and why, and that the person responsible was being punished? Cecilia still felt rage at a preschool teacher who had once made Isabel cry. Isabel didn't even remember it, for heaven's sake. So how must Rachel feel? Cecilia's stomach churned. She put her tea back down.

"You've gone completely white," said Tess.

"I guess I've got a virus," said Cecilia. *My husband has given me a virus. A really nasty virus.* Ha! To her horror, she actually laughed out loud. "Or something. I've got something, that's for sure."

TWENTY-SEVEN

A s Tess drove Cecilia's car up to the school to drop off Polly's sports shoes, it occurred to her that if Polly was having PE today, then Liam would be too, because weren't they in the same class? And of course *he* wasn't wearing sports shoes. Nobody had told Tess it was PE day. Or perhaps they had, but she hadn't registered it. She wondered if she should stop at her mother's house and pick up Liam's sneakers. She wavered. Nobody ever told you that being a mother is all about making what seemed like thousands of tiny decisions. Tess had always considered herself quite a decisive person before she had Liam.

Well, it was past ten o'clock. She'd better not risk getting Polly's shoes there late. It seemed to matter so much, and Tess didn't want to let Cecilia down. The poor woman really did seem very sick.

Cecilia had said to take the shoes either to Polly's classroom or straight to the PE teacher. "You'll probably see

Connor Whitby on the oval," she'd said. "That might be easiest."

"I know Connor," Tess had surprised herself by saying. "I actually went out with him for a while. Years ago. Ancient history now, of course." She cringed, remembering the "ancient history" part. Why had she said that? So pointless and nerdy.

Cecilia had seemed quite impressed. "Well, he's currently St. Angela's most eligible bachelor. I won't tell Polly that you once dated him, or else she'll have to kill you." But then she'd given another one of those disconcerting, high-pitched giggles and said she was very sorry, but she had to go and lie down right that very second.

When Tess found him, Connor was in the process of carefully placing basketballs in the center of each colored segment of a giant, multicolored parachute laid out on the oval. He was wearing a very white T-shirt and black tracksuit pants, and looked less intimidating than the night before at the petrol station. The sunlight showed the deep lines around his eyes.

"Hello again." He smiled as she handed over the shoes. "For Liam, I assume."

You kissed me for the first time on a beach, thought Tess.

"No, these are for Polly Fitzpatrick. Cecilia is sick, and I offered to bring them up for her. Liam doesn't have any of his PE gear, actually. You won't put him in detention, will you?"

There it was again: that mildly flirtatious sound in her voice. Why was she flirting with him? Because she'd just remembered their first kiss? Because Felicity had never liked him? Because her marriage had fallen apart and she needed urgent proof that she was still pretty? Because she was angry? Because she was sad? Because why the hell not?

"I'll go gentle on him." Connor carefully placed Polly's little shoes off to the side of the parachute. "Does Liam like PE?"

"He likes running," said Tess. "Running for no reason at all."

She thought of Will. He was an obsessive football fan, and when Liam was a baby he'd talked so excitedly about how he'd take Liam along to matches, but so far Liam had zero interest in Will's passion. Tess knew he had to be bitterly disappointed, but he laughed it off, made the joke on himself. Once they'd been watching a match together on TV, and Tess had heard Liam say, "Let's go outside and *run*, Dad!" Will, who didn't really enjoy running at all, had sighed with comic resignation, and next thing the TV was off and they were running in circles around the backyard.

She would not let Felicity ruin that relationship. She would not have Liam one day making awkward conversation with a father who didn't really know him.

"Is he okay about starting at a new school?" asked Connor.

"I thought he was," said Tess. She fiddled with Cecilia's car keys. "But he was upset this morning. He misses his dad. His dad and I are . . . Anyway, I stupidly thought Liam was oblivious to some things that were going on."

"They surprise you with how smart they are," said Connor. He took another two basketballs from the cloth bag and held them against his chest. "Then next thing they surprise you with how stupid they are. But if it makes you feel better, this is a lovely school. I've never taught at such a caring school. It comes from the school principal. She's a nutcase, but the children come first."

"It must be a very different world from accounting." Tess watched the bright primary colors of the parachute gently rippling in the breeze.

"Ha! You knew me when I was an accountant," said Connor. He gave her a friendly, tender smile, as if he was much fonder of her than he could possibly be after all this time. "I forgot that for some reason."

Clontarf Beach, thought Tess suddenly. *That's where you kissed me for the first time. It was a good first kiss.*

"It was all such a long time ago," she said. Her heart rate had picked up. "I can hardly remember so much."

I can hardly remember so much. It didn't even make sense.

"Really?" said Connor. He squatted down and placed one of the balls on the red segment of the parachute. As he straightened, he shot her a look. "I actually remember quite a lot."

What did he mean? That he remembered a lot about their relationship, or just that he remembered a lot about the nineties?

"I'd better go," she said. She met his eyes and looked away fast, as if she'd done something wildly inappropriate. "Get out of your way."

"All right." Connor bounced the basketball back and forth between his palms. "Still up for that coffee sometime?"

"Sure," said Tess. She smiled in his general direction. "Have fun parachuting, or whatever it is you're doing."

"Will do. And I promise I'll keep an eye on Liam."

She started to walk off, and as she did, she remembered how much Felicity liked watching football with Will. It was something they had in common. A shared interest. Tess would sit and read her book while they shouted together at the TV. She turned around. "Let's make it a drink," she said, and this time she did meet his eyes. It felt like physical contact. "I mean, instead of a coffee."

Connor shifted one of the balls on the parachute with the side of his foot. "How about tonight?"

TWENTY-EIGHT

Cecilia sat weeping on the floor of her pantry, her arms wrapped around her knees. She reached up for the roll of paper towels on the bottom shelf, ripped one off and blew her nose furiously.

She couldn't remember why she'd come into the pantry in the first place. Maybe she'd come in for no other reason than to calm her mind by looking at her Tupperware containers. The pleasing, purposeful geometry of their interlocking shapes. Their blue airtight lids keeping everything fresh and crisp. There were no rotting secrets in Cecilia's pantry.

She could smell a hint of sesame oil. She was always so careful to wipe the bottle of sesame oil, but still that faint scent lingered. Maybe she should throw it out, but John-Paul loved her sesame chicken.

Who cared what John-Paul liked? The marital scales would never be even again. She had the upper hand and the last word forever.

The doorbell rang and Cecilia gasped. *The police!* she thought.

But there was no reason for the police to turn up now, after all these years, just because Cecilia knew. *I hate you for this, John-Paul Fitzpatrick,* she thought as she got to her feet. Her neck ached. She took the bottle of sesame oil and tossed it into the rubbish bin on her way to the front door. It wasn't the police. It was John-Paul's mother. Cecilia blinked, disoriented.

"Were you in the bathroom?" said Virginia. "I was just thinking I might have to sit down on the step. My legs were getting all wobbly."

Virginia's specialty was making you feel just a little bad about anything she could. She had five sons and five daughters-in-law, and Cecilia was the only daughter-in-law who hadn't at one time been reduced to tears of rage and frustration by Virginia. It was due to Cecilia's unshakable confidence in her abilities as a wife, mother and housewife. *Bring it on, Virginia,* she sometimes thought to herself as Virginia's gaze swept over everything from John-Paul's crease-free shirts to Cecilia's dust-free skirting boards.

Virginia "dropped by" at Cecilia's every Wednesday after her tai chi class for a cup of tea and something freshly baked. "How do you stand it?" Cecilia's sisters-in-law moaned, but Cecilia didn't really mind all that much. It was like taking part in a weekly battle with an unspecified goal that Cecilia felt she generally won.

But not today. She didn't have the strength for it today.

"What's that smell?" said Virginia as she presented her cheek to be kissed. "Is it sesame oil?"

"Yes." Cecilia sniffed her hands. "Come and sit down. I'll put the kettle on."

"I'm really not fond of the smell of sesame," said Virginia. "It's very Asian, isn't it?" She settled herself down at the table and looked about the kitchen for grime or errors of judgment. "How was John-Paul last night? He called this morning. That was nice that he rushed back earlier than expected. The girls must be happy. They're all such *daddy's* girls, your three, aren't they? But I couldn't believe it when I heard he had to go straight back into the office this morning after flying back only last night! He must have terrible jet lag. The poor man."

John-Paul had wanted to stay home today. "I don't want to leave you alone to deal with this," he had said. "I won't go into the office at all. We can talk. We can keep talking."

Cecilia could think of nothing worse than more talking. She'd insisted that he go in to work, virtually pushing him out the door. She needed to be away from him. She needed to think. He'd been calling all morning, leaving frantic-sounding messages. Was he worried she was going to turn him in?

"John-Paul has a good work ethic," she told her mother-in-law as she made tea. *Imagine if you knew what your precious son did. Just imagine.*

She felt Virginia's eyes shrewdly assessing her. She was no fool, Virginia. That was the mistake Cecilia's sisters-in-law made. They underestimated the enemy.

"You don't look very well," said Virginia. "You're washed out. Probably exhausted, are you? You take on far too much. I hear you did a party last night. I was chatting to Marla Evans at tai chi and she said it was a great success. Everyone got tipsy, apparently. She mentioned that you drove Rachel Crowley home."

"Rachel is very nice," said Cecilia. She put Virginia's tea in front of her, along with a selection of baked treats. (Virginia's weakness. It helped give Cecilia the edge.) Could she talk about her without feeling nauseated? "I actually asked her to Polly's pirate party next weekend."

Which is just wonderful.

"Did you?" said Virginia. There was a pause. "Does John-Paul know that?"

"Yes," said Cecilia. "He does, actually." It was an odd question for Virginia to ask. She knew perfectly well that John-Paul didn't get involved in the planning of birthday parties. She put the milk back in the fridge and turned around to look at Virginia. "Why do you ask?"

Virginia helped herself to a piece of coconut slice. "He didn't mind?"

"Why should he mind?" Cecilia carefully pulled a chair out and sat down at the table. She felt like someone was pushing their thumb right through the center of her forehead, as if her head were made of dough. Her eyes met Virginia's. She had John-Paul's eyes. She'd been a beauty once, and had never forgiven one of her hapless daughters-in-law for not recognizing her in a photo hanging in the family room.

Virginia looked away first. "I just thought he might prefer not to have too many outsiders at his daughter's party." Her voice was off-key. She took a bite of coconut slice and chewed it awkwardly, as if she were only pretending to chew.

She knows. The thought dropped straight into Cecilia's head with a thud.

John-Paul said nobody knew. He was adamant that nobody knew.

They were silent for a few moments. Cecilia heard the refrigerator hum. She felt her heart thud. Virginia couldn't know, could she? She swallowed: a sudden involuntary gulp for air.

"I talked to Rachel about her daughter," said Cecilia. She sounded breathless. "About Janie. On the way home." She paused, took a breath to calm herself. Virginia had put down the coconut slice and was scrabbling for something in her handbag. "Do you remember much about . . . when it happened?"

"I remember it very well," said Virginia. She pulled a tissue from her bag and blew her nose. "The papers loved it. They had pages and pages of photos. They even showed a photo of the . . ." She crumpled the tissue in her hand and cleared her throat. "The rosary beads. The crucifix was made of mother-of-pearl."

The rosary beads. John-Paul had said that his mother had lent him her rosary beads because he had an exam that day. She must have recognized them and never said a word, never asked the question so she'd never need to hear the answer, but she knew. She absolutely knew. Cecilia felt a clammy, shivery sensation creeping up her legs, like the start of the flu.

"But that was all such a very long time ago," said Virginia.

"Yes. Although it must be so distressing for Rachel," said Cecilia. "Not knowing. Not knowing what happened."

Their eyes locked across the table. This time Virginia didn't look away. Cecilia could see tiny particles of orange face powder embedded in the drawstring of wrinkles around Virginia's mouth. Outside the house she could hear the soft midweek sounds of her neighborhood: the chatter of cockatoos, the twitter of sparrows, the far-off buzz of someone's leaf blower, a slam of a car door.

"Although it wouldn't really change anything, would it? It wouldn't bring Janie back." Virginia patted Cecilia's arm. "You've got enough on your mind without worrying about that. Your family comes first. Your husband and your daughters. They come first."

"Yes, of course," began Cecilia, and stopped abruptly. The message was loud and clear. The taint of evil was all through her house. It smelled like sesame oil.

Virginia smiled sweetly and picked up the coconut slice again between her fingertips. "I don't need to tell you this, do I? You're a mother. You'd do anything for your children, just like I'd do anything for mine."

TWENTY-NINE

The school day was nearly over, and Rachel was busy typing up the school newsletter, her fingers moving rapidly over the keyboard. "Sushi is now available in the cafeteria. Healthy and yummy! More volunteers are needed to cover library books. Don't forget the *Eggscellent* Easter Hat Parade tomorrow! Connor Whitby has been charged with the murder of Rachel Crowley's daughter. Hooray! Our warmest wishes to Rachel. Applications now open for the position of PE Teacher."

Her little finger hit the Delete key. *Delete. Delete.*

Her mobile phone buzzed and vibrated on the desk next to her computer, and she snatched it up.

"Mrs. Crowley, it's Rodney Bellach."

"Rodney," said Rachel. "Do you have good news for me?"

"Well. Not . . . Well, I just wanted to let you know that I've given the tape to a good mate at the Homicide Squad," said Rodney. He sounded stilted, as if he'd carefully scripted his remarks before he picked up the phone. "So it's absolutely in the right hands."

"That's good," said Rachel. "That's a start! They'll reopen the case!"

"Well, Mrs. Crowley, the thing is, Janie's case isn't closed," said Rodney. "It's still open. When the coroner returns an open finding—as they did with Janie, as you know—well, it stays open. So what I'm saying is the boys will take a look at the tape. They'll certainly look at it."

"And they'll interview Connor again," said Rachel. She pressed the phone hard against her ear.

"I guess that's a possibility," said Rodney. "But please don't get your hopes up too high, Mrs. Crowley. Please don't."

The disappointment felt personal, as if she were being told she'd failed some test. She wasn't good enough. She'd failed to help her daughter. She'd failed her again.

"But look, that's just my opinion. The new guys are younger and smarter than me. Someone from the Homicide Squad will call you this week and let you know what they think."

As she put down the phone and returned to the computer, Rachel's eyes blurred. She realized she'd had a warm sense of anticipation all day, as if finding the tape was going to set into motion a series of events that would lead to something wonderful, almost as if she'd thought that the tape was going to bring Janie back. An infantile part of her mind had never accepted that this could truly happen, that your daughter could be murdered. Surely one day some respectable authority figure would take charge and put it right. Maybe God was the reasonable, respectable figure she'd always assumed was going to step in. Could she really have been that deluded? Even subconsciously?

God didn't care. God couldn't care less. God gave Connor Whitby free will, and Connor used that free will to strangle Janie.

Rachel pushed her chair back from her desk and looked out the window at the school yard. She had a bird's-eye view from up here and could see everything that was going on. It was nearly school pickup time. Parents were scattered about the place: little groups of mums deep in conversation, the occasional father lurking in the background, checking his e-mail on his mobile phone. She watched one of the fathers quickly step aside for someone in a wheelchair. It was Lucy O'Leary. Her daughter, Tess, was pushing the chair. As Rachel watched, Tess bent down to hear something that her mother said, then threw back her head and laughed. There was something quietly subversive about those two.

You could become friends with your grown-up daughter in a way that didn't seem possible with your grown-up son. That was what Connor took away from Rachel: all the future relationships she could have had with Janie.

I am not the first mother to lose a child, Rachel kept telling herself that first year. *I am not the first. I will not be the last.*

It made no difference, of course.

The buzzer went for the end of the school day, and seconds later the children tumbled out of their classrooms. There was that familiar afternoon babble of childish voices:

laughing, shouting, crying. Rachel saw Lucy O'Leary's grandson run to his mother and grandmother. He nearly tripped because he was using both hands to awkwardly carry a giant cardboard construction covered in aluminum foil. Tess bent down next to her mother's wheelchair, and all three of them examined whatever it was—a spaceship, perhaps? No doubt it was Trudy McDuff's doing. Forget the syllabus. If Trudy decided Year 1 was making spaceships that day, so it would be. Lauren and Rob were going to end up staying in New York. Jacob would have an American accent. He'd eat pancakes for breakfast. Rachel would never see him run out of his school carrying something made out of cardboard and aluminum foil. The police wouldn't do anything with the videotape. They'd put it on file. They probably didn't even have a VCR to watch it on.

Rachel turned back to her computer screen and let her hands splay limply on the keys. She'd been waiting twenty-eight years for something that was never going to happen.

THIRTY

It had been a mistake suggesting a drink. What was she thinking? The bar was crowded with young, beautiful drunk people. Tess kept staring at them. They all looked like high school students to her, who should have been at home studying, not out on a school night, shrieking and squawking. Connor had found them a table, which was lucky, but it was right next to a row of flashing, beeping poker machines and it was clear from the panicked concentration on Connor's face each time she spoke that he was having difficulty hearing what she was saying. Tess sipped a glass of not especially good wine and felt her head begin to ache. Her legs were sore after that long walk up the hill from Cecilia's place. She did that one body combat class with Felicity on Tuesday nights, but she couldn't seem to manage to fit in any other time for exercise between work and school and all of Liam's activities. She remembered suddenly that she'd just paid one hundred and ninety dollars for a martial arts course that Liam was meant to have started in Melbourne *today*. Shit, shit, shit.

What was she doing here, anyway? She'd forgotten how bad Sydney's bars were compared to Melbourne's. That's why there wasn't anyone over thirty in this place. If you lived on the North Shore you had to do your drinking at home and be tucked up in bed by ten o'clock.

She missed Melbourne. She missed Will. She missed Felicity. She missed her life.

Connor leaned forward. "Liam has pretty good hand-eye coordination," he shouted. For God's sake, was this a parent-teacher conference now?

When Tess had picked Liam up from school this afternoon, he'd seemed elated and hadn't mentioned anything about Will or Felicity. Instead, he'd talked nonstop about how he was definitely the best at the Easter egg hunt, and how he'd shared some of his eggs with Polly Fitzpatrick, who was going to have this amazing pirate party and everyone in the class was invited, and how he'd done this really fun game with a parachute on the oval, and there was an Easter Hat Parade the next day, and their teacher was going to dress up like an Easter egg! Tess didn't know if it was just the novelty factor or the chocolate high that was making him so happy, but for now at least Liam was definitely not missing his old life.

"Did you wish Marcus was here too?" she'd asked him.

"Not really," answered Liam. "Marcus was pretty mean."

He'd refused help making his Easter hat and had made

his own weird and wonderful creation out of an old straw hat of Lucy's, incorporating fake flowers and a toy rabbit. Then he ate all his dinner, sang in the bath and was sound asleep by seven thirty. Whatever happened, he wasn't going back to that school in Melbourne.

"He gets it from his father," Tess said with a sigh. "The good hand-eye coordination." She took a big mouthful of the bad wine. Will would never take her anywhere like this. He knew all the best bars in Melbourne: tiny, stylish, soft-lit bars where he'd sit across the table from her and they'd talk. The conversation never faltered. They still made each other laugh. They went out every couple of months. Just the two of them. Saw a show or had dinner. Wasn't that what you were meant to do? To invest in your marriage with nice, regular "date nights"? (She couldn't stand that phrase.)

Felicity took care of Liam when they went out. They always had a drink with her when they got home and told her about their night. Sometimes, if it was too late, she stayed the night, and they all had breakfast together in the morning.

Yes, Felicity had been an integral part of date night.

Did she lie in the spare bedroom wishing she were in Tess's place? Had Tess's behavior been unwittingly, yet unspeakably, cruel to Felicity?

"What's that?" Connor leaned forward, squinting at her.

"He gets it—"

"Booya!" There was an explosion of noise around one of the poker machines.

"You bitch, you total bitch!" One of the pretty young

girls ("skanky," Felicity would have described her) slapped her friend's back while a torrent of coins cascaded from the machine.

"Booya, booya, booya!" A broad-chested young boy pummeling his chest like a gorilla lurched sideways against Tess.

"Watch it, mate," said Connor.

"Man, I'm so sorry! We just won—" The boy turned around, and his face lit up. "Mr. *Whitby*! Hey, guys, this is my primary school PE teacher! He was, like, the best PE teacher *ever*." He stuck out his hand and Connor stood and shook it, shooting a rueful look at Tess.

"How the hell *are* you, Mr. Whitby?" The boy shoved his hands in his jeans pockets and shook his head as he looked at Connor, seemingly overcome with a sort of paternal emotion.

"I'm good, Daniel," said Connor. "How are you?"

The boy was suddenly struck by an astonishing thought. "You know what? I'm going to buy you a drink, Mr. Whitby. It would be my fucking pleasure. Seriously. Excuse my language. I may be intoxicated. What are you drinking, Mr. Whitby?"

"You know what, Daniel, that would have been great, but we were actually just leaving."

Connor held out his hand to Tess and she automatically picked up her bag, got to her feet and took it, as naturally as if they'd been in a relationship for years.

"Is this *Mrs*. Whitby?" The boy looked Tess up and down, entranced. He turned to Connor and gave him a big sly wink and a thumbs-up. He turned to Tess. "Mrs.

Whitby, your husband is a legend. An absolute legend. He taught me, like, long jump, and *hockey*, and cricket, and, and, like, every sport in the fucking universe, and you know, I look athletic, I know, and I am, but it might surprise you to know that I'm not that coordinated, but Mr. Whitby, he—"

"Gotta go, Daniel." Connor clapped the boy on the shoulder. "It was good seeing you."

"Oh, likewise, man. Likewise."

Connor led Tess out of the bar and into the wonderfully quiet night air.

"Sorry," he said. "I was just losing my mind in there. I think I'm going deaf. And then a drunk ex-student offering to buy me drinks . . . Geez. So, it looks like I'm still holding your hand."

"It looks like you are."

What are you doing, Tess? But she didn't let go. If Will could fall in love with Felicity, if Felicity could fall in love with Will, she could spend a few moments holding hands with an ex-boyfriend. Why not?

"I remember that I always loved your hands," said Connor. He cleared his throat. "I guess that's bordering on inappropriate."

"Oh, well," said Tess.

He moved his thumb so gently across her knuckle, it was almost imperceptible.

She had forgotten this: the way your senses exploded and your pulse raced, as if you were properly awake after a long sleep. She had forgotten the thrill, the desire, the melting sensation. It just wasn't possible after ten years of marriage. Everyone knew that. It was part of the deal. She'd accepted the deal. It had never been a problem. She hadn't even known she'd missed it. If she ever thought about it, it felt childish, silly—"sparks flying"—whatever, who cares, she had a child to care for, a business to run. But, my God, she'd forgotten the power of it. How nothing else felt important. This was what Will had been experiencing with Felicity while Tess was busy with mundane married life.

Connor increased the pressure of his thumb just fractionally, and Tess felt a shot of desire.

Maybe the only reason Tess had never cheated on Will was that she'd never had the opportunity. Actually, she'd never cheated on any of her boyfriends. Her sexual history was unimpeachable. She'd never had a one-night stand with an inappropriate boy, never drunkenly kissed someone else's boyfriend, never woken up with a single regret. She'd always done the right thing. Why? For what? Who cared?

Tess kept her eyes on Connor's thumb and watched, hypnotized and astonished, as it ever so gently grazed her knuckle.

———

June 1987, Berlin: U.S. president Ronald Reagan spoke in West Berlin, saying, "General Secretary Gorbachev, if you seek peace, if you seek prosperity for the Soviet Union and Eastern Europe, if you seek liberalization: Come here to this gate! Mr. Gorbachev, open this gate! Mr. Gorbachev, tear down this wall!"

In Sydney, Andrew and Lucy O'Leary spoke quietly and with brutal honesty across their kitchen table, while their ten-

year-old daughter slept upstairs. "It's not that I can't forgive you," said Andrew. "It's that I don't care. I don't even care."

"I only did it to make you look at me," said Lucy.

But Andrew's eyes were already looking past her, at the door.

THIRTY-ONE

How come we're not having lamb?" asked Polly. "We always have a lamb roast when Daddy comes home." She poked her fork discontentedly at the piece of overcooked fish on her plate.

"Why did you cook fish for dinner?" said Isabel to Cecilia. "Dad hates fish."

"I don't *hate* fish," said John-Paul.

"You do so," said Esther.

"Well, okay, it's not my favorite," said John-Paul. "But this is actually very nice."

"Um, it's not actually very nice." Polly put down her fork and sighed.

"Polly Fitzpatrick, where are your manners?" said John-Paul. "Your mother went to all the trouble of cooking this—"

"Don't." Cecilia held up her hand.

There was silence around the table for a moment as

everyone waited for her to say something else. She put down her fork and had a large mouthful of her wine.

"I thought you gave up wine for Lent," said Isabel.

"Changed my mind," said Cecilia.

"You can't just *change your mind*!" Polly was scandalized.

"Did everybody have a good day today?" asked John-Paul.

"This house smells of sesame oil," said Esther, sniffing.

"Yeah, I thought we were having sesame chicken," said Isabel.

"Fish is brain food," said John-Paul. "It makes us smart."

"So why aren't Eskimos, like, the smartest people in the world?" said Esther.

"Maybe they are," said John-Paul.

"This fish tastes really *bad*," said Polly.

"Has an Eskimo ever won the Nobel Prize?" asked Esther.

"It does taste a bit funny, Mum," said Isabel.

Cecilia stood up and began clearing their full plates away. Her daughters looked stunned. "You can all have toast."

"It's fine!" protested John-Paul, holding on to the edge of his plate with his fingertips. "I was quite enjoying it."

Cecilia pulled his plate away. "No, you weren't." She avoided his eyes. She hadn't made eye contact with him since he'd come home. If she behaved normally, if she let life just continue on, wasn't she condoning it? Accepting it? Betraying Rachel Crowley's daughter?

Except wasn't that exactly what she'd already decided to do? To do nothing? So what difference did it make if she was cold toward John-Paul? Did she really think that made a difference?

Don't worry, Rachel, I'm being so mean to your daughter's murderer. No lamb roast for him! No sirree!

Her glass was empty again. Gosh. That went down fast. She took the bottle of wine from the fridge and refilled it to the very brim.

—

Tess and Connor lay on their backs, breathing raggedly.

"Well," said Connor finally.

"Well indeed," said Tess.

"We seem to be in the hallway," said Connor.

"We do seem to be."

"I was trying to get us to the living room at least," said Connor.

"It seems like a very nice hallway," said Tess. "Not that I can see all that much."

They were in Connor's dark apartment, lying on the hallway floor. She could feel a thin rug beneath her back, and possibly floorboards. The apartment smelled pleasantly of garlic and laundry powder.

She'd followed him home in her mother's car. He kissed her at the security door to the building, then he'd kissed her again in the stairwell, and for quite a long time at the front door, and then once he got the key in the door, they were suddenly doing that crazy, tear-each-other's-clothes-off, banging-into-walls thing that you never do once you're in a long-term relationship because it seems too theatrical and not really worth the bother anyway, especially if there's something good on TV.

"I'd better get a condom," Connor had said in her ear at a crucial point in the proceedings, and Tess said, "I'm on the pill. You seem disease-free, so, just, please, oh, *God*, please, just go right ahead."

"Rightio," he said, and did just that.

Now Tess readjusted her clothes and waited to feel ashamed. She was a married woman. She was not in love with this man. The only reason she was here was because her husband had fallen in love with someone else. Just a few days earlier this scenario would have been laughable, inconceivable. She should be filled with self-loathing. She should feel seedy and slutty and sinful, but actually what she felt right now was . . . cheerful. Really cheerful. Almost absurdly cheerful, in fact. She thought of Will and Felicity and their sad, earnest faces just before she threw cold coffee at them. She recalled that Felicity had been wearing a new white silk blouse. That coffee stain would never come out.

Her eyes adjusted, but Connor was still just a shadowy silhouette lying next to her. She could feel the warmth of his body all along her right side. He was bigger, stronger and in much better shape than Will. She thought of Will's short, stocky, hairy body—so familiar and dear, the body of a family member, although always sexy to her. She had thought Will was the last bullet point in her sexual history. She had thought she wouldn't sleep with anyone else for the rest of her life. She remembered the morning after she

and Will were engaged, when that thought had first occurred to her. The glorious sense of relief. No more new,
unfamiliar bodies. No more awkward conversations about
contraception. Just Will. He was all she needed, all she
wanted.

And now here she was, lying in an ex-boyfriend's hallway.

"Life sure can surprise you," her grandmother used to
say, mostly about quite unsurprising developments such as
a bad cold, the price of bananas and so on.

"Why did we break up?" she asked Connor.

"You and Felicity decided to move to Melbourne," said
Connor. "And you never asked if I wanted to go too. So I
thought, *Right. Looks like I just got dumped*."

Tess winced. "Was I horrible? It sounds like I was horrible."

"You broke my heart," said Connor pitifully.

"Really?"

"Possibly," said Connor. "Either you did, or this other
girl I dated for a while around the same time called Teresa.
I always get the two of you mixed up."

Tess pushed her elbow into his side.

"You were a good memory," said Connor in a more
serious voice. "I was happy to see you again the other day."

"Me too," said Tess. "I was happy to see you."

"Liar. You looked horrified."

"I was surprised." She changed the subject. "Do you
still have a water bed?"

"Sadly, the water bed didn't make it into the new mil-
lennium," said Connor. "I think it made Teresa seasick."

"Stop talking about Teresa," said Tess.

"All right. Do you want to move somewhere more comfortable?"

"I'm okay."

They lay in companionable silence for a few moments, and then Tess said, "Um. What are you doing?"

"Just seeing if I still know my way around the place."

"That's a bit, I don't know, rude? Sexist? Oh. Oh, well."

"Do you like that, Teresa? Wait, what was your name again?"

"Stop talking, please."

THIRTY-TWO

Cecilia sat on the couch next to Esther, watching YouTube videos of the cold, clear November night in 1989 when the Berlin Wall came down. She was becoming obsessed with the Wall herself. After John-Paul's mother had left, she'd stayed sitting at the kitchen table, reading one of Esther's books until it was time to pick the girls up from school. There were so many things she should have been doing—Tupperware deliveries, preparations for Easter Sunday, the pirate party—but reading about the Wall was a good way of pretending she wasn't thinking about what she was really thinking about.

Esther was drinking warm milk. Cecilia was drinking her third—or fourth?—glass of sauvignon blanc. John-Paul was listening to Polly do her reading. Isabel sat at the computer in the family room downloading music onto her iPod. Their house was a cozy lamp-lit bubble of domesticity. Cecilia sniffed. The scent of sesame oil seemed to have pervaded the whole house now.

"Look, Mum." Esther elbowed her.

"I'm watching," said Cecilia.

Cecilia's memories of the news footage she'd seen back in 1989 were rowdier than this. She remembered crowds of people dancing on top of the wall, fists punching the air. Wasn't David Hasselhoff singing at some point? But there was a strange, eerie quietness to the clips Esther had found. The people walking out from East Berlin seemed quietly stunned, exhilarated but calm, filing out in such an orderly fashion. (They were Germans after all. Cecilia's sort of people.) Men and women with eighties hairstyles drank champagne straight from the bottle, tipping their heads back and smiling at the cameras. They hooted and hugged and wept, they tooted the horns of their cars, but they all seemed so well-behaved, so very *nice* about it. Even the people slamming sledgehammers against the wall seemed to do so with controlled jubilation, not vicious fury. Cecilia watched a woman of about her own age dance in circles with a bearded man in a leather jacket.

"Why are you crying, Mum?" asked Esther.

"Because they're so happy," said Cecilia.

Because they endured this unacceptable thing. Because that woman probably thought, like so many people had, that the Wall would eventually come down, but not in their lifetimes, and that she would never see this day, and yet she had, and now she was dancing.

"It's weird how you always cry about happy things," said Esther.

"I know," said Cecilia.

Happy endings always made her cry. It was the relief.

"Would you like a cup of tea?" John-Paul stood up from the dining room table, while Polly put away her book. He looked at Cecilia anxiously. All evening she'd been aware of his timid, solicitous glances. It was driving her crazy.

"No," said Cecilia sharply, avoiding his eyes. She felt the perplexed gaze of her daughters. "I do not want a cup of tea."

THIRTY-THREE

remember Felicity," said Connor. "She was funny. Quick-witted. A bit scary."

They'd moved to Connor's bed. It was an ordinary queen-size mattress with plain white Egyptian cotton sheets. (She'd forgotten that: how he loved good sheets, like in a hotel.) Connor had heated up some leftover pasta he'd made the night before and they were eating it in bed.

"We could be civilized and sit at the table," Connor had offered. "I could make a salad. Put out place mats."

"Let's just stay here," said Tess. "I might remember to feel awkward about this."

"Good point," said Connor.

The pasta was very good. Tess ate hungrily. She felt that ravenous sensation she used to feel when Liam was a baby and she'd been up all night breast-feeding.

Except instead of a night innocently suckling her son, she'd just had two very boisterous, highly satisfying sexual encounters with a man who was not her husband. She should have lost her appetite, not regained it.

"So she and your husband are having an affair," said Connor.

"No," said Tess. "They just fell in love. It's all very pure and romantic."

"That's horrible."

"I know," said Tess. "I only found out on Monday, and here I am." She waved her fork around the room, and at herself and her own state of undress. (She was wearing nothing but a T-shirt of Connor's, which he'd taken from a drawer and handed her, without comment, before he went off to make the pasta. It smelled very clean.)

"Eating pasta," finished Connor.

"Eating excellent pasta," agreed Tess.

"Wasn't Felicity quite a . . ." Connor searched for the right word. "How can I put this without sounding . . . Wasn't she quite a sturdy girl?"

"She was morbidly obese," said Tess. "It is relevant, because this year she lost forty kilos and became extremely beautiful."

"Ah," said Connor. He paused. "So what do you think is going to happen?"

"I have no idea," said Tess. "Last week I thought my marriage was good. As good as a marriage can be. And then they made this announcement. I was in shock. I'm still in shock. But then again, look at me, within three days. Actually *two* days. I'm with an ex-boyfriend . . . eating pasta."

"Things just happen sometimes," said Connor. "Don't worry about it."

Tess finished the pasta and ran her finger around the bowl. "Why are you single? You can cook, and you can do other things"—she gestured vaguely at the bed—"very well."

"I've been pining for you all these years." He was straight-faced.

"No you haven't," said Tess. She frowned. "That is, you haven't, have you?"

Connor took her empty bowl and placed it inside his own bowl. He put them both on the bedside table. Then he lay back against his pillow.

"I did actually pine for you for a while," he admitted.

Tess's cheerful feeling began to slip. "I'm sorry, I had no idea—"

"Tess," interrupted Connor. "Relax. It was a long time ago, and we didn't even go out for that long. It was the age difference. I was a boring accountant, and you were young and ready for adventures. But I did sometimes wonder what could have been."

Tess had never wondered. Not even once. She'd barely thought of Connor.

"So you were never married?" asked Tess.

"I lived with a woman for a number of years. A lawyer. We were both on track for partnership, and marriage, I guess. But then my sister died, and everything changed. I was looking after Ben. I lost interest in accounting around the same time that Antonia lost interest in me. And then I decided to do my degree in physical education."

"But I still don't get it. There's a single dad at Liam's school in Melbourne, and the women *swarm* all over him. It's embarrassing to watch."

"Well," said Connor. "I never said they didn't swarm."

"So you've just been playing the field all these years," said Tess.

"Sort of," said Connor. He went to speak and then stopped.

"What?"

"No. Nothing."

"Go on."

"I was just going to admit something."

"Something juicy?" guessed Tess. "Don't worry, I've become very open-minded ever since my husband suggested I live in the same house as him and his lover."

Connor gave her a sympathetic smile. "Not that juicy. I was going to say that I've been seeing a therapist for the last year. I've been—how do people put it—'working through' some stuff."

"Oh," said Tess carefully.

"You've got that careful look on your face," said Connor. "I'm not crazy. I just had a few issues I needed to . . . cover off."

"Serious issues?" asked Tess, not sure if she really wanted to know. This was meant to be an interlude from all the serious stuff, a crazy little escapade. She was letting off steam. (She was aware of herself already trying to define it, to package it in a way that made it acceptable. Perhaps the self-loathing was about to hit.)

"When we were going out," said Connor, "did I ever

tell you that I was the last person to see Janie Crowley alive? Rachel Crowley's daughter?"

"I know who she is," said Tess. "I'm pretty sure you never told me that."

"Actually, I know I wouldn't have told you," said Connor. "Because I never talked about it. Hardly anyone knew. Except for the police. And Janie's mother. I sometimes think that Rachel Crowley thinks I did it. She looks at me in this intense way."

Tess felt a chill. He murdered Janie Crowley, and now he was about to murder Tess, and then everyone would know that she'd used her husband's romantic predicament as an excuse to jump into bed with an ex-boyfriend.

"And did you?" she asked.

Connor looked up, startled. "Tess! No! Of course not!"

"Sorry." Tess relaxed back against her pillow. Of course he didn't.

"Geez, I can't believe you would think—"

"Sorry, sorry, so was Janie a friend? Girlfriend?"

"I wanted her to be my girlfriend," said Connor. "I was pretty hung up on her. She'd come over to my place after school and we'd make out on my bed, and then I'd get all serious and say, 'Okay, this means you're my girlfriend, right?' I was desperate for commitment. I wanted everything signed and sealed. My first girlfriend. Only she'd hem and haw and was all, 'Well, I don't know, I'm still deciding.' I was losing my mind over it all, but then, on the morning of the day she died, she told me that she'd decided. I got the job, so to speak. I was stoked. Thought I'd won the lottery."

"Connor," said Tess. "I'm so sorry."

"She came over that afternoon, and we ate fish and chips in my room and kissed for about thirty hours or so, and then I saw her off at the railway station, and next morning I heard on the radio that a girl had been found strangled at Wattle Valley Park."

"My God," said Tess uselessly. She felt out of her depth, similar to the way she'd felt when she and her mother were sitting across the desk from Rachel Crowley the other day, filling in Liam's enrollment forms, and she kept thinking to herself, *Her daughter was murdered*. She couldn't link Connor's experience to anything even remotely similar in her own life, and so she didn't seem able to converse with him in any normal way.

Finally she said, "I can't believe you never told me any of this when we were together."

Although, really, why should he have? They only went out for six months. Even married couples didn't share everything. She never told Will about her self-diagnosis of social anxiety. The very thought of telling him made her toes curl with embarrassment.

"I lived with Antonia for years before I finally told her," said Connor. "She was offended. We seemed to talk more about how offended she was than what actually happened. I think that's probably why we broke up in the end. My failure to *share*."

"I guess girls like to know stuff," said Tess.

"There was one part of the story that I never told Antonia," said Connor. "I never told anyone until I told this therapist woman. My 'shrink.'"

He stopped.

"You don't have to tell me," said Tess nobly.

"Okay, let's talk about something else," said Connor.
Tess swatted at him.

"My mother lied for me," said Connor.

"What do you mean?"

"You never had the pleasure of meeting my mother, did
you? She died before we met."

Another memory of her time with Connor floated to
the surface of Tess's mind. She'd asked him about his parents, and he said, "My father left when I was a baby. My
mother died when I was twenty-one. My mother was a
drunk. That's all I have to say about her."

"Mother issues," said Felicity, when Tess repeated this
conversation. "Run a mile."

"My mother and her boyfriend told the police that I was
home with them from five o'clock that night. I wasn't. I
was home alone. They were out getting drunk somewhere.
It was tricky, because I never asked them to lie for me. My
mother just did it. Automatically. And she *loved* it. Lying
to the police. When the police left, she winked at me as she
held the front door for them. Winked! As if she and I were
in cahoots. It made me feel as if I had done it. But what
could I do? I couldn't tell them that Mum had just lied for
me, because that would make it look as if she thought I
had something to hide."

"But you're not saying she actually thought you did it,"
said Tess.

"After the police left she held up a finger like this and
said, 'Connor, baby, I don't want to know,' as if she were
in a movie, and I said, 'Mum, *I didn't do it*,' and she just

said, 'Pour me a wine, darl.' After that, whenever she got nasty-drunk, she'd say, 'You owe me, you ungrateful little bastard.' It gave me a permanent sense of guilt. Almost as if I *had* done it." He shuddered. "Anyway. I grew up. Mum died. I never talked about Janie. I never even let myself think about her. And then my sister died, and I got Ben, and straight after my teaching degree, I got offered the job at St. Angela's. I didn't even know that Janie's mother was working there until my second day of work."

"That must be strange."

"We don't run into each other that often. I did try to talk to her about Janie in the very beginning, but she made it clear she wasn't interested in being chatty. So. I started telling you all this because you asked why I was single. My very expensive *therapist* thinks I've been subconsciously sabotaging these relationships because I don't think I deserve to be happy, because of my guilt over what I didn't actually do to Janie." He smiled shamefacedly at Tess. "So there you go. I'm extremely *damaged*. Not your run-of-the-mill accountant turned PE teacher."

Tess took his hand in hers and laced her fingers through his. She looked at their interlocked hands, struck by the fact that she was holding another man's hand, even though just moments before she'd been doing things that most people would have considered far more intimate.

"I'm sorry," she said.

"Why are you sorry?"

"I'm sorry about Janie. And your sister dying." She paused. "And I'm really sorry I broke up with you like I did."

Connor made the sign of the cross over her head. "I

absolve you of your sins. My child. Or whatever it is they say. It's been a while since my last confession."

"Mine too," said Tess. "I think you were meant to give me penance before you absolved me."

"Ooh, I can think of penance, baby."

Tess giggled. She unlaced her fingers. "I should go."

"I've scared you off with all my 'issues,'" said Connor.

"No you haven't. I just don't want my mother getting worried. She'll wait up for me and she won't expect me to be that late." She remembered suddenly why they were meant to be getting together. "Hey, we never talked about your nephew. You wanted to ask me some career advice or something?"

Connor smiled. "Ben's already got a job. I just wanted an excuse to see you."

"Really?" Tess felt a flare of happiness. Was there anything better than to be wanted? Was that all anyone really needed?

"Yep."

They looked at each other.

"Connor—" she began.

"Don't worry," he said. "I don't have any expectations. I know exactly what this is."

"What is it?" asked Tess with interest.

He paused. "I'm not sure. I'll check with my therapist and let you know."

Tess snorted.

"I really should go," she said again.

But it was another half hour before she finally put her clothes back on.

THIRTY-FOUR

Cecilia went into the en suite bathroom where John-Paul was brushing his teeth. She picked up her toothbrush, squeezed toothpaste on it and began to brush, her eyes not meeting his in the mirror.

She stopped brushing.

"Your mother knows," she said.

John-Paul bent down to the basin and spat. "What do you mean?" He straightened, patted his mouth with the hand towel and shoved it back on the handrail in such a haphazard way that you'd think he was deliberately trying to avoid keeping it straight.

"She knows," said Cecilia again.

He spun around. "You *told* her?"

"No, I—"

"Why would you do that?" The color had drained from his face. He didn't seem angry so much as utterly baffled and astonished.

"John-Paul, I didn't tell her. I mentioned Rachel was

coming to Polly's party, and she asked how you felt about that. I could just tell."

John-Paul's shoulders relaxed. "You must have imagined it."

He sounded so certain. Whenever they had an argument about a point of fact, he was always so utterly confident that he had it right and she had it wrong. He never even entertained the possibility that he might be mistaken. It drove her bananas. She struggled with an irresistible urge to slap him across the face.

This was the problem. All his flaws seemed more significant now. It was one thing for a gentle, law-abiding husband and father to have failings: a certain inflexibility that manifested itself just when it was most inconvenient, those occasional (also inconvenient) black moods, the frustrating implacability during arguments, the untidiness, the constant losing of his possessions. They all seemed innocuous enough, common even, but now that these faults belonged to a murderer, they seemed to matter so much more, to define him. His good qualities now seemed irrelevant and probably fraudulent: a cover identity. How could she ever look at him again in the same way? How could she still love him? She didn't know him. She'd been in love with an optical illusion. The blue eyes that had looked at her with tenderness and passion and laughter were the same eyes that Janie had seen in those terrifying few moments before she died. Those lovely strong hands that had cupped the soft, fragile heads of Cecilia's baby daughters were the same hands that he held around Janie's neck.

"Your mother knows," she told him. "She recognized

her rosary beads in the newspaper picture. She basically told me that a mother would do anything for her children, and that I should do the same for my children and pretend it never happened. It was creepy. *Your mother is creepy.*"

It felt like crossing a line to say that. John-Paul did not take criticism of his mother kindly. Cecilia normally tried to respect that, even though it annoyed her.

John-Paul sank down on the side of the bath, knocking the hand towel off the rail with his knees in the process. "You really think she knows?"

"Yes," said Cecilia. "So there you go. Mummy's golden boy really can get away with murder."

John-Paul blinked, and Cecilia almost considered apologizing, before she remembered that this wasn't an ordinary disagreement about packing the dishwasher. The rules had changed. She could be just as nasty and snarky as she pleased.

She picked up her toothbrush again and began to clean her teeth with harsh, mechanical movements. Her dentist had told her just last week that she was brushing too hard, wearing away the enamel. "Hold your toothbrush with your fingertips, like the bow of a violin," he'd said, demonstrating. Should she get another electric toothbrush? she'd wondered, and he said he wasn't a believer, except for the old and arthritic, but Cecilia said she liked the nice, clean feeling it gave her—and oh, it had all genuinely *mattered*, she had been completely involved in that conversation, a conversation about the maintenance of her teeth, back then, back in last week.

She rinsed and spat and put the toothbrush away and

picked up the towel that John-Paul had knocked onto the floor and put it back on the railing.

She glanced at John-Paul. He flinched.

"The way you look at me now," he said. "It's . . ." He stopped and took a shaky breath.

"What do you expect?" asked Cecilia, astounded.

"I'm so sorry," said John-Paul. "I'm so sorry for putting you through this. For making you part of it. I'm such an *idiot* for writing that letter. But I'm still me, Cecilia. I promise you. Please don't think I'm some evil monster. I was seventeen, Cecilia. I made one terrible, terrible mistake."

"Which you never paid for," said Cecilia.

"I know I didn't." He met her eyes unflinchingly. "I know that."

They stood in silence for a few moments.

"Shit!" Cecilia slammed the side of her hand to her head. "Fuck it."

"What is it?" John-Paul reeled back. She never swore. All these years there had been a Tupperware container of bad language sitting off to the side in her head, and now she'd opened it and all those crisp, crunchy words were lovely and fresh, ready to be used.

"Easter hats," she said. "Polly and Esther need fucking Easter hats for tomorrow morning."

THIRTY-FIVE

Janie very nearly changed her mind when she looked out the window of the train and saw John-Paul waiting for her on the platform. He was reading a book, his long legs stuck out in front of him, and when he saw the train pulling in he stood up and stuck the book in his back pocket, and with a sudden, almost furtive movement he smoothed down his hair with the palm of his hand. He was *gorgeous*.

She got up from her seat, holding the pole for balance, and slung her bag over her shoulder.

It was funny—the way he'd smoothed down his hair then, it had been an insecure gesture for a boy like John-Paul. You'd almost think that he was nervous about seeing Janie, that he was worried about impressing her.

"Next stop Asquith, then all stations to Berowra."

The train clattered to a stop.

So this was it. She was going to tell him that she couldn't see him anymore. She could have stood him up, just left him waiting for her, but she wasn't that type of girl. She could have telephoned him, but that didn't seem right either. And besides, they'd never called each other. Both of them had mothers who liked to lurk about when they were on the phone.

If only she could have e-mailed or texted him, that would have solved everything, but mobile phones and the Internet were still in the future.

She'd been thinking that this would be unpleasant and that maybe John-Paul's pride would be hurt, and that he might say something nasty like, "I never liked you that much anyway," but until she saw him smoothing down his hair, it hadn't occurred to her that she might be about to hurt him. She felt sick at the thought.

She got off the train, and John-Paul lifted a hand and smiled. Janie waved back, and as she walked down the railway platform toward him, it came to her with a tiny, bitter shock of self-revelation that it wasn't that she liked Connor more than John-Paul, it was that she liked John-Paul far too much. It was a strain being with someone so good-looking and smart and funny and nice. She was dazzled by John-Paul. Connor was dazzled by her. And it was more fun doing the dazzling. Girls were meant to do the dazzling.

John-Paul's interest felt like a trick. A practical joke. Because surely he knew that she wasn't good enough for him. She kept waiting for a gaggle of teenage girls to appear, laughing and jeering and pointing. "You didn't *really* think he'd be interested in *you*?" That's why she hadn't even told any of her friends about his existence. They knew about Connor, of course, but not John-Paul Fitzpatrick. They wouldn't believe that a Fitzpatrick boy would be interested in her, and she didn't really believe it either.

She thought of Connor's big goofy smile on the bus when she told him he was now officially her boyfriend. He was her friend. Losing her virginity to Connor would be sweet and funny and tender. She couldn't possibly take her clothes off in front of John-Paul. The very thought made her heart stop. Besides, he deserved a girl with a body that matched his. He might laugh if he saw her strange, skinny white body. He might notice that her arms were disproportionately long for her body. He might sneer or snort at her concave chest.

"Hi," she said to him.

"Hi," he said, and she caught her breath, because as their eyes met she got that feeling again, that sensation of there being something huge between them, something that she couldn't quite define, something that her twenty-year-old self might have called passion and her thirty-year-old self might have more cynically called chemistry. A tiny speck of her, a tiny speck of the woman she could have become, thought, *Come on, Janie, you're being a coward. You like him more than Connor. Choose him. This could be big. This could be huge. This could be love.*

But her heart was hammering so hard it was horrible, scary and painful; she could barely breathe. There was a painful crushing sensation in the center of her chest, as if someone were trying to flatten her. She just wanted to feel normal again.

"I need to talk to you about something," she said, and she made her voice cold and hard, sealing her fate like an envelope.

THIRTY-SIX

Cecilia! Did you get my messages? I've been trying to call!"

"Cecilia, you were right about those raffle tickets."

"Cecilia! You weren't at Zumba yesterday!"

"Cecilia! My sister-in-law wants to book a party with you."

"Cecilia, is there any chance I could drop off Harriet just for an hour after ballet next week?"

"Cecilia!"

"Cecilia!"

"Cecilia!"

It was the Easter Hat Parade, and the St. Angela's mothers were out in force, dressed up in honor of Easter and the first truly autumnal day of the new season. Soft, pretty scarves looped necks, skinny jeans encased skinny and not-so-skinny thighs, spike-heeled boots tapped across the playground. It had been a humid summer, and the crispness of the breeze and the anticipation of a four-day, chocolate-filled weekend had put everyone in good moods. The mothers, sitting in a big double-rowed circle of blue fold-up chairs around the quadrangle, were frisky and high-spirited.

The older children who weren't taking part in the Easter Hat Parade had been brought outside of the classrooms to watch, and they hung over the balconies with dangling, nonchalant arms and mature, tolerant expressions to indicate that of course they were now far too old for this sort of thing, but weren't the little ones cute?

Cecilia looked for Isabel on the Year 6 balcony and saw her standing in between her best friends, Marie and Laura. The three girls had their arms slung around one another, indicating that their tumultuous three-way relationship was currently at a high point, where nobody was being ganged up on by the other two and their love for one another was pure and intense. It was lucky that there was no school for the next four days, because their intense times were inevitably followed by tears and betrayal and long, exhausting stories of she said, she texted, she posted and I said, I texted, I posted.

One of the mothers discreetly passed around a basket of Belgian chocolate balls, and there were moans of drunken, sensual pleasure.

I'm a murderer's wife, thought Cecilia while Belgian chocolate melted in her mouth. *I'm an accessory to murder,* she thought as she set up playdates and pickups and Tupperware parties, as she scheduled and organized and set things in action. *I'm Cecilia Fitzpatrick, and my husband is a murderer, and look at me, talking and chatting and laughing and hugging my kids. You'd never know.*

This was how it could be done. This was how you lived with a terrible secret. You just did it. You pretended everything was fine. You ignored the deep, cramplike pain in your stomach. You somehow anesthetized yourself so that nothing felt that bad, but nothing felt that good either. Yesterday, she'd thrown up in the gutter and cried in the pantry, but this morning she'd woken up at six a.m. and made two lasagnas to go into the freezer, ready for Easter Sunday, and ironed a basket of clothes, and sent three e-mails inquiring about tennis lessons for Polly, and answered fourteen e-mails about various school matters, and put in her Tupperware order from the party the other night, and put a load of laundry on the line, all before the girls and John-Paul were out of bed. She was back on her skates, twirling expertly about the slippery surface of her life.

"Give me strength. What is that woman *wearing*?" said someone as the school principal appeared in the center of the yard. Trudy was wearing long rabbit ears and a fluffy tail pinned to her bottom. She looked like a motherly Playboy Bunny.

Trudy hopped to the microphone in the middle of the yard with her hands curled up in front of her like paws. The mothers rocked with fond laughter. The kids on the balconies cheered.

"Ladies and jelly beans, girls and boys!" One of Trudy's rabbit ears slipped down over her face, and she brushed it away. "Welcome to the St. Angela's Easter Hat Parade!"

"I love her to death," said Mahalia, who was sitting on Cecilia's right. "But it really is hard to believe she runs a school."

"*Trudy* doesn't run the school," said Laura Marks, who was sitting on her other side. "Rachel Crowley runs the school. Together with the lovely lady on your left." Laura Marks leaned in front of Mahalia and waggled her fingers at Cecilia.

"Now, now, you know that's not true." Cecilia smiled roguishly. She felt like a demented parody of herself. Surely she was overdoing it? Everything she did felt exaggerated and clownlike, but nobody seemed to notice.

The music began, pounding out through the state-of-the-art sound system that Cecilia's highly successful art show raffle had paid for last year.

The conversation rippled around Cecilia.

"Who chose the playlist? It's quite good."

"I know. Makes me feel like dancing."

"Yes, but is anybody listening to the lyrics? Do you know what this song is *about*?"

"Best not to."

"My kids know them all anyway."

The kindergarten class was first to file out, led by their teacher, the rather beautiful busty brunette Miss Parker, who had made the best use of her natural assets by dressing up in a fairy princess dress that was two sizes too small for her, and was dancing along to the music in a manner perhaps not quite befitting a kindergarten teacher. The tiny kindergarteners followed her, grinning proudly and self-consciously, carefully balancing the familiar Easter hat creations on their heads.

The mothers congratulated one another on their children's Easter hats.

"Ooh, *Sandra*, creative!"

"Found it on the Internet. Took me ten minutes."

"Sure it did."

"Seriously, I swear!"

"Does Miss Parker realize this is an Easter Hat Parade, not a nightclub?"

"Do fairy princesses normally show that much cleavage?"

"And by the way, does a tiara really count as an Easter hat?"

"I think she's trying to get Mr. Whitby's attention, poor girl. He's not even looking."

Cecilia adored events just like these. An Easter Hat Parade summed up everything she loved about her life. The sweetness and simplicity of it all. The sense of community. But today the parade seemed pointless, the children snotty-nosed, the mothers bitchy. She stifled a yawn and smelled sesame oil on her fingers. It was the scent of her life now. Another yawn overtook her. She and John-Paul had been up late making the girls' Easter hats in strained silence.

Polly's class made their appearance, led by the adorable Mrs. Jeffers, who had gone to a tremendous lot of trouble to dress as a gigantic shiny-pink-foil-wrapped Easter egg. Polly was right behind her teacher, strutting along like a supermodel, wearing her Easter hat tilted rakishly over one eye. John-Paul had made her a bird's nest out of sticks from the garden and filled it with Easter eggs. A fluffy yellow toy chick emerged from one of the eggs as if it were hatching.

"My *Lord*, Cecilia, you're an absolute freak." Erica Edgecliff, who was sitting in the row in front of Cecilia, turned around. "Polly's hat looks amazing."

"John-Paul made it." Cecilia waved at Polly.

"Seriously? That man is a catch," said Erica.

"He's a catch, all right," agreed Cecilia, hearing a weird lilt in her voice. She sensed Mahalia turning to look at her.

Erica said, "You know me. Forgot all about the Easter Hat Parade until this morning at breakfast, then I stuck an old egg carton on Emily's head and said, 'That'll have to do, kid.'" Erica took pride in her slapdash approach to mothering. "There she is! Em! Whoo-hoo!" Erica half stood, waving frantically, and then subsided. "Did you see that death stare she sent me? She knows it's the worst hat in the parade. Someone give me another one of those chocolate balls before I shoot myself."

"Are you feeling okay, Cecilia?" Mahalia leaned closer so that Cecilia could smell the familiar musky scent of her perfume.

Cecilia glanced over at Mahalia and looked quickly away.

Oh, no, don't you dare be nice to me, Mahalia, with your smooth skin and the whites of your eyes so pearly white. Cecilia had noticed tiny splotches of red in the whites of her eyes this morning. Wasn't that what happened when someone tried to strangle you? The capillaries in your eyes burst? How did she know that? She shuddered.

"You're shivering!" said Mahalia. "That breeze *is* icy."

"I'm fine," said Cecilia. The longing to confide in some-one, anyone, felt like a raging thirst. She cleared her throat. "Might be coming down with a cold."

"Here, put this around you." Mahalia pulled the scarf from around her neck and settled it over Cecilia's shoulders. It was a beautiful scarf, and Mahalia's beautiful scent drifted all around her.

"No, no," said Cecilia ineffectually.

She knew exactly what Mahalia would say if she told her. *It's very simple, Cecilia; tell your husband he has twenty-four hours to confess or you're going to the police yourself. Yes, you love your husband, and yes, your children will suffer as a result, but none of that is the point. It's very simple.* Mahalia was very fond of the word "simple."

"Horseradish and garlic," said Mahalia. "Simple."

"What? Oh, yes. For my cold. Absolutely. I've got some at home."

Cecilia caught sight of Tess Curtis sitting on the other side of the quadrangle, with her mother's wheelchair parked at the end of the row of chairs. Cecilia reminded herself that she must thank Tess for everything she'd done yester-day and apologize for not even offering to call a taxi. The poor girl must have walked all the way back up the hill to her mother's house. Also, she'd promised to make a lasagna for Lucy! Maybe she wasn't skating so expertly over life as she thought. She was making lots of tiny mistakes that would eventually cause everything to fall apart.

Was it only Tuesday that Cecilia had been driving Polly to ballet and longing for some huge wave of emotion to sweep her off her feet? The Cecilia of two days ago had been a fool. She'd wanted the wave of clean, beautiful emotion you felt when you saw a heart-swelling movie scene with a magnificent sound track. She hadn't wanted anything that would actually hurt.

"Oops, oops, it's going to go!" said Erica. A boy from the other Year 1 class was wearing an actual birdcage on his head. The little boy, Luke Lehaney (Mary Lehaney's son; Mary often overstepped the mark, and had once made the mistake of running against Cecilia for the role of P&F president), was walking along like the Leaning Tower of Pisa, with his whole body tipped to one side in a desperate attempt to keep the birdcage upright. Suddenly, inevitably, it slipped from his head, crashing to the ground and causing Bonnie Emerson to trip and lose her own hat. Bonnie's face crumpled, while Luke stared in bewildered horror at his mangled birdcage.

I want my mother too, thought Cecilia as she watched Luke's and Bonnie's mothers rush to retrieve their children. *I want my mother to comfort me, to tell me that everything is going to be okay and that there's no need to cry.*

Normally her mother would be at the Easter Hat Parade, snapping blurry, headless photos of the girls with her disposable camera, but this year she'd gone to Sam's parade at the exclusive preschool. There was going to be champagne for the grown-ups. "Isn't that the silliest thing you've ever heard?" she said to Cecilia. "Champagne at an Easter Hat Parade! That's where Bridget's fees are going." Cecilia's mother loved champagne. She'd be having the time of her life hobnobbing with a better class of grandmas than you got at St. Angela's. She'd always made a point of pretending not to be interested in money, because she was, in fact, very interested in it.

What would her mother say if she told her about John-Paul? Cecilia had noticed that as her mother got older, whenever she heard anything distressing, or just too complicated, there was a disturbing moment where her face became dull and slack, like a stroke victim's, as if her mind had momentarily closed down from the shock.

"John-Paul committed a crime," Cecilia would begin.

"Oh, darling, I'm sure he didn't," her mother would interrupt.

What would Cecilia's dad say? He had high blood pressure. It might actually kill him. She imagined the flash of terror that would cross his soft, wrinkled face before he recovered himself, frowning ferociously while he tried to slot the information into the right box in his mind. "What does John-Paul think?" he'd probably say automatically, because the older her parents got, the more they seemed to rely on John-Paul's opinion.

Her parents couldn't cope without John-Paul in their lives, and they would never cope with the knowledge of what he'd done and the shame in the community.

You had to weigh up the greater good. Life wasn't black-and-white. Confessing wouldn't bring back Janie. It would achieve nothing. It would hurt Cecilia's daughters. It would hurt Cecilia's parents. It would hurt John-Paul for a mistake (she hurried over that soft little word "mistake," knowing that it wasn't right, that there had to be a bigger word for what John-Paul had done) he'd made when he was seventeen years old.

"There's Esther!" Cecilia startled as Mahalia nudged her. She'd forgotten where she was. She looked up in time to see Esther nod coolly at her as she walked by, her hat stuck right on the back of her head, the sleeves of her cardigan pulled right down to cover her hands like mittens. She was wearing an old straw hat of Cecilia's with fake flowers and tiny chocolate eggs stuck all over it. Not Cecilia's best effort, but it didn't matter, because Esther thought Easter hat parades were a waste of her valuable time. "What does the Easter Hat Parade actually teach us?" she'd said to Cecilia that morning in the car.

"Nothing about the Berlin Wall," said Isabel smartly.

Cecilia had pretended not to notice that Isabel was wearing mascara this morning. She'd done a good job of it. Only one tiny blue-black smudge just below her perfect eyebrow.

She looked up to the Year 6 balcony and saw Isabel and her friends dancing to the music.

If a nice young boy murdered Isabel and got away with it, and if that boy felt very remorseful and turned out to be a fine, upstanding member of the community, a good father and a good son-in-law, Cecilia would still want him jailed. Executed. She'd want to kill him with her own bare hands.

The world tipped.

She heard Mahalia say from a very long way away, "Cecilia?"

THIRTY-SEVEN

Tess shifted in her seat and felt a pleasurable ache in her groin. *Just how superficial are you? What happened to your supposedly broken heart? So, what, it takes you TWO DAYS to get over a marriage breakup?* She was sitting at the St. Angela's Easter Hat Parade thinking about sex with one of the three parade judges, who was right now on the other side of the school yard, wearing a giant pink baby's hat tied under his chin and doing the chicken dance with a group of Year 6 boys.

"Isn't this lovely?" said her mother beside her. "This is just lovely. I wish . . ."

She stopped, and Tess turned to study her.

"You wish what?"

Lucy looked guilty. "I was just wishing that the circumstances were happier—that you and Will had decided to move to Sydney and that Liam was at St. Angela's and I could always come to his Easter hat parades. Sorry."

"You don't need to be sorry," said Tess. "I wish that too."

Did she wish that?

She turned her gaze back to Connor. The Year 6 boys were now laughing with such crazy abandon at something Connor had just said that Tess suspected fart jokes must be involved.

"How was last night?" said Lucy. "I forgot to ask. Actually, I didn't even hear you come in."

"It was nice," said Tess. "Nice to catch up." She had a sudden image of Connor flipping her over and saying in her ear, "I seem to remember this used to work quite well for us."

Even before, when he was a young boring accountant with a nerdy hairstyle, before he got the killer body and the motorbike, he'd been good in bed. Tess had been too young to appreciate it. She thought all sex was as good as that. She shifted again in her seat. She was probably about to get a bladder infection. That would teach her. The last time she'd had sex three times in a row—and, not so coincidentally, the last time she'd had a bladder infection—was when she and Will had first started dating.

Thinking about Will and their early days together should hurt, but it didn't, not right now at least. She felt light-headed with wicked, delicious sexual satisfaction and . . . what else? Vengeance, that was it. Vengeance is mine, sayeth Tess. Will and Felicity thought she was up here in Sydney nursing a broken heart, when in fact she was having excellent sex with her ex-boyfriend. Sex with an ex. It left married sex for dead. So *there*, Will.

"Tess, my darling?" said her mother.

"Mmmm?"

Her mother lowered her voice. "Did something happen last night between you and Connor?"

"Of course not," said Tess.

"I couldn't possibly," she'd said to Connor that third time, and he'd said, "I bet you could," and she'd murmured, "I couldn't, I couldn't, I couldn't," over and over, until it was established that she could.

"Tess O'Leary!" said her mother, just as a Year 1 boy's birdcage hat slipped from his head. Tess met her mother's eyes and laughed.

"Oh, darling." Lucy grabbed hold of her arm. "Good on you. The man is an absolute *hottie*."

THIRTY-EIGHT

"Connor Whitby is in a very good mood today," said Samantha Green. "I wonder if that means he's finally got himself a woman?"

Samantha Green, whose oldest child was in Year 6, did part-time bookkeeping work at the school. She charged by the hour, and Rachel suspected that St. Angela's would still pay for the time that Samantha was spending outside the office next to Rachel, watching the Easter Hat Parade. That was the problem with having one of the mums work for the school. Rachel couldn't very well say, "Will you be billing us for this, Samantha?" When she was only there for three hours, it really didn't seem necessary for her to stop work to watch the parade. It wasn't like her daughter was taking part. Of course, Rachel didn't have a child taking part either, and *she'd* stopped work to watch. Rachel sighed. She was feeling itchy and bitchy.

Rachel looked at Connor sitting at the judges' table, wearing his pink baby's hat. There was something perverted about a grown man dressed up as a baby. He was making some of the older boys laugh. She thought of his malevolent face on that video. The murderous way he'd looked at Janie. Yes, it *had* been murderous. The police should arrange for a psychologist to look at the tape. Or some expert in face reading. There were experts in everything these days.

"I know the kids love him," said Samantha, who liked to wring a topic dry before she moved on to the next one. "And he's always perfectly nice to us parents, but I always sensed something *not quite right* about that Connor Whitby. You know what I mean? Ooh! Look at Cecilia Fitzpatrick's little girl! She's just beautiful, isn't she? I won-der where she gets it from. Anyway, my friend Janet Tyler went out with Connor a few times after her divorce, and she said Connor was like a depressed person pretending not to be depressed. He dumped Janet in the end."

"Hmmm," said Rachel.

"My mother remembers his mother," said Samantha. "She was an alcoholic. Neglected the kids. Father ran off when Connor was a baby. Gosh, who's that with the bird-cage on his head? The poor kid is going to lose it in a mo-ment."

Rachel could vaguely remember Trish Whitby turning up at church sometimes. The children were grubby. Trish scolded them too loudly during the service, and people turned to stare.

"I mean, a childhood like that has to have an impact on your personality, doesn't it? Connor's, I mean."

"Yes," said Rachel so adamantly that Samantha looked startled.

"But he's in a good mood today," said Samantha, getting herself back on track. "I saw him in the car park earlier and I asked him how he was, and he said, 'Top of the world!' Now, that sounds to me like a man in love. Or at least a man who got lucky last night. I must tell Janet. Well, I probably shouldn't tell poor Janet. I think she quite liked him, even if he was strange. Oops! There goes the birdcage. Saw that coming."

Top of the world.

Tomorrow was the anniversary of Janie's death, and Connor Whitby was feeling on top of the world.

THIRTY-NINE

Cecilia decided to leave the parade early. She needed to be moving. When she sat still, she thought, and thinking was dangerous. Polly and Esther had both seen that she was there, and there was only the judging to follow, and Cecilia's daughters weren't going to win, because she'd told the judges last week (a thousand years ago) to make sure they didn't. If the Fitzpatrick girls won too many accolades, people got resentful and suspected favoritism, making them less likely to volunteer their time to the school.

She wouldn't run again for P&F president after this year. The thought struck her with absolute certainty as she bent down to pick up her bag from next to her chair. It was a relief to know one thing for sure about her future. No matter what happened next, even if nothing happened, she would not run again. It simply wasn't possible. She was no longer Cecilia Fitzpatrick. She'd ceased to exist the moment she read that letter.

"I'm going," she said to Mahalia.

"Yes, go home and rest," said Mahalia. "I thought you were about to faint away for a moment there. Keep the scarf. It looks lovely on you."

As she walked through the quadrangle, Cecilia saw Rachel Crowley watching the parade with Samantha Green on the balcony outside the school office. They were looking the other way. If she was quick about it, she'd get by without their seeing her.

"Cecilia!" cried Samantha.

"Hi!" cried Cecilia, and let loose a string of violent profanities in her head. She walked toward them with her keys held prominently in her hand, so that they'd know she was in a rush, and stood as far away from them as could be considered polite.

"Just the person I wanted to see!" called Samantha, leaning over the balcony. "I thought you said I'd get that Tupperware order before Easter? It's just that we're having a picnic on Sunday, assuming this lovely weather holds! And so I thought—"

"Of course," interrupted Cecilia. She stepped closer to them. Was this where she would normally stand? She'd completely forgotten about the deliveries she'd intended to do yesterday. "I'm so sorry. This week has been . . . tricky. I'll come by this afternoon after I pick up the girls."

"Wonderful," said Samantha. "I mean, you just got me so excited about that picnic set, I can't wait to get my hands on it! Have you ever been to one of Cecilia's Tupperware parties, Rachel? The woman could sell ice to Eskimos!"

"I actually went to one of Cecilia's parties the night

before last," said Rachel. She smiled at Cecilia. "I had no idea how much Tupperware was missing from my life!"

"Actually, I can drop your order off at the same time if you like?" said Cecilia.

"Really?" said Rachel. "I wasn't expecting it so soon. Don't you have to order it in?"

"I keep extra stock of everything," said Cecilia. "Just in case." *Why was she doing this?*

"Special overnight service for VIPs, eh?" said Samantha, who would no doubt be storing this information away for future reference.

"It's no trouble," said Cecilia. She went to meet Rachel's eyes and found it was impossible, even from a safe distance like this. She was such a nice woman. Would it be easier to justify if she weren't nice? She pretended to be distracted by Mahalia's scarf slipping from her shoulders.

"If it suits, that would be lovely," said Rachel. "I'm taking a pavlova to my daughter-in-law's place for lunch on Easter Sunday, so one of those storage thingummies would come in handy."

Cecilia was pretty sure that Rachel hadn't ordered anything that would be suitable for transporting a pavlova. She'd find something and give it to her for free. *It's okay, John-Paul, I gave your murder victim's mother some free Tupperware, so everything is all squared up.*

"I'll see you both this afternoon!" she cried, waving her keys so energetically that they flew from her hand.

"Oops-a-daisy!" called Samantha.

FORTY

iam won second prize in the Easter Hat Parade.

"Look what happens when you sleep with one of the judges," whispered Lucy.

"Mum, shhh!" hissed Tess, glancing over her shoulder for scandalized eavesdroppers. Besides, she didn't want to think about Liam in relation to Connor. That confused everything. Liam and Connor belonged in separate boxes, on separate shelves, far, far away from each other.

She watched her small son shuffle across the playground to accept his gold trophy cup filled with tiny Easter eggs. He turned to look for Tess and Lucy with a thrilled, self-conscious smile.

Tess couldn't wait to tell Will about it when they saw him this afternoon.

Wait. They wouldn't be seeing him.

Well. They would ring him. Tess would speak in that cheerful, cold voice women used when they spoke to their ex-husbands in front of their children. Her own mother had used it. "Liam has good news!" she'd tell Will, and then she'd pass Liam the phone and say, "Tell your dad what happened today!" He wouldn't be Daddy anymore. He'd be "your dad." Tess knew the drill. Oh God, did she know the drill.

It was hopeless to try to save the marriage for Liam's sake. How ridiculous she'd been. Deluded. Thinking that it was simply a matter of strategy. From now on Tess would behave with dignity. She'd act as if this were an ordinary, run-of-the-mill, amicable separation that had been in the cards for years. Maybe it *had* been in the cards.

Because otherwise how could she have behaved the way she had last night? And how could Will have fallen in love with Felicity? There *had* to be problems in their marriage; problems that had been completely invisible to her, problems she still couldn't name, but problems nonetheless.

What was the last thing she and Will had argued about? It would be useful right now to focus on the most negative aspects of her marriage. She forced her mind back. Their last argument was over Liam. The Marcus problem. "Maybe we should consider changing schools," Will had said, after Liam had seemed particularly down about some incident in the school yard, and Tess had snapped, "That seems a bit dramatic!" They'd had a heated disagreement while they were packing the dishwasher after dinner. Tess had slammed a few drawers. Will had made an ostentatious point of re-packing the frying pan she'd just put in the dishwasher. She'd ended up saying something silly like, "So are you saying I don't care about Liam as much as you do?" and Will had yelled, "Don't be an idiot!"

But they'd made up just a few hours later. They'd both apologized, and there had been no lingering bitterness. Will wasn't a sulker. He was actually pretty good at negotiating a compromise. And he rarely lost his sense of humor or ability to laugh at himself. "Did you see the way I repacked your frying pan?" he said. "That was a masterstroke, eh? Put you in your place, didn't it?"

For a moment Tess felt her strange, inappropriate happiness teeter. It was as though she were balanced on a narrow crevice surrounded by chasms of grief. One wrong thought and down she'd tumble.

Do not think about Will. Think about Connor. Think about sex. Think wicked, earthy, primal thoughts. Think about the orgasm that ripped through your body last night, cleansing your mind.

She watched Liam walk back to his class. He stood next to the one child that Tess knew: Polly Fitzpatrick, Cecilia's youngest daughter, who was shockingly beautiful and seemed positively Amazonian next to spindly little Liam. Polly gave Liam a high five, and Liam looked almost incandescent with happiness.

Damn it. Will had been right too. Liam *did* need to change schools.

Tess's eyes filled with tears, and she felt suddenly ashamed.

Why the shame? she wondered as she pulled a tissue from her bag and blew her nose. Because her husband had fallen in love with someone else? Because she wasn't lovable enough, or sexy enough, or something enough, to keep her child's father satisfied?

Or was she actually ashamed about last night? Because she'd found a selfish way to make the pain disappear? Because right now she was longing to see Connor again—or, more specifically, to sleep with him again, to have his tongue, his body, his hands obliterate the memory of Will and Felicity sitting on either side of her, telling her their horrible secret? She remembered the feel of the length of her spine being flattened against the floorboards in Connor's hallway. He was fucking her, but really he was fucking them.

There was a burst of sweet feminine laughter from the row of pretty, chatty mothers sitting alongside Tess. Mothers who had proper married sex with their husbands in the marital bed. Mothers who were not thinking the word "fuck" while they were watching their children's Easter Hat Parade. Tess was ashamed because she wasn't behaving like a selfless mother should.

Or perhaps she was ashamed because deep down she wasn't that ashamed at all.

"Thank you so much for joining us today, mums and dads, grandmas and grandpas! That concludes our Easter Hat Parade!" said the school principal into the microphone. She tilted her head to one side and waggled her fingers around an imaginary carrot stick like Bugs Bunny. "That's all, folks!"

"What do you want to do this afternoon?" asked Lucy as everyone applauded and laughed.

"There are a few things I need at the shops." Tess stood

and stretched and looked down at her mother in her wheel-chair. She could feel Connor's eyes on her from the opposite side of the yard.

New lingerie was what she needed. Extremely expensive lingerie that her husband would never see.

FORTY-ONE

Happy Easter!" said Trudy to Rachel as they packed up the office that afternoon. "Here, I got you a little something."

"Oh!" said Rachel, touched and annoyed, because it hadn't occurred to her to get a present for Trudy. There had never been any exchanging of gifts with the old school principal. They'd rarely exchanged pleasantries.

Trudy handed over a charming little basket filled with a variety of delicious and expensive-looking eggs. It looked like the sort of thing Rachel's daughter-in-law would buy her: expensive, elegant and just right.

"Thank you so much, Trudy. I didn't . . ." She waved her hand to indicate her absence of a gift.

"No, no." Trudy waved back to indicate it wasn't necessary. She'd stayed in her bunny suit for the entire day and looked, Rachel thought, perfectly ridiculous. "I just want you to know how much I appreciate the work you do, Rachel. You carry this whole office, and you let me be . . .

me." She lifted one of her rabbit ears out of her eyes and gave Rachel a level look. "I've had some secretaries who found my working approach somewhat unusual."

I bet they did, thought Rachel.

"You make it all about the children," said Rachel. "That's who we're here for."

"Well, you have a lovely Easter break," said Trudy. "Enjoy some time with that scrumptious grandson of yours."

"I will," said Rachel. "Are you . . . going away?"

Trudy didn't have a husband or children or any interests that Rachel knew of outside of the school. There were never any phone calls of a personal nature. It was hard to imagine how she'd be spending the Easter break.

"Just gadding about," said Trudy. "I read a lot. Love a good whodunit! I pride myself on guessing who the murderer is—oh!"

Her face turned bright pink with distress.

"I quite like historical fiction myself," said Rachel quickly, avoiding her eye and pretending to be busily distracted with picking up her bag and coat and Easter basket.

"Ah." Trudy couldn't recover her equilibrium. Her eyes filled with tears.

The poor girl was only fifty, not that much older than what Janie would have been. Her kooky gray wispy hair made her look like an elderly toddler.

"It's fine, Trudy," said Rachel softly. "You didn't upset me. It's perfectly fine."

FORTY-TWO

Hi," Tess answered her phone. It was Connor. Her body responded instantly to his voice, like Pavlov's salivating dog.

"What are you doing?" he asked.

"I'm buying hot cross buns," said Tess. She'd picked up Liam from school and taken him up to the shops for a treat. Unlike yesterday, he seemed quiet and moody after school and not interested in talking about his Easter hat win. She was also buying a whole list of things for her mother, who had suddenly realized the shops would be closed the next day, for *one whole day*, and had gone into a panic about the state of her pantry.

"I love hot cross buns," said Connor.

"Me too."

"Really? We've got so much in common."

Tess laughed. She noticed Liam looking up at her curiously, and she turned slightly away from him so that he couldn't see her flushed face.

"Anyway," said Connor, "I wasn't calling for any particular reason. I just wanted to say that last night was really . . . nice." He coughed. "That's an understatement, actually."

Oh, God, thought Tess. She pressed the palm of her hand to her burning cheek.

"I know things are really complicated for you right now," continued Connor. "I don't have any, ah, expectations, I promise you. I'm not going to make your life more complicated. But I just wanted you to know that I'd love to see you again. Anytime."

"Mum?" Liam pulled on the edge of her cardigan. "Is that Dad?"

Tess shook her head.

"Who is it?" demanded Liam. His eyes were big and worried.

Tess pulled the phone away from her ear and put a finger to her lip. "It's a client." Liam lost interest immediately. He was used to conversations with clients.

Tess took a few steps away from the crowd of customers waiting to be served at the bakery.

"It's okay," said Connor. "Like I said, I really don't have any—"

"Are you free tonight?" interrupted Tess.

"God, yes."

She put her lips close to the phone, as if she were a secret agent. "I'll come over after Liam is asleep. I'll bring hot cross buns."

———

Rachel was walking toward her car when she saw her daughter's murderer.

He was talking on his mobile phone, swinging his motorbike helmet held loosely in his fingertips. As she got closer, he suddenly tipped back his head to the sun as if he'd just received unexpectedly wonderful news. The afternoon light glinted off his sunglasses. He snapped the phone shut and slid it in his jacket pocket, smiling to himself.

Rachel thought again of the video and remembered the expression on his face when he'd turned on Janie. She could see it so clearly. The face of a monster: leering, malicious, cruel.

And now look at him. Connor Whitby was very alive and very happy, and why wouldn't he be, because *he'd gotten away with it*. If the police did nothing, as it seemed likely, he would never pay for what he'd done.

As she got closer, Connor caught sight of Rachel and his smile vanished instantly, as if a light had been snapped off.

Guilty, thought Rachel. *Guilty. Guilty. Guilty.*

———

This came by overnight courier for you," said Lucy when Tess was home unpacking the groceries. "Looks like it's from your father. Fancy him managing to send something by *courier*."

Intrigued, Tess sat down at the kitchen table with her mother and unwrapped the small bubble-wrapped package. Inside was a flat square box.

"He hasn't sent you jewelry, has he?" asked her mother. She peered over to look.

"It's a compass," said Tess. It was a beautiful old-fashioned wooden compass. "It's like something Captain Cook would have used."

"How peculiar," said her mother with a sniff.

As Tess lifted up the compass she saw a small handwritten yellow Post-it note stuck to the bottom of the box.

"Dear Tess," she read. "This is probably a silly gift for a girl. I never did know the right thing to buy you. I was trying to think of something that would help when you're feeling lost. I remember feeling lost. It was bloody awful. But I always had you. Hope you find your way. Love, Dad."

Tess felt something rise within her chest.

"I guess it's quite pretty," said Lucy, taking the compass and turning it this way and that.

Tess imagined her father searching the shops for the right gift for his adult daughter. The expression of mild terror that would have crossed his leathery, lined face each time someone asked, "Can I help you?" Most of the shop assistants would have thought him rude, a grumpy, gruff old man who refused to meet their eye.

"Why did you and Dad split up?" Tess used to ask her mother, and Lucy would say airily, a little glint in her eye, "Oh, darling, we were just two very *different* people." She meant: Your father was different. (When Tess asked her father the same question, he'd shrug and cough and say, "You'll have to ask your mum about that one, love.")

It occurred to Tess that her father probably suffered from social anxiety too.

Before their divorce, her mother had been driven to distraction by his lack of interest in socializing. "But we *never* go *anywhere*!" she would say, full of frustration, when Tess's father once again refused to attend some event.

"Tess is a bit shy," her mother used to tell people in an audible whisper, her hand over her mouth. "Gets it from her father, I'm afraid." Tess had heard the cheerful disrespect in her mother's voice and had come to believe that any form of shyness was wrong—morally wrong, in fact. You *should* want to go to parties. You *should* want to be surrounded by people.

No wonder she felt so ashamed of her shyness, as if it were an embarrassing physical ailment that needed to be hidden at all costs.

She looked at her mother. "Why didn't you just go on your own?"

"What?" Lucy looked up from the compass. "Go where?"

"Nothing," said Tess. She held out her hand. "Give me back my compass. I love it."

———

Cecilia parked her car in front of Rachel Crowley's house and wondered why she was doing this to herself. She could have dropped Rachel's Tupperware order off at the school after Easter. The guests from Marla's party weren't promised delivery until after the break. It seemed she simultaneously wanted to seek Rachel out and avoid her at all costs.

Perhaps she wanted to see her because Rachel was the only person in the world with the right and the authority to speak out on Cecilia's current dilemma. "Dilemma" was too gentle a word. Too selfish a word. It implied that Cecilia's feelings actually mattered.

She lifted the plastic bag of Tupperware from the passenger seat and opened the car door. Perhaps the real reason she was here was because she knew Rachel had every reason in the world to hate her, and she couldn't bear the thought of anyone hating her. *I'm a child,* she thought as she knocked on the door. *A middle-aged, perimenopausal child.*

The door opened faster than Cecilia had expected. She was still preparing her face.

"Oh," said Rachel, and her face dropped. "Cecilia."

"I'm sorry," said Cecilia. *So very, very sorry.* "Are you expecting someone?"

"Not really," said Rachel. She recovered herself. "How are you? My Tupperware! How exciting. Thank you so much. Would you like to come in? Where are your girls?"

"They're at my mother's place," said Cecilia. "She felt bad because she missed their Easter Hat Parade today. So she's giving them afternoon tea. Anyway. That's neither here nor there! I won't come in, I'll just—"

"You sure? I've just put the kettle on."

Cecilia felt too weak to argue. She would do whatever Rachel wanted. Her legs could barely hold her up, they were trembling so badly. If Rachel shouted, "Confess!" she would confess. She almost longed for that.

She walked across the threshold with her heart in her mouth, as if she were in physical danger. The house was very similar to Cecilia's family home, like so many of the homes on the North Shore.

"Come into the kitchen," said Rachel. "I've got the heater on in there. It's getting chilly in the afternoon."

"*We* had that linoleum!" said Cecilia when she followed her into the kitchen.

"I'm sure it was the height of fashion all those years ago," said Rachel as she put tea bags into cups. "I'm not one of those renovating types, as you can see. Just can't get myself interested in tiles and carpets, paint colors and back-splashes. Here you go. Milk? Sugar? Help yourself."

"Is this Janie?" asked Cecilia. She'd stopped in front of the refrigerator. It was a relief to say Janie's name. Her presence was so gigantic in Cecilia's head. It felt like if she didn't say her name normally, it would suddenly burst out of her mouth in the middle of a sentence.

The photo on Rachel's fridge was casually held with a magnet advertising Pete the 24-Hour Plumber. It was a small, faded, off-center color photo of Janie and her younger brother holding cans of Coke and standing in front of a barbecue. They'd both turned around with blank, slack-mouthed expressions on their faces, as if the photographer had surprised them. It wasn't a particularly good photo. Somehow its very casualness made it seem all the more impossible that Janie was dead.

"Yes, that's Janie," said Rachel. "That photo was up on the fridge when she died, and I've never taken it down.

Silly, really. I've got much better ones of her. Have a seat. I've got these biscuits called macarons. Not macaroons, oh, no, if that's what you're thinking. Macarons. You probably know all about them. I'm not very sophisticated." Cecilia saw that she took pride in not being sophisticated. "Have one! They're really very good."

"Thank you," said Cecilia. She sat down and took a macaron. It tasted like nothing, like dust. She sipped her tea too fast and burnt her tongue.

"Thank you for dropping off the Tupperware," said Rachel. "I'm looking forward to using it. The thing is that tomorrow is the anniversary of Janie's death. Twenty-eight years."

It took Cecilia a moment to comprehend what Rachel had said. She couldn't work out the link between the Tupperware and the anniversary.

"I'm sorry," said Cecilia. She noticed with almost scientific interest that her hand was visibly trembling, and she carefully placed her teacup back in its saucer.

"No, I'm sorry," said Rachel. "I don't know why I told you that. I've just been thinking about her a lot today. Even more than usual. I sometimes wonder how often I would have thought about her if she'd lived. I don't think about poor Rob that often. I don't worry about him. You'd think after losing one child that I'd be worried about something happening to my other child. But I'm not particularly worried. Isn't that awful? I do worry about something happening to my grandson. To Jacob."

"I think that's natural," said Cecilia, and suddenly she

was overcome by her own breathtaking *audacity*. To be sitting here in this kitchen, delivering platitudes along with Tupperware.

"I do love my son," murmured Rachel into her mug. She shot Cecilia a shamefaced look over the rim. "I'd hate you to think I didn't care for him."

"Of course I don't think that!" Cecilia saw to her horror that Rachel had a triangle of blue macaron right in the center of her bottom lip. It was horribly undignified and made Rachel seem suddenly elderly, almost like a dementia patient.

"I just feel like he belongs to Lauren now. What's that old saying? 'A son is a son until he takes him a wife; a daughter is a daughter for all of her life.'"

"I've—heard that. I don't know if it's true."

Cecilia was in agony. She couldn't tell Rachel about the crumb on her lip. Not when she was talking about Janie.

Rachel lifted her teacup for another sip, and Cecilia tensed. Surely it would be gone now. Rachel lowered the cup. The crumb had moved off center and was even more obvious. She had to say something.

"I really don't know why I'm rambling on like this," said Rachel. "You're probably thinking I've lost the plot! I'm not myself, you see. When I came home from your Tupperware party the other night, I found something."

She licked her lips and the blue crumb vanished. Cecilia sagged with relief.

"Found something?" she repeated. She took a big mouthful of her tea. The faster she drank, the faster she could leave. It was very hot. The water must have been boiling when Rachel poured. Cecilia's mother made the tea too hot as well.

"Something that proves who killed Janie," said Rachel. "It's evidence. New evidence. I've given it to the police— Oh! Oh, dear, Cecilia, are you okay? Quickly! Come and run your hand under the tap."

FORTY-THREE

Tess tightened her arms around Connor's waist as his bike swooped and dipped around corners. The streetlights and shop fronts were blurry streaks of colored light in her peripheral vision. The wind roared in her ears. Each time they took off at a set of traffic lights, her stomach lurched thrillingly the way it did when she was in a plane taking off from the runway.

"Don't worry, I'm a safe, boring, middle-aged bike rider," Connor had told her as he adjusted her helmet for her. "I stay under the speed limit. Especially when I've got precious cargo." Then he'd dropped his head and gently banged his helmet against hers. Tess felt touched and cherished and also idiotic. She was too old, surely, for helmet-clinking and flirty little remarks like that. She was too married.

But perhaps not.

She tried to remember what she'd been doing the previous Thursday night, back home in Melbourne, back when she was still Will's wife and Felicity's cousin. She'd made apple muffins, she remembered. Liam liked them for his morning tea at school. And then she and Will had watched TV with their laptops on their knees. She'd caught up with some invoicing. He'd been working on the Cough Stop campaign. They'd read their books and gone to bed. Wait. No. Yes. Yes, they definitely did. They'd had sex. Quick and comforting and perfectly nice, like a muffin; nothing like sex in the hallway of Connor's apartment, of course. But that was marriage. Marriage was a warm apple muffin.

And all that ordinary Thursday night, Will had been thinking to himself: *I'm in love with Felicity. I don't want Tess. I want Felicity. I don't want this woman in my bed. I want someone else.*

The hurt spread instantaneously throughout her body like ice cracking. She squeezed her legs tighter around Connor's body and leaned forward as if she could press herself into him. When they got to the next set of lights, Connor put back his hand and caressed her thigh, giving her an instant jolt of sexual pleasure. It occurred to her that the pain she was feeling over Will and Felicity was intensifying every sensation, so that what felt good, like the swoop of the bike and Connor's hand on her thigh, felt even better. Last Thursday night she was leading a soft, muffled, pain-free little life. This Thursday night felt like adolescence: exquisitely painful and sharply beautiful.

But no matter how badly it hurt, she didn't want to be home in Melbourne, baking and watching television and doing invoices. She wanted to be right here, soaring along on this bike, her heart thumping, letting her know she was alive.

———

I t was after nine p.m., and Cecilia and John-Paul were in the backyard, sitting in the cabana next to the pool. This was the only place where they were safe from eavesdroppers. Their daughters had an extraordinary ability to hear things they weren't meant to hear. From where she sat, Cecilia could see them through the French doors, their faces illuminated by the flickering light of the television. It was a tradition that they were allowed to stay up as late as they wanted on the first night of a school holiday, eating popcorn and watching movies.

Cecilia turned her gaze away from the girls and looked at the shimmering blue of their kidney-shaped swimming pool with its powerful underwater light: the perfect symbol of suburban bliss. Except for that strange intermittent sound, like a baby choking, that was coming from the pool filter. She could hear it right now. Cecilia had asked John-Paul to look at it weeks before he went to Chicago, and he never got around to it, but he would have been furious if she'd arranged for some repair guy to come and fix it. It would have indicated lack of faith in his abilities. Of course, when he *did* finally look at it, he wouldn't be able to fix it, and she'd have to get the guy in anyway. It was frustrating. Why hadn't that been part of his stupid lifelong redemption program: *Do what my wife asks immediately so she doesn't feel like a nag.*

She longed to be out here having an ordinary argument with John-Paul about the damned pool filter. Even a really bad ordinary argument, where feelings were hurt, would be so much better than this permanent sense of dread. She could feel it everywhere: in her stomach, her chest, even her mouth had a horrible taste to it. What was it doing to her health?

She cleared her throat. "I need to tell you something." She was going to tell him what Rachel Crowley had said today about finding new evidence. How would he react? Would he be frightened? Would he *run*? Become an instant fugitive?

Rachel had never told her the exact nature of this evidence because she'd been distracted by Cecilia's spilling her tea, and Cecilia had been in such a state of panic, it hadn't occurred to her to ask. She *should* have asked, she realized now. It might have been useful to know. She wasn't doing too well in her new role as a criminal's wife.

Rachel couldn't possibly know exactly *whom* the evidence implicated, or she wouldn't have told Cecilia. Would she? It was so hard to think clearly.

"What's that?" asked John-Paul. He was sitting on the wooden bench opposite her, wearing jeans and a long-sleeved striped jersey the girls had bought him last Father's Day. He leaned forward, his hands hanging limply between his knees. There was something odd about his tone of voice. It was like the gentle, fiercely strained way he would have replied to one of the girls when he was in the early stages of a migraine and still hoping that it wasn't going to take hold.

"Have you got a migraine coming on?" she asked.

He shook his head. "I'm fine."

"Good. Listen, today when I was at the Easter Hat Parade, I saw—"

"Are *you* okay?"

"I'm fine," she said impatiently.

"You don't look fine. You look terrible. It's like I've made you sick." His voice trembled. "The only thing that ever mattered to me was making you and the girls happy, and now I've put you in this intolerable position."

"Yes," said Cecilia. She curled her fingers around the slats of the bench seat and watched her daughters as their faces simultaneously dissolved into laughter over something they'd seen on the television. "'Intolerable' is a pretty good word for it."

"All day at work, I was thinking, how can I fix this? How can I make it better for you?" He came over and sat next to her. She felt the welcoming warmth of his body next to hers. "Obviously I can't make it better. Not really. But I wanted to say this to you: If you want me to turn myself in, I will. I'm not going to ask you to carry this too, if you can't carry it."

He took her hand and squeezed it. "I'll do whatever you want me to do, Cecilia. If you want me to go straight to the police or to Rachel Crowley, then that's what I'll do. If you want me to leave, if you can't bear to live in the same house as me, then I'll leave. I'll tell the girls we're separating because . . . I don't know what I'll tell the girls, but I'd take the blame, obviously."

Cecilia could feel John-Paul's whole body shaking. His palm was sweaty over hers.

"So you're prepared to go to jail. What about your claustrophobia?" she asked.

"I'd just have to deal with it," he said. His palm got sweatier. "It's all in my head anyway. It's not real."

She flicked his hand away with a sudden feeling of revulsion and stood.

"So why didn't you put up with it before? Why didn't you turn yourself in before I even knew you?"

He lifted his palms and looked up at her with a contorted, pleading face. "I can't really answer that, Cecilia. I've tried to explain. I'm sorry—"

"And now you're saying I get to make the decision. It's nothing to do with you anymore. Now it's *my* responsibility whether Rachel gets closure or not!" She thought of the blue crumb on Rachel's mouth and shuddered.

"Not if you don't want it to be!" John-Paul was almost in tears now. "I was trying to make things easier for you."

"Can't you see that you're making it my problem?" cried Cecilia, but the rage was already fading, to be replaced by a great wave of despair. John-Paul's offer to confess made no difference. Not really. She was already accountable. The moment she opened that letter, she became accountable.

She sank back down on the bench on the opposite side of the cabana.

"I saw Rachel Crowley today," she said. "I dropped off her Tupperware. She said she had new evidence that implicates Janie's murderer."

John-Paul's head jerked up. "She couldn't have. There's nothing. There is no evidence."

"I'm just telling you what she said."

"Well then," said John-Paul. He swayed a little as if he was having a dizzy spell and briefly closed his eyes. He opened them again. "Maybe the decision will be made for us. For me."

Cecilia thought back to exactly what Rachel had said. Something like "I've found something that proves who killed Janie."

"This evidence she's found," said Cecilia suddenly. "It might actually implicate *someone else*."

"In that case, I'd have to turn myself in," said John-Paul flatly. "Obviously I would."

"Obviously," repeated Cecilia.

"It just seems unlikely," said John-Paul. He sounded exhausted. "Doesn't it? After all these years."

"It does," agreed Cecilia. She watched as he lifted his head and turned toward the back of the house to look at the girls. In the silence, the sound of the pool filter became loud. It didn't sound like a choking baby. It sounded like the wheezing breaths of something monstrous, like an ogre from a child's nightmare, creeping around their house.

"I'll look at that filter tomorrow," said John-Paul, his eyes fixed on his daughters.

Cecilia said nothing. She sat and breathed in time with the ogre.

FORTY-FOUR

his is sort of the ultimate second date," said Tess.
She and Connor were sitting on a low brick wall
overlooking Dee Why Beach, drinking hot chocolate in takeaway cups. The bike was parked behind them,
the chrome gleaming in the moonlight. The night was
cold, but Tess was warm in the big leather jacket Connor
had lent her. It smelled of aftershave. "Yeah, it normally
works like a charm," said Connor.

"Except you already scored with me on the first date,"
said Tess. "So you know, you don't need to waste all your
seductive charms."

She sounded odd, as if she were trying out someone
else's personality: one of those sassy, feisty girls. Actually
it was like she was trying to be Felicity and not doing a very
good job of it. The magical, heightened sensations she'd
felt on the bike seemed to have dissipated, and now she felt
awkward. It was too much. The moonlight, the bike, the

leather jacket and the hot chocolate. It was horribly romantic. She'd never been fond of classic romantic moments. They made her snicker.

Connor turned to look at her with a deadly serious expression. "So you're saying the other night was a first date." He had gray, serious eyes. Unlike Will, Connor didn't laugh a lot. It made his occasional deep chuckles all the more precious. *See*, quality, *not quantity, Will.*

"Oh, well," said Tess. Did he think they were *dating*? "I don't know. I mean—"

Connor put his hand on her arm. "I was joking. Relax. I told you. I'm just happy to spend time with you."

Tess drank some of the hot chocolate and changed the subject. "What did you do this afternoon? After school?"

Connor squinted, as if considering his answer, and then shrugged. "I went for a run, had a coffee with Ben and his girlfriend and ah, well, I saw my shrink. Thursday evenings I see her. At six p.m. There's an Indian restaurant next door. I always have a curry afterward. Therapy and an excellent lamb curry. I don't know why I keep telling you about my therapy."

"Did you tell your therapist about me?" said Tess.

"Of course not." He smiled.

"You did." She poked his leg gently with her finger.

"All right, I did. Sorry. It was news. I like to make myself interesting for her."

Tess put her cup of hot chocolate down on the wall next to her. "What did she say?"

He glanced at her. "You've obviously never been in

therapy. They don't say a word. They say things like, 'And how did that make you feel?' and 'Why do you think you did that?'"

"I bet she didn't approve of me," said Tess. She saw herself through the therapist's eyes: An ex-girlfriend who broke his heart years ago suddenly reappears in his life when she's right in the middle of a marriage crisis. Tess felt defensive. *But I'm not leading him on. He's a grown man. Anyway, maybe it will go somewhere. It's true I never thought about him since then, but maybe I could fall in love with him. In fact, maybe I am falling in love with him. I know he's all messed up about his murdered first girlfriend. I'm not going to break his heart. I'm a good person.*

Wasn't she a good person? She felt a dim awareness of something almost shameful about the way she'd lived her life. Wasn't there something closed off, even small-minded and mean, about the way she cut herself off from people, ducking down behind the convenient wall of her shyness, her social anxiety? When she sensed overtures of friendship, she took too long to respond to phone calls and e-mails, and eventually people gave up, and Tess was always relieved. If she were a better mother, a more social mother, she would have helped Liam cultivate friendships with kids other than Marcus. But no, she'd just sat back with Felicity, giggling over their wine and sniping. She and Felicity didn't tolerate the overly skinny, the overly sporty, the overly rich or the overly intellectual. They laughed at people with personal trainers and small dogs, people who put overly intellectual or misspelled comments on Facebook, people who used the phrase "I'm in a very good place right now" and people who always got "involved"—people like Cecilia Fitzpatrick.

Tess and Felicity sat on the sidelines of life smirking at the players.

If Tess had a wider social network, then perhaps Will wouldn't have fallen in love with Felicity. Or at least he would have had a wider range of potential mistresses at his disposal.

When her life fell apart there hadn't been one friend whom Tess could call. Not one friend. That's why she was behaving like this with Connor. She needed a *friend*.

"I fit the pattern, don't I?" said Tess suddenly. "You keep choosing the wrong women. I'm another wrong woman. I'm terrible for you."

"Mmmm," said Connor. "Also, you didn't even bring the hot cross buns you promised."

He tipped back his paper cup and drained the last of his hot chocolate. He put it down on the ledge next to him and shifted closer to her.

"I'm using you," said Tess. "I'm a bad person."

He put one warm hand on the back of her neck and pulled her close enough that she could smell the chocolate on his breath. He took the paper cup from her unresisting hand.

"I'm using you to help me not think about my husband," she clarified. She wanted him to understand.

"Tess. Honey. Do you think I don't know that?" Then he kissed her so deeply and so completely that she felt like she was falling, floating, spiraling down, down, down, like Alice in Wonderland.

FORTY-FIVE

Janie didn't know that boys could blush. Her brother, Rob, blushed, but obviously he didn't count as a proper boy. She didn't know that a smart, good-looking, private-school boy like John-Paul Fitzpatrick could blush. It was late in the afternoon, and the light was changing, making everything indistinct and shadowy, but she still could see that John-Paul's face was glowing. Even his ears, she noticed, were a translucent pink.

She'd just said her little speech about how there was this other guy she'd been seeing and he wanted her to be his "sort of, um, girlfriend." So she really couldn't see John-Paul anymore, because the other guy wanted to "make things sort of official."

She'd had this vague idea that it would be better to make it sound as if it were Connor's fault, as if he were making her break up with John-Paul, but now, as John-Paul's face reddened, she wondered if it had been a mistake to mention another boy at all. She could have blamed it on her father. She could have said that she was too nervous about his finding out that she was seeing a boy.

But part of her had wanted John-Paul to know that she was in demand.

"But, Janie." John-Paul's voice sounded girly and squeaky, as if he was about to cry. "I thought you were *my* girlfriend."

Janie was horrified. Her own face flushed in sympathy, and she looked away toward the swings and heard herself giggle. A strange, high-pitched giggle. It was a terrible habit she had, of laughing when she was nervous, when she didn't find anything funny about a particular situation. It had happened, for example, when Janie was thirteen and the school principal had come in to their homeroom with such a somber, mournful expression on his normally jolly face and told them that their geography teacher's husband had died. Janie had been so shocked and distressed, and then she'd laughed. It was inexplicable. The whole class had turned to look at her accusingly, and she'd just about died of shame.

John-Paul lunged at her. Her first fleeting thought was that he was going to kiss her, and this was his odd yet masterful technique, and she was pleased and excited. He wasn't going to *let* her break up with him. He wasn't going to stand for it!

But then his hands grabbed her *neck*. She tried to say, "That's hurting, John-Paul," but she couldn't speak, and she wanted to clear up this dreadful misunderstanding, to explain that she actually liked him *more* than Connor, and she'd never meant to hurt his feelings, and she wanted to be his girlfriend, and she tried to convey that with her eyes, which were staring straight into his, his beautiful eyes, and she thought for a second that she saw a shift, a shocked recognition, and she felt a loosening of hands, but there was something else happening; something very wrong and unfamiliar was happening to her body, and at that instant, a far-off part of her mind remembered that her mother had been going to pick her up from school today to take her to a doctor's appointment, and she'd forgotten all about it and gone to Connor's house instead. Her mother would be furious.

Her last properly articulated thought was: *Oh, shit.*

After that there were no more thoughts, just helpless, flailing panic.

FORTY-SIX

J uice!" demanded Jacob.

"What do you want, sweetie?" whispered Lauren.

Juice, thought Rachel. *He wants a juice. Are you deaf?*

It was only just light, and Rachel, Rob and Lauren were standing in a shivery little circle at Wattle Valley Park, rubbing their hands together and stamping their feet, while Jacob slithered in and out between their legs. He was bundled up in a parka that Rachel suspected was too small for him, his arms sticking straight out like a snowman's.

As expected, Lauren was wearing her trench coat, although her ponytail didn't look quite as perfect as normal—there were a few strands escaping from her hair band—and she looked tired. She was carrying a single red rose, which Rachel thought was a silly choice. It was like those roses in long plastic cylinders that young men gave to their girl-friends on Valentine's Day.

Rachel herself was carrying a small posy of sweet peas she'd picked from her own backyard, tied up with a piece of green velvet ribbon like Janie used to wear when she was very little.

"Do you leave the flowers where she was found? At the bottom of the slide?" Marla had once asked.

"Yes, Marla, I leave them there to be trampled by hundreds of little feet," said Rachel.

"Oh, yes, good point," said Marla, not at all offended.

It wasn't even the same slide. All the clunky old metal equipment had been replaced by fancy, space-age-looking stuff, just like the park near Rachel's house where she took Jacob, and the ground had a rubbery surface that gave an astronautlike bounce to your step.

"Juice!" said Jacob again.

"I don't understand, sweetie." Lauren flipped her ponytail back over one shoulder. "Moose? Loose? You want me to loosen your jacket?"

For heaven's sake. Rachel sighed. It wasn't like she ever really felt Janie's presence when she came here. She couldn't imagine her here, couldn't conceive how she had come to be here. None of Janie's friends had ever known her to come to this particular park. It was a boy, obviously, who had brought her here. A boy called Connor Whitby. He probably wanted sex, and Janie said no. She should have had sex with him. That was Rachel's fault, for going on about it so much, as if losing her virginity was this momentous event. Dying was far more momentous. She should have said to her, "Have sex with whomever you want, Janie. Just stay safe."

Ed had never wanted to come to the park where she was found. "What's the bloody point of that?" he said. "Too bloody late to go there now, isn't it? She's not bloody there, is she?"

You're bloody right, Ed.

But Rachel felt like she owed it to Janie to turn up each year with her posy of flowers, to apologize for not being there, to be there now, to imagine her last few moments, to honor the last place she'd been alive, the last place where she'd breathed. If only Rachel could have been there to see her for those last precious minutes, to drink in the sight of those ridiculously long, skinny legs and arms, the awkward, angular beauty of her face. It was a silly thought, because if Rachel had been there, then she would have been busy saving her life, but still, she longed to have been there, even if she wouldn't have been able to change the outcome.

Maybe Ed had been right. It was pointless to come here each year like this. It felt particularly pointless this year with Rob and Lauren and Jacob standing around like people waiting for something to happen, the entertainment to start, the bus to arrive.

"Juice!" said Jacob.

"I'm sorry, sweetie, I just don't understand," said Lauren.

"He wants a juice," said Rob so gruffly that Rachel almost felt sorry for Lauren. Rob had sounded just like Ed when he got grumpy. The Crowley men were such grumps. "We don't have any, mate. Here. We've got your water bottle. Have some water."

"We don't drink juice, Jakey," said Lauren. "It's bad for your teeth."

Jacob held his water bottle with fat little hands, tipped back his head and drank thirstily, giving Rachel a look that said, *We won't tell her about all the juice I drink at your place.*

Lauren tightened the belt of her trench coat and turned to Rachel. "Do you normally say anything? Or, um—"

"No, I just think of her," said Rachel in a flat, shut-the-hell-up voice. She certainly wasn't going to let her feelings loose in front of Lauren. "We can go in a moment. It's very nippy. We don't want Jacob getting a chill."

It was *ridiculous* bringing Jacob here. On this day. To this park. Perhaps in the future she'd do something else to mark the anniversary of Janie's death. Go to her grave like they did on her birthday.

She just had to get through this endless day, and then it would be done for another year. *Let's just move it along. Come on, minutes. March on by until it's midnight.*

"Do you want to say something, honey?" Lauren asked Rob.

Rachel nearly said, "Of course he doesn't," but she stopped herself in time. She looked at Rob and saw he was looking up at the sky, stretching his neck out like a turkey, gritting those strong, white teeth, his hands awkwardly clenched across his stomach as if he were having a fit.

He hasn't been here, realized Rachel. *He hasn't been to the park since she was found.* She took a step toward him, but Lauren got there first and took his hand.

"It's okay," she murmured. "You're okay. Just breathe, honey. Breathe."

Rachel watched, helpless, as this young woman she didn't really know that well comforted her son, whom she probably didn't know that well either. She watched how Rob leaned toward his wife, and she thought of how little she knew, had never really wanted to know, about her son's grief. Did he wake Lauren with nightmares that twisted the sheets? Did he speak quietly in the darkness to her, telling stories about his sister?

Rachel felt a hand on her knee and looked down.

"Grandma," said Jacob. He beckoned to her.

"What is it?" She bent down and he cupped a hand over her ear.

"Juice," he whispered. "Please?"

The Fitzpatrick family slept late. Cecilia woke first. She reached for her iPhone sitting on the bedside table and saw that it was half past nine. Dishwater-gray morning light flooded through their bedroom windows.

Good Friday and Boxing Day were the two precious days of the year when they never scheduled anything. Tomorrow she'd be frantic preparing for the Easter Sunday lunch, but today there would be no guests, no homework, no rushing, not even grocery shopping. The air was chilly, the bed warm.

John-Paul murdered Rachel Crowley's daughter. The thought settled on her chest, compressing her heart. She would never again lie in bed on a Good Friday morning and relax in the blissful knowledge that there was nothing to do and nowhere to be, because for the rest of her life, there would always, always be something left undone. An unmade confession. An ugly secret.

She was lying on her side with her back up against John-Paul. She could feel the warm weight of his arm across her waist. Her husband. Her husband, the murderer. Should she have known? Should she have guessed? The nightmares, the migraines, the times when he was so . . . stubborn and strange. It wouldn't have made any difference, but it made her feel somehow negligent. "That's just him," she'd tell herself. She kept replaying memories of their marriage in light of what she now knew. She remembered, for example, how he'd refused to try for a fourth child. "Let's try for a boy," Cecilia had said to him when Polly was a toddler, knowing that both of them would have been perfectly happy if they'd ended up with four girls. John-Paul had mystified her with his stubborn refusal to consider it. It was probably yet another example of his self-flagellation. He'd probably been desperate for a boy.

Think of something else. Maybe she should get up and make a start on some of the baking for Sunday. How would she cope with all those guests, all that conversation, all that happiness? John-Paul's mother would sit in her favorite armchair, full of righteousness, holding court, sharing the secret. "It was all such a long time ago," she'd said. But it must feel like yesterday to Rachel.

Cecilia remembered with a lurch that Rachel had said today was the anniversary of Janie's death. Did John-Paul know that? Probably not. He was terrible with dates. He didn't remember his own wedding anniversary unless she reminded him; why would he remember the day he killed a girl?

"Jesus Christ," she said softly to herself, as all the physical symptoms of her new disease came rushing back: the nausea, the headache. She had to get up. She had to somehow escape from it. She went to move to throw back the covers and felt John-Paul's arms tighten around her.

"I'm getting up," she said, without turning to face him.

"How do you think we'd cope financially?" he said into her neck. He sounded hoarse, as if he had a terrible cold. "If I do go to . . . without my salary? We'd have to sell the house, right?"

"We'd survive," answered Cecilia shortly. She took care of the finances. Always had. John-Paul was happy to be oblivious to bills and mortgage payments.

"Really? We would?" He sounded doubtful. The Fitzpatricks were relatively wealthy, and John-Paul had grown up expecting to be better off than most people he knew. If there was money around, he quite naturally assumed it must emanate from him. Cecilia hadn't deliberately misled him about how much money she'd been earning the last few years; she just hadn't gotten around to mentioning it.

He said, "I was thinking that if I'm not here, we could get one of Pete's boys to come around and do odd jobs for you. Like clearing the gutters. That's really important. You can't let that go, Cecilia. Especially around bushfire season. I'll have to do a list. I keep thinking of things."

She lay still. Her heart thudded. How could this be? It was absurd. Impossible. Were they actually lying in bed, talking about John-Paul going to jail?

"I really wanted to be the one to teach the girls how to drive," he said. His voice broke. "They've got to know how to handle wet roads. You don't know how to brake properly when the roads are wet."

"I do so," protested Cecilia.

She turned around to face him and saw that he was sobbing, his cheeks crumpled into ugly grizzled folds. He twisted his head to bury his face in the pillow, as if to hide his tears. "I know I have no right. No right to cry. I just can't imagine not seeing them each morning."

Rachel Crowley never gets to see her daughter again.

But she couldn't harden her heart enough. The part of him she loved best was the part that loved his daughters. Their children had bound them together in a way that she knew didn't always happen to other couples. Sharing stories about their children—laughing about them, wondering about their futures—was one of the greatest pleasures of her marriage. She'd married John-Paul because of the father she knew he would one day be.

"What will they think of me?" He pressed his hands to his face. "They'll hate me."

"It's all right," said Cecilia. This was unbearable. "It will be all right. Nothing is going to happen. Nothing is going to change."

"But I don't know, now that I've actually said it out loud, now that *you* know, after all these years, it feels so real, much more real than ever before. It's today, you know." He ran the back of his hand across his nose and looked at her. "Today is the day. The day I did it. I remember every year. I hate autumn. But this year it seems even more shocking than ever. I can't believe it was me. I can't believe I did that to someone's daughter. And now my girls, my girls . . . my girls have to pay."

The remorse racked his whole body, like the worst sort of pain. Her every instinct was to ease it, to rescue him, to somehow make the pain stop. She gathered him to her like a child and whispered soothing words. "Shhhh. It's all right. Everything is going to be all right. There couldn't possibly be new evidence after all these years. Rachel must be mistaken. Come on, now. Deep breaths."

He buried his face in her shoulder and she felt his tears soaking through her nightie.

"Everything is going to be fine," she told him. She knew this couldn't possibly be true, but as she stroked the military-straight line of John-Paul's graying hair on his neck, she finally understood something about herself.

She would never ask him to confess.

It seemed that all her vomiting in gutters and crying in pantries had been for show, because as long as nobody else was accused, she would keep his secret. Cecilia Fitzpatrick, who always volunteered first, who never sat quietly when something needed to be done, who always brought casseroles and gave up her time, who knew the difference between right and wrong, was prepared to look the other way. She could and she would allow another mother to suffer.

Her goodness had limits. She could have easily gone her whole life without knowing those limits, but now she knew exactly where they lay.

FORTY-SEVEN

D on't be so stingy with the butter!" demanded Lucy. "Hot cross buns are meant to be served dripping with butter. Have I taught you nothing?"

"Have you heard nothing of the word 'cholesterol'?" said Tess, but she picked up the butter knife. She and her mother and Liam were sitting in the backyard in the morning sun, drinking tea and eating toasted hot cross buns. Tess's mother was wearing her pink quilted dressing gown over her nightie, and Tess and Liam were wearing their pajamas.

The day had started out suitably dour for a Good Friday, but had suddenly changed its mind and decided to twirl about and show off its autumn colors after all. There was a brisk, flirty breeze, and the sun was pouring through the red leaves of her mother's flame tree.

"Mum?" said Liam with his mouth full.

"Mmm?" said Tess. She held her face up to the sun, her eyes closed. She felt peaceful and sleepy. There had been more sex last night in Connor's apartment after they'd gone back on the bike from the beach. It was even more spectacular than the previous night. He had certain skills that were really quite . . . outstanding. Had he read a book, perhaps? *Will* had never read that book. It was curious how last week sex was just a pleasant semiregular pastime she never really thought about. And now, this week, it was all-consuming, as if it were all that really mattered about life, as if these moments in between sexual encounters were irrelevant, not really living.

She felt like she was becoming addicted to Connor and the particular curve of his upper lip and the breadth of his shoulders and his—

"Mum!" said Liam again.

"Yeah."

"When are—"

"Finish what's in your mouth."

"When are Daddy and Felicity coming? For Easter?"

Tess opened her eyes and glanced at her mother, who raised her eyebrows.

"I'm not sure," she said to Liam. "I have to talk to them. They might have to work."

"They can't work at Easter! I want to see Dad head-butt my rabbit egg."

Somehow they'd started the somewhat violent Easter Sunday tradition of beginning the day with the ceremonial head-butting of a chocolate Easter Bunny. Will and Liam both found the poor bunny's caved-in face to be hysterically funny.

"Well," said Tess. She had no idea what to do about

Easter. Was there any point in putting on a happy family show for Liam's benefit? They weren't good enough actors. He'd see right through it. Nobody would expect that of her, surely?

Unless she invited Connor? Sat on his lap like a high school girl proving to her ex-boyfriend that she'd moved on to no less than the muscly-armed school jock? She could ask him to roar up on his bike. *He* could do the head-butting of Liam's chocolate rabbit. He could out-head-butt Will.

"We'll call Daddy later on," she told Liam. Her peaceful feeling had vanished.

"Let's call him now!" He ran inside the house.

"No!" said Tess, but he'd gone.

"Dearie me," said her mother with a sigh, putting down her hot cross bun.

"I don't know what to do," began Tess, but Liam came running straight back with her mobile phone in her outstretched hand. It beeped with a text message as he went to hand it over.

"Is that a message from Dad?" said Liam.

Tess grabbed for the phone in panic. "No. I don't know. Let me see."

The message was from Connor. *Thinking of you. xx.* Tess smiled. As soon as she read it, the phone beeped again.

"This one is probably from Dad!" Liam bounced in front of her on the balls of his feet as if he were playing soccer.

Tess read the text. It was another one from Connor.

It's a good kite day if you want to bring Liam up to the oval for a quick run. I'll supply the kite! (But understand if you think it's not a good idea.)

"They're not from your dad," Tess said to Liam. "They're from Mr. Whitby. You know. Your new PE teacher."

Liam looked blank. Lucy cleared her throat.

"Mr. Whitby," said Tess again. "You had him for—"

"Why is he texting you?" said Liam.

"Are you going to finish your hot cross bun, Liam?" asked Lucy.

"Mr. Whitby is actually an old friend of mine," said Tess. "Remember how I saw him in the school office? I knew him years ago. Before you were born."

"Tess," said her mother. There was a warning note in her voice.

"What?" said Tess irritably. Why shouldn't she tell Liam that Connor was an old friend? What was the harm in that?

"Does Daddy know him too?" said Liam.

Children seemed so clueless about grown-up relationships, and then all of a sudden they'd say something like that, something that showed that on some level they understood everything.

"No," said Tess. "It was before I knew your dad. Anyway, Mr. Whitby texted because he's got this great kite and he wondered if you and I would like to go up to the oval to fly it."

"Huh?" Liam scowled, as if she'd suggested he clean up his room.

"Tess, my love, do you really think that's—you know." Tess's mother held up the side of her hand as a shield and silently mouthed, *Appropriate?*

Tess ignored her. She would not be made to feel guilty

about this. Why should she and Liam stay at home here doing nothing, while Will and Felicity did whatever the hell it was they were doing today? Anyway, she wanted to show that therapist, that invisible critical presence in Connor's life, that Tess wasn't just some crazy, damaged woman using Connor for sex. She was good. She was *nice*.

"He's got this amazing kite," improvised Tess. "He just thought you might like to have a turn flying it, that's all." She glanced at her mother. "He's being *friendly* because we're new at the school." She turned back at Liam. "Shall we go meet him? Just for half an hour?"

"All right," said Liam grudgingly. "But I want to call Dad first."

"Once you're dressed," said Tess. "Go put your jeans on. And your rugby top. It's chillier than I thought."

"All *right*," said Liam, and slouched off.

She tapped out a text to Connor: *We'll see you on the oval in half an hour. xx.*

Just before she was about to hit Send, she deleted the kisses. In case the therapist thought that was leading him on. Then she thought of all the *actual* kissing they'd done last night. Ridiculous. She may just as well kiss him in a text message. She made it three kisses and went to hit Send, but then she wondered if three kisses were over the top and changed it to one kiss, but that seemed stingy compared to his two, as if she was trying to make a point. She made a *tch* sound, added back in the second kiss and hit Send. She looked up to see her mother watching her.

"What?" she said.

"Careful," said her mother.

"What do you mean by that exactly?" There was a truc-
ulent tone in Tess's voice she recognized from her teenage
years.

"I just mean you don't want to go so far down a path
you can't come back," said her mother.

Tess glanced at the back door to check that Liam was
inside. "There's nothing to come back for! Obviously,
there must have been something badly wrong with our
marriage—"

"Rubbish!" interrupted her mother with such vehe-
mence that Tess was taken aback. "Bollocks! That's a total
fallacy. That's the sort of rubbish you read in women's
magazines. This is what happens in life. People mess up.
We're designed to be attracted to one another. It absolutely
does not mean there was something wrong with your marriage. I've seen you and Will together. I know how much
you love each other."

"But, Mum, Will *fell in love* with Felicity. It wasn't just
a drunken kiss at an office party. It's love." She frowned at
her fingernails and lowered her voice to a whisper. "And
maybe I'm falling in love with Connor."

"So what? People fall in and out of love all the time. I
fell in love with Beryl's son-in-law just the other week. It's
not some sign that your marriage was damaged." Lucy took
a bite of her hot cross bun and spoke with her mouth full.
"Of course, it's very badly damaged *now*."

Tess guffawed and lifted her palms. "So there you go.
We're stuffed."

"Not if you're both prepared to let go of your egos."

"It's not just about our egos," said Tess irritably. This

was ridiculous. Her mother wasn't making any sense. *Beryl's son-in-law*, for heaven's sake.

"Oh, Tess, my darling, at your age everything is about your ego."

"So, what are you saying? I should forget my ego and *beg* Will to come back to me?"

Lucy rolled her eyes. "Of course not. I'm just saying don't burn your bridges by jumping straight into a relationship with Connor. You have to think about Liam. He—"

Tess was outraged. "I *am* thinking about Liam!" She paused. "Did you think about me when you and Dad split up?"

Her mother gave her a small, humble smile. "Maybe not as much as we should have." She lifted her teacup and put it back down again. "Sometimes I look back, and think, goodness me, we took our feelings so *seriously*. Everything was black-and-white. We got into our positions and that was that. We wouldn't budge. Whatever happens, don't get all rigid, Tess. Be prepared to be a bit . . . bendy."

"Bendy," repeated Tess.

Her mother held up one hand and tilted her head.

"Was that the doorbell?"

"I didn't hear it," said Tess.

"If that's my damned sister showing up here unannounced again, I'll be so cross." Lucy straightened and narrowed her eyes. "Don't offer her a cup of tea, whatever you do!"

"I think you imagined it," said Tess.

"Mum! Grandma!"

The screen door at the back of the house flew open and

Liam tumbled out, still wearing his pajamas, his face alight. "Look who's here!" He held the screen door wide open and made a big game-show-host gesture. "Ta-daaa!"

A beautiful blond woman stepped through the open door. There was a split second where Tess genuinely didn't recognize her and simply admired the stylish effect she created in the autumn leaves. She was wearing one of those chunky white knit cardigans with brown wooden buttons, a brown leather belt, skinny blue jeans and boots.

"It's *Felicity*!" crowed Liam.

FORTY-EIGHT

Just sit with your mum and relax," said Lauren to Rob. "I'll bring out some hot cross buns and coffee. Jacob. You come with me, mister."

Rachel let herself sink into a cushiony couch next to a woodstove. It was comfortable. The couch had the exact right level of softness, which was to be expected. Thanks to Lauren's impeccable taste, everything in their beautifully restored two-bedroom Federation cottage was exactly right.

The café that Lauren had originally suggested had been closed, much to her chagrin. "I called and double-checked what time they were opening just *yesterday*," she'd said when they saw the "Closed" sign across the door. Rachel had watched with interest as she almost lost her equilibrium, but she'd managed to recover herself and suggest that they go back to their place. It was closer than Rachel's place, and Rachel couldn't think of a reason to refuse without seeming churlish.

Rob sat down in a red-and-white-striped armchair opposite her and yawned. Rachel caught the yawn and immediately sat up straighter. She did not want to nod off in Lauren's house, like an old lady.

She looked at her watch. It was only just after eight a.m. There were still hours and hours to endure before the day was done. At this time twenty-eight years ago, Janie had been eating her very last breakfast. Half a Weet-Bix, probably. She'd never liked breakfast.

Rachel ran her palm over the fabric of the couch. "What will you do with all your lovely furniture when you move to New York?" she said to Rob, chattily, coolly. She could talk about the upcoming move to New York on the anniversary of Janie's death. Oh, yes, she could.

Rob took a few moments to answer. He stared at his knees. She was about to say "Rob?" when he finally spoke. "We might rent this place out furnished," he said, as if speaking was an effort. "We're still thinking about all those logistics."

"Yes, a lot to think about, I imagine," said Rachel snappily. *Yes, Rob, quite a lot of logistics involved in taking my grandson to New York*. She dug her fingernails into the cloth of the couch, as if it were a soft, fat animal she was abusing.

"Do you dream about Janie, Mum?" asked Rob.

Rachel looked up. She released the flesh of the couch. "Yes," she said. "Do you?"

"Sort of," said Rob. "I have nightmares that I'm being strangled. I guess I'm dreaming that I'm Janie. It's always the same. I wake up choking for air. The dreams are always worse around this time of year. Autumn. Lauren thought maybe going to the park with you—might—be good. To face up to it. I don't know. I didn't really like being there. That's the wrong way to put it. Obviously you don't *like* being there either. But I just found that really hard. Thinking of what she went through. How scared she must have been. Jesus." He looked up at the ceiling and his face buckled. Rachel remembered how Ed would fiercely resist tears in exactly the same way.

Ed used to have nightmares too. Rachel would wake up to hear him yelling, over and over, "Run, Janie! *Run!* For God's sake, darling, run!"

"I'm sorry. I didn't know you had nightmares," said Rachel. What could she have done about it?

Rob got his face back under control.

"They're just dreams. They're no big deal. But you shouldn't have to go to the park every year on your own, Mum. I'm sorry I never offered to go with you before. I should have."

"Sweetheart, you did offer," said Rachel. "Don't you remember? Many times. And I always said no. It was my thing. Your dad thought I was crazy. He never went back to that park. Never even drove along the same street."

Rob wiped the back of his hand across his nose and sniffed.

"Sorry," he said. "You'd think after all these years—" He stopped abruptly.

They could hear Jacob in the kitchen singing the words to the "Bob the Builder" song. Lauren was singing along. Rob smiled tenderly at the sound. The smell of hot cross buns drifted into the room.

Rachel studied his face. He was a good dad. A better dad than his own father had been. That was the way these days, all the men were better fathers, but Rob had always been a softhearted boy. Even as a baby he'd been a loving little thing. She used to pick him up from his cot after a nap and he'd snuggle against her chest and actually pat her back as if to thank her for picking him up. He'd been the most chuckly, kissable baby. She remembered Ed saying, without resentment, "For God's sake, woman, you're besotted with that child."

It was strange, remembering Rob as a baby, like picking up a much-loved book she'd hadn't read in years. She so rarely bothered to think about memories of Rob. Instead, she was always trying to scrape up new memories of Janie's childhood, as if Rob's childhood didn't matter, because he got to live.

"You were the most beautiful baby," she said to Rob. "People used to stop me in the street to compliment me. Have I told you that before? Probably a hundred times."

Rob shook his head slowly. "You never told me that, Mum."

"Didn't I?" said Rachel. "Not even when Jacob was born?"

"No." There was an expression of wonder on his face.

"Well, I should have," said Rachel. She sighed. "I probably should have done a lot of things."

Rob leaned forward, his elbows resting on his knees. "So I was pretty cute, eh?"

"You were gorgeous, darling," said Rachel. "You still are, of course."

Rob snorted. "Yeah, right, Mum." But he couldn't hide the delight that suddenly wreathed his face, and Rachel bit down hard on her lower lip with regret for all the ways she'd let him down.

"Hot cross buns!" Lauren appeared carrying a beautiful platter of perfectly toasted and evenly buttered buns, which she placed in front of them.

"Let me help," said Rachel.

"Absolutely not," said Lauren over her shoulder as she returned to the kitchen. "You never let me help at your place."

"Ah." Rachel felt strangely exposed. She always assumed that Lauren didn't really notice her actions, or actually register her as a person at all. She thought of her age as a shield that protected her from the eyes of the young.

She always pretended to herself that she didn't let Lauren help because she was trying to be the perfect mother-in-law, but really, when you didn't let a woman help, it was a way of keeping her at a distance, of letting her know that she wasn't family, of saying *I don't like you enough to let you into my kitchen.*

Lauren reappeared with another tray containing three coffee cups. The coffee would be perfect, made exactly the way Rachel liked it: hot with two sugars. Lauren was the perfect daughter-in-law. Rachel was the perfect mother-in-law. All that perfection hiding all that dislike.

But Lauren had won. New York was her ace. She'd played it. Good on her.

"Where's Jacob?" asked Rachel.

"He's drawing," said Lauren as she sat down. She lifted

her mug and shot Rob a wry look. "Hopefully not on the walls."

Rob grinned at her, and Rachel got another glimpse of the private world of their marriage. It seemed like it was a good marriage, as far as marriages went.

Would Janie have liked Lauren? Would Rachel have been a nice, ordinary, overbearing mother-in-law if Janie had lived? It was impossible to imagine. The world with Lauren in it was so vastly different from the world when Janie had been alive. It seemed impossible that Lauren would still have existed if Janie had lived.

She looked at Lauren, strands of fair hair escaping from her ponytail. It was nearly the same blond as Janie's. Janie's hair was blonder. Perhaps hers would have darkened as she'd aged.

Ever since that first morning after Janie died, when Rachel woke up and the horror of what had happened crashed down upon her, she had been obsessively imagining another life running alongside her own, her real life, the one that was stolen from her, the one where Janie was warm in her bed.

But as the years had gone by it had become harder and harder to imagine it. Lauren was sitting right in front of her and she was so *alive*, the blood pumping through her veins, her chest rising and falling.

"You okay, Mum?" said Rob.

"I'm fine," said Rachel. She went to reach for her cup of coffee and found that she didn't have the energy to even lift her arm.

Sometimes there was the pure, primal pain of grief, and

other times there was anger, the frantic desire to claw and hit and kill, and sometimes, like right now, there was just ordinary, dull sadness, settling itself softly, suffocatingly over her like a heavy fog.

She was just so damned sad.

FORTY-NINE

Hello," said Felicity.

Tess smiled at her. She couldn't help it. It was like the way you automatically, politely say "thank you" to a police officer who is handing you a speeding ticket you don't want and can't afford. She was automatically happy to see Felicity because she loved her, and she looked so nice, and because a *lot* had been happening to her over the last few days, and she had so much to tell her.

In the very next instant she remembered, and the shock and betrayal felt brand-new. Tess battled a desire to fly at Felicity, to knock her to the ground and scratch and pummel and bite. But nice, middle-class women like Tess didn't behave like that, especially not in front of their impressionable small children, so she did nothing except lick her greasy lips from the buttery hot cross buns and move forward in her chair, tugging at the front of her pajama top.

"What are you doing here?" she asked.

"I'm sorry for just . . ." Felicity's voice disappeared on

her. She tried to clear her throat and said huskily, ". . . turning up like this. Without calling."

"Yes, it might have been better if you had called," said Lucy. Tess knew her mother was trying her best to look forbidding, but she just looked distraught. In spite of all the things Lucy had said about Felicity, Tess knew that she loved her niece.

"How is your ankle?" Felicity asked her.

"Is Dad coming too?" said Liam.

Tess straightened. Felicity met her eyes and quickly looked away. *That's right. Ask Felicity.* Felicity *will know what Will's plans are.*

"He's coming soon," Felicity told Liam. "I'm not actually staying long. I just wanted to talk to your mum first about a few things, and then I've got to go. I'm, ah, going away, actually."

"Where to?" asked Liam.

"I'm going to England," said Felicity. "I'm going to do this amazing walk. It's called the Coast to Coast Walk. And then I'm going to Spain, and America— Well, anyway, I'm going to be away for quite a long time."

"Are you going to Disneyland?" asked Liam.

Tess stared at Felicity. "I don't get it." Was Will going with her on some romantic adventure?

Red painful blotches stained Felicity's neck. "Could you and I talk?"

Tess stood up. "Come on."

"I'll come too," said Liam.

"No," said Tess.

"You stay out here with me, darling," said Lucy. "Let's eat chocolate."

Tess took her to her old bedroom. It was the only room with a lock. They stood next to her bed, looking at each other. Tess's heart hammered. She hadn't realized that you could spend your whole life looking at the people you loved in an oblique, halfhearted way, as if you were deliberately blurring your vision, until something like this happened, and then just looking at that person could be terrifying.

"What's going on?" said Tess.

"It's over," said Felicity.

"Over?"

"Well, it never got started really. Once you and Liam were gone, it just—"

"Wasn't as thrilling anymore?"

"Can I sit down?" said Felicity. "My legs are shaking."

Tess's legs were shaking too.

She shrugged. "Sure. Sit."

There was nowhere to sit but on the bed or the floor. Felicity sank to the floor. She sat cross-legged with her back against the chest of drawers. Tess sat also, with her back against the bed.

"Still the same rug." Felicity put her hand on the blue-and-white rug.

"Yep." Tess looked at Felicity's slim legs and fine-boned wrists. She thought of the little fat girl who had sat in that exact same position so many times throughout their childhood. Her beautiful green almond eyes shining out from her plump face. Tess always knew there was a fairy princess trapped within there. Perhaps Tess had liked the fact that she was trapped.

"You look beautiful," said Tess. For some reason, it just had to be said.

"Don't," said Felicity.

"I wasn't trying to make a point."

"I know."

They sat in silence for a few moments.

"So tell me," said Tess finally.

"He's not in love with me," said Felicity. "I don't think he was ever in love with me. It was just a crush. The whole thing was just pathetic, really. I knew straightaway. As soon as you and Liam were gone, I knew that nothing was going to happen."

"But . . ." Tess lifted her hands helplessly. She felt a rush of humiliation. The events of the past week all seemed so *stupid*.

"It wasn't just a crush for me," said Felicity. She lifted her chin. "It was real for me. I love him. I've loved him for years. Ever since the first moment we met."

"Is that right?" said Tess dully, but it wasn't a surprise. Not really. Maybe she'd always known it. In fact, maybe she'd even *liked* the fact that she sensed Felicity was in love with Will, because it made Will seem all the more desirable, and because it was perfectly safe. There was no way that Will could be sexually attracted to Felicity. Had Tess not really seen her cousin at all? Had she been just like everyone else who didn't see past Felicity's weight?

Tess said, "But all those years. Spending so much time

with us. It must have been horrible." It was as though she'd thought that Felicity's fatness cushioned her feelings, as though she believed that Felicity must surely know and accept that no ordinary man could really love her! And yet Tess would have killed anyone who would have said that out loud.

"It was just how I felt." Felicity pleated the fabric of her jeans between her fingers. "I knew he just thought of me as a friend. I knew Will liked me. Loved me, even, like a sister. It was enough to spend time with him."

"You should have—" began Tess.

"What? Told you? How could I tell you? What could you have done except feel sorry for me? What I should have done was gone off and lived my own life, instead of just being your faithful fat sidekick."

"I never thought of you like that!" Tess was stung.

"I'm not saying you thought of me like that. It was more that I saw myself as your sidekick. As if I wasn't thin enough to have a real life. But then when I lost the weight, I started to notice men looking at me. I know as good feminists we're not meant to like it, being objectified, but when you've never experienced it, it's like, I don't know, cocaine. I loved it. I felt so powerful. It was like in those movies when the superhero first discovers his powers. And then I thought, *I wonder if I could get Will to notice me now, like those men notice me*—and then, well, then . . ."

She stopped. She'd become caught up in the telling of her story and forgotten that it wasn't really an appropriate one for Tess to hear. Tess had only had a few days of not being able to talk to Felicity, whereas Felicity had all those years of not being able to share the biggest thing on her mind.

"And then he noticed you," finished Tess. "You tried out your superpowers and they worked."

Felicity gave a pretty, self-deprecating shrug. It was funny how all her gestures were different now. Tess was sure she'd never seen that particular shrug before—sort of French and flirty.

"I think Will felt so bad about feeling, you know, a little bit attracted to me that he convinced himself that he was in love with me," said Felicity. "Once you and Liam were gone, everything changed. I think he lost interest in me the moment you walked out the door."

"The moment I walked out the door," repeated Tess.

"Yup."

"Bullshit."

Felicity lifted her head. "It's true."

"No it's not."

It seemed as though Felicity was trying to absolve Will of all wrongdoing, to imply that he'd been briefly led astray, as if what had happened was no different than the betrayal of a drunken kiss at an office party.

Tess thought of Will's dead-white face on Monday evening. He wasn't that shallow or stupid. His feelings for Felicity had been real enough for him to begin the process of dismantling his whole life.

It was Liam, she thought. The moment Tess walked out the door with Liam, Will finally understood what he was sacrificing. If there had been no child involved, this conversation wouldn't be taking place. He loved Tess—presumably he did—but right now he was *in* love with Felicity, and everyone knew which was the more powerful feeling. It wasn't a fair fight. It was why marriages fell apart. It was why, if you valued your marriage, you kept a barricade around yourself and your feelings and your thoughts. You didn't let your eyes linger. You didn't stay for the second drink. You kept the flirting safe. You just didn't go there. At some point, Will made a choice to look at Felicity with the eyes of a single man. That was the moment he betrayed Tess.

"Obviously I'm not asking for your forgiveness," said Felicity.

Yes, you are, thought Tess. *But you're not getting it.*

"Because I could have done it," said Felicity. "I want you to know that. For some reason it's really important to me that you know that I was serious. I felt terrible, but not so terrible that I couldn't have done it. I could have lived with myself."

Tess stared at her, appalled.

"I just want to be totally honest with you," said Felicity.

"Thanks, I guess."

Felicity dropped her eyes first. "Anyway. I thought the best thing would be for me to just leave the country, to get as far away as possible. So you and Will can work things out. He wanted to talk to you first, but I thought it would make more sense if—"

"So where is he now?" said Tess. There was a strident

note to her voice. Felicity's knowledge of Will's where-abouts and plans was infuriating. "Is he in Sydney? Did you fly up together?"

"Well, yes, we did, but—" began Felicity.

"That must have been very traumatic for you both. Your last moments together. Did you hold hands on the plane?"

The flicker in Felicity's eyes was indisputable.

"You did, didn't you?" said Tess. She could just imagine it. The *agony*. The star-crossed lovers clinging to each other, wondering if they should keep on running—fly to Paris!—or do the right thing, the boring thing. Tess was the boring thing.

"I don't want him," she told Felicity. She couldn't stand her role as the stodgy, wronged wife. She wanted Felicity to know that there was nothing stodgy about Tess. "You can have him. Keep him! I've been sleeping with Connor Whitby."

Felicity's mouth dropped open. "Seriously?"

"Seriously."

Felicity exhaled. "Well, Tess, that's—I don't know." She looked around the room for inspiration and returned her gaze to Tess. "Three days ago you said you would not have Liam growing up with divorced parents. You said *you wanted your husband back*. You made me feel like the worst person in the world. And now you tell me that you've just jumped straight into an affair with Connor Whitby, while Will and I . . . we never even—*God*!" She thumped her fist on the side of Tess's bed, her color high, her eyes shining with fury.

The injustice, and perhaps the justice, of Felicity's words took Tess's breath away.

"Don't be so pious." She shoved Felicity's skinny thigh as hard as she could, childishly, like a kid on a bus. It felt strangely good. She did it again, harder. "You *are* the worst person in the world. Do you think I would have even *looked* at Connor if you and Will hadn't made your announcement?"

"You didn't muck about, though, did you? Bloody hell, stop *hitting* me!"

Tess gave her one final shove and sat back. She had never felt such an overwhelming desire to hit someone before. She had certainly never given in to it. It seemed that all the niceties that made her a socially acceptable grown-up had been stripped away. Last week she was a school mum and a professional. Now she was having sex in hallways and hitting her cousin. What next?

She took a deep, shaky breath. "In the heat of the moment," they called it. She had never realized just how hot the heat of the moment could get.

"Anyway," said Felicity. "Will wants to work things out, and I'm leaving the country. So do whatever you want to do."

"Thanks," said Tess. "Thanks very much. Thanks for everything." She could feel the anger almost physically draining from her body, leaving her limp and detached.

There was silence for a moment.

"He wants another baby," said Felicity.

"Don't tell me what he wants."

"He *really* wants another baby."

"And I suppose you would have liked to have given him one," said Tess nastily.

Felicity's eyes filled. "Yes. I'm sorry, but yes."

"For God's sake, Felicity. Don't make me feel bad for you. It's not fair. Why did you have to fall in love with *my* husband? Why couldn't you have fallen in love with someone else's husband?"

"We never really saw anyone else." Felicity laughed as the tears rolled down her face. She wiped the back of her hand across her nose.

That was true.

"He doesn't think he can ask you to go through another pregnancy because of how sick you got," said Felicity. "But it might not be as bad with a second pregnancy, right? Every pregnancy is different, isn't it? You should have another baby."

"Do you really think we're going to have a baby now and live happily ever after?" said Tess. "A baby doesn't fix a marriage. Not that I even knew my marriage needed fixing."

"I know, I just thought—"

"It's not really because of the sickness that I didn't want a baby," she said to Felicity. "It's because of the people."

"The people?"

"The other mothers, the teachers, the *people*. I didn't realize that having a child was so social. You're always *talking* to people."

"So what?" Felicity looked mystified.

"I have this disorder. I did a quiz in a magazine. I have . . ." Tess lowered her voice. "I have social anxiety."

"You do not," said Felicity dismissively.

"I do so! I did the quiz—"

"You're seriously diagnosing yourself based on some quiz in a magazine?"

"It was *Reader's Digest*, not *Cosmopolitan*. And it's true! I can't stand meeting new people. I get sick. I have heart palpitations. I can't stand parties."

"Lots of people don't like parties. Get over yourself."

Tess was taken aback. She had expected hushed pity.

"You're shy," said Felicity. "You're not one of those loudmouthed extroverts. But people like you. People really like you. Haven't you ever noticed that? I mean, God, Tess, how could you have had all those boyfriends if you were supposedly such a shy, nervy little thing? You had about thirty boyfriends before you were twenty-five."

Tess rolled her eyes. "I did not."

How could she explain to Felicity that her anxiety was like a strange, mercurial little pet she was forced to look after? Sometimes it was quiet and pliable; other days it was crazy, running around in circles, yapping in her ear. Besides, dating was different. Dating had its own definite set of rules. She could do dating. A first date with a new man had never been a problem. (As long as he asked her out, of course. She never did the asking.) It was when the man asked her to meet his family and friends that her anxiety reared its freaky little head.

"And by the way, if you really had this 'social anxiety,' why did you never tell me?" said Felicity with total confidence that she knew everything there was to know about Tess, even if the reverse was not true.

"I never had a name for it before," said Tess. "I never had words to describe this feeling until a few months ago."

And because you were part of my cover identity, she thought. *Because you and I pretended together that we didn't care what other people thought of us, that we were superior to just about the whole world. If I'd admitted to you how I felt, I would have had to admit that not only did I care what other people thought, I cared far too much.*

"You know what? I walked into an aerobics class when I was at least double the size of every person in the room." Felicity leaned forward and looked at her fiercely. "People couldn't look at me. I saw one girl nudging her friend to check me out, and then they both fell about laughing. I heard a guy say, 'Watch out for the heifer.' Don't you talk to *me* about social anxiety, Tess O'Leary."

There was a banging on the door.

"Mum! Felicity!" shouted Liam. "Why have you locked the door? Let me in!"

"Go away, Liam!" called back Tess.

"No! Have you made up yet?"

Tess and Felicity looked at each other. Felicity smiled faintly, and Tess looked away.

Lucy's voice came from the other end of the house. "Liam, come back here! I said to leave your mother alone!" She was at a disadvantage on her crutches.

Felicity stood. "I have to go. My flight is at two o'clock. Mum is taking me to the airport. She's in a state. Dad isn't speaking to me, apparently."

"You're seriously leaving today?" Tess looked up at her from the floor. She thought briefly of the business: the clients she'd worked so hard to win over, the cash flow they'd tried so hard to maintain, fussing and fretting over the profit and loss like a delicate little plant, the "work in progress" spreadsheet they'd studied each morning. Was this the end for TWF Advertising? All those dreams. All that stationery.

"Yes," said Felicity. "It's what I should have done years ago."

Tess stood as well. "I don't forgive you."

"I know," said Felicity. "I don't forgive me either."

"Mum!" yelled Liam.

"Hold your horses, Liam!" called out Felicity. She grabbed Tess's arm and said in her ear. "Don't tell Will about Connor."

For one fleeting, strange moment they hugged, and then Felicity turned and opened the door.

FIFTY

There's no butter," announced Isabel. "No margarine either."

She turned from the fridge and looked at her mother expectantly.

"Are you sure?" asked Cecilia. How could that have happened? She never forgot a staple. Her system was fool-proof. Her refrigerator and pantry were always perfectly stocked. Sometimes John-Paul rang on his way home and asked if she needed him to "pick up milk or anything," and she'd always reply, "Uh, *no*?"

"But aren't we having hot cross buns?" said Esther. "We always have hot cross buns for breakfast on Good Friday."

"We can still have them," said John-Paul. He brushed his fingers automatically across Cecilia's lower back as he walked past her to the kitchen table. "Your mother's hot cross buns are so good, they don't need butter."

Cecilia watched him. He was pale and a little shaky, as

if he were recovering from the flu, and he seemed in a tremulous, tender mood.

She found herself waiting for something to happen: the shrill ring of the phone, a heavy knock on the door, but the day continued to be cloaked in soft, safe silence. Nothing would happen on a Good Friday. Good Friday was in its own protective little bubble.

"We always have our hot cross buns with lots and lots of butter," said Polly, who was sitting at the kitchen table in her pink flannelette pajamas, her black hair rumpled, her cheeks flushed with sleep. "It's a family *tradition*. Just go to the shop, Mum, and get some butter."

"Don't speak to your mother like that. She's not your slave," said John-Paul, at the same time as Esther glanced up from her library book and said, "The shops are closed, stupid."

"Whatever." Isabel sighed. "I'm going to go Skype with—"

"No, you're not," said Cecilia. "We're *all* going to eat some porridge, and then we're *all* going to walk up to the school oval."

"Walk?" said Polly disdainfully.

"Yes, walk. It's turned into a beautiful day. Or ride your bikes. We'll take the soccer ball."

"I'm on Dad's team," said Isabel.

"And then on the way back we'll stop by the BP service station and pick up some butter, and we'll have hot cross buns when we get home."

"Perfect," said John-Paul. "That sounds perfect."

"Did you know that some people wish the Berlin Wall had never come down?" said Esther. "That's weird, isn't it? Why would you want to be stuck behind a wall?"

———

Well, that was lovely, but I really should go," said Rachel. She placed her coffee mug back down on the coffee table. Her duty was done. She shifted herself forward and took a breath. It was another one of those impossibly low couches. Could she stand up on her own? Lauren would get there first if she saw Rachel was having difficulty. Rob was always just a moment too late.

"What are you doing for the rest of the day?" asked Lauren.

"I'll just putter about," said Rachel. *I'll just count the minutes.* She held out a hand to Rob. "Give me a hand, will you, love?"

As Rob went to help her, Jacob toddled over with a framed photo he'd picked up from the bookcase and brought it over to Rachel. "Daddy," he said clearly.

"That's right," said Rachel. It was a photo of Rob and Janie on a camping trip they'd taken on the south coast the year before Janie died. They were standing in front of a tent, and Rob had held his fingers up like rabbit ears behind Janie's head. Why did children insist on doing that?

Rob came and stood next to them and pointed at his sister. "And who's that, buddy?"

"Auntie Janie," said Jacob clearly.

Rachel caught her breath. She'd never heard him say "Auntie Janie" before, although she and Rob had been pointing her out in photos to him since he was a tiny baby.

"Clever boy." She ruffled his hair. "Your Aunt Janie would have loved you."

Although, in truth, Janie had never been particularly interested in children. She'd preferred constructing cities with Rob's Legos to playing with dolls.

Jacob gave her a cynical look, as if he knew this, and wandered off with the photo frame swinging precariously between his fingertips. Rachel put her hand in Rob's and he helped her to her feet.

"Well, thank you so much, Lauren . . ." she began, and was startled to see that Lauren was staring at the floor with a fixed expression, as if she were pretending not to be there.

"Sorry." She gave them a watery smile. "It was just hearing Jacob say 'Auntie Janie' for the first time. I don't know how you get through this day, Rachel, every year, I really don't. I just wish I could *do* something."

You could not take my grandson to New York, thought Rachel. *You could stay here and have another baby*. But she just smiled politely and said, "Thank you, darling. I'm perfectly all right."

Lauren stood. "I wish I'd known her. My sister-in-law. I always wanted a sister." Her face was pink and soft. Rachel looked away. She couldn't bear it. She didn't want to see evidence of Lauren's vulnerability.

"I'm sure she would have loved you." Rachel sounded so perfunctory to her own ears that she coughed, embarrassed. "Well. I'll be off. Thank you for coming to the park with me today. It meant a lot to me. I'll look forward to seeing you on Easter Sunday. At your parents' house!"

She tried her best to inject some enthusiasm into her voice, but Lauren had closed her face back up and recovered her poise.

"Lovely," Lauren said coolly, and leaned forward to brush her lips against her cheek. "By the way, Rachel, Rob said he told you to bring a pavlova, but that's *really* not necessary."

"It's no trouble at all, *Lauren*," said Rachel.

She thought she heard Rob sigh.

———

So, now Will is going to make an appearance?" Lucy leaned heavily on Tess's arm as they stood on the front porch, watching Felicity's taxi turn the corner at the end of the street. Liam had disappeared inside somewhere. "This is like a play. Evil mistress exits stage right. Enter chastened husband."

"She's not really an evil mistress," said Tess. "She said she's been in love with him for years."

"For heaven's sake," said Lucy. "Silly girl. Plenty of fish in the sea! Why must she want your fish?"

"He's a pretty good fish, I guess."

"Do I take it you forgive him, then?"

"I don't know. I don't know if I can. I feel like he's only choosing me because of Liam. I feel like he's settling for me. For second best."

The thought of seeing Will filled her with almost unbearable confusion. Would she cry? Yell? Fall into his arms? Slap him across the face? Offer him a hot cross bun? He loved hot cross buns. Obviously he did not deserve one. "You're not getting a bun, babe." That was the thing. It was just *Will*. It was impossible to imagine how she'd maintain the level of drama and gravitas the situation required. Especially with Liam there. But then again, he wasn't Will, because the real Will would never have allowed this to happen. So this was a stranger.

Her mother studied her. Tess waited for a wise, loving comment.

"I assume you're not going to see him in those raggedy old *pajamas* are you, darling? And you are going to give your hair a good brush, I hope?"

Tess rolled her eyes. "He's my husband. He knows what I look like first thing in the morning. And if he's *that* superficial, then I don't want him."

"Yes, you're right, of course," said Lucy. She tapped her lower lip. "Gosh, Felicity was looking *particularly* lovely today, wasn't she?"

Tess laughed. Maybe she would feel more resilient if she were dressed. "Fine, Mum, I'll go put a ribbon in my hair and pinch my cheeks. Come on, cripple. I don't know why you had to come outside to see her off."

"I didn't want to miss any of the action."

"They never did sleep together, you know," whispered Tess as she held the screen door with one hand and her mother's elbow with the other.

"Seriously?" said Lucy. "How peculiar. In my day infidelity was a much raunchier affair."

"I'm ready!" Liam came running down the hallway.

"For what?" said Tess.

"To go fly a kite with that teacher. Mr. Whatby or what-ever his name is."

"Connor," breathed Tess, and nearly lost hold of her mother. "Shit. What time is it? I'd forgotten."

———

Rachel's mobile rang just as she got to the end of Rob and Lauren's street. She pulled the car over to answer it. It was probably Marla, ringing for Janie's anniversary. Rachel was happy to talk to her. She felt like complaining about Lauren's perfectly toasted hot cross buns.

"Mrs. Crowley?" It wasn't Marla. It was a woman's voice. She sounded like a snooty doctor's receptionist: nasal and self-important. "This is Detective-Sergeant Strout from the Homicide Squad. I meant to call you last night, but I ran out of time, so I thought I would try to catch you this morning."

Rachel's heart leapt. The video. She was calling on Good Friday. A public holiday. It had to be good news.

"Hello," she said warmly. "Thank you for calling."

"Well. I wanted to let you know that we received the video from Detective Bellach and we have, er, reviewed it." Detective-Sergeant Strout was younger than she'd first sounded. She was putting on her best professional voice for the call. "Mrs. Crowley, I understand you may have had high expectations, that you even thought this might have been something of a breakthrough. So I'm sorry if this is disappointing news, but I have to tell you that at this stage, we won't be questioning Connor Whitby again. We don't think the video justifies it."

"But it's his motive," said Rachel desperately. She looked through the car windshield at a magnificent gold-leafed tree soaring up to the sky. "Can't you see that?" As she watched, a single gold leaf detached itself and began to fall, circling rapidly through the air.

"I'm so sorry, Mrs. Crowley. At this stage there's really nothing further we can do." There was sympathy there, yes, but Rachel could also hear a young professional's condescension toward an elderly layperson. *The victim's mother. Obviously far too emotional to be objective. Didn't understand police procedure. Part of the job to try to soothe her.*

Rachel's eyes filled with tears. The leaf vanished from sight.

"If you'd like me to come around and talk to you after the Easter break," said Detective-Sergeant Strout, "I'd be happy to make a time that suits."

"That won't be necessary," said Rachel icily. "Thank you for the call."

She hung up and threw the phone so that it landed on the floor in front of the passenger seat.

"Useless, patronizing, miserable little . . ." Her throat closed up. She turned the keys in the ignition.

———

Look at that man's kite!" said Isabel.

Cecilia looked up to see a man on the crest of the

hill carrying an enormous kite in the shape of a tropical fish. He was letting it bob about behind him like a balloon.

"It's like he's taking his fish for a walk," huffed John-Paul. He was leaned over almost double, pushing Polly on her bike because she'd just complained that her legs had turned to jelly. She was sitting upright, wearing a glittery pink helmet and plastic rock-star sunglasses with star-shaped lenses. As Cecilia watched, Polly leaned forward to take a sip of lemon cordial from the purple water bottle she'd packed for herself in the white mesh basket.

"Fish can't walk," said Esther, without looking up from her book. She had a remarkable ability to walk and read at the same time.

"You could at least pedal a bit, Princess Polly," said Cecilia.

"My legs still feel like jelly," said Polly delicately.

John-Paul grinned at Cecilia. "It's okay. Good workout for me."

Cecilia breathed in deeply. There was something comical and wonderful about the sight of the fish-shaped kite swimming jauntily through the air behind the man in front of them. The air smelled sweet. The sun was warm on her back. Isabel was pulling tiny yellow dandelions from hedges and sticking them in between the strands of Esther's plait. It reminded Cecilia of something. A book or a movie from her childhood. Something to do with a little girl who lived in the mountains who wore flowers in her braid. Heidi?

"Beautiful day!" called out a man who was sitting on

his front porch drinking tea. Cecilia knew his face vaguely from church.

"Gorgeous!" she called back warmly.

The man ahead of them with the kite stopped. He pulled a phone from his pocket and held it to his ear.

"That's not a man." Polly straightened. "That's Mr. Whitby!"

———

Rachel drove robotically toward home, trying to keep her mind completely empty of thoughts.

She stopped at a red light and looked at the time on the dashboard clock. It was ten o'clock. At this time twenty-eight years ago, Janie would have been at school, and Rachel was probably ironing her dress for her appointment with Toby Murphy. The bloody dress that Marla had convinced her to buy because it showed off her legs.

Just seven minutes late. It probably made no difference. She would never know.

"We won't be taking any further action." She heard again the prim voice of Detective-Sergeant Strout. She saw Connor Whitby's frozen face when she paused the video. She thought of the unmistakable guilt in his eyes.

He *did* it.

She screamed. An ugly, bloodcurdling scream that reverberated around the car. She beat her fists just once on the steering wheel. It both frightened and embarrassed her.

The lights changed. She put her foot on the accelerator.

Was today the worst anniversary yet, or was it always this bad? It was probably always this bad. It was so easy to forget how bad things were. Like winter. Like the flu. Like childbirth.

She could feel the sun on her face. It was a beautiful day, like the day Janie died. The streets were deserted. Nobody appeared to be about. What did people do on Good Friday?

Rachel's mother used to do the Stations of the Cross. Would Janie have stayed a Catholic? Probably not.

Don't think about the woman Janie would have been.

Think nothing. Think nothing. Think nothing.

When they take Jacob to New York, there will be nothing. It will be like death. Every day will feel as bad as this. Don't think about Jacob either.

Her eyes followed a squall of fluttering red leaves like tiny, frantic birds.

Marla said she always thought of Janie whenever she saw a rainbow. And Rachel said, "Why?"

The empty road unfurled in front of her, and the sun brightened. She squinted and lowered the sun visor. She always forgot her sunglasses.

There was somebody out and about after all.

She grabbed hold of the distraction. It was a man. He was standing on the sidewalk, carrying a brightly colored balloon. It looked like a fish. Like the fish in *Finding Nemo*. Jacob would love that balloon.

The man was talking on a mobile phone, looking up at his balloon.

It wasn't a balloon. It was a kite.

———

'm sorry. We can't meet you after all," said Tess.

"That's all right," said Connor. "Another time." The reception was crystal clear. She could hear the very weight and timbre of his voice, deeper than in person, a bit gravelly. She pressed the phone to her ear, as if she could wrap his voice around her.

"Where are you?" she asked.

"Standing on a footpath, carrying a fish kite."

She felt a flood of regret, and also plain, kidlike disappointment, as if she'd missed a birthday party because of a piano lesson. She wanted to sleep with him one more time. She didn't want to sit in her mother's chilly house having a complicated, painful conversation with her husband. She wanted to run around her old school oval in the sunshine with a fish kite. She wanted to be falling in love, not trying to fix a broken relationship. She wanted to be someone's first choice, not their second.

"I'm so sorry," she said.

"You don't need to be sorry."

There was a pause.

"What's going on?" he asked.

"My husband is on his way here."

"Ah."

"Apparently he and Felicity are over before it's even begun."

"So I guess we are too." He didn't make it sound like a question.

She could see Liam playing in the front garden. She'd told him that Will was on his way. He was racing back and forth across the yard, tipping first the hedge and then the fence, as if he were in training for some life-and-death event.

"I don't know what's going to happen. It's just that with Liam, you see, I have to at least try. At least give it a go." She thought of Will and Felicity sitting on the plane from Melbourne, hands gripped, faces stoic. For fuck's sake.

"Of course you do." He sounded so warm and lovely. "You don't need to explain."

"I should never have—"

"Please don't regret it."

"Okay."

"Tell him if he treats you badly again, I'll break his knees."

"Yes."

"Seriously, Tess. Don't give him any more chances."

"No."

"And if things don't work out, well. You know. Keep my application on file."

"Connor, someone will—"

"Don't do that," he said sharply. He tried to soften his voice. "No worries. I told you, I've got the chicks lining the streets for me."

She laughed.

"I should let you go," he said, "if this bloke of yours is on his way."

She could hear his disappointment so clearly now. It made him sound abrupt, almost aggressive, and part of her wanted to keep him on the line, to flirt with him, to make sure that the last thing he said was gentle and sexy, and then she could be the one to put an end to the conversation, so that she could file these last few days away in her memory under the category that suited her. (What was that category? "Fun flings where nobody got hurt"?)

But he was entitled to be abrupt, and she'd already exploited him enough.

"Okay. Well. 'Bye."

"'Bye, Tess. Take care."

———

Mr. Whitby!" shouted Polly.

"Oh my God. Mum, make her stop!" Isabel lowered her head and hid her eyes.

"Mr. *Whitby*!" screeched Polly.

"He's too far away to hear you." Isabel sighed.

"Darling, leave him alone. He's talking on the phone," said Cecilia.

"Mr. Whitby! It's me! Hello! Hello!"

"It's outside of his work hours," commented Esther. "He's not obliged to talk to you."

"He *likes* talking to me!" Polly grabbed hold of her handlebars and pedaled away from her father's grasp, her wheels wobbling precariously along the footpath. "Mr. Whitby!"

"Looks like her legs have recovered." John-Paul massaged his lower back.

"Poor man," said Cecilia. "Enjoying his Good Friday and he's accosted by a student."

"I guess it's an occupational hazard if he chooses to live in the same area," said John-Paul.

"Mr. Whitby!" Polly gained ground. Her legs pumped. Her pink wheels spun.

"At least she's getting some exercise," said John-Paul.

"This is so embarrassing," said Isabel. She hung back and kicked at someone's fence. "I'm waiting here."

Cecilia stopped and looked back at her. "Come on. We're not going to let her bother him for long. Stop kicking that fence."

"Why are you embarrassed, Isabel?" asked Esther. "Are you in love with Mr. Whitby too?"

"No, I'm not! Don't be disgusting!" Isabel turned purple. John-Paul and Cecilia exchanged looks.

"Why is this guy so special, anyway?" asked John-Paul. He nudged Cecilia. "Are you in love with him too?"

"Mothers can't be in love," said Esther. "They're too old."

"Thanks very much," said Cecilia. "Come on, Isabel." She turned to look back at Polly, just as Connor Whitby stepped off the footpath and onto the curb of the road, the kite floating above him.

Polly swung her bike down a steep driveway toward the road.

"Polly!" she called, at the same time as John-Paul yelled, "Stop right there, Polly!"

FIFTY-ONE

Rachel watched the man with the kite step off the curb. *Look out for traffic, matey. That's not a pedestrian crossing.*

He turned his head in her direction.

It was Connor Whitby.

He was looking right at her, but it was as though Rachel's car were invisible, as if she didn't exist, as if she were completely irrelevant to him, as if he could choose to inconvenience her by making her slow down if it suited him. He stepped briskly, happily across the road, with every confidence that she would stop. His kite caught a gust of wind and spun in lazy circles.

Rachel's foot lifted from the accelerator and hovered over the brake.

Then it slammed like a brick on the accelerator.

t didn't happen in slow motion. It happened in an instant.

There was no car. The street was empty. And then, just like that, there was a car. A small blue car. John-Paul would say afterward that he knew there was a car coming from behind them, but to Cecilia, it just materialized out of nowhere.

No car. Car.

The little blue car was like a bullet. Not so much because of its speed, but because it seemed as if it were on some unstoppable trajectory, as if it had been shot from something.

Cecilia saw Connor Whitby run. Like a man in a movie chase scene leaping from one building to another.

A second later, Polly rode her bike directly in front of the car and vanished beneath it.

The sounds were small. A thump. A crunch. The long, thin squeal of brakes.

And then silence. Ordinariness. The sound of a bird.

Cecilia didn't feel anything except confusion. What just happened?

She heard heavy footsteps and turned to see John-Paul running. He ran straight past her. Esther was screaming. Over and over. A terrible, ugly sound. Cecilia thought, *Stop it, Esther.*

Isabel grabbed Cecilia's arm. "The car hit her!"

A chasm cracked open in her chest.

She shook Isabel's hand free and ran.

—

A little girl. A little girl on a bike.

Rachel's hands were still on the steering wheel. Her foot was still pressed hard on the brake pedal. It was compressed all the way to the floor of the car.

Slowly, painstakingly, she lifted her trembling left hand from the steering wheel and wrenched on the handbrake. She placed her left hand back on the steering wheel and used her right hand to turn off the ignition. Then she cautiously lifted her foot from the brake pedal.

She looked in the rearview mirror. Maybe the little girl was all right.

(Except she'd felt it. The soft speed bump beneath her wheels. She knew with perfect sick certainty what she'd done. What she'd deliberately done.)

She could see a woman running, her arms dangling oddly from her body, as if they were paralyzed. It was Cecilia Fitzpatrick.

Little girl. Pink sparkly helmet. Black ponytail. Brake. Brake. *Brake*. Her face in profile. The girl was Polly Fitzpatrick. Gorgeous little Polly Fitzpatrick.

Rachel whimpered like a dog. Somewhere in the distance, someone was screaming over and over.

———

Hello?"

"Will?"

Liam had kept asking when his dad was arriving, and Tess had felt all at once infuriated by her passive role, waiting for Felicity and Will to make their scheduled appearances. She'd called Will on his mobile. She was going to be icy and controlled and give him his first inkling of the almighty task that lay ahead of him.

"Tess," said Will. He sounded distracted and strange.

"According to Felicity, you're on your way over here—"

"I am," interrupted Will. "I was. In a taxi. We had to stop. There was an accident just around the corner from your mum's place. I saw it happen. We're waiting for an ambulance." His voice broke, and his voice became muffled. "It's terrible, Tess. Little girl on a bike. About the same age as Liam. I think she's dead."

FIFTY-TWO

The doctor reminded Cecilia of a priest or a politician. He specialized in professional compassion. His eyes were warm and sympathetic, and he spoke slowly and clearly, authoritatively and patiently, as if Cecilia and John-Paul were his students and he needed them to fully understand a tricky concept. Cecilia wanted to throw herself at his feet and hug his knees. As far as she was concerned, this man had absolute power. He was God. This man, this soft-spoken, bespectacled Asian man in a blue-and-white-striped shirt that was very similar to one John-Paul owned, was God.

Throughout the previous day and night there had been so many people talking at them: the paramedics, the doctors and nurses in the emergency department. Everyone had been nice, but rushed and tired, their eyes slipping and sliding. There was noise and bright white lights constantly shining in her peripheral vision, but now they were talking to Dr. Yue in the hushed, churchlike environment of Intensive Care. They were standing outside the glass-paneled room where Polly was lying on a high, single bed, attached to a plethora of equipment. She was heavily sedated. An intravenous drip had been inserted in her left arm. Her right arm was wrapped in gauze bandages. At some point one of the nurses had brushed her hair away from her forehead, pinning it off to one side so that she didn't look quite like herself.

Dr. Yue seemed highly intelligent because he wore glasses, and perhaps because he was Asian, which was racial stereotyping, but Cecilia didn't care. She hoped that Dr. Yue's mother had been one of those pushy tiger mothers. She hoped poor Dr. Yue didn't have any other interests apart from medicine. She loved Dr. Yue. She loved Dr. Yue's mother.

But John-bloody-Paul! John-Paul didn't seem to understand that they were speaking to God. He kept interrupting. He sounded too brusque. Rude, almost! If John-Paul offended Dr. Yue, he might not try as hard for Polly. Cecilia knew that this was just a job for Dr. Yue, and Polly was just another one of his patients, and that they were just another pair of distraught parents, and everyone knew that doctors, like airline pilots, were overworked and got exhausted and made tiny errors that turned out to be catastrophic. Cecilia and John-Paul had to differentiate themselves in some way. They had to make him see that Polly wasn't just another patient, she was *Polly*, she was Cecilia's baby girl, she was her funny, infuriating, charming little girl. Cecilia's breath caught, and for a moment she couldn't breathe.

Dr. Yue patted her arm. "This is incredibly distressing for you, Mrs. Fitzpatrick, and I know you've had a long night with no sleep."

John-Paul glanced sideways at Cecilia, as if he'd forgotten she was there too. He took her hand. "Please just go on," he said.

Cecilia smiled obsequiously at Dr. Yue. "I'm fine," she said. "Thank you." *Look how very nice and undemanding we are!*

Dr. Yue ran through Polly's injuries. A serious concussion, but the CT scan had showed no sign of a serious brain injury. The pink sparkly helmet had done its job. As they already knew, internal bleeding was a concern, but they were monitoring and so far, so good. They already knew that Polly had suffered severe skin abrasions, a fractured tibia and a ruptured spleen. The spleen had already been removed. Many people lived without their spleens. She might have some danger of reduced immunity, and they would recommend antibiotics in the case of—

"Her arm," interrupted John-Paul. "The main concern through the night seemed to be her right arm."

"Yes." Dr. Yue locked eyes with Cecilia and breathed in and out, as if he were a yoga teacher demonstrating breathing techniques. "I'm very sorry to say that the limb is not salvageable."

"Pardon?" said Cecilia.

"Oh God," said John-Paul.

"I'm sorry," said Cecilia, still trying to be nice, but feeling a surge of fury. "What do you mean 'not salvageable'?" It sounded like Polly's arm was at the bottom of the ocean.

"She's suffered irreparable tissue damage, a double fracture, and there's no longer sufficient blood supply. We'd like to do the procedure this afternoon."

"Procedure?" echoed Cecilia. "By 'procedure' you mean . . ."

She couldn't say the word. It was unspeakably obscene.

"Amputation," said Dr. Yue. "Just above the elbow. I know this is terrible news for you, and I've arranged for a counselor to see you—"

"No," said Cecilia firmly. She would not stand for this. She had no idea what a spleen did, but she knew what a right arm did. "She's right-handed, you see, Dr. Yue. She's six years old. She can't live without *her arm*!" Her voice skidded into the ugly maternal hysteria she'd been trying so hard to spare him.

Why wasn't John-Paul saying anything? The brusque interruptions had stopped. He had turned away from Dr. Yue and was looking back through the glass panels at Polly.

"She can, Mrs. Fitzpatrick," said Dr. Yue. "I'm so very sorry, but she can."

———

There was a long, wide passageway outside the heavy wooden doors that led to Intensive Care, beyond which only family members were allowed. A row of high windows let in dust-flecked rays of sunlight, reminding Rachel of church. People sat in brown leather chairs all the way along the passageway: reading, texting, talking on their mobile phones. It was like a quieter version of an airport terminal. People enduring impossibly long waits, their faces tense and tired. Sudden muffled explosions of emotion.

Rachel sat in one of the brown leather chairs facing the wooden doors, her eyes continually watching for Cecilia or John-Paul Fitzpatrick.

What did you say to the parents of a child you'd hit with your car, nearly killed?

The words "I'm sorry" felt like an insult. You said "I'm sorry" when you bumped against someone's supermarket trolley. There needed to be bigger words.

I am profoundly sorry. I am filled with terrible regret. Please know that I will never forgive myself.

What did you say when you knew the true extent of your own culpability, which was so much more than that assigned to her by the freakishly young paramedics and police officers who had arrived at the accident yesterday. They treated her like a doddering old woman involved in a tragic accident. Words kept forming in her head: *I saw Connor Whitby and I put my foot on the accelerator. I saw the man who murdered my daughter and I wanted to hurt him.*

Yet some instinct for self-preservation must have prevented her from speaking out loud, because otherwise, surely, she would be locked up for attempted murder.

All she remembered saying out loud was, "I didn't see Polly. I didn't see her until it was too late."

"How fast were you going, Mrs. Crowley?" they asked her, so gently and respectfully.

"I don't know," she said. "I'm sorry. I don't know."

It was true. She didn't know. But she knew there had been plenty of time to put her foot on the brake to let Connor Whitby cross the road.

They told her that it was unlikely she would be charged. It seemed that a man in a taxi had seen the little girl ride her bike directly in front of the car. They asked her whom they could call to come and collect her. They insisted on this, even though a second ambulance had been called just for her, and the paramedic had checked her over and said that there was no need for her to go to the hospital. Rachel gave the police Rob's number, and he arrived far too quickly (he must have been speeding) with Lauren and Jacob in the car. Rob was white-faced. Jacob grinned and waved a chubby hand from the backseat. The paramedic told Rob and Lauren that Rachel was probably suffering from mild shock, and that she should rest and stay warm, and not be left alone. She should see her regular doctor as soon as possible for a checkup.

It was terrible. Rob and Lauren dutifully followed orders, and Rachel couldn't get rid of them, no matter how hard she tried. She couldn't get her thoughts straight while they hovered about, bringing her cups of tea and cushions. Next thing, that perky young Father Joe turned up, very upset about members of his flock running each other over. "Shouldn't you be at Good Friday services?" said Rachel ungratefully. "All under control, Mrs. Crowley," he said. Then he'd taken her hand and said, "Now, you know this was an accident, don't you, Mrs. Crowley? Accidents happen. Every day. You must not blame yourself."

She thought, *Oh, you sweet, innocent young man, you know nothing about blame. You have no idea of what your parishioners are capable. Do you think any of us really confess our real sins to you? Our terrible sins?*

At least he was useful for information. He promised her that he would keep her constantly informed about Polly's progress, and he'd been as good as his word.

She's still alive, Rachel kept telling herself as each update came. *I didn't kill her.* This is not irretrievable.

Lauren and Rob had finally taken Jacob home after dinner, and Rachel had spent the night replaying those few moments over and over.

The fish-shaped kite. Connor Whitby stepping out onto the road, ignoring her. Her foot on the accelerator. Polly's pink sparkly helmet. Brake. Brake. Brake.

Connor was fine. Not a scratch on him.

Father Joe had called this morning to say that there was no further news, except that Polly was in Intensive Care at Westmead Children's Hospital and receiving the very best of treatment.

Rachel had thanked him, put down the phone and then immediately picked it up again to call a cab to take her to the hospital. She had no idea if she would be able to see either of Polly's parents or if they would want to see her—they probably wouldn't—but she felt that she had to be there. She couldn't just sit comfortably at home, as if life went on.

The double doors leading into Intensive Care flew open and Cecilia Fitzpatrick barreled through, as if she were a surgeon off to save a life. She walked rapidly down the passageway, past Rachel, then stopped and gazed about her, baffled and blinking, like a sleepwalker waking up.

Rachel stood.

———

"Cecilia?"

An elderly, white-haired woman materialized in front of Cecilia. She seemed wobbly, and Cecilia instinctively put out her hand toward the woman's elbow.

"Hello, Rachel," Cecilia said, suddenly recognizing her, and for a moment she saw only Rachel Crowley, the kindly but distant and always efficient school secretary. Then a giant chunk of her memory crashed back into place: John-Paul, Janie, the rosary beads placed in her hands. She hadn't thought about any of it since the accident.

"I know I'm the last person who you want to see right now," said Rachel. "But I had to come."

Cecilia remembered dully that Rachel Crowley had been driving the car that hit Polly. She'd registered it at the time, but it had no particular relevance to her. The little blue car had been like a force of nature: a tsunami, an avalanche. It was as if it were driven by no one.

"I'm so sorry," said Rachel. "So terribly, dreadfully sorry."

Cecilia couldn't quite comprehend what she meant. She was too sluggish with exhaustion and the shock of what Dr. Yue had just said. Her normally reliable brain cells

lumbered about, and it was with the greatest of difficulty
that she corralled them into one place.

The person driving the car would feel terrible.

You need to make them feel better.

"It was an accident," she said, with the relief of someone
remembering the perfect phrase in a foreign language.

"Yes," said Rachel. "But—"

"Polly was chasing Mr. Whitby," said Cecilia. The words
flowed easier now. "She didn't look." She closed her eyes
briefly and saw Polly disappear beneath the car. She opened
them again. Another perfect phrase came to her. "You must
not blame yourself."

Rachel shook her head impatiently and batted at the air
as if an insect were bugging her. She grabbed hold of Cecilia's forearm and held it tight. "Please just tell me. How
is she? How serious are her—her injuries?"

Cecilia stared at Rachel's wrinkly, knuckly hand clutching her forearm. She saw Polly's beautiful, healthy, skinny
little-girl arm and found herself coming up against a spongy
wall of resistance. It was unacceptable. It simply could not
happen. Why not *Cecilia's* arm? Her ordinary, unappealing
arm with its faded freckles and sunspots. They could take
that if the bastards had to have an arm.

"They said she has to lose her arm," she whispered.

"No." Rachel's hand tightened.

"I can't. I just can't."

"Does she know?"

"No."

This thing was endless and enormous, with tentacles

that crept and curled and snarled, because she hadn't even begun to think about how she would tell Polly, or really, in fact, what this barbaric act would mean to *Polly*, because she was consumed with what it meant to her, how *she* couldn't bear it, how it felt like a violent crime was being committed upon *Cecilia*. This was the price for the sensual, delicious pleasure and pride she'd always taken in her children's bodies.

What did Polly's arm look like right now, beneath the bandages? *The limb was not salvageable.* Dr. Yue had assured her that they were managing Polly's pain.

It took Cecilia a moment to realize that Rachel was crumpling, her legs folding at the knees. She caught her just in time, grabbing her arms and taking her full weight. Rachel's body felt surprisingly insubstantial for a tall woman; it was as though her bones were porous. But it was still tricky keeping her upright, as if she'd just been handed a large, awkward package.

A man walking by carrying a bunch of pink carnations stopped, stuck the flowers under his arm and helped Cecilia get Rachel to a nearby seat.

"Shall I find you a doctor?" he asked. "Should be able to track one down. We're in the right spot!"

Rachel shook her head adamantly. She was pale and shaky. "Just dizzy."

Cecilia knelt down next to Rachel and smiled politely up at the man. "Thank you for your help."

"No problems. I'll get going. My wife just had our first baby. Three hours old. Little girl."

"Congratulations!" said Cecilia a moment too late. He

was already gone, walking joyfully off, right in the middle of the happiest day of his life.

"Are you sure you're okay?" said Cecilia to Rachel.

"I'm so sorry."

"It's not your fault," said Cecilia, and felt a hint of impatience. She'd come out for air, to stop herself from screaming, but she needed to get back now. She needed to start collecting facts. She did not need to talk to a bloody counselor, thanks very much, she needed to see Dr. Yue again, and this time, she would take notes and ask questions and not worry about being nice.

"You don't understand," said Rachel. She fixed Cecilia with red, watery eyes. Her voice was high and weak. "It *is* my fault. I put my foot on the accelerator. I was trying to kill him, because he killed Janie."

Cecilia grabbed for the side of Rachel's seat, as if it were a precipice she'd been pushed from.

"You were trying to kill John-Paul?"

"Of course not. I was trying to kill Connor Whitby. He murdered Janie. I found this video, you see. It was proof."

It was like somebody had grabbed Cecilia by the shoulders, spun her around and forced her to come face-to-face with the evidence of an atrocity.

There was no grappling for comprehension. She understood everything in an instant.

What John-Paul had done.

What she had done.

Their accountability to their daughter. The penalty she would pay for their crime.

Her entire body felt hollowed by the bright white light

of a nuclear blast. She was a shell of her former self. Yet she didn't shake. Her legs didn't give way. She remained perfectly still.

Nothing really mattered anymore. Nothing could be worse than this.

The important thing now was complete and utter truth. It would not save Polly. It would not redeem them in any way. But it was absolutely necessary. It was an urgent task that Cecilia needed to cross off her list *this very moment*.

"Connor didn't kill Janie," said Cecilia. She could feel her jaw moving up and down as she talked. She was a puppet made of wood.

Rachel became very still. The texture of her soft, wet eyes changed, visibly hardening. "What do you mean?"

Cecilia heard the words come out of her dry, sour-tasting mouth. "My husband killed your daughter."

FIFTY-THREE

Cecilia was crouched down next to Rachel's chair, talking softly but clearly, her eyes just inches away. Rachel could hear and comprehend every word she said, but she couldn't seem to keep up. It wouldn't sink in. The words were slipping straight off the surface of her mind. She felt a terrifying sensation, as if she were running desperately to catch something of vital importance.

Wait, she wanted to say. *Wait. Cecilia. What?*

"I only found out the other night," said Cecilia. "The night of the Tupperware party."

John-Paul Fitzpatrick. Was she trying to tell her that John-Paul Fitzpatrick murdered Janie? Rachel grabbed at Cecilia's arm. "You're saying it wasn't Connor," she said. "You know for a fact that it wasn't Connor. That he had nothing to do with it?"

A profound sadness crossed Cecilia's face. "I know this for a fact," she said. "It wasn't Connor. It was John-Paul."

John-Paul Fitzpatrick. Virginia's son. Cecilia's husband.

A tall, handsome, well-dressed, courteous man. A well-known, respected member of the school community. Rachel would greet him with a smile and a wave if she saw him at the local shops or a school event. John-Paul always led the parent volunteer building projects at the school. He wore a tool belt and a plain black baseball cap and held up a slide rule with impressive assurance. Last month, Rachel had watched Isabel Fitzpatrick run straight into her father's arms when he picked her up after the Year 6 camp. It had struck Rachel because of the sheer joy on Isabel's face when she saw John-Paul, and also because of Isabel's resemblance to Janie. John-Paul had swung Isabel around in an arc, her legs flying, like she was a much younger child, and Rachel had felt a searing regret that Janie had never been that sort of daughter, and Ed had never been that sort of father. Their uptight concerns about what other people thought seemed like such a waste. Why had they been so careful and contained with their love?

"I should have told you," said Cecilia. "I should have told you the moment I knew."

John-Paul Fitzpatrick.

He had such nice *hair*. Respectable-looking hair. Not like Connor Whitby's shifty-looking bald head. John-Paul drove a shiny, clean family car. Connor roared about on his grimy motorbike. It couldn't be right. Cecilia must have it wrong. Rachel couldn't seem to shift her hatred over from Connor. She'd hated Connor Whitby for so long, even when she didn't know for sure, even when she just suspected, she'd hated him for the *possibility* of what he'd done.

She'd hated him for his very existence in Janie's life. She'd hated him for being the last one to see Janie alive.

"I don't understand," she said to Cecilia. "Did Janie know John-Paul?"

"They were in a sort of a secret relationship. They were dating, I guess you'd call it," said Cecilia. She was still crouched on the floor next to Rachel, and her face, which had been drained of color, was now flooded with it. "John-Paul was in love with Janie, but then Janie said there was another boy, and she'd chosen the other boy, and then, he . . . Well. He lost his temper." Her words faded. "He was seventeen. It was a moment of madness. That makes it sound like I'm trying to excuse him. I promise I am absolutely not trying to excuse him, or what he did. *Obviously.* Of course there is no excuse. I'm sorry. I have to stand up. My knees. My knees are hurting."

Rachel watched Cecilia rise to her feet with difficulty, look around for another chair and drag it closer to Rachel's before sitting down and leaning toward her with her brows knitted so fiercely, she looked like a constipated baby.

Janie told John-Paul there was another boy. So the other boy was Connor Whitby.

Janie had *two* boys interested in her, and Rachel had been completely unaware of it. Where had Rachel gone wrong as a mother that she'd had such little knowledge of her daughter's life? Why hadn't they exchanged confidences over milk and cookies in the afternoon after school like a mother and daughter in an American sitcom? Rachel had only ever baked under duress. Janie used to eat buttered crackers for her afternoon tea. If only she'd *baked* for Janie, she thought with a sudden burst of savage self-loathing. Why *hadn't* she baked? If she'd baked, and if Ed had swung Janie in joyful circles, then maybe everything could have been different.

"Cecilia?"

Both women looked up. It was John-Paul.

"Cecilia. They want us to sign some forms . . ." He saw Rachel and stopped. "Hello, Mrs. Crowley," he said.

"Hello," said Rachel.

She couldn't move. It was as though she were anesthetized. Here was her daughter's murderer standing in front of her. An exhausted, distressed, middle-aged father, with red-rimmed eyes and gray stubble. It was impossible. He had nothing to do with Janie. He was much too old. Too grown-up.

Cecilia said, "I told her, John-Paul."

John-Paul took a step back, as if someone had tried to hit him.

He briefly closed his eyes, and then he opened them and looked straight down at Rachel with such sick regret in his eyes, there was no longer any doubt in her mind.

"But why?" Rachel said, and she was struck by how civilized and ordinary she sounded, discussing her daughter's murder in the middle of the day, while dozens of people walked by, ignoring them, assuming theirs was just another unremarkable conversation. "Could you please tell me why you would do such a thing? She was just a little girl."

John-Paul ducked his head and ran both his hands

through his nice, respectable hair, and when he looked up again, it was as though his face had shattered into a thousand pieces. "It was an accident, Mrs. Crowley. I never meant to hurt her because, you see, I loved her. I really loved her." He wiped the back of his hand across his nose in a careless, hopeless gesture, like a drunk on a street corner. "I was a stupid teenage boy. She told me she was seeing someone else, and then she laughed at me. I'm so sorry, but that's the only reason I have. I know it's no reason at all. I loved her, and then she laughed at me."

———

Cecilia was dimly aware that people continued to move through the corridor where they sat. They hurried or strolled by, they gesticulated and laughed, they talked animatedly into mobile phones. Nobody stopped to observe the white-haired woman sitting straight-backed in the brown leather chair, her gnarled hands gripping the sides, her eyes fixed on the middle-aged man who stood in front of her, with his head bowed in deep contrition, his neck exposed, his shoulders slumped. Nobody seemed to notice anything extraordinary about their frozen bodies, their silence. They were in their own little bubble, separated from the rest of humanity.

Cecilia felt the cool, smooth leather of the chair beneath her hands, and suddenly the air rushed from her lungs.

"I need to get back to Polly," she said, and stood up so fast that her head swam.

How much time had passed? How long had they been

out here? She felt a panicky sensation, as if she'd deserted Polly. She looked at Rachel and thought, *I can't care about you right now.*

"I need to talk to Polly's doctor again," she said to Rachel.

"Of course you do," said Rachel.

John-Paul held out his palms to Rachel, his wrists upward, as if he were waiting to be handcuffed. "I know that I don't have any right to ask you this, Rachel, Mrs. Crowley, I have no right to ask you for anything, but, you see, Polly needs us both right now, so I just need time—"

"I'm not taking you away from your daughter," interrupted Rachel. She sounded brisk and furious, as if Cecilia and John-Paul were badly behaved teenagers. "I've already . . ." She stopped, swallowed and looked up at the ceiling, as if she were trying to suppress the urge to be sick. She shooed them away. "Go. Just go to your little girl. Both of you."

FIFTY-FOUR

It was late Saturday night, and Will and Tess were hiding Easter eggs in her mother's backyard. They both held bags of tiny eggs, the ones wrapped in shiny colored foil.

When Liam was very little, they used to put the eggs in plain sight, or even just scatter them across the grass; but as he grew older, he preferred the challenge of a tricky Easter egg hunt, with Tess humming the theme song to *Mission: Impossible* while Will timed him on a stopwatch.

"I suppose we could put some of them in the gutter." Will looked up at the roof. "We could leave a ladder somewhere handy."

Tess gave the sort of polite chuckle she'd give to an acquaintance or a client.

"Guess not," said Will. He sighed and carefully placed a blue one in the corner of a windowsill that Liam would have to stand on tippy-toes to reach.

Tess unwrapped an egg and ate it. The last thing Liam needed was more chocolate. Sweetness filled her mouth.

She herself had eaten so much chocolate this week, if she didn't watch it she'd be the size of Felicity.

The casually cruel thought came automatically into her head like an old song lyric, and she realized how often she must have thought it. "The size of Felicity" was still her definition of unacceptably fat, even now, when Felicity had a slim, gorgeous body that was better than hers.

"I can't believe you thought we could all three just live together!" she exploded. She saw Will steel himself.

This was the way it had been ever since he had finally turned up at her mother's house the previous day, pale and discernibly thinner-looking than the last time she'd seen him. Her mood kept swinging about precariously. One minute she was cool and sarcastic, the next she was hysterical and weepy. She couldn't seem to get ahold of herself.

Will turned to face her, the bag of chocolate eggs in the palm of his hand. "I didn't really think that," he said.

"But you said it! On Monday, you said it."

"It was idiotic. I'm sorry," he said. "All I can do is keep saying I'm sorry."

"You sound robotic," said Tess. "You don't even mean it anymore. You're just saying the words in the hope I'll finally shut up." She spoke in a monotone. " 'I'm sorry. I'm sorry. I'm sorry.' "

"I do mean it," said Will wearily.

"Shhh," said Tess, although he hadn't really spoken that loudly. "You'll wake them." Liam and her mother were both in bed asleep. Their rooms were at the front of the house, and they were both deep sleepers. Tess and Will probably wouldn't wake them even if they started yelling at each other.

There had been no yelling. Not yet. Just these short, useless conversations that traveled bitterly down one-way streets. Their reunion the previous day had been both surreal and mundane, an exasperating clash of personalities and emotion. For a start there was Liam, who was almost deranged with excitement. It was like he'd sensed the danger of losing his father, and the safe little structure of his life, and now his relief at Will's return manifested itself in six-year-old craziness. He spoke in annoying silly voices, he giggled maniacally, he wanted to wrestle constantly with Will. Will, on the other hand, was completely traumatized by witnessing Polly Fitzpatrick's accident. "You should have seen the expressions on the parents' faces," he kept saying quietly to Tess. "Imagine if that was Liam. If that was us."

The shocking news about Polly's accident should have put everything into perspective for Tess, and in a way it did. If something like that had happened to Liam, then nothing else would have mattered. But at the same time it was as if her own feelings were now a trivial matter, and that made her feel defensive and aggressive.

She couldn't find big enough words to describe the enormous breadth and depth of her emotions. *You hurt me. You really hurt me. How could you hurt me like that?* It was so simple in her head but so strangely complex each time she opened her mouth.

"You wish you were on a plane with Felicity right now," said Tess. He did. She knew that he did, because she wished she were in Connor's apartment right now. "Flying to Paris."

"You keep saying Paris," said Will. "Why Paris?" She heard a hint of ordinary Will, the Will she loved, in his voice. The Will who found the humor in everyday stuff. "Do *you* want to go to Paris?"

"No," said Tess.

"Liam does love his croissants."

"No."

"Except we'd have to bring our own Vegemite."

"I don't want to go to Paris."

She walked across the lawn to the back fence and went to hide an egg near a post, and then changed her mind, worried about spiders.

"I should mow that lawn for your mother tomorrow," said Will from the courtyard.

"A boy down the road does it once every two weeks," said Tess.

"Okay."

"I know that you're only here because of Liam," she said.

"What?"

"You heard me."

She'd said this before, last night in bed and again when they'd gone for a walk today. She was repeating herself. Acting like an irrational, crazy bitch, as if she wanted to make him regret his decision. Why did she keep bringing it up? She was here for the same reason. She knew that if it weren't for Liam, she'd be in bed with Connor right now.

She wouldn't have bothered to try to fix it. She would have let herself fall into something fresh and new and delicious.

"I am here because of Liam," said Will. "And I'm here because of you. You and Liam are my family. You mean everything to me."

"If we meant everything to you, then you wouldn't have fallen in love with Felicity in the first place," said Tess. It was so easy being the victim. The accusing words rolled with delightful, irresistible ease off the tongue.

The words wouldn't roll so easily if she told him what she'd been doing with Connor, while he and Felicity were heroically resisting temptation. She presumed it would hurt him, and she wanted to hurt him. The information was like a secret weapon hidden in her pocket, which she held in the palm of her hand, caressing its contours, considering its power.

"Don't tell him about Connor," her mother had said urgently in her ear, pulling her aside as Will's cab pulled up at the house and Liam ran out to greet him. "It will only upset him. It's pointless. Honesty is overrated. Take it from me."

Take it from her. Was her mother speaking from personal experience? One day she would ask her. Right now she didn't particularly want to know, or even care.

"I didn't really fall in love with Felicity," said Will.

"Yes, you did," said Tess, although the words "falling in love" suddenly seemed juvenile and ridiculous, as if she and Will were far too old to be using such terms. When you were young, you talked about falling in love with such amusing gravity, as if it were an actual, recordable event, when what was it really? Chemicals. Hormones. A trick of the mind. She could have fallen in love with Connor. Easily. Falling in love was easy. Anyone could *fall*. It was holding on that was tricky.

She could tear up her marriage right now if she chose; tear up Liam's life with a few simple words. *Guess what, Will? I fell in love with somebody else too. So everything is just fine and dandy. Off you go.* All it would take was words, and they could both be on their way.

What she couldn't forgive was the revolting *purity* of what had gone on between Will and Felicity. Unconsummated love was so powerful. Tess had left Melbourne so that they could have their affair, damn it. Instead, *she* was the one left lugging around a sleazy secret.

"I don't think I can do this," she said quietly.

"What?"

Will looked up from where he was squatting down, carefully pushing eggs into the latticework at the back of one of her mother's chairs.

"Nothing," she said.

She walked over to the side fence and placed a row of eggs at careful intervals all the way along the middle paling hidden beneath the ivy.

"Felicity said you wanted another baby," she said.

"Yeah, well, you knew that," said Will. He sounded exhausted.

"Was it just because she got so pretty? Felicity? Was that it?"

"Huh? What?" Tess almost laughed at his panicky expression. Poor Will. Even on a normal day he preferred his conversations to follow a linear structure, and now he couldn't complain like he normally would and say, "Make sense, woman!"

"There wasn't anything really wrong with our marriage, was there?" she said. "We didn't fight. We were in the middle of watching season five of *Dexter*! How could you break up with me when we were in the middle of season five?"

Will smiled warily and clutched his bag of eggs.

Suddenly she couldn't stop talking. It was like she was drunk. "And wasn't our sex life okay? I thought it was okay. I thought it was pretty good." She remembered Connor's fingertips running so slowly and softly all the way down her back and shivered violently. Will's forehead was knitting and furrowing, as if someone had taken hold of his balls and was squeezing, just gently at first, but then gradually harder and harder. Soon she would cause him to topple to the ground.

"We didn't fight. Or we did fight, but weren't they just normal, run-of-the-mill fights? What did we fight about? The dishwasher? The way I put the frying pan in so it hits the thingamabob? You think we come to Sydney too often? But that's just run-of-the-mill stuff, isn't it? Weren't we happy? I was happy. I thought we were both happy. You must have thought I was such an idiot." She lifted her arms and legs up and down like a puppet. "Here comes dopey Tess dopily going about her day. Ooh, tra-la-la, I'm so happily married, yes I am!"

"Tess. Don't do that." Will's eyes were shiny.

She stopped and noticed that there was a salty taste in her mouth now along with the chocolate. She wiped the backs of her hands impatiently across her face. She hadn't even been aware that she'd been crying. Will took a step toward her as if to comfort her, and she held up both her palms to stop him from coming any closer.

"And now Felicity is gone. I haven't been apart from her for more than two weeks since, my God, since we were born. That's weird, isn't it? No wonder you thought you could have both of us. We were like Siamese twins."

That's why she was so furious with him for thinking they could all three live together: because it wasn't entirely preposterous, not for them. She *understood* why they thought it would be possible, and that made it all the more infuriating, because how could that be?

"We should finish hiding these stupid eggs," she said.

"Wait. Can we sit for a moment?" Will took her hand and pulled her to the table where she'd sat eating hot cross buns and texting Connor in the sunlight the previous morning, a million years ago. Tess sat down and put the bag of eggs on the table and folded her arms, tucking her hands into her armpits.

"Are you too cold?" asked Will anxiously.

"It's not exactly balmy," snapped Tess. She was all dry-eyed detachment now. "But it's fine. Go ahead. Say your thing."

Will said, "You're right. There wasn't anything wrong with our marriage. I was happy with us. It's just that I was sort of unhappy with me."

"How? Why?" Tess lifted her chin. She already felt defensive. If he was unhappy, then it had to be her fault. Her cooking, her conversation, her body. Something wasn't up to scratch.

"This will sound so lame," said Will. He looked up to the sky and took a breath. "This is in *no way* an excuse. Don't think that for a second. But about six months ago, after my fortieth, I started to feel so . . . the only word I can think of is 'bland.' Or 'flat' might be a better word."

"Flat," repeated Tess.

"Remember how I had all those troubles with my knee? And then my back went? I thought, *Jesus, is this life now? Doctors and pills and pain and bloody* heat packs? *Already? It's all over?* So there was that, and then one day . . . Okay, so this is embarrassing." He chewed his lip and continued. "I got my hair cut, right? And my normal guy wasn't there, and for some reason, the girl held up this little *mirror* to show me the back of my head. I don't know why she would feel the need to do that. I swear to you, I nearly fell off my chair when I saw my bald spot. I thought it was some other bloke's head. I looked like Friar bloody Tuck. I had no idea."

Tess burst out laughing and Will grinned ruefully. "I know," he said. "I know. I just started feeling so . . . middle-aged."

"You *are* middle-aged," said Tess.

He winced. "Thank you. I know. Anyway, this flat feeling. It came and went. It was no big deal. I was waiting for it to pass. Hoping it would pass. And then . . ." He stopped.

"And then Felicity," supplied Tess.

"Felicity," said Will. "I always cared about Felicity. You know how we were together. That sort of banter thing we did. Almost flirting. It was never serious. But then, after she lost the weight, I started to sense this . . . vibe from her. And I guess I was flattered, and it didn't seem to count, because it was *Felicity*, not some random woman. It was safe. It didn't feel like I was betraying you. It felt almost like she was you. But then, somehow, it got out of hand and I found myself . . ." He stopped himself.

"Falling in love with her," said Tess.

"No, not really. I don't think it was really love. It was nothing. As soon as you and Liam walked out the door, I knew it was nothing. It was just a stupid crush, a—"

"Stop." Tess held up her palm as if to put it across his mouth. She didn't want lies, even if they were white lies, or even if he didn't know they were lies, and she also felt a peculiar sense of loyalty toward Felicity. How could he say it was nothing when Felicity's feelings had been so real and powerful? Will was right. She wasn't just some random girl. She was Felicity.

"Why didn't you ever tell me about the flat feeling?" she asked.

"I don't know," said Will. "Because it was idiotic. Feeling depressed about my bald spot. *Jesus*." He shrugged. She wasn't sure if it was just the lighting, but his color seemed high. "Because I didn't want to lose your respect."

Tess laid her hands down on the table and looked at them.

She thought about how one of the jobs of advertising was to give the consumer rational reasons for their irrational purchases. Had Will looked back on his "thing" with Felicity and thought, *Why did I do that*? And then he created this story for himself, which was loosely based on the truth? In the same way that she was still trying to rationalize exactly why she'd risked everything by sleeping with Connor?

"Well, anyway, I have social anxiety," she said chattily.

"Pardon?" Will frowned, as if he'd just been presented with a tricky riddle.

"I get very anxious, over-the-top anxious, about certain social activities. Not everything. Just some things. It's not a big deal. But sometimes it is."

Will pressed his fingertips to his forehead. He seemed puzzled and almost fearful. "I mean, I know you don't like parties much, but I'm not that keen on standing around making small talk myself."

"I have heart palpitations about the school trivia night," said Tess. She looked him squarely in the eye. She felt naked. More naked than she'd ever been in front of him.

"But we don't go to the school trivia night."

"I know. That's why we don't go."

Will lifted his palms. "We don't have to go! I don't care if we don't go."

Tess smiled. "But I sort of care. Who knows? It might be fun. It might be boring. I'd like to start being a little more . . . open to my life."

Will said, "I don't get it. You're not an extrovert, but you go out and get new business for us! *I'd* find that hard!"

"It frightens me half to death," said Tess. "I hate it, and I also love it. I just wish I didn't waste so much time feeling sick."

"But—"

"I read this article recently. There are thousands of us walking around with this neurotic little secret. People you wouldn't expect: CEOs who can do big presentations to shareholders, but can't handle small talk at the Christmas party; actors with crippling shyness; doctors who are terrified of making eye contact. I felt like I had to hide it from everyone, and the more I hid it, the bigger it seemed. I told Felicity today, and she just dismissed it. She said, 'Get over it.' It was strangely liberating, actually, hearing her say that. It was like I finally took this big hairy spider out of a box and someone looked at it and said, 'That's not a spider.'"

"I don't want to dismiss it," said Will. "I want to squash your spider. I want to kill the damned thing."

Tess felt the tears rise again. "I don't want to dismiss your flat feeling either."

Will reached across the table and held out his hand, palm up. She looked at it for a moment, considering, and then she laid her hand in his. The sudden warmth of his hand, its simultaneous familiarity and strangeness, the way it enfolded hers, reminded her of the first time they met, when they were introduced in the reception area of the company where Tess worked, and her usual anxiety about meeting new people was overwhelmed by a powerful attraction to this shortish, grinning man with the laughing gold eyes looking straight into hers.

They sat silently, holding hands, not looking at each other, and Tess thought of the way Felicity's eyes flickered when she asked her if she and Will had held hands on the plane from Melbourne, and she nearly pulled her hand away; but then she remembered standing outside the pub with Connor, his thumb caressing her palm, and for some reason she thought also of Cecilia Fitzpatrick sitting in a hospital room with poor little beautiful Polly right now, and of Liam, safe upstairs, in his blue flannel pajamas, dreaming of chocolate eggs. She looked up at the clear, starry night sky and imagined Felicity on a plane somewhere high above them, flying off into a different day, a different season, a different life, watching the in-flight movie, reading her book, wondering how in the world it had come to this.

The sensor light on her mother's back porch flickered, and suddenly they were plunged into darkness. Neither of them moved.

There were so many decisions to be made. How would they manage the next part of their lives? Would they stay in Sydney? Keep Liam at St. Angela's? Impossible. She'd see Connor every day. What about the business? Would they replace Felicity? That seemed impossible too. In fact, it all seemed impossible. Insurmountable.

What if Will and Felicity really were meant to be together? What if she and Connor were meant to be together? Perhaps there were no answers to questions like that. Perhaps nothing was ever "meant to be." There was just life, and right now, and doing your best. Being a bit "bendy."

"We'll give it until Christmas," said Tess after a moment. "If you still miss her by Christmas, if you still want her by then, you should go to her."

"Don't say that. I've told you. I don't—"

"Shhh." She held his hand tighter, and they sat in the moonlight, clinging to the wreckage of their marriage.

FIFTY-FIVE

I t was done.

Cecilia and John-Paul sat side by side watching Polly's closed eyelids flutter and smooth, flutter and smooth, as if they were tracking the progress of her dreams.

Cecilia held on to Polly's left hand, ignoring the tears sliding down her face and dripping off her chin. She remembered sitting with John-Paul at another hospital, at the dawn of another autumn day, after two hours of intense labor. (Cecilia gave birth efficiently; a little too efficiently with their third daughter.) She and John-Paul were counting Polly's fingers and toes, as they'd done with Isabel and Esther, a ritual like opening and inspecting a marvelous, magical gift.

Now their eyes kept returning to the space where Polly's right arm should have been. It was an anomaly, an oddness, an optical discrepancy. From now on it wouldn't be her beauty that would cause people to stare at her in shopping centers.

Cecilia let the tears slide on and on. She needed to get all her crying out of the way, because she was determined that Polly would never see her shed a tear. Cecilia was about to step into a new life: her life as an amputee's mother. Even as she cried, she could feel her muscles tensing in readiness, as if she were an athlete about to begin a marathon. Soon she would be fluent in a new language of stumps and prostheses and God knows what else. She'd move heaven and earth and bake muffins and pay fraudulent compliments to get the best results for her daughter. No one was better qualified than Cecilia for this role.

But was Polly qualified? That was the question. Was any six-year-old qualified? Did she have the strength of character to live with this sort of injury in a world that put such value on a woman's looks? *She's* still *beautiful*, thought Cecilia furiously, as if someone had denied it.

"She's tough," she said to John-Paul. "Remember that day at the pool when she wanted to prove she could swim as far as Esther?"

She thought of Polly's arms slicing through sunlit chlorinated blue water.

"Jesus. *Swimming*." John-Paul's whole body heaved, and he pressed his palm to the center of his chest as if he were in the throes of a heart attack.

"Don't drop dead on me," said Cecilia sharply.

She pushed the heels of her hands deep into her eye sockets and turned them in a circular motion. She could taste so much salt from all her tears, it was like she'd been swimming in the sea.

"Why did you tell Rachel?" said John-Paul. "Why now?"

She dropped her hands from her face and looked at him. She lowered her voice to a whisper. "Because she thought Connor Whitby killed Janie. She was trying to *hit* Connor."

She watched John-Paul's face as his mind traveled from A to B and finally to the horrendous responsibility of C.

He pressed his fist to his mouth. "Fuck," he said quietly into his knuckles, and he began to rock back and forth like an autistic child.

"This was my fault," he mumbled into his hand. "I made this happen. Oh God, Cecilia. I should have confessed. I should have told Rachel Crowley."

"Stop it," hissed Cecilia. "She might hear."

He stood up and walked toward the door of the hospital room. He turned back and looked at Polly, his face ravaged with despair. He looked away, plucked helplessly at the fabric of his shirt. Then he suddenly crouched down, his head bent, his hands interlocked at the back of his neck.

Cecilia watched him dispassionately. She remembered how he'd sobbed on Good Friday morning. The pain and regret he felt for what he'd done to another man's daughter was nothing compared to what he felt for his own daughter.

She looked away from him and back at Polly. You could try as hard as you could to imagine someone else's tragedy—drowning in icy waters, living in a city split by a wall—but nothing truly hurts until it happens to you. Most of all, to your child.

"Get up, John-Paul," she said without looking at him. Her eyes stayed on Polly.

She thought of Isabel and Esther, who were at home with her parents right now. The siblings always got neglected when something like this happened to a family. She would have to make sure she found a way to be a mother to all three of her daughters through this. The P&F would go. The Tupperware would go. They didn't need the money.

She turned to look again at John-Paul, who was still hunkered down on the floor, as if protecting himself from a bomb blast.

"Get up," she said again. "You can't fall apart. Polly needs you. We all need you."

John-Paul removed his hands from his neck and looked up at her with bloodshot eyes. "But I'm not going to be here for you," he said. "Rachel will tell the police."

"Maybe," said Cecilia. "Maybe she will. But I don't think so. I don't think Rachel is going to take you away from your family." There was no real evidence for this, except somehow she felt, or she did for now, that it was true. "Not right now, anyway."

"But—"

"I think we've paid," said Cecilia, her voice low and vicious. She gestured at Polly. "Look how we've paid."

FIFTY-SIX

Rachel sat in front of the television watching the colorful, hypnotic flicker of images and faces. If someone had turned the TV off and asked her what she'd been watching, she couldn't have answered.

She could pick up the phone right now and have John-Paul Fitzpatrick arrested for murder. She could do it right now, or in an hour's time, or in the morning. She could wait until Polly was home from the hospital, or she could wait a few months. Six months. A year. Give her a year with her father and then take him away. She could wait until the accident was far enough in the past for it to be a memory. She could wait for those Fitzpatrick girls to grow a little older, to get their driver's licenses, to not need a daddy.

It was like she'd been handed a loaded gun, along with permission to shoot Janie's murderer at any time. If Ed were still alive, the trigger would have been pulled already. The police would have been called hours ago.

She thought of John-Paul's hands around Janie's neck

and felt that old familiar rage blossom across her chest. *My little girl.*

She thought of his little girl. The glittery pink helmet. *Brake. Brake. Brake.*

If she told the police about John-Paul's confession, would the Fitzpatricks tell them about her own confession? Would she be arrested for attempted murder? It was only luck that she hadn't killed Connor. Was her foot on the accelerator an equal sin to his hands around Janie's neck? But what happened to Polly was an accident. Everyone knew that. She rode her bike straight in front of her car. It should have been Connor. What if Connor had been dead tonight? *His* family receiving that phone call, the call that meant for the rest of your life you never heard a phone ring or a knock on the door without a chill of fear.

Connor was alive. Polly was alive. Janie was the only one who was dead.

What if he hurt someone else? She remembered his face at the hospital, ravaged with worry over his daughter's mangled body. "She laughed at me." *She* laughed *at you? You stupid, egotistical little bastard. That was enough to make you kill her? To take away her life? To take away all the days she could have lived, the degrees she never earned, the countries she never visited, the husband she never married, the children she never had?* Rachel shook so hard, she felt her teeth chatter.

She stood. She went to the phone and picked it up. Her thumb hovered over the keys. A memory came to her of teaching Janie how to call the police if there was an emergency. They'd still had that old green rotary-dial phone then. She'd let Janie practice by dialing the numbers, and then she'd hang up before it actually rang. Janie wanted to act out a whole little performance. She made Rob lie on the kitchen floor while she yelled into the phone, "I need an ambulance! My brother isn't breathing! Stop breathing," she ordered Rob. "Rob. I can see you breathing." Rob nearly passed out trying to please her.

Little Polly Fitzpatrick wouldn't have a right hand anymore. Was she right-handed? Probably. Most people were right-handed. Janie had been left-handed. One of the nuns tried to make her write with her right hand, and Ed went up to the school and said, "Sister, with all due respect, who do you think made her left-handed? God did! So let's leave her that way."

Rachel pressed a key.

"Hello?" The phone was answered much quicker than she expected.

"Lauren," said Rachel.

"Rachel. Rob's just coming out of the shower," said Lauren. "Is everything all right?"

"I know it's late," said Rachel. She hadn't even looked at the time. "And I know I shouldn't impose like this, after all the time you spent with me yesterday, but I wondered if I could come over and stay the night there? Just this once. For some reason, I don't know why, but I just find myself unable to—"

"Of *course* you can," said Lauren, and suddenly she shrieked, "Rob!" Rachel heard the deep rumble of Rob's voice in the background. She heard Lauren say, "Go and pick up your mother."

Poor dear Rob. Under the thumb, Ed would have said.

"No, no," said Rachel. "He's only just stepped out of the shower. I'll drive myself."

"Absolutely not," said Lauren. "He's on his way. He wasn't doing anything! I'll make up the sofa bed. It's surprisingly comfy! Jacob will be so happy to see you tomorrow morning. I can't wait to see his face."

"Thank you," said Rachel. She felt all at once warm and sleepy, as if someone had placed a blanket over her.

"Lauren?" she said before she hung up. "You don't have any more of those macarons, do you? Like the ones you brought for me on Monday night? They were divine. Absolutely divine."

There was the briefest of pauses. "Actually, I do." There was a quiver in Lauren's voice. "We can have some with a cup of tea."

FIFTY-SEVEN

EASTER SUNDAY

Tess woke to the sound of heavy rain. It was still dark, about five a.m., she guessed. Will lay on his side next to her, facing the wall and snoring gently. The shape and smell and feel of him were so ordinary and familiar; the events of the past week seemed inconceivable. She could have made Will sleep on her mother's couch, but then she would have had to deal with Liam's questions. He was already far too aware that things were not quite normal; at the dinner table tonight she'd noticed his eyes darting constantly back and forth between herself and Will, monitoring their conversation. His wary little face broke her heart, and made her so furious with Will she could barely look at him.

She shifted slightly away from Will's body so that they weren't touching. It was handy that she had her own guilty secret. It helped bring her breathing back to normal during those sudden bursts of rage. He'd wronged her. She'd wronged him right back.

Had they both been suffering a form of temporary insanity? It was a defense for murder, after all; why not for married couples? Marriage was a form of insanity; love hovering permanently on the edge of aggravation.

Connor would be asleep now, in his neat apartment smelling of garlic and laundry powder, already beginning the process of moving on and forgetting her for the second time. Was he kicking himself for falling for that no-good, coldhearted woman yet again?

Why was she making herself sound like a woman in a country song? To soften it, presumably; to make her behavior seem tender and melancholy, not slutty. She had a feeling that Connor liked country music, but she might have been making it up, confusing him with another ex-boyfriend. She didn't really know him.

Will couldn't stand country music.

That was why the sex had been so good with Connor: because they were essentially strangers. It was his otherness. It made everything—their bodies, their personalities, their feelings—seem more sharply defined, and therefore superior. It wasn't logical, but the better you knew someone, the more blurry they became. The accumulation of facts made them disappear. It was more interesting wondering if someone did or didn't like country music than knowing one way or the other.

She and Will must have made love, what, a thousand

times? At least. She started to calculate it, but she was too tired. The rain got harder, as if someone had turned up the volume. Liam would have to do his Easter egg hunt with an umbrella and rain boots. It must have rained on Easter Sunday before in her lifetime, but all her memories were sun-dappled and blue-skied, as if this were the first sad, rainy Easter Sunday of her life.

Liam wouldn't care about the rain. He'd probably love it. She and Will would look at each other and laugh, and then they'd look away again, fast, and they'd both be thinking about Felicity and how strange it was without her. Could they do this? Could they make it work on behalf of one beautiful little six-year-old boy?

She began to slip toward sleep.

Maybe Mum was right, she thought hazily. *It's all about our egos.* She felt she was on the edge of understanding something important. They could fall in love with fresh, new people, or they could have the courage and humility to tear off some essential layer of themselves and reveal to each other a whole new level of otherness, a level far beyond what sort of music they liked. It seemed to her everyone had too much self-protective pride to truly strip down to their souls in front of their long-term partners. It was easier to pretend there was nothing more to know, to fall into an easygoing companionship. It was almost embarrassing to be truly intimate with your spouse; how could you watch someone floss one minute, and the next minute share your deepest passion or most ridiculous, trite little fears? It was almost easier to talk about that sort of thing *before* you'd shared a bathroom and a bank account and argued over the packing of the dishwasher. But now that this had happened, she and Will had no choice; otherwise they'd hate each other for what they were sacrificing for Liam.

And maybe they'd already begun, when they shared their stories last night about bald spots and school trivia nights. She felt equal parts hilarity and tenderness at the thought of Will's face dropping when the hairdresser held up the mirror to show him the back of his head.

The compass her father had sent her was sitting on the bedside table. She wondered what would have happened to her parents' marriage if they'd decided to stay together for her. If they'd really tried, out of love for her, could they have done it? Probably not. But she was convinced that Liam's happiness was the most valid reason in the world for her and Will to be here right now.

She remembered how Will had said that he wanted to squash her spider. He wanted to kill it.

Maybe he wasn't here entirely for Liam's sake.

Maybe she wasn't either.

The wind howled and the glass of her bedroom window rattled. The temperature in the room seemed to plunge, and Tess felt all at once violently cold. Thank God Liam was wearing his warm pajamas and she'd put that extra blanket on him; otherwise she'd have to get up in the cold and go check on him. She rolled toward Will and pressed the length of her body against his back. The warmth was an exquisite relief, and she felt herself begin to slide back into sleep, but at the same time she pressed her lips to the back of his neck, accidentally, reflexively. She felt Will stir and put his hand back to caress her hip, and without either of them making a decision or asking the question, they found themselves making love, quiet, sleepy, married love, and every move felt sweet and simple and familiar, except that they didn't usually cry.

FIFTY-EIGHT

Grandma! Grandma!"

Rachel emerged slowly from a deep, dreamless sleep. It was the first time in years that she'd slept without the lights on. Jacob's room had heavy dark drapes across the window, like in a hotel, and Rachel had fallen asleep almost instantly on the sofa bed pulled out next to his toddler bed. Lauren was right; the sofa bed was surprisingly comfy. She couldn't remember the last time she'd slept so deeply; it felt like a skill from her past she'd assumed she'd lost forever, like turning a cartwheel.

"Hello," she said. She could just make out the shape of Jacob's little body standing next to her bed. His face was level with hers, his eyes shining in the darkness.

"You *here*!" He was amazed.

"I know," she said. She was amazed herself. Lauren and Rob had offered for her to stay the night so many times, and she'd always refused instantly and adamantly, as if she had a religious objection to the idea.

"Raining," said Jacob solemnly, and she registered the sound of heavy, settled rain.

There was no clock in the room, but it felt like it was about six o'clock, too early to start the day. She remembered with a slight sinking of the heart that she'd said she'd go to Lauren's family's house for Easter lunch. Perhaps she'd feign illness. She'd stayed the night after all; they would have had enough of her by lunchtime, and she would have had enough of them.

"Do you want to hop in with me?" she said to Jacob.

Jacob chortled, as if she were one crazy grandma, and hauled himself up into the bed. He climbed on top of her and buried his face in her neck. His little body was warm and heavy. She pressed her lips against the silken skin of his cheek.

"I wonder if . . ." She caught herself just in time before she said, *I wonder if the Easter Bunny has been.* He would have hurled himself from the bed and run through the house searching for eggs, waking up Rob and Lauren, and Rachel would have been the annoying houseguest and mother-in-law who reminded the child it was Easter.

"I wonder if we should go back to sleep," she said instead, thinking it highly unlikely for both of them.

"Nah," he said. Rachel felt the soft flutter of his eyelashes against her neck.

"Do you know how much I'll miss you when you're in New York?" she said in his ear. It made no sense to him, of course. He ignored the question and wriggled himself into a more comfortable position.

"Grandma," he said happily.

"Oof," she said as he dug his knee into her stomach.

The rain got harder, and the room felt suddenly colder. She pulled the blankets tighter around their bodies and held Jacob closer, and sang into his ear, "It's raining, it's pouring, the old man is snoring; went to bed and bumped his head and couldn't get up in the morning."

"Again," demanded Jacob.

She sang again.

Little Polly Fitzpatrick was waking up this morning with a body that would never be the same because of what Rachel had done. It would seem outrageous to John-Paul and Cecilia. They'd be shocked for months, before they finally learned, like Rachel had, that the unthinkable happened, and the world kept turning, and people still talked at length about the weather, and there were still traffic jams and electricity bills, celebrity scandals and political coups.

At some point, when Polly was home from the hospital, Rachel would ask John-Paul to come to her home and describe Janie's last moments to her. She could see exactly how it would be. His strained, frightened face when she opened her door. She would make her daughter's murderer a cup of tea, and he would sit at her kitchen table and talk. She wouldn't grant him absolution, but she'd make him tea. She would never forgive him, but perhaps she would never report him or ask him to give himself up. After he left, she would sit on her couch and she would rock and keen and howl. One last time. She would never stop crying for Janie, but that would be the last time she cried like that.

Then she would make a fresh pot of tea and she'd decide. She would make her final decision about what needed to be done, what price needed to be paid, or if, in fact, it had already been paid.

". . . went to bed and bumped his head and couldn't get up in the morning."

Jacob was asleep. She shifted his weight off her and moved him over, so his head was sharing her pillow.

On Tuesday she would tell Trudy that she was retiring from St. Angela's. She couldn't go back to school and risk seeing little Polly Fitzpatrick or her father. It was impossible. It was time to sell the house, sell the memories, sell the pain.

Her thoughts turned to Connor Whitby. Was there a moment when his eyes met hers as he ran across the road? A moment when he recognized her murderous intent and ran for his life? Or was she imagining it? He was the boy that Janie had chosen over John-Paul Fitzpatrick. *You chose the wrong boy, darling.* She would have lived if she'd chosen John-Paul.

She wondered if Janie had truly loved Connor. Was Connor the son-in-law Rachel was meant to have in that fantasy parallel life she never got to live? And did Rachel therefore owe it to Janie's memory to do something nice for Connor? Have him over for dinner? She shuddered at the thought. Absolutely not. She couldn't turn off her feelings like a tap. She could still see the fury on Connor's face in that video, and the way Janie had shrunk from him. She knew, intellectually at least, that it was nothing more than an ordinary teenage boy desperate for a straight answer from a teenage girl, but that didn't mean she forgave him.

She thought of the way Connor had smiled at Janie in

the video before he lost his temper. The genuinely smitten smile. She remembered too the photo in Janie's album: the one where Connor had been laughing so fondly over something Janie said.

Perhaps one day she'd mail Connor Whitby a copy of that photo with a card. *Thought you might like to have this.* A subtle apology for the way she'd treated him over the years, and, oh yes, a subtle apology for trying to kill him. Let's not forget that. She grimaced in the darkness, and turned her head and pressed her lips against Jacob's scalp for comfort.

Tomorrow, I'll go to the post office and pick up a passport application, she thought. *I'll visit them in New York. Maybe I'll even do one of those damned Alaskan cruises. Marla and Mac can come with me. They don't mind the cold.*

Go back to sleep now, Mum, said Janie. For a moment, Rachel could see her so clearly. The middle-aged woman she would have become, so sure of herself and her place in the world, bossy and loving, condescending and impatient with her dear old mum, helping her get her first-ever passport.

Can't sleep, said Rachel.

Yes, you can, said Janie.

Rachel slept.

FIFTY-NINE

The official demolition of the Berlin Wall happened as effi-
ciently as its construction. On June 22, 1990, Checkpoint
Charlie, the famous symbol of the Cold War, was dismantled
in a strangely prosaic ceremony. A giant crane lifted out the
famous beige metal shack in one piece, watched by foreign
ministers and other dignitaries seated on rows of plastic
chairs.

On the same day, in another hemisphere, Cecilia Bell, fresh
back from her trip to Europe with her friend Sarah Sacks and
in an extreme state of readiness for a boyfriend and a prop-
erly structured life, went to a housewarming party in a
crowded two-bedroom unit in Lane Cove.

"You probably know John-Paul Fitzpatrick, don't you,
Cecilia?" the party's host shouted over the thump of the music.

"Hi," said John-Paul. Cecilia took his hand, met his
grave eyes and smiled as though she'd just been granted her
freedom.

—

M ummy."

Cecilia woke with a giant gasp, as if she'd been drowning. She'd been dreaming of the little Spider-Man boy. Except in the dream he was Polly. Her mouth felt dry and hollowed out. She must have been asleep with her head tipped back against the chair next to Polly's bed, her mouth gaping. John-Paul had gone home to be with the girls and get them both some clean clothes. Later on this morning, if Cecilia gave the word, he would bring Isabel and Esther in for a visit.

"Polly," she said frantically.

"Try to watch your body language," the social worker had said to her last night. "Children read you much better than you think. Your tone of voice. Your facial expressions. Your gestures."

Yes, thank you, I know what body language is, thought Cecilia. The social worker had her hair pushed back with a pair of oversize sunglasses, as if she were at a beach party, not at the hospital at six o'clock at night, talking to parents in the middle of their own worst nightmares. Cecilia couldn't forgive her for the flippancy of those damned sunglasses.

Of course, wouldn't you know it, Good Friday was the worst time for your child to suffer a traumatic injury. A lot of the regular staff were off for the Easter break, so it would be a few days before Cecilia met all the members of Polly's "rehabilitation team," including a physical therapist, an occupational therapist, a psychologist and a prosthesis specialist. It was both comforting and horrifying to know that there were procedures in place for this with information packs and "top tips" and that they would be traveling a path already trod by so many other parents. Each time someone talked with matter-of-fact authority to Cecilia about what lay ahead, there would be a moment when she lost the thread of what they were saying, because she would suddenly feel immobilized by shock. No one at the hospital was sufficiently *surprised* by what had happened to Polly. None of the nurses or doctors clutched Cecilia's arm and said, "My God, I can't believe it. I just can't believe it." It would be disconcerting if they did, but it was also somehow disconcerting that they didn't.

That's why it was comforting to listen to the dozens of messages on her mobile phone from her family and friends; to hear her sister, Bridget, practically incoherent with shock; to hear the normally unflappable Mahalia's voice breaking in two; to hear the school principal, dear Trudy McDuff, burst into tears, apologize, and then call back and do it again. (Her mother said no fewer than *fourteen* casseroles had already been delivered by school mums. All those casseroles she'd made over the years finally coming home to roost.)

"Mummy," muttered Polly again, but her eyes were shut. She seemed to be talking in her sleep. She shuddered, and her head moved from side to side agitatedly, as if in pain or fear. Cecilia's hand hovered over the call button for the nurse, but then Polly's face calmed.

Cecilia breathed out. She hadn't realized she was holding her breath. This kept happening too. She had to remember to breathe.

She sat back in the chair and wondered how John-Paul was doing with the girls, and without warning she was racked with a violent spasm of hatred like nothing she'd ever felt in her life. She hated him for what he'd done to Janie Crowley all those years ago. He was responsible for Rachel Crowley's foot on the accelerator. The hatred spread throughout her body like fast-acting poison. She wanted to kick him, to punch him, to kill him. Dear God. She couldn't bear to be in the same room as him. She breathed shallowly and looked around her desperately for something to break or hit. *Now is not the time,* she told herself. *This will not help Polly.*

He blames himself, she reminded herself. The thought of his suffering gave her some relief. The hatred gradually eased to a manageable level. She knew that it would come again, that as Polly suffered through each new stage, Cecilia would look for someone to blame—other than herself. That was the root of the hatred: the knowledge of her own responsibility. Her decision to sacrifice Rachel Crowley for her family had led to this moment in this hospital room.

She knew that her marriage was damaged at its very core, but she knew also that they would keep limping along together like wounded soldiers for Polly's sake. She'd learn how to live with the waves of hatred. It would be her secret. Her loathsome secret.

And once the waves passed, there would still be love. It was an entirely different feeling from the uncomplicated, unstinting adoration she'd felt as a young bride, walking down the aisle to that serious, handsome man; but she knew that no matter how much she hated him for what he'd done, the love was still there, like a deep seam of gold in her heart. It would always be there.

Think about something else. She pulled out her iPhone and began making a list. First up, Polly's seventh birthday. Could they have a pirate party in the hospital? Of course they could. It would be the most wonderful, magical party ever. She'd make the nurses wear eye patches.

"Mum?" Polly opened her eyes.

"Hello, Princess Polly," said Cecilia. This time she was ready, like an actress about to sweep onto a stage. "Guess who dropped off something for you last night?" She produced an Easter egg from under Polly's pillow. It was wrapped in shimmering gold, with a red velvet ribbon tied around the middle.

Polly smiled. "The Easter Bunny?"

"Even better. Mr. Whitby."

Polly went to hold out her hand for the egg, and an expression of mild bemusement crossed her beautiful face. She frowned at her mother and waited for her to fix things.

Cecilia cleared her throat, smiled and took Polly's left hand firmly in her own.

"Darling," she said.

So it began.

EPILOGUE

There are so many secrets about our lives we'll never know.

Rachel Crowley will never know that her husband wasn't, as he said, seeing clients in Adelaide the day that Janie was killed. He was on a tennis court, taking part in an intensive tennis workshop he hoped would teach him how to break bloody Toby Murphy's serve. Ed hadn't told Rachel beforehand because he was embarrassed by his motivations (he'd seen the way Toby looked at his wife, and the way Rachel looked back), and he never told her afterward because he was deeply ashamed and blamed himself, however illogically, for not being there for Janie. He never picked up his racquet again, and took his silly secret to his death.

Speaking of tennis, Polly Fitzpatrick will never know that if she hadn't ridden her bike in front of Rachel Crowley's car that day, she would have received a tennis racquet for her seventh birthday from her Auntie Bridget. Two weeks later she would have turned up for her first tennis lesson, where after twenty minutes her coach would have gone over to his boss on the next court and said quietly, "Come and see this kid's forehand," and the swing of her racquet would have changed her future as swiftly as it changed when she swung the handlebars of her bike to follow Mr. Whitby.

Polly will also never know that Mr. Whitby did hear her call out to him that terrible Good Friday, but pretended not to, because he was desperate to get home and put his ludicrous fish kite back in the cupboard, along with his equally ludicrous hopes about another chance at a relationship with his goddamned ex-girlfriend Tess O'Leary. Connor's crippling guilt over Polly's accident will help put his therapist's daughter through Year 9 of private school, and will only begin to ease on the day he finally raises his eyes to meet those of the beautiful woman who owns the Indian restaurant where he has his post-therapy curry.

Tess will never know for sure whether her husband, Will, is the biological father of their second child, the result of an accidental pregnancy conceived one strange April week in Sydney. The pill works only when you take it, and she'd left the packet behind in Melbourne when she flew to Sydney. Not a word will ever be spoken of the possibility, although when Tess's adored teenage daughter mentions one year at Christmas lunch that she's decided to be a PE teacher, her grandmother will choke on a mouthful of turkey and her mother's cousin will spill champagne all over her handsome French husband's lap.

John-Paul Fitzpatrick will never know that if Janie had

remembered the doctor's appointment that day in 1984, her doctor would have listened to her describe her symptoms and, after observing her unusually tall, long, skinny body, would have tentatively diagnosed her with a condition called Marfan syndrome, an incurable genetic disorder of the connective tissues thought to have been suffered by Abraham Lincoln, involving elongated limbs, long thin fingers and cardiovascular complications. Symptoms include fatigue, shortness of breath, a racing heartbeat and cold hands and feet due to poor circulation, all of which Janie experienced on the day she died. It's a hereditary condition, probably also suffered by Rachel's Auntie Petra, who dropped dead when she was twenty. The GP, who, thanks to an overbearing mother, was a high achiever and an excellent doctor, would have arranged an urgent appointment at the hospital for Janie, where an ultrasound would have confirmed her concerns and saved Janie's life.

John-Paul will never know that it was an aortic aneurysm that killed Janie, not traumatic asphyxiation, and that if the forensic pathologist who did Janie's autopsy hadn't been suffering from a debilitating flu that day, he would not have been so willing to acquiesce to the Crowley family's request for a limited autopsy if possible. Another pathologist would have done the full autopsy and seen the evidence, clear as day, of an aortic dissection, the indisputable cause of Janie's death.

If it had been any other girl but Janie Crowley in the park that day, she would have staggered, gasping for air, when John-Paul realized what he was doing before the seven to fourteen seconds it takes for the average man to strangle the average woman and dropped his hands, and she would have run, tears streaming, ignoring his shouted apologies. Another girl would have reported John-Paul to the police, who would have charged him with assault, sending his life ricocheting in an entirely different direction.

John-Paul will never know that if Janie had gone to her doctor's appointment that afternoon, she would have had urgent lifesaving surgery that very night, and while her heart was recovering, she would have phoned John-Paul and broken his heart over the phone. She would have married Connor Whitby far too young and divorced him ten days after their second wedding anniversary.

Less than six months later, Janie would have bumped into John-Paul Fitzpatrick at a housewarming party in Lane Cove, just moments before Cecilia Bell walked in the door.

None of us ever know all the possible courses our lives could have and maybe should have taken. It's probably just as well. Some secrets are meant to stay secret forever. Just ask Pandora.

ACKNOWLEDGMENTS

I had only a handful of readers in the United States until I was fortunate enough to be taken under the wing of the talented and wonderful Amy Einhorn. Thank you so much to everyone at Amy Einhorn Books for all your support, with special thanks to Elizabeth Stein. Thank you also to my agent, Faye Bender, and to Cate Paterson, Samantha Sainsbury and Alexandra Nahlous in Australia, Samantha Humphreys and Celine Kelly in the UK and Daniela Jarzynka in Germany.

I'm very grateful to my friend Lena Spark, who gave me expert medical advice and answered my mildly gruesome questions while we pushed our children in the swings at the park. Any mistakes are most definitely mine.

Thank you to my sisters for being my sisters: Jaclyn Moriarty, Katrina Harrington, Fiona Ostric and Nicola Moriarty. Thank you to Adam for the cups of tea, and to George and Anna for letting me "work on the computer." Thank you to Anna Kuper for gently encouraging George and Anna to let me work on the computer.

Thank you to my fellow authors and friends, Dianne Blacklock and Ber Carroll. Touring with you two by my side is always so much fun.

Most important of all, thank you to the readers who take the time to write to me. I'm addicted to your e-mails, your Facebook and blog comments. I think I must have the loveliest, most generous readers in the world.

The book *Berlin: The Biography of a City* by Anthony Read and David Fisher was invaluable to me in writing this novel.

THE
HUSBAND'S SECRET

DISCUSSION QUESTIONS

1. When Cecilia finds the letter addressed to her from her husband, "*To be opened only in the event of my death*," she is tormented by the ethics of opening it. Do you agree with her ultimate decision? What would you have done?

2. Consider the title *The Husband's Secret*. Several characters in the book have secrets they hold on to that they eventually reveal. Felicity and Will share the secret of their affair with Tess; John-Paul guards his secret from Cecilia until he is forced to admit it. What are the ramifications of their secrets? Is secrecy in a marriage ever warranted or justifiable?

3. Tess has suffered her whole life from crippling social anxiety. How has this made everyday situations a challenge for her? Why has she never confronted her problem? Why doesn't she tell anyone about it?

4. The Berlin Wall is referred to throughout the novel as Esther works on her school project. And, in fact, we learn that Cecilia met John-Paul on the day the Wall finally came down. What does the Wall signify in the book?

5. Grief is a major theme in the novel, and many of the characters have suffered as a result of their losses. How has grief affected Rachel? Rob? Tess? John-Paul? How do they each cope? In what ways have their lives been irrevocably altered as a result of their grieving? Do you think people can fully stop grieving and move on with their lives?

6. The concept of guilt also plays a major role in the novel. Rachel feels that because of a brief flirtation with Toby Murphy she was absent when Janie died. John-Paul continues to sacrifice things that he loves, out of guilt for what he did to Janie. It seems that these characters have never been able to recover from the feelings of guilt caused by their actions. Yet at the same time, other characters in the book do not appear to feel guilt in the same way. Consider Felicity and Will. Do they have remorse for their affair? Does Tess regret her fling with Connor? What determines how guilty one feels—is it the situation, or is it determined by an individual's character?

7. Tess and Felicity have a history of making snide comments about other people. Tess realizes this only once she is out of the comfort zone she's shared with Felicity for so many years. How has such negative energy affected her relationships with others? Do you think she and Felicity are actually cruel, or is there another reason for their unkind behavior?

8. Ethics and morals are important themes in the book. Discuss how John-Paul, Cecilia, Tess, Will, and Rachel

have each done something they would not have thought possible. Have you ever acted in a way that seems entirely out of character? How did you feel? Does love cause people to do things they wouldn't normally do?

9. Consider the notion of betrayal in this book. Which characters have betrayed someone they love? Are their acts of betrayal premeditated, or are they unplanned decisions that become regrettable actions? When one person betrays another, can that person be forgiven? Or is the damage irreparable?

10. The novel is narrated in third-person and in past tense. Given the intense focus on three women, why did the author choose to tell the story from this point of view? How does this perspective add a sense of mystery and foreboding?

11. Cecilia has been married to John-Paul for fifteen years and has three children with him. Until she opens his letter, she seems to trust him and believe him to be the wonderful husband and father she's always thought him to be. But when she discovers his terrible, sinful secret, she begins to question him. How well can one know one's spouse? Is it possible to ever completely know another person?

TURN THE PAGE FOR A SPECIAL PREVIEW OF THE #1 *NEW YORK TIMES* BESTSELLER

"Irresistible...Will keep you turning the pages."—*People*

"Reading one [of Liane Moriarty's novels] is a bit like drinking a pink cosmo laced with arsenic...[*Big Little Lies*] is a fun, engaging, and sometimes disturbing read."—*USA Today*

lianemoriarty.com
penguin.com

Penguin Random House

ONE

"That doesn't sound like a school trivia night," said Mrs. Patty Ponder to Marie Antoinette. "That sounds like a riot."

The cat didn't respond. She was dozing on the couch and found school trivia nights to be trivial.

"Not interested, eh? Let them eat cake! Is that what you're thinking? They do eat a lot of cake, don't they? All those cake stalls. Goodness me. Although I don't think any of the mothers ever actually eat them. They're all so sleek and skinny, aren't they? Like you."

Marie Antoinette sneered at the compliment. The "let them eat cake" thing had grown old a long time ago, and she'd recently heard one of Mrs. Ponder's grandchildren say it was meant to be "let them eat brioche" and also that Marie Antoinette never said it in the first place.

Mrs. Ponder picked up her television remote and turned down the volume on *Dancing with the Stars*. She'd turned it up loud earlier because of the sound of the heavy rain, but the downpour had eased now.

She could hear people shouting. Angry hollers crashed through the quiet, cold night air. It was somehow hurtful for Mrs. Ponder to hear, as if all that rage were directed at her. (Mrs. Ponder had grown up with an angry mother.)

"Goodness me. Do you think they're arguing over the capital of Guatemala? Do you know the capital of Guatemala? No? I don't either. We should Google it. Don't sneer at me."

Marie Antoinette sniffed.

"Let's go see what's going on," said Mrs. Ponder briskly. She was feeling nervous and therefore behaving briskly in front of the cat, the same way she'd once done with her children when her husband was away and there were strange noises in the night.

Mrs. Ponder heaved herself up with the help of her walker. Marie Antoinette slid her slippery body comfortingly in between Mrs. Ponder's legs (she wasn't falling for the brisk act) as she pushed the walker down the hallway to the back of the house.

Her sewing room looked straight out onto the school yard of Pirriwee Public.

"Mum, are you mad? You can't live this close to a primary school," her daughter had said when she was first looking at buying the house.

But Mrs. Ponder loved to hear the crazy babble of children's voices at intervals throughout the day, and she no longer drove, so she couldn't care less that the street was jammed with those giant, truck-like cars they all drove these days, with women in big sunglasses leaning across their steering wheels to call out terribly urgent information about Harriett's ballet and Charlie's speech therapy.

Mothers took their mothering so seriously now. Their frantic little faces. Their busy little bottoms strutting into the school in their tight gym gear. Ponytails swinging. Eyes fixed on the mobile phones held in the palms of their hands like compasses. It made Mrs. Ponder laugh. Fondly though. Her three daughters, although older, were exactly the same. And they were all so pretty.

"How are you this morning?" she always called out if she was on the front porch with a cup of tea or watering the front garden as they went by.

"Busy, Mrs. Ponder! Frantic!" they always called back, trotting along, yanking their children's arms. They were pleasant and friendly and just a touch condescending because they couldn't help it. She was so old! They were so busy!

The fathers, and there were more and more of them doing the school run these days, were different. They rarely hurried, strolling past with a measured casualness. No big deal. All under control. That was the message. Mrs Ponder chuckled fondly at them too.

But now it seemed the Pirriwee Public parents were misbehaving. She got to the window and pushed aside the lace curtain. The school had recently paid for a window guard after a cricket ball had smashed the glass and nearly knocked out Marie Antoinette. (A group of Year 3 boys had given her a hand-painted apology card, which she kept on her fridge.)

There was a two-story sandstone building on the other side of the playground with an event room on the second level and a big balcony with ocean views. Mrs. Ponder had been there for a few functions: a talk by a local historian, a lunch hosted by the Friends of the Library. It was quite a beautiful room. Sometimes ex-students had their wedding receptions there. That's where they'd be having the school trivia night. They were raising funds for SMART Boards, whatever they were. Mrs. Ponder had been invited as a matter of course. Her proximity to the school gave her a funny sort of honorary status, even though she'd never had a child or grandchild attend. She'd said no thank you to the school trivia night invitation. She thought school events without the children in attendance were pointless.

The children had their weekly school assembly in the same room. Each Friday morning, Mrs. Ponder set herself up in the sewing room with a cup of English Breakfast and a ginger-nut biscuit. The sound of the children singing floating down from the second floor of the building always made her weep. She'd never believed in God, except when she heard children singing.

There was no singing now.

Mrs. Ponder could hear a lot of bad language. She wasn't a prude about bad language—her eldest daughter swore like a trooper—but it was upsetting and disconcerting to hear someone maniacally screaming that particular four-letter word in a place that was normally filled with childish laughter and shouts.

"Are you all drunk?" she said.

Her rain-splattered window was at eye level with the

entrance doors to the building, and suddenly people began to spill out. Security lights illuminated the paved area around the entrance like a stage set for a play. Clouds of mist added to the effect.

It was a strange sight.

The parents at Pirriwee Public had a baffling fondness for costume parties. It wasn't enough that they should have an ordinary trivia night; she knew from the invitation that some bright spark had decided to make it an "Audrey and Elvis" trivia night, which meant that the women all had to dress up as Audrey Hepburn and the men had to dress up as Elvis Presley. (That was another reason Mrs. Ponder had turned down the invitation. She'd always abhorred costume parties.) It seemed that the most popular rendition of Audrey Hepburn was the *Breakfast at Tiffany's* look. All the women were wearing long black dresses, white gloves and pearl chokers. Meanwhile, the men had mostly chosen to pay tribute to the Elvis of the latter years. They were all wearing shiny white jumpsuits, glittery gemstones and plunging necklines. The women looked lovely. The poor men looked perfectly ridiculous.

As Mrs. Ponder watched, one Elvis punched another across the jaw. He staggered back into an Audrey. Two Elvises grabbed him from behind and pulled him away. An Audrey buried her face in her hands and turned aside, as though she couldn't bear to watch. Someone shouted, "Stop this!"

Indeed. What would your beautiful children think?

"Should I call the police?" wondered Mrs. Ponder out loud, but then she heard the wail of a siren in the distance, at the same time as a woman on the balcony began to scream and scream.

Gabrielle: It wasn't like it was just the mothers, you know. It wouldn't have happened without the dads. I guess it *started* with the mothers. We were the main players, so to speak. The mums. I can't stand the word "mum." It's a frumpy word. "Mom" is better. With an *o*. It sounds skinnier. We should change to the American spelling. I have body-image issues, by the way. Who doesn't, right?

Bonnie: It was all just a terrible misunderstanding. People's feelings got hurt, and then everything just spiraled out of control. The way it does. All conflict can be traced back to someone's feelings getting hurt, don't you think? Divorce. World wars. Legal action. Well, maybe not every legal action. Can I offer you an herbal tea?

Stu: I'll tell you exactly why it happened: *Women don't let things go.* Not saying the blokes don't share part of the blame. But if the girls hadn't gotten their knickers in a knot . . . And that might sound sexist, but it's not, it's just a fact of life. Ask any man—not some new-age, artsy-fartsy, I-wear-moisturizer type, I mean a real man—ask a real man, then he'll tell you that women are like the Olympic athletes of grudges.

You should see my wife in action. And she's not even the worst of them.

Miss Barnes: Helicopter parents. Before I started at Pirriwee Public, I thought it was an exaggeration, this thing about parents being overly involved with their kids. I mean, my mum and dad loved me, they were, like, *interested* in me when I was growing up in the nineties, but they weren't, like, *obsessed* with me.

Mrs. Lipmann: It's a tragedy, and deeply regrettable, and we're all trying to move forward. I have no further comment.

Carol: I blame the Erotic Book Club. But that's just me.

Jonathan: There was nothing erotic about the Erotic Book Club, I'll tell you that for free.

Jackie: You know what? I see this as a feminist issue.

Harper: Who said it was a feminist issue? What the heck? I'll tell you what started it: the *incident* at the kindergarten orientation day.

Graeme: My understanding was that it all goes back to the stay-at-home mums battling it out with the career mums. What do they call it? The Mummy Wars. My wife wasn't involved. She doesn't have time for that sort of thing.

Thea: You journalists are just loving the French-nanny angle. I heard someone on the radio today talking about the "French maid," which Juliette was certainly not. Renata had a housekeeper as well. Lucky for some. I have four children, and no staff to help out! Of course, I don't have a problem *per se* with working mothers, I just wonder why they bothered having children in the first place.

Melissa: You know what I think got everyone all hot and bothered? The head lice. Oh my gosh, don't let me get started on the head lice.

Samantha: The head lice? What did that have to do with anything? Who told you that? I bet it was Melissa, right? That poor girl suffered post-traumatic stress disorder after her kids kept getting reinfected. Sorry. It's not funny. It's not funny at all.

Detective-Sergeant Adrian Quinlan: Let me be clear: This is not a circus. This is a murder investigation.

TWO

orty. Madeline Martha Mackenzie was forty years old today.

"I am forty," she said out loud as she drove. She drew the word out in slow motion, like a sound effect. *"Fooorty."*

She caught the eye of her daughter in the rearview mirror. Chloe grinned and imitated her mother. "I am five. *Fiiiive.*"

"Forty!" trilled Madeline like an opera singer. "Tra la la la!"

"Five!" trilled Chloe.

Madeline tried a rap version, beating out the rhythm on the steering wheel. "I'm forty, yeah, forty—"

"That's enough now, Mummy," said Chloe firmly.

"Sorry," said Madeline.

She was taking Chloe to her kindergarten—"Let's Get

Kindy Ready!"—orientation. Not that Chloe required any orientation before starting school next January. She was already very firmly oriented at Pirriwee Public. At this morning's drop-off Chloe had been busy taking charge of her brother, Fred, who was two years older but often seemed younger. "Fred, you forgot to put your book bag in the basket! That's it. In there. Good boy."

Fred had obediently dropped his book bag in the appropriate basket before running off to put Jackson in a headlock. Madeline had pretended not to see the headlock. Jackson probably deserved it. Jackson's mother, Renata, hadn't seen it either, because she was deep in conversation with Harper, both of them frowning earnestly over the stress of educating their gifted children. Renata and Harper attended the same weekly support group for parents of gifted children. Madeline imagined them all sitting in a circle, wringing their hands while their eyes shone with secret pride.

While Chloe was busy bossing the other children around at orientation (her gift was bossiness; she was going to run a corporation one day), Madeline was going to have coffee and cake with her friend Celeste. Celeste's twin boys were starting school next year too, so they'd be running amuck at orientation. (Their gift was shouting. Madeline had a headache after five minutes in their company.) Celeste always bought exquisite and very expensive birthday presents, so that would be nice. After that, Madeline was going to drop Chloe off with her mother-in-law, and then have lunch with some friends before they all rushed off for school pickup. The sun was shining. She was wearing her gorgeous new Dolce & Gabbana stilettos (bought online, thirty percent off). It was going to be a lovely, lovely day.

"Let the Festival of Madeline begin!" her husband, Ed, had said this morning when he brought her coffee in bed. Madeline was famous for her fondness of birthdays and celebrations of all kinds. Any excuse for champagne.

Still. Forty.

As she drove the familiar route to the school, she considered her magnificent new age. Forty. She could still feel "forty" the way it felt when she was fifteen. Such a colorless age. Marooned in the middle of your life. Nothing would matter all that much when you were forty. You wouldn't have real feelings when you were forty, because you'd be safely cushioned by your frumpy forty-ness.

Forty-year-old woman found dead. Oh dear.

Twenty-year-old woman found dead. Tragedy! Sadness! Find that murderer!

Madeline had recently been forced to do a minor shift in her head when she heard something on the news about a woman dying in her forties. *But, wait, that could be me! That would be sad! People would be sad if I was dead! Devastated, even. So there, age-obsessed world. I might be forty, but I am cherished.*

On the other hand, it was probably perfectly natural to feel sadder over the death of a twenty-year-old than a forty-year-old. The forty-year-old had enjoyed twenty years more of life. That's why, if there was a gunman on the loose, Madeline would feel obligated to throw her middle-aged self in front of the twenty-year-old. Take a bullet for youth. It was only fair.

Well, she would, if she could be sure it was a nice young person. Not one of those insufferable ones, like the child driving the little blue Mitsubishi in front of Madeline. She wasn't even bothering to hide the fact that she was using her mobile phone while she drove, probably *texting* or updating her Facebook status.

See! This kid wouldn't have even noticed the loose gunman! She would have been staring vacantly at her phone, while Madeline sacrificed her life for her! It was infuriating.

The little car appeared to be jammed with young people. At least three in the back, their heads bobbing about, hands gesticulating. Was that somebody's foot waving about? It was a tragedy waiting to happen. They all needed to concentrate. Just last week, Madeline had been having a quick coffee after her ShockWave class and was reading a story in the paper about how all the young people were killing themselves by sending texts while they drove. *On my way. Nearly there!* These were their last foolish (and often misspelled) words. Madeline had cried over the picture of one teenager's grief-stricken mother, absurdly holding up her daughter's mobile phone to the camera as a warning to readers.

"Silly little idiots," she said out loud as the car weaved dangerously into the next lane.

"Who is an idiot?" said her daughter from the backseat.

"The girl driving the car in front of me is an idiot because she's driving her car and using her phone at the same time," said Madeline.

"Like when you need to call Daddy when we're running late?" said Chloe.

"I only did that one time!" protested Madeline. "And I was very careful and very quick! And I'm *forty* years old!"

"Today," said Chloe knowledgeably. "You're forty years old today."

"Yes! Also, I made a quick call, I didn't send a text! You have to take your eyes off the road to text. Texting while driving is illegal and naughty, and you must promise to never ever do it when you're a teenager."

Her voice quivered at the thought of Chloe being a teenager and driving a car.

"But you're allowed to make a quick phone call?" checked Chloe.

"No! That's illegal too," said Madeline.

"So that means you broke the law," said Chloe with satisfaction. "Like a *robber.*"

Chloe was currently in love with the idea of robbers. She was definitely going to date bad boys one day. Bad boys on motorcycles.

"Stick with the nice boys, Chloe!" said Madeline after a moment. "Like Daddy. Bad boys don't bring you coffee in bed, I'll tell you that for free."

"What are you babbling on about, woman?" sighed Chloe. She'd picked this phrase up from her father and imitated his weary tone perfectly. They'd made the mistake of laughing the first time she did it, so she'd kept it up, and said it just often enough, and with perfect timing, so that they couldn't help but keep laughing.

This time Madeline managed not to laugh. Chloe currently trod a very fine line between adorable and obnoxious. Madeline probably trod the same line herself.

Madeline pulled up behind the little blue Mitsubishi at a red light. The young driver was *still* looking at her mobile phone. Madeline banged on her car horn. She saw the driver glance in her rearview mirror, while all her passengers craned around to look.

"Put down your phone!" she yelled. She mimicked texting by jabbing her finger in her palm. "It's illegal! It's dangerous!"

The girl stuck her finger up in the classic up-yours gesture.

"Right!" Madeline pulled on her emergency brake and put on her hazard lights.

"What are you doing?" said Chloe.

Madeline undid her seat belt and threw open the car door.

"But we've got to go to orientation!" said Chloe in a panic. "We'll be late! Oh, *calamity*!"

"Oh, calamity" was a line from a children's book that they used to read to Fred when he was little. The whole family said it now. Even Madeline's parents had picked it up, and some of Madeline's friends. It was a very contagious phrase.

"It's all right," said Madeline. "This will only take a second. I'm saving young lives."

She stalked up to the girl's car on her new stilettos and banged on the window.

The window slid down, and the driver metamorphosed from a shadowy silhouette into a real young girl with white skin, sparkly nose ring and badly applied, clumpy mascara. She looked up at Madeline with a mixture of aggression and fear. "What is your *problem*?" Her mobile phone was still held casually in her left hand.

"Put down that phone! You could kill yourself and your friends!" Madeline used the exact same tone she used on Chloe when she was being extremely naughty. She reached in the car, grabbed the phone and tossed it to the open-mouthed girl in the passenger seat. "OK? Just stop it!"

She could hear their gales of laughter as she walked back to her SUV. She didn't care. She felt pleasantly stimulated. A car pulled up behind hers. Madeline smiled, lifted her hand apologetically and hurried back to be in her car before the lights changed.

Her ankle turned. One second it was doing what an ankle was meant to do, and the next it was flipping out at a sickeningly wrong angle. She fell heavily on one side. Oh, calamity.

That was almost certainly the moment the story began. With the ungainly flip of an ankle.

THREE

Jane pulled up at a red light behind a big shiny SUV with its hazard lights blinking and watched a dark-haired woman hurry along the side of the road back to it. She wore a floaty, blue summer dress and high strappy heels, and she waved apologetically, charmingly at Jane. The morning sun caught one of the woman's earrings, and it shone as if she'd been touched by something celestial.

A glittery girl. Older than Jane but definitely still glittery. All her life Jane had watched girls like that with scientific interest. Maybe a little awe. Maybe a little envy. They weren't necessarily the prettiest, but they decorated themselves so affectionately, like Christmas trees, with dangling earrings, jangling bangles and delicate, pointless scarves. They touched your arm a lot when they spoke. Jane's best friend at school had been a glittery girl. Jane had a weakness for them.

Then the woman fell, as if something had been pulled out from underneath her.

"Ouch," said Jane, and she looked away fast to save the woman's dignity.

"Did you hurt yourself, Mummy?" asked Ziggy from the backseat. He was always very worried about her hurting herself.

"No," said Jane. "That lady over there hurt herself. She tripped."

She waited for the woman to get up and get back in her car, but she was still on the ground. She'd tipped back her head to the sky, and her face had that compressed look of someone in great pain. The traffic light turned green, and a little blue Mitsubishi that had been in front of the SUV zoomed off with a squeal of tires.

Jane put her signal on to drive around the car. They were on their way to Ziggy's orientation day at the new school, and she had no idea where she was going. She and Ziggy were both nervous and pretending not to be. She wanted to get there in plenty of time.

"Is the lady OK?" said Ziggy.

Jane felt that strange lurch she sometimes experienced when she got distracted by her life, and then something (it was often Ziggy) made her remember just in time the appropriate way for a nice, ordinary, well-mannered grown-up to behave.

If it weren't for Ziggy she would have driven off. She would have been so focused on her goal of getting him to his kindergarten orientation that she would have *left a woman sitting on the road, writhing in pain.*

"I'll just check on her," said Jane, as if that were her intention all along. She flicked on her own hazard lights and opened the car door, aware as she did of a selfish sense of resistance. *You are an inconvenience, glittery lady!*

"Are you all right?" she called.

"I'm fine!" The woman tried to sit up straighter and whimpered, her hand on her ankle. "Ow. Shit. I've rolled my ankle, that's all. I'm such an *idiot*. I got out of the car to go tell the girl in front of me to stop texting. Serves me right for behaving like a school prefect."

Jane crouched down next to her. The woman had shoulder-length, well-cut dark hair and the faintest sprinkle of freckles across her nose. There was something aesthetically pleasing about those freckles, like a childhood memory of summer, and they were very nicely complemented by the fine lines around her eyes and the absurd swinging earrings.

Jane's resistance vanished entirely.

She liked this woman. She wanted to help her.

(Although, what did that say? If the woman had been a toothless, warty-nosed crone she would have continued to feel resentful? The injustice of it. The cruelty of it. She was going to be nicer to this woman because she liked her freckles.)

The woman's dress had an intricately embroidered cut-out pattern of flowers all along the neckline. Jane could see tanned freckly skin through the petals.

"We need to get some ice on it straightaway," said Jane. She knew about ankle injuries from her netball days and she could see this woman's ankle was already beginning to swell. "And keep it elevated." She chewed her lip and looked about hopefully for someone else. She had no idea how to handle the logistics of making this actually happen.

"It's my birthday," said the woman sadly. "My fortieth."

"Happy birthday," said Jane. It was sort of cute that a woman of *forty* would even bother to mention that it was her birthday.

She looked at the woman's strappy shoes. Her toenails were painted a lustrous turquoise. The stiletto heels were as thin as toothpicks and perilously high.

"No wonder you did your ankle," said Jane. "No one could walk in those shoes!"

"I know, but aren't they gorgeous?" The woman turned her foot at an angle to admire them. "Ouch! *Fuck*, that hurts. Sorry. Excuse my language."

"Mummy!" A little girl with dark curly hair, wearing a sparkling tiara, stuck her head out the window of the car. "What are you doing? Get up! We'll be late!"

Glittery mother. Glittery daughter.

"Thanks for the sympathy, darling!" said the woman. She smiled ruefully at Jane. "We're on our way to her kindergarten orientation. She's very excited."

"At Pirriwee Public?" said Jane. She was astonished. "But that's where I'm going. My son, Ziggy, is starting school next year. We're moving here in December." It didn't seem possible that she and this woman could have anything in common, or that their lives could intersect in any way.

"Ziggy! Like Ziggy Stardust? What a great name!" said the woman. "I'm Madeline, by the way. Madeline Martha

Mackenzie. I always mention the Martha for some reason. Don't ask me why." She held out her hand.

"Jane," said Jane. "Jane no-middle-name Chapman."

Gabrielle: The school ended up split in two. It was, like, I don't know, a civil war. You were either on Team Madeline or Team Renata.

Bonnie: No, no, that's awful. That never happened. There were no *sides*. We're a very close-knit community. There was too much alcohol. Also, it was a full moon. Everyone goes a little crazy when it's a full moon. I'm serious. It's an actual verifiable phenomenon.

Samantha: Was it a full moon? It was pouring rain, I know that. My hair was all boofy.

Mrs. Lipmann: That's ridiculous and highly defamatory. I have no further comment.

Carol: I know I keep harping on about the Erotic Book Club, but I'm sure something happened at one of their little quote-unquote meetings.

Harper: Listen, I *cried* when we learned Emily was gifted. I thought, *Here we go again!* I'd been through it all before with Sophia, so I knew what I was in for! Renata was in the same boat. *Two* gifted children. Nobody understands the stress. Renata was worried about how Amabella would settle in at school, whether she'd get enough stimulation and so on. So when that child with the ridiculous name, that Ziggy, did what he did, and it was only the orientation morning! Well, she was understandably very distressed. That's what started it all.